I0652726

HERETICS IN OCCUPIED EDEN

HERETICS IN OCCUPIED EDEN

BOOK ONE

THE FLOATING BOY

A NOVEL BY
KENNETH ALAN MOE

STRANGE ANGEL PRESS
Phoenix, Arizona

Copyright © 2012
Kenneth Alan Moe

Cover and interior design by Ethan Moe
Cover model Emma Fry
Cover photo is the White Tank Mountains, west of Phoenix, AZ

All rights reserved under International and Pan-American Copyright Conventions.

Printed in the United States of America
Third Printing

This is a work of fiction. Characters, conversations, organizations, and incidents herein are products of the author's imagination. Any resemblance to real people, living or dead, is coincidental. Historical events described are accurate as to time and place, but the real individuals named in connection with them do not function as characters. Some actual place names are used, including names of schools and military bases, but events described in connection with those places are fictional. Bible verses quoted are from the King James Version or are the author's translation.

ISBN: 978-0615591551

For Shelly

Twice or thrice had I loved thee
Before I knew thy face or name.
John Donne

Eden is that old-fashioned House
We dwell in every day
Without suspecting our abode
Until we drive away.
Emily Dickinson

The heresy of one age becomes the orthodoxy of
the next.
Helen Keller

CONTENTS

I

THE OLD ONE

This World is not Conclusion.
A Species stands beyond
Invisible, as Music
But positive, as Sound
                          Emily Dickinson

Our truest life is when we are in dreams awake.
                          Henry David Thoreau

Sweet is the dream, divinely sweet, when absent
souls in fancy meet.
                          Thomas More

CHAPTER ONE

Spewing dirt with its tires, the 1940 Ford rumbled across open desert west of Phoenix. The decade old car carried four teenage boys, one of them more or less using the steering wheel to aim the vehicle as he pressed his right foot firmly against the accelerator.

The boy riding shotgun shouted, "This looks like a good spot. Stop the car."

The driver jammed in the clutch and stomped on the brake pedal, creating a huge dust storm outside that blew over the car as it skidded to rest, briefly engulfing the encapsulated joyriders in total darkness. When the cloud of dirt cleared, the front doors and the rear suicide doors swung open and the boys jumped out.

The tall one looked northwestward and said, "That's the White Tanks over there." The small range of treeless mountains shone in the midday sun. The skinny one opened the trunk and pulled out a case of A-1 beer. The bottles had warmed up during the trip from town and were cool now rather than ice cold. He handed a bottle to each of the others, uncapped his with a church key then passed the opener around.

The short one removed a 22 rifle from the trunk and said, "Finish 'em off quick and put the empties over there on that rock and we'll plunk at 'em."

The fat one finished chugging his beer first and set out for the designated flat boulder twenty yards away. As he positioned the empty bottle he looked at the depression of land beyond and spotted a wooden shack a quarter mile down the slope.

"Hey guys, there's a cabin down there!" he yelled. "Let's go take a look." They scrambled after him. A few yards past the target rock, the short one pivoted and shot at the fat one's bottle, shattering the glass with a bullet.

"Good shot," the tall one said and threw his now empty beer bottle at the rock, producing more shattered glass.

"Wow, look way over there at that big lizard doing pushups on that granite outcrop," the skinny one said. The short one spun around and fired his rifle at it, missing by a great margin. The skinny one had not finished his beer, and while laughing at the unsuccessful attack against the desert reptile, he dropped the half-full bottle. "Oh shit! I'm watering the cactuses with my beer. I was planning to do that with my piss," he said.

"Ya know, there's Bighorn sheep up there in the White Tanks," said the short one. "Maybe I can shoot one of them."

The fat one said, "Those Bighorns won't come down here, asshole, and you couldn't nail one with a 22 anyway. You'd need a 30 odd six."

"If I got him between the eyes, I could do it with my 22," the short one responded. "Six ain't odd. It's 30 *aught* six, dodo."

"*Ought* six? Fat chance! That don't make any sense," the fat one said.

The four boys resumed their trek toward the shack. "Hey, I bet it's a miner's shack," the tall one said. "There might be gold dust hid in there."

As they approached within ten yards of the place, odd feelings engulfed them. The broken down hovel seemed to radiate a pulsing resonance. The fat one started to make a joke about the foot-long chuckwalla the short one had taken a shot at. The lizard was inside the door plotting its revenge, he was going to say, but then thought better of it and held his tongue. No doubt *something* alive was in there!

The scene did not induce fear but was far beyond anything they knew as normal. An aura of rainbow colors now arced over the shack, creating an eerie tableau. Warily, they walked a little closer, and the aura grew brighter and stronger. Now they could feel their own bodies pulsate. Science fiction images filled their minds. Were they approaching a creature from outer space?

No one spoke. Amid the silence, each boy experienced a tingling sensation of awe that quickly spread until it enveloped every inch of his being. Simultaneously they stopped moving and began listening to the wordless conversations that had begun running through their minds. To this point in their lives, none of these boys had been in any way self-reflective, but suddenly all four became aware of themselves as individual creatures and yet indistinguishable from the entirety of creation.

A microsecond later (or had an eternity passed?), each boy, the tall one, the short one, the fat one and the skinny one, saw vividly projected on the screen within his brain the failures of his unique life, including this current escapade. They understood their errors but felt no guilt. Rather, each felt affirmation of his own value tinged with sadness at the ways he had diminished himself and others through various thoughtless behaviors. And they all felt loved by something beyond themselves and in turn fell in love -at least temporarily- with the desert flora and fauna they perceived all around them.

The boys watched a giant tumbleweed blow across the landscape and saw it come to a stop in front of the wooden shack. Quivering in the bright April sunlight, the tumbleweed looked like it was on fire. Another gust picked it up and carried it over the shack and off toward the White Tank Mountains. As it disappeared from sight it seemed to turn purple.

The short one dropped the rifle. The tall one said, "Let's go home." As they turned to head back to the car, the skinny one retrieved the 22 from the dust, saying to the short one, "Your dad's gonna beat the shit out of you if you leave this here."

As the Ford peeled out across the dirt track, the deep voice of Vaughn Monroe rose through the car radio speaker over station KOY. The haunting sounds of the musical cowboy legend "Ghost Riders in the Sky" filled the boys' ears, and they listened in rapt silence, wondering if the threat of chasing a ghost herd across the sky might be an omen.

The sentient being inside the shack also heard the western ballad and thought: This would be understood as a clear plea for vegetarianism in my society, but that view is lost on these young men. The song's real message is the need to adopt better ecological habits and practice genuine equality between the sexes and among all races or suffer hell on earth, but they will think the warning is about drinking and illicit sex.

The return drive to Phoenix was considerably more subdued than the trip out. Nevertheless, by the time they reached the city limits they were already scheming about what to do with the unopened beer bottles. They decided to hide them in an alley behind the tall one's house.

All four boys had been changed by their desert experiences, but apart from a day or two of uncharacteristic pensiveness, their families did not notice. By the time they returned to classes at Phoenix Union High School the following Monday, they were as rowdy as ever. Yet they would remember.

The Old One, abiding in the shack, produced an enigmatic smile from a tiny mouth. If the boys had dared to open the door and peer inside, they would have encountered someone of indeterminate sex, with long, fine, white hair, robed in a tent-like garment of unbleached canvas cloth.

The Old One's face was triangular, bracketed with large and long-lobed ears. Bright turquoise eyes, deep set and round, radiated intelligence seemingly beyond human capacity. A broad cranium added to the effect of intellect, dominating the top part of the creature's head. A thimble shaped nose and a thin-lipped mouth decorated the lower facial surface that tapered to a sharp chin.

No furniture graced the single room where the Old One sat on bare ground. Scorpions scuttled across the dirt floor, and in the corner, a black widow spider was at work on a web. Red ants were carrying away breadcrumbs from the folds in the Old One's garment, and wasps hovered around the rim of a clay mug that had once contained some sweet liquid. The Old One paid no mind to any of these creatures.

At that moment, the Old One returned attention to another boy in Phoenix, younger than these four who were fleeing the desert by car. This one was six years old, and he was in grave danger.

II

CLOUD

Over the tree-tops I float thee a song.
Walt Whitman

That with this bright, believing band
I have no right to be,
That faith by which my comrades stand
Seems fantasies to me.
Thomas Hardy

My Wars are laid away in Books
I have one Battle more
Emily Dickinson

CHAPTER TWO

Narcissa Morgan was scared. Her six year-old son had the measles, and his fever had just spiked to a dangerous level. She called her husband at his office. "Lloyd, you better come home. Cloud's running a temperature of a hundred and five. We may have to take him over to Good Sam."

"Now, calm down, Narcissa. You don't take a kid to the hospital for measles. How high does it have to get before he could die?" he said.

"A hundred and five, you son of a bitch. Bring the car home as fast as you can!"

Cloud lay in bed in his darkened room. His mother wouldn't let him pore over the fascinating illustrations in his folio edition of L. Frank Baum's *The Wizard of Oz*, because it would damage his eyes. The overhead light would also hurt his eyes while he was suffering from measles, she told him, so he had to lie there in the shadows, with only his imagination to keep him occupied. Fortunately, he possessed a precociously ample imagination.

He imagined, for example, that he wasn't in his bed at all but floating close to the ceiling, looking down at his own naked body and the sweat-drenched pajamas he had peeled off and tossed aside because he was so hot. From this hovering perch, he took inventory of his toys scattered about the room. The toys had been important to him yesterday when he had played with them on the floor. From his aerial perspective now they looked nice, but he felt no desire for them. Ah, but it seemed so pleasant on the ceiling, unlike the feverish bed below. He liked floating in the air. Cloud also liked talking with his friend.

The friend didn't have a name and didn't have a shape or body either. The friend lived only inside Cloud's brain and didn't so much use words to communicate as feelings. All Cloud knew was that his friend was very old, much older than grandma and grandpa, whom he barely knew but perceived to be as old as people could get. And now his friend was feeling sad and didn't want to float with Cloud anymore. This wasn't a good time to float. Some other day Cloud and his friend would float through the air together. Maybe next time they would do it outdoors and look at the whole world. With gentle firmness his friend said it was time for the boy to swoop down under the covers and sleep. The old friend promised to teach him some new feelings another day.

Lloyd stood at the side of his son's bed, holding a thermometer. "A hundred and one," he said. "Are you sure it was a hundred and five?"

"I'm absolutely sure that twenty minutes ago that same damn thermometer you just pulled out of Cloud's rectum said one hundred and five degrees Fahrenheit," Narcissa said, her voice laden with irritation and relief. "Thank God the fever broke. You can go back to work now, if you're so worried about goings-on at your precious bank when you're away."

Silently, Lloyd left, returning to the branch office he managed. Next-door, peering around picture window drapes, Miss Listerbaum noted his coming home at an odd hour and quick departure and wondered what was happening. She knew Cloud had measles and hoped he was recovering. Maybe they're having marital problems, she thought.

Three weeks later, Cloud ambled into the kitchen as his mother was preparing dinner and saw that she was making bacon and pancakes. He had dreamed this scene two days earlier and it had struck him as strange. She usually made pancakes and bacon for Saturday morning breakfast but had never served them at dinner. Well, he thought, if my dream is true, Dad will come home with strawberries.

Lloyd did indeed have strawberries. "They were all out of blueberries at Bayless," he explained, "so I got the next best thing. They look really good, don't they?"

Narcissa was indignant. "How can I make blueberry pancakes with strawberries? I've had my heart set on blueberry pancakes all day. Couldn't you have gone to another store? Bashas is only another mile."

Cloud's parents then entered into a prolonged conversation that soon grew into existential questions about the nature of their marriage. Ignoring the scene, Cloud fell into a reverie, contemplating his dream come true. While in this otherworldly state, he strode to the kitchen garbage can, stepped on the pedal that lifted the lid, unbuttoned his pants, and urinated into the container. Without awareness of the peculiar nature of this deed, he wandered back to his bedroom in search of a comic book about Scrooge McDuck.

This peculiar use of the garbage can caused his parents momentarily to stop bickering and turn silent. Narcissa watched her son with dismay, while Lloyd observed the scene with amusement.

Lloyd Morgan and Narcissa Cloud met in the summer of 1942 in front of the Westward Ho Hotel on Central Avenue in Phoenix. He had enlisted in the Army a month after the Pearl Harbor attack and following basic training was sent to an air base in Arizona for flight training. Narcissa spotted Lloyd, looking dapper in well-fitted khakis, as he exited the swank hotel.

He was waiting for a ride back to Thunderbird Field and the Westward Ho was a convenient landmark for the pick-up. Curious about the place, he had wandered in and inspected the plush lobby. As he emerged, Narcissa, who was walking northbound on the sidewalk, noted to her co-worker how handsome the air cadet looked. The colleague dared her to strike up a conversation with the soldier, and Narcissa met the dare.

After chatting briefly, they made a date for the next Saturday. When the day came, they met in front of the hotel and went inside for dinner and dancing in the Fiesta Room. Both proved to be good dancers as they swirled to the big band music of the Phoenicians. Lloyd noticed Narcissa's great legs as her skirt flared when she whirled. She enjoyed showing off her gams. Narcissa was a good talker too. Lloyd liked it when a girl would talk, because then he didn't have to say much.

Being seen on the arm of this handsome soon-to-be pilot from the East pleased Narcissa. She felt his coming from Pennsylvania automatically made him more sophisticated than any of the local boys. And he seemed to like her and wanted to hear about her life. He had never met anyone from exotic Bagdad, Arizona and thought that was something to be proud of, although Narcissa assured him it was not.

On their first date, Narcissa and Lloyd became smitten with one another dancing to "Where or When" in the Fiesta Room. At midnight, she invited him to walk her home to her studio apartment on McKinley a few blocks west and north of the hotel.

"My dad's a mining engineer," she explained as they walked along the still warm sidewalk. "He can afford nice things but doesn't believe in extravagance. The house I grew up in has bare walls. Not a single painting or decoration. No color. Just dirty yellow paint in every room of the house. It was originally off-white, but it's darkened with age. Every time we came to Phoenix to shop, when I was a kid, I tried to get them to buy a few decorative items, but he always said no. I can still hear him saying, 'Don't you know there's a Depression, young lady?' That's how he shut me up."

"Sounds creepy," offered Lloyd. "Like something out of Dickens."

"I used to go to the company movie theater a lot. I love Fred Astaire and Ginger Rogers. I saved my babysitting money, and on my thirteenth birthday I got a little more money, so I bought a portable radio for my bedroom. Dad said it was a foolish waste, since they had a radio console in the living room and reception in Bagdad wasn't that good anyway. But it was the best purchase I ever made."

"How so?" asked Lloyd. "And by the way, when's your birthday?"

"I was born on the tenth anniversary of statehood, February 14, 1922. The thing about that radio is it connected me to the world. I wanted to get out of that mining town in the worst way. On clear nights I'd curl up in bed and listen to dance bands on KTAR. On Sunday nights when the atmospheric conditions were right I listened to Major Bowes' Original Amateur Hour and on Mondays the Voice of Firestone. I think the Firestone Symphony Orchestra is so sophisticated, don't you?"

At this point, they reached her front door, and without another word, she opened it and ushered Lloyd inside. After turning on a lamp, she snapped on her radio and set the volume to allow for conversation.

"As soon as I graduated from high school," Narcissa continued, "I headed for Phoenix and got a job right away at Korricks, where I sell fine home furnishings and art work to people of refined tastes. That's only till I save enough for modeling school. Someday I'm going to be a model."

Lloyd noticed a painting on the wall above Narcissa's bed.

She saw his eyes fixed on the piece and said, "I got an employee discount on that. I had to put it on lay-away for a couple of months but couldn't resist it. It's beautiful, don't you think?"

The painting depicted an Indian maiden, following the romantic Old West style of Edward Mason Eggleston. The maiden, striking a pose managing to convey a demure yet heroic attitude, was nude except for a feathered war bonnet and beaded leather moccasins. Her face, however, was that of a woman of European ancestry.

"She doesn't look like any of the Indians I've seen sitting on rugs along the sidewalk on Washington, selling baskets and jewelry," said Lloyd.

"I think she's a Canadian Indian," said Narcissa. "I've heard they look more British than the Pimas and Maricopas around here. And speaking of sitting on blankets, I apologize for not having a couch. I usually sit on the bed and rest my back against the wall. Care to join me?"

Narcissa turned up the volume on her radio, and with their shoes removed the two nestled sideways on the bed. Lloyd put his arm around Narcissa as the Inkspots warbled "My Prayer" via KOY. After hearing Dinah Shore croon "He Wears a Pair of Silver Wings" they began kissing and disrobing at the same time. Lloyd stayed the night.

Sunday morning, the lovers walked to the Coffee Pot restaurant at 7th Street and McDowell for breakfast. The popular eatery, shaped like a giant coffee pot, was another convenient landmark. An air cadet with a car met the couple at the restaurant, and after delivering Narcissa to her front door, took Lloyd back to Thunderbird Field.

Six weeks later Narcissa and Lloyd stood in front of a justice of the peace in the Phoenix City Hall. The bride's co-worker, who had initiated the relationship through a dare, acted as witness to the wedding. Though they were invited, Narcissa's parents declined to drive down from Bagdad for the occasion.

Evan Cloud Morgan was conceived early in 1943 during what passed for winter in Phoenix. At the time, Lloyd was stationed at Davis-Monthan Field in Tucson, learning to fly B-24 bombers. Narcissa did not join him in Tucson but stayed in her apartment in Phoenix, and Lloyd came up whenever he could get leave. Before his son was born in the fall, Lloyd was transferred to Camp Kilmer, New Jersey and from there shipped overseas to England to join a squadron in the Eighth Air Force.

Thus he was not at home to see his son as a prune-faced newborn, and didn't see him learn to crawl, or see his first steps, or hear him talk for the first time. He monitored his son's development through the photographs Narcissa sent him.

With Lloyd based in England, Narcissa eagerly followed the United News newsreels at the Fox Theater. Footage of brave pilots belly-landing flak-damaged bombers and panoramas of obliterated Luftwaffe bases thrilled her. She boasted to strangers that her husband was a pilot. It never entered her mind to worry about Lloyd's safety. She knew with certainty that he was a hero and by extension she was a heroine.

Their son had been named Evan, after his paternal grandfather, but in Lloyd's absence, Narcissa started calling him by his middle name -her maiden name- and it stuck. Cloud seemed to suit the boy perfectly.

When he returned from the war, Lloyd was hurt to discover the abandonment of his son's first name, for Narcissa had not mentioned this in any of her letters. She referred always to "our son" or "our boy" and used neither Evan nor Cloud when writing to him. He felt then that some part of his son had been taken from him, and occasionally he wondered if another man might be the boy's biological father.

Lloyd never expressed this doubt to his wife, however, and anyone could see that Evan Cloud Morgan had inherited more physical features from his father than his mother. Yet the name switch caused Lloyd to feel some distance from Cloud as the boy grew up.

Transition from Army Air Force officer to civilian was easy for Lloyd but hard for Narcissa. He found work as a teller at the Maricopa National Bank and quickly moved through the chairs to loan officer, assistant manager, branch manager, and vice-president (which was the title for manager of a larger branch office). Lloyd did not miss the sleety winters of Central Pennsylvania and found being part of a burgeoning city in the desert Southwest much to his liking.

Until Lloyd returned to Phoenix wearing a ruptured duck lapel pin, the symbol of his rebirth as a civilian, Narcissa had never known her husband as other than a military man, and at that, they had spent most of their married lives apart. Now that he was around all the time, she began to wonder if she had made the right choice. She preferred having him as a weekend visitor, entering and leaving the house with his officer's insignia gleaming for everyone to see. Somehow, a white shirt, dull banker's tie, and fedora didn't project the same effect in her mind. And the aura of East Coast sophistication she had seen in him in 1942 now seemed to have been a mirage.

His lack of judgment became clear to her late in 1946, when he suggested that they invest in land north of Phoenix. Large parcels were available on the far side of Shadow Mountain, he told her, for a dollar an acre.

She laughed at his gullibility. "We're not spending hard earned cash on worthless desert land!" she insisted. "I grew up in a mining town. Unless there's minerals under the land, it's not worth a nickel an acre. And I guarantee you, there's no gold in this valley."

Lloyd pressed his case for several weeks, but Narcissa was convinced that buying arid acreage was akin to buying the Brooklyn Bridge, and she adamantly refused to invest family resources in so foolhardy an enterprise. Lloyd conceded defeat and decided that he would never again speak with his wife about buying land. And at the time, losing an opportunity to buy acreage was not the greatest disappointment occupying his mind.

A more immediate concern was Narcissa's lack of interest in intimate marital relations. His first week home after the war, they had had sex nine times, but this would not become a pattern. They fell into a routine of having intercourse once a month and then once every three or four months. In 1946, Lloyd had wanted to try for another child but Narcissa thought the time wasn't right. As years passed, Lloyd came to feel fortunate that they did not have a second child to complicate the family dynamics.

Lloyd spent little time with his son, leaving Cloud to play by himself. When other boys were playing catch with their dads, Cloud was constructing imaginary forts out of mud from the puddle at the edge of the front yard. When other boys sat on the couch with their dads to watch baseball and football, Cloud was alone in his room reading comic books.

At the start of third grade, Cloud played in a school soft ball game for the first time. However, he had no concept of the general flow of the game much less the rules. Nevertheless, after watching other boys swing their bats at the ball and run around the bases when they managed to get a hit, Cloud confidently took his turn in the batter's box.

The first pitch came wobbling toward him, and Cloud swung with all his might, knocking the ball into short right field. As his teammates cheered, he ran toward first base, arriving there in time to see that the opposing player assigned to that base was having difficulty getting the ball, having let the right fielder's throw roll between his legs. Cloud, being a polite and helpful youngster, trotted over and scooped it up and handed it to the first baseman. Cloud's teammates were not impressed with his sportsmanship.

A pretty girl in his class, however, took note of this behavior. Prudy told Cloud she thought the way he played the game was the sign of a true gentleman. She didn't know anything about baseball either, but she had heard her mother describe her father as a true gentleman, so this was the highest compliment she knew, and she freely applied it to this cute boy. During the lunch recess, Cloud and Prudy held hands as they waded through the blanket of pecan nuts that had fallen from the stately trees lining the perimeter of Grand Avenue Elementary School. The feeling of their fingers intertwined sent a pleasant electric buzz all through his skin. After school, he stuffed the cuffs of his Levis with nuts and when he got home stored them in a cigar box he kept in the bottom drawer of his dresser. Though Prudy moved on to another cute boy a week later, Cloud kept the pecans for several years as a remembrance of this moment of bliss.

— ☺ —

Cloud discovered his favorite word in the fourth grade. He was browsing through the card catalog in the school library, looking for anything that might strike his fancy and found a Dewey Decimal System tab labeled Metaphysics. The library had no books in this section, and this absence intrigued him. If the school library did not have anything on a certain subject, he reasoned, that meant they wanted to keep kids away from it, which of course made it even more interesting.

Metaphysics. He spoke the word in his mind and then whispered it to himself. He liked the look and sound of the word. An aura of mystery seemed to surround its letters. Something about it beckoned his imagination, although he did not know its meaning.

The librarian walked by and noticed Cloud's finger marking a spot in the card catalog. "Are you looking for something, Cloud?" she asked. "May I help you find it?"

Startled by the teacher's presence, his first thought was to decline help. But he could not resist asking. "I saw this tab for metaphysics, and I don't know what that is."

"A fourth grader wouldn't have encountered that word," she explained. "It's the philosophy of the universe. Not science, but ideas about the nature of existence."

"You mean like why are we here?" Cloud asked. "I mean, not here in the library but why is there an earth and why do humans exist?"

"Yes," she said, surprised that he had been thinking such thoughts. "Metaphysics includes psychic and mysterious occurrences too. Do you know what psychic means?"

"Mental," he answered. "Things that a mind knows or can make happen that can't be explained by science." Cloud blushed at these words, recognizing himself in them and strongly desiring to protect this inner identity from exposure. "I'd like to learn about metaphysics, but there aren't any metaphysics books listed in here," Cloud added.

"No, not in an elementary school, but I'll tell you where you can find plenty of them," she said conspiratorially. "Do you know where the Phoenix Public Library is?"

"Oh sure. Central and McDowell," he said. "I've been there many times. I'll look up metaphysics next time I go. Thanks."

"You're most welcome," she said, producing a wide smile. Though she would never tell him, Cloud had made her very happy to be a grade school librarian.

When he was ten, Cloud discovered a pair of his father's brown combat boots, tucked away on a shelf in the tool room off the back porch. He had never seen them before, and his father had never mentioned having them. In fact, Lloyd rarely spoke of the war or his experiences overseas, and the only thing Cloud knew was that his father had been stationed in England and had been a B-24 pilot.

Mud clung to the sides of the boots, and Cloud imagined it must have come from an airfield in England. He put the boots on his feet and tightened the straps as far as they would go, and although they were much too big for him, he managed to march around clumsily in his father's boots. As he tramped back and forth across the back porch, he thought about the heroic deeds his old man must have accomplished in the war.

Carefully, almost reverently, he put the boots away, but every once in a while, when no one else was home, he got them down and marched around in them. The second time, he put on three pairs of socks to make them fit better. He thought about going out into the back yard to expand his parade but was afraid he might mix ordinary Phoenix dirt with knightly English mud, and that would spoil the boots.

The reality, which Cloud would never learn, was that the boots were not military issue. Lloyd had gotten them from a British officer who had bought them in Cairo. He had not worn them on any bombing missions, and the mud was from his back yard in Phoenix. Cloud's fervently imagined connection with his father's heroic past was based on a false assumption, and not the last one he would entertain.

At the moment Cloud first traipsed around his back porch in his father's boots, a young girl with fine tan skin and straight black hair walked with demure grace through the Ben Thanh Market in Saigon. Bombed by the Allies during the war, the market was restored in 1950. The girl's mother had taken her shopping in the huge indoor maze of a thousand stalls, an errand seven year-old Xuan loved to help with. On this cool morning in the dry season, Xuan stopped to admire a basket of fresh, plump figs.

For no reason that she could understand, Xuan became fixated on this basket of fruit. She could not look away from it and noticed that some bruised figs were carefully nestled in with good ones. The entrancing scene suddenly shimmered and shifted, and she saw the basket lying outside in the street, and a large dark-green truck came barreling toward it. Odd white men -certainly not French- rode in the back of the truck singing boisterously. Then she saw the dark-green *xe van-tai* crush the basket of *qua va*. Its wheels ran right over the figs, and her body jerked in reaction. Immediately, the scene reverted to the fruit basket resting securely on the stall table. Nothing in reality had happened, except that her mother was now tugging at her arm, urging her to come along.

By fifth grade, things were not going well for Cloud in school. His academic grades were fine, but his deportment grades were disastrous. He talked when he should listen and squirmed in his seat when he should be still. On bright, sunny afternoons, he gazed through the steel-framed classroom windows, intent upon the rounded, bleached white shapes of clouds floating at leisure across an otherwise clear blue sky instead of paying attention to his teacher. Other students stole glances at the playground, but Cloud's mental truancy was blatant as he imagined running across the cumulus tops.

On a warm spring morning, his music teacher introduced the class to an old spiritual, "Deep River." One line was, "Lord, I want to pass over into campground." Cloud raised his hand and asked what campground was. The teacher looked at him scornfully and said, "Oh Cloud, what's the matter with you? Don't you go to church?"

"No, ma'am," he said. This response provided the teacher with the warrant she needed to ignore his question. Cloud felt that everyone in the room was staring at him and thinking: Cloud doesn't know what campground is. How stupid. He doesn't go to church. How shameful. The following day the music teacher moved him from the second seat to the last seat in the row, according to her talent ranking system. Cloud inferred from this that he couldn't sing, for despite trying to improve, he never again moved up.

In homeroom, the teacher read a short story to the class each day. Cloud loved the stories and doodled imaginatively while listening to the words, allowing them to wander through his mind. Among his doodling habits was writing what he heard backwards, from right to left on the pages in his tablet. He had been doing this ever since he learned to write in cursive in the third grade. He had no idea where the skill had come from, but while doodling aimlessly one afternoon he discovered that he could write from right to left both ways. That is, he could write the letters in the words in the correct orientation but running from right to left, so they had to be read from right to left, and he could also write them backward, so that when held up to a mirror they could be read from left to right. Cloud could do this as easily as writing left to right.

One day during story time the girl beside him leaned over to look at the strange inscriptions Cloud was making on paper. The teacher perceived the interruption and slammed her book shut and marched up to Cloud's desk.

"What are you doing, young man? Let me see your tablet!" she demanded. Cloud handed it to her. "What's this nonsense?"

"It's backwards. I write backwards," Cloud answered.

"Where did you learn this?" she wanted to know. "Are you Jewish?"

"No, ma'am," he said.

"Well, stop it, Cloud! In America we write from left to right." She grabbed his ears and twisted hard. His comfortably large ears turned bright red in response to the friction, followed shortly by his face flushing in response to the humiliation.

The day got worse from there. Going home from school, Cloud detoured over to 19th Avenue to look for golf balls in the irrigation ditch next to the Encanto Golf Course. He found four balls, and in the process smeared considerable mud on his Levis and shirt.

When Narcissa saw his clothing, she shrieked, "Have you been playing in the ditch again?" She didn't wait for a reply. "How many times have I told you to stay away from irrigation ditches? Young man, you seem bound and determined to get polio! I swear, if you get polio I think I'll let them keep you in an iron lung permanently!"

Cloud hung his head penitently to await the verdict on his punishment.

"You'll eat dinner by yourself in your room," Narcissa

pronounced.

This was no punishment in Cloud's view, but he knew there was more coming.

"And no television tonight! Now get in the bathroom this minute and take a bath!" she ordered. "I'll wash your filthy clothes to get the polio germs out."

While Cloud was in the tub making a bar of Ivory soap into an imaginary speedboat, Narcissa came in wearing rubber gloves and retrieved his clothing.

Later that evening, sitting alone in his room, Cloud switched on the radio that had once belonged to his mother. The calm crooning voice of Margaret Whiting emanated from the speaker, singing "Far Away Places." Without intention, Cloud slipped into a deep state of altered consciousness and was filled with desire to see the other side of the world. Though he had never been outside Arizona, the desire was tinged with nostalgia and wrapped in a sense of inevitability. How long he remained in the trance he had no idea, but suddenly he became aware that the radio was no longer on and his mother was standing next to his bed waving a hand in front of his face.

"Answer me, Cloud!" she said impatiently.

"What?" he responded, embarrassed that she had caught him this way.

"How many times do I have to ask? Are you finished with your dinner tray?"

"Yes, thank you," he mumbled and yawned theatrically in an attempt to cover his meditative state. "I'm tired. I think I'll go to bed early."

"You better not be sick," Narcissa said.

CHAPTER THREE

Tom Person was very excited about the airplanes. He had driven his family from New Jersey to Arizona on vacation, and he was about to show them some B-24s, like the ones he had flown in during World War II.

His hands grasped both sides of the wheel of his new 1957 Chevrolet the way he had seen pilots hold the control wheels of the bombers he had crewed during the war. Tom had been a bombardier, but he often fantasized about his missed opportunity to become a pilot. The car sped westward on Buckeye Road.

"This town is Goodyear," he announced. "Down the road a bit you'll see the planes, miles of them, stored out in the desert so they won't rust."

When they came in sight of thousands of mothballed planes, it did seem like they stretched for miles across the desert. Tom parked his sleek car beside the road and hustled everyone out to peer through the chain link fence at the rows of Army Air Corps B-17 Flying Fortresses, B-24 Liberators, and Navy pontoon planes.

"I was a B-24 man," he said. "Look, there's a row of them over there!" They knew this, because he had talked of little else on the long drive through Oklahoma, Texas, New Mexico, and through northeastern Arizona down to Phoenix. "These are rare," Tom added. "Most Liberators were scrapped right after the war."

Tom's wife Penny had been listening to his tales of aerial combat since December 1945, when he had been shipped from England to Camp Kilmer to be released from the Army Air Force. She was eighteen and not long out of high school, working for the USO as a Kilmer Sweetheart. During his two days in camp before release, he charmed her with stories of life in England, and so smitten was she with her dashing lieutenant that throughout their ensuing courtship she could listen for hours to his detailed accounts about everything from bomb trajectories to aircraft maintenance.

He had a romantic side too, she discovered. Tom savored Lorenz Hart lyrics. On their first date, he knelt in the grass in front of her house and serenaded her with a slightly off-key but sincere rendition of "My Heart Stood Still."

Penny was eight years younger than Tom. In high school she had dreamed of becoming a Broadway dancer, and it was her theatrical aspirations that sparked his initial attraction to her. But when it came to practice, Penny was unexacting, and in truth, she lacked the driving energy necessary to pursue a professional dancing career. Soon after meeting Tom at Camp Kilmer, she gave up any ideas of life on the stage and focused her attention exclusively on him.

As years passed, Tom's war stories continued. Hundreds of times he narrated that if a bomb accidentally fell off the rack, the bomb bay doors would open and let it out, because it took only a hundred pounds of pressure to open the doors. A man stepping off the catwalk onto the doors would fall right through. He'd never seen it himself, but he'd heard about it happening. Not long before he joined his crew, a bombardier had slipped and the bay doors popped right open and the crewman fell into the night and was never seen again.

Tom Person grew up in Edison, New Jersey and went off to college at Swarthmore in Pennsylvania. He graduated in the spring of 1941 with a degree in English and two firm beliefs. After four years studying among the Quakers of Swarthmore, he had become firmly convinced that pacifism was naïve and attending church served no useful purpose. He spent the next six months bussing tables in a Manhattan restaurant by night while trying to write a play by day.

After Pearl Harbor, he enlisted in the Army and qualified for pilot training. But then a Washington bureaucrat noticed a disproportionate number of pilot candidates compared with other crew positions, so Tom was arbitrarily reassigned to bombardier school. Since he had no choice in the matter, outwardly he accepted this change with good humor, but inside he seethed. He had gladly set aside his goal of being a playwright for the greater purpose of serving his country, but now his dream of becoming a pilot had been thwarted as well. Though he would be an officer, the Bombardier Badge felt like a consolation prize. On long bombing runs over Germany during the war, Tom filled his mental solitude by inventing dialog and scenes for plays he would one day write.

Tom's best friend in high school had been killed on Iwo Jima. Soon after Tom returned to New Jersey, his friend's father asked Tom to fill in for the dead son, helping to manage his restaurant equipment and cleaning supplies business. Tom wanted to write but knew he would need to generate some money to support himself and a new wife, so he agreed to help out for a year. It soon became clear that the owner was unable to overcome grieving for his son and had trouble concentrating on important matters. Feeling overwhelmed, he chose to retire. At the end of the promised year, rather than quit to write plays, Tom bought the company at very favorable terms. Together, he and Penny applied themselves to running and expanding the business. Consequently, they agreed to delay starting a family until they were financially secure. Then Penny could devote herself to motherhood, and Tom could let others manage day-to-day operations while he wrote for the stage. Penny's day eventually came but not Tom's.

Eleven years into the marriage, the days of rapt attention to his war stories were gone, but Penny still loved Tom dearly, cherishing his essential gentleness and boyish deference to women. Their two girls, soon-to-be five year-old Terp and two year-old Mary, were less interested in their father's stories but were for the moment fascinated by the row upon row of obsolete military aircraft.

"We used to call B-24s constipated lumberers," Tom told his daughters, "because they were so heavy and ungainly when loaded with bombs. That was a pun on their manufacturer's name, Consolidated Liberator."

"Tom!" retorted Penny. "That's a gross image to use in front of the girls." She tried to sound serious but could not entirely suppress a laugh.

"It's a medical term," Tom said. "Terp, do you know what constipated means?"

"So full of poop you have to squeeze hard to get it out," she replied and then wrinkled her brow with another idea. "Or maybe so full of bombs it's hard to take off."

"See, Penny," Tom said. "Terp understands the metaphor."

"What's a metaphor?" Terp asked.

"When you call bombs poop," Tom answered.

"That's easy to remember," Terp said. She found the concept captivating.

After more minutes gazing at mothballed planes, the girls grew bored and wanted to do something else.

"Mom's packed a picnic," Tom announced. "We'll find a spot out in the desert."

They found their places in the car and headed further west, until Tom swerved onto a farm road that led to a dirt road that seemed to take them toward a small range of mountains to the north. A few minutes later Tom pulled into a dry wash, announcing that it looked like a perfect place to set out a picnic blanket.

If this had been July or August, when thunderstorms filled dry washes with flash floods, they might have been washed away in a lightning quick torrent. But it was late April, the sky was empty and the earth was dry.

While Penny was laying out the food and Tom was connecting an awning to the side of the car, Mary brushed by a jumping cactus and screamed with pain as multiple needles pierced her skin. Mom and dad dropped everything to tend to her wounds, and since no one was paying attention to Terp, she decided to explore the desert on her own. The bend in the wash captured her interest, so she wended her way around it. Terp followed the sandy bed a while, then stepped up over the bank and down into a depression to her left.

Something shiny a short distance away caught her eye. It was a wooden shack, and its bleached white boards reflected all kinds of color, as if they formed a prism radiating into the surrounding crystal blue sky. Fascinated, she approached it, following a line of triangular shards of sun-dyed blue glass that pointed the way. As she neared the place, Terp experienced a sense of euphoria that made her skip and dance in sweeping circles, spiraling her way toward the open door.

Sunlight from the south poured in through the door, dispelling any sense of darkness inside, and so without fear she danced up to it and said, "Anybody home?" No answer. "Yoo hoo, anybody there?" No words, but she heard a soft chuckle followed by a rattle. Terp stepped through the door and immediately stopped as she saw someone sitting on the floor. She couldn't tell if this was a man or a woman, but whoever it was had long, straight white hair draped over a very big head and was clad in an elegant purple robe.

Rather than startled, Terp felt at ease, as if she had known the Old One would be sitting there with a welcoming smile, in the same place as the last time they had talked. Except she had never been there before, and they had not met, at least not face to face.

"What's your name?" she asked.

"Never mind my name," the Old One said. "You couldn't pronounce it."

"I'm a very good pronouncer for my age," Terp replied. "I'll be five next month."

"Even an adult could not pronounce my name," the Old One countered.

"Do you live here?" she continued.

"I stop by now and again," the Old One answered. "I was hoping you would visit here today. I have something to tell you. When you grow up, look for the floating boy. When all seems lost, seek the floating boy."

Terp said, "I don't know what you mean."

The Old One said, "Don't worry about what I mean. Remember the floating boy. You'll know what it means when the dark time comes. Now turn around and follow the wash back to your parents. They are very worried about you, Terry."

She extended her right index finger and touched the Old One's open left palm. It was soft, dry, and warm to the touch. She spied a snake with a rattle on its tail coiled next to the bigheaded person and reached out to pet it, but the Old One intercepted her hand. Without another thought, she spun around and skipped out into the desert. Halfway back it struck her that the strange person knew her real name, but she had no time to reflect on that, because her father spotted her and ran forward to sweep her into his arms.

"Where have you been?" he cried. "We were so worried."

"I know," she said, and intuitively decided not to tell her parents about the shack and what she had seen inside.

Cloud was being followed again. For the second time that week Quincy Queensbury was stalking him as he walked home from school. The first time Quincy had hit him in the arm and demanded a quarter, which Cloud didn't have, and the bully had settled for fifteen cents. Now Quincy wanted to escort Cloud home and take his pick of Cloud's comic book collection. He had heard that Cloud owned some Superman comics from the 1940s, and he wanted them. He didn't worry that Cloud's mom might interfere in the extortion, because she got home from work around five o'clock, and Cloud would be the only one in the house until then.

But skinny, agile Cloud jumped across the irrigation ditch and ran home through the weed-covered vacant lot, and pudgy Quincy couldn't sprint fast enough to catch him. The taps on Cloud's loafers clacked rapid fire when he reached his driveway and clattered to the front door. He shoved the key into the lock, twisted it, pushed on the door, dashed in and slammed it shut just as Quincy reached the corner of Cloud's front lawn.

A moment later the teenage extortionist huffed and pounded on the door. "Open up, you queer! Bring me your comic books!"

"Go away, Quincy!" Cloud shouted. "I'm calling the cops."

"What a chickenshit! Cloudy's calling the cops. Call my dad. He's a cop. He'll laugh at you." Silence followed this announcement, so the bully continued, "I don't have time for this, but I'll be back and I want those Supermans." Quincy left.

Quincy may seem an unlikely name for the son of a police officer, but in this case the boy was named after John Quincy Adams, a distant relative. Quincy's father was proud of his family genealogical tie with two presidents of the United States -even though the connection was through his wife's lineage- and he spoke of it frequently.

Cloud was thirteen and a month away from graduating from the eighth grade. That morning he learned he had been chosen to give the class speech at the commencement ceremony and had been pleased with himself. Now he was ashamed that he couldn't handle a plodding bully. Every one at school would know it too. So he would have to stand in front of the whole class and deliver a speech while they all giggled and smirked because he was such a sissy.

Adrenaline still coursing through his system, he walked into his bedroom and shut the door. With the curtains drawn shut and the light off, the room was dark, which was what Cloud wanted. He removed his clothes and lay supine on a thin rug, through which he could feel the coolness of the concrete floor permeating into his back, and his body immediately relaxed in response to the familiar setting. He closed his eyes and began breathing slowly and deeply. Although he didn't know it, his breathing approximated a widely used yoga technique.

A few moments later Cloud was floating around the room, looking down at the floor rather than up at the ceiling. No particular thoughts graced his mind. He paid no attention to the items scattered about his room, nor to the naked body of a slender adolescent boy lying on the rug. He merely hovered near the ceiling, basking in the safety of the air. As long as he was aloft, life was peaceful and happy.

An image of his mother driving down Villa Verde Street flickered into his consciousness, so he sailed down into his body, slowly got up, then dressed. He opened the curtains and the bedroom door just as his mother pulled into the driveway. He was setting the kitchen table when she walked through the side door.

"What's for dinner?" he asked.

"Whatever your father brings home," she replied in a voice registering indifference to the meal and annoyance with her husband. "How was school, Cloud?"

"OK. Same as usual." He had no intention of revealing that he had been selected to deliver the class speech, for she would squeal with delight and call neighbors and coworkers to boast about her son's accomplishment. And he was certainly not going to tell her that the same day the principal asked him to do the speech, his home room teacher rapped his knuckles with a ruler because he had been staring out the window, daydreaming again. And he would never tell either parent that the school bully had chased him. He did not trust their ability to protect him, and anything they might do if they knew would only make things worse.

Dinner was creamed chipped beef on toast, prepared by Lloyd Morgan. "During the war we called this stuff shit on a shingle," he chortled. For the first time in years, Lloyd reminisced about the war. As they ate, Lloyd talked while Cloud and Narcissa nodded in polite attention. In the end, all his talk was about stateside service, disappointing Cloud, who yearned to hear about bombs over Germany.

That night, Cloud dreamed that Quincy Queensbury fell down concrete steps and broke his leg. He had to use crutches for two months. The next morning, Quincy was in school, uninjured and as full of malice as ever. It would be four weeks before the event actually occurred and Quincy had to be taken to Good Samaritan Hospital to have the fracture set. It happened the day before graduation, and Cloud reasoned that he thus would have most of the summer free from Quincy's harassment.

The drive back to New Jersey was a blur for Terp. The new Chevrolet transported the Person family through what her father called spectacular scenery, but she didn't remember much of it. She was lost in a five year-old's version of nostalgic reverie. Terp sat in her personal space in the back seat feeling homesick for a desert place where she had spent only one afternoon. She longed to return to a time that seemed like eons ago but was in measured chronology just two weeks past.

Her reverie contained little conceptual content. She basked in remembering the joy she felt dancing in front of the white cabin. She savored the image of Big Head, for in lieu of a withheld unpronounceable name, that was the name she had given to the Old One. This memory filled her tender brain with personal confidence and affection for the whole world. And then there was that lingering anticipation that someday she would see a boy float in the air. Since she loved the Jersey shore, she might have imagined a boy floating in water, but somehow, she conceived of him swimming through sky.

Staring out the window as the car sped along Route 66 through the Painted Desert, Terp focused not on the multi-hued landscape but on a large cumulus cloud overhead, and she conjured the sight of a naked boy sailing and gamboling on top of its fluffy white puffs.

Why he was naked she had no idea; she just knew he would be naked. Terp felt these scenes were her private treasure, and she told no one.

At the eighth grade graduation ceremony, students were arranged in rows alphabetically, so by this plan Quincy should be six seats from Cloud and Cloud could safely ignore him. As it happened, Cloud sat in the first seat in his row, but because of his crutches, Quincy was placed out of order in the end seat immediately behind Cloud.

Quincy jabbed Cloud in the back. "I'm gonna have lots of time to read comic books this summer, so you better get them over to me or else," the bully said.

"Shut up, jerk," Cloud whispered. "If you don't leave me alone I'll break your other leg too then put you on rubber crutches. What a hoot!"

"You and what ten guys?" Quincy boomed, eliciting an icy stare from the principal, who leaned on the podium while grandly introducing the faculty.

To his left Cloud perceived his mother approaching in a crouched walk so she wouldn't block the view from the parents' section. Her appearance peremptorily ended the exchange between the bully and the bullied. Cloud groaned silently, knowing what she was about to say.

"Look here at the program, Cloud. Why didn't you tell me you were giving a speech?" she said, managing to cram delight and indignation into the same words.

"I wanted it to be a surprise," he whispered. "Please, Mom, go back to your seat. You're embarrassing me."

"Pardon me for living. I was only trying to congratulate you," she huffed sarcastically. As she snuck back, Narcissa's ears registered one word of an exchange between Quincy and her son.

Again, Quincy punched Cloud hard in the back. "Hey you *queer*, what did you mean about breaking my other leg *too*?" he demanded.

"Be quiet! You're interrupting the ceremony *too*. All I'm going to say, spastic ass, is if you should happen to break your other leg, remember I told you so first."

Thirty minutes later, the diplomatic niceties and bureaucratic pronouncements now completed, Cloud was summoned to the podium to speak.

While taking the family on an outing to the shore, Tom made a brief detour to his company's warehouse, and Penny decided to wait in the office with the girls.

"Can I go in the warehouse with you, Dad?" Terp asked.

Penny shook her head at Tom, saying, "Not with those cheesecake pinups on every wall."

Terp did not remember pictures of dessert from a visit when she was three and mused aloud, "That's a metaphor, isn't it? Does cheesecake mean naked lady?"

Penny grimaced. "Sometimes. Terp, do you remember *everything* you see and hear?"

"I guess so," Terp said. "Is that bad?"

"No," Penny answered but thought that it *was* disconcerting.

CHAPTER FOUR

Most of Cloud's speech was as trite and as forgettable as such speeches are meant to be. But near the end of his allotted ten minutes, nodding heads lifted and ears turned to listen more carefully.

Cloud said, "Now we look forward to high school. In a few minutes we will no longer be grade schoolers but freshmen. When we get to high school, most of the kids there won't know us. They won't know what boys got paddled by the teacher in shop class. They won't know who walked through the breezeway making loud burps. They won't know which girls showed their health class pamphlets to the boys, even though they were supposed to keep them secret. They won't know what girl wrote in lipstick on the mirror in the boys' bathroom. They won't even know who the class bully was.

"This is an opportunity for all of us to start over. High school is our chance to become who we want to be and not who everyone knows we are. Everyone can grow up. Everyone can change, even the belchers and bullies.

"So, dream of better things, class of '57. West High here we come! Thank you."

This was more or less what Cloud had submitted to the principal a week earlier for editorial assistance and pre-approval, except for the references to specific behaviors. The principal took a deep breath and sighed. As Cloud returned to his seat, the principal rose to introduce the District Superintendent, who would hand out the diplomas, and he said in a half bemused half stern way, "Thank you, Cloud. I see that you've already begun to *change* things in your life."

Life was about to change for Cloud in a way that despite his prescient tendencies he could not have anticipated. His mother got religion and began attending church. In an effort to salvage her never strong marriage, she decided to take Jesus Christ as her personal possession. Now she insisted that her family sit with her in the pew. Lloyd agreed to try it for a while. He had been contemplating leaving her for several years, and calculated that his willingness to attend church with his wife would be looked upon favorably by the judge when the divorce proceedings eventually began. Cloud had no choice in the matter, and he went along without protest.

The vehicle for this excursion into the world of religion was an independent congregation called the Disciples' Angelic Fundamentalist Temple, which Narcissa chose not on the basis of its doctrine but because it was the nearest church to her home.

The pastor, T. C. Smith, was a self-ordained tenth grade dropout. He grew up in the town of Coolidge, south of the Pima Indian community on the Gila River Reservation, having had the ill luck to be born a few months before the stock market crash of 1929 that ushered in the Great Depression. T. C.'s chronically unemployed father was in the habit during those bleak economic times of getting roaring drunk and taking out his anger on his son. A mesquite switch was his generally preferred corporal punishment tool. Smith senior was drafted during World War II and was killed in a bar fight in Wahiawa, near Schofield Barracks, Hawaii.

Wanting to feel like he had become the man in the family, T. C. quit school in the spring of 1945 and moved to Phoenix, where he took a job helping to deliver ice to bars around the city. He stuck with that till he turned twenty-one and could legally drink in those places where he had been hauling ice. But he was bored with ice, and with vivid memories of being terrorized by an alcoholic father, he had no interest in consuming alcohol.

Lacking any better plan for his life, he enlisted in the US Army in 1950. T. C. landed in Korea in 1951, where he suffered massive emotional wounds in combat and was given a medical discharge on the basis of battle fatigue.

Because of the nature of his release from the service, T. C. could not find a job. Looking for something to do with his ample free time, he wandered into a B. B. Buckshot tent revival at the fairgrounds in Phoenix. Buckshot wore cowboy boots and a fancy silver studded cowboy shirt. His wavy blond hair bounced as he strutted back and forth across the stage. Stopping in the center of the stage, he planted his boots firmly on the boards and slowly turned to face the audience.

Clasping an open Bible in his left hand, he poked his right index finger onto the page (which by sheer coincidence was a portion of Ecclesiastes) and drawled, "Jesus. It says right here in the Holy Bible, Jeeeeesus wants you to say no to the devil."

B. B. spoke at length, describing what the Bible said about this and that personal behavior, intoning from memory a list of unconnected words and phrases, which if not quoted precisely from the King James Version, sounded authentic. Ten minutes into his spiel, the sweat on his forehead triggered a chemical reaction with a powder he had previously applied to his skin. A glowing red cross appeared above his eyes, eliciting gasps from the audience.

After twenty minutes of increasingly intense verbal devotion to the word of God, the tent evangelist shifted thematically to the matter of stewardship. That is, he began to talk, softly at first, about giving money to the B. B. Buckshot Ministries.

"I'm going to take this town for Jeeeeesus," he said. "But I need your help. I need help from believers. There's a handful of believers here tonight; I know it. Are you one of 'em? I'm gonna take Phoenix for the Lord, if you will help me. It takes green stuff to fight the devil, but if you dig deep enough, I will take this damned town!"

There was another audible gasp when he said damned. He knew it was coming, so he paused for it. The gasp was not as loud in Phoenix as it was in Tulsa or Amarillo, but it was louder than Las Vegas. Vegas was a tough town, he mused, and he may have to drop it from his circuit.

""D'ya hear me friends? I said DAMNED town. That's right,

and I'll say it again. Phoenix is damned, damned, damned! But I'm not gonna let Satan have you. I'm gonna take every damned soul in Phoeeeeenix and give them all to Jeeeeesus. And here's the deal, friends. If you give me ten dollars, God will bless you, and I will ask God to turn the one-dollar bills in your pocket into tens. I know he can do that. I promise you, God wants to multiply your money. If you give me twenty, think of the riches God will give you! Are you with me?"

T. C. was with him. He was excited. He knew clearly now what he was going to do with his life. As the ushers began circulating through the crowd with their deep cloth bags attached to long poles, efficiently lifting the offering, T. C. stood up and slipped out of the tent. Once outside, he leaped up in the air and shouted, "Whoopee!"

Two uniformed security guards immediately confronted T. C. Their caps and sleeves bore horseshoe shaped patches with crossed shotguns and the red-lettered name of their master: B. B. Buckshot Ministries.

"Hey buddy boy, we're gonna run you in for disturbing a religious ceremony," the larger of the two said in a menacing manner.

"Aw gee, I didn't mean to," T. C. said. "I'm just excited for the Lord, and I'm gonna go get some of my buddies right now and bring 'em back here." This was an instinctual lie. He wasn't going to have any of his friends give money to B. B. Buckshot. They were going to give it to him. In that tent T. C. had experienced a mystical vision in which he saw ten and twenty-dollar bills showered upon him by eager parishioners. The guards stood aside and let him pass.

T. C. Smith walked out of the fairgrounds and into his destiny, which was conveniently located right across the street. He began preaching in the parking lot of the Union 76 gas station at Six Points, attracting a small band of disciples, who soon tired of sitting on folding chairs in the sun and built a small concrete block sanctuary a few blocks up 19th Avenue at Granada.

In 1954, Smith legally changed his name from Thomas Charles Smith to Ten Commandments Smith. Using his initials for general identity, he developed a sermon for a private ceremony to induct new members into DAFT. In this sermon he dramatically revealed how he had been born in an adobe hut on the Pima Indian reservation, because his parents had been traveling to Phoenix at the time, and his mother's water had burst before they could get to a hospital.

Two Indian women appeared out of the morning mist and attended the birth, and then God spoke to his father, telling him to name his son Ten Commandments. The midwives who brought T. C. into the world told his father that their village had a secret Indian name, which translated into English meant burning bush.

It was an inspiring account, which Smith concluded by telling his new disciples that his name was to be kept strictly secret. Only members of the church were allowed to know his real name. Since he had been born in the desert and did not have a birth certificate, the satanic officials who had infiltrated the Arizona state government could not control his destiny. They must never reveal to outsiders what T. C. stood for, even to regular visitors. Therefore, knowledge of this hidden name soon spread well beyond the congregation, although members faithfully concealed the sacred method of its conferral.

The Morgans were not members of DAFT. They attended services regularly during the summer of 1957, but Narcissa was disinclined to join until she could see how it would benefit her, and Lloyd was not interested in taking on the commitment to tithe the pre-tax family income, which was a requirement for membership.

In addition to Sunday morning services, the temple conducted a vacation Bible school on Saturday mornings led by the preacher's plump and obedient wife, Anjelina. Narcissa made Cloud attend. At nearly fourteen, he was the oldest child there, but he dutifully made little temples out of Popsicle sticks and helped the younger ones paste "Jesus loves me" stickers onto their workbook pages.

Anjelina was as gentle and affectionate as her husband was strident and fiery. She told them stories about Jesus, how Jesus loved children, and how he was the kindest and gentlest person who ever lived, only he wasn't a real person. He only pretended to be human. He was actually God in disguise. And the reason God came to earth in disguise was to teach people how to love one another.

Anjelina, nee Cordero, had been raised -begrudgingly- by her maternal aunt and uncle, after her mother died in childbirth and her father disappeared. She was one of T. C.'s first converts in the parking lot at Six Points, and the unhappy teenager quickly fell under the spell of his seductive personality. She was sixteen when she wed T. C. Smith.

Over time, Smith developed a peculiar ecclesiastical garb for Sunday morning. He appeared before the congregation wearing immaculate white suede shoes, tight navy blue slacks, and a billowing bright red dress shirt. In lieu of a tie, an ivory crucifix on a gold rope chain dangled from his neck. Keenly aware that his chin and nose were long and sharp, T. C. sought to soften these features with bushy wide sideburns and a lush crop of brown hair combed back and carefully shaped into a ducktail at the base of his skull.

Worship began with singing a few gospel songs, and then T. C. opened his Bible and began to preach, without addressing any specific text. As he spoke, he would read whatever came into his sight on the pages open before him, occasionally leafing through the chapters, selecting snippets of text at random. After reading a few lines from the Psalms, or Malachi, or Luke, or Revelation, he would call on the Holy Ghost to use him to explain God's word to the people.

One Sunday Smith opened his Bible to First Samuel 28:17 and read, "For the Lord hath rent the kingdom out of thine hand, and given it to thy neighbor." He looked up from the text, scanned the congregation with piercing eyes and interpreted the words of scripture. "Praise the Lord, good friends. The Holy Ghost has led me to this passage for certain this very hour. This is a warning about paying for the temple. It means you gotta take good care of this temple where you sit all cozy out of the blazing sun. This is why tithing is absolutely necessary. Friends, if you don't give enough money to pay the mortgage on this temple, God will rent it to someone else. The mortgage payment is due next Wednesday and we're short of funds. If we don't come up with the money for the bankers, God's gonna take this church away from us and rent it to the neighbors out there who have never once darkened the door of this place. Heathens the lot of them! But God will punish this congregation if you're stingy. Therefore I say unto you, be generous with your gifts, lest God smite you and all those you love with his mighty hand. Hallelujah!"

With rapid finger movements, he turned pages in his Bible until the Holy Ghost apparently caused him to stop near the end of the Song of Solomon, and he read from the eighth chapter, eighth verse, "We have a little sister and she hath no breasts." Smith pointed his finger toward heaven and intoned, "God has a reason for depriving this poor creature of her breasts. This little girl has done something wicked, and God is punishing her. Jesus said so. Here, let me find you the proof."

For a minute or two he paged through his Bible looking for a particular text. "Ah, here it is," he said triumphantly. "Suffer the children to come unto me." He stared right at Cloud. "Do you know who said that? It was Jesus. Jesus is not afraid of suffering. He suffered on the cross for your salvation. But this passage right here, Luke 18:16, says he was not afraid to make even children suffer if they disobey their parents. Suffer the little children, Jesus said, for such is the kingdom of God."

Cloud noticed that no matter what words the preacher read from the Bible, the Holy Ghost always seemed to produce the same interpretation of the text. That basic message was that God was exceedingly angry with people, especially children, who did all sorts of secret sinful things when their parents weren't around. God was so angry he was going to destroy the world. He had done it once before by flood, and saved only members of Noah's family, but next time God's anger was going to be assuaged by fire.

Sometimes Smith used the language of warfare he had learned in Korea to embellish his picture of God's planned destruction. "Gooood," he proclaimed, stretching out the word for the Deity into four syllables, "is coming to Phoenix with his holy machine guns, and he's gonna mow down every unbeliever in town. He's gonna strafe this neighborhood right here with angelic power from the skies. You better put on your bulletproof vests, my friends, and put on your Jesus helmets. You better shield yourselves on the Word of God, if you want to survive the invasion of Satan's army."

At other times, T. C. added comments about how the Book of Revelation predicted American and Soviet nuclear test explosions. These were signs that the end was near for unbelievers. Only those who stopped their secret sinning and joined the Disciples' Angelic Fundamentalist Temple and tithed their pre-tax income would be saved from God's mighty wrath. "Duck Satan and cover yourself in the Bible!" he railed.

Occasionally he offered a softer, more encouraging variation on this theme, extolling how grateful he was to be part of this good and faithful fellowship, rather than lost out there in the wicked neighborhoods of Phoenix.

For many DAFT worshipers, the highlight of the service was the pastor's long prayer, which Smith delivered in stream-of-consciousness fashion. With tearful emotion, he named people with various illnesses and infirmities, praying for God to heal them. This was a great source of gossip for parishioners who craved such material. But the best part of the prayer came at the end, when all eyes were piously closed but all ears acutely attentive. Smith bravely begged God to forgive unnamed members who had backslid in certain evil ways. He vividly described the ways, and it became great lunchtime sport for congregants to speculate on who had committed which specific sins. Sexual sins were the highlight, stimulating a great deal of fantasy and regret among the faithful worshipers.

One Sunday Smith's Bible opened to the second chapter of John, the story of Jesus at a wedding at Cana in Galilee. The guests exhausted the supply of wine, and Mary, Jesus' mother, exhorted the servants to do whatever Jesus told them to do. Jesus ordered them to fill ritual bathing vessels with water, which Jesus then turned into wine.

After reading the passage, T. C. looked up with a grin of triumph. "Here it is, folks. Children did you hear the word of God? Mary told them to do what Jesus ordered. This is plain as the nose on your face. Obey your mother! You have to obey Jesus. Everybody knows that. But the Bible teaches right here in John chapter two: Do what your mother tells you. Jesus obeyed his mother, and so should you!"

"Amen," Narcissa whispered into Cloud's ear. "Mother knows best." She was beginning to appreciate Smith's approach to biblical interpretation.

Mary just wanted Jesus to show off, Cloud thought, to make her look good. She nagged Jesus into turning that water into wine.

Cloud was not impressed with Smith's preaching, and one day in vacation Bible school, he said to Anjelina, "If Jesus and God are the same being, then how is it possible for Jesus to be always loving and God always angry?"

She was taken by surprise by the question, which had never occurred to her, and she tried to formulate an answer but only succeeded in confusing herself. Finally she said, "My husband understands these things. He's a man of God. You need to ask him."

The next day in church Cloud mentally rehearsed ways he could ask his question at the end of the service. He soon fell into a meditative state in which his eyes fell on the head of T. C. Smith in a diffused way, and Cloud saw an aura surrounding the preacher. Extending up from his shoulders, it circled his head like a solid halo. The aura was dark red and black. Its colors formed a repository for fear and malice, anger and confusion.

Then something entered Cloud's consciousness. It was not a voice. There was no sound inside his head, but a command appeared in his mind: Do not ask this man your question. Leave this place now and do not come back.

During Smith's scripture reading performance, Cloud abruptly stood and sidled past his parents in the pew, walked down the aisle and out the door into the hot, dry air of a late morning in mid-July. The enveloping heat felt good to him, cleansing and reassuring. He walked the few blocks to his home, and then had to sit on the front porch awaiting his parents' arrival, because he had left his key on his dresser.

Narcissa was furious. "How dare you humiliate me in front of the whole congregation. You will march right back to the temple and apologize to Pastor Smith."

"I'm not going back there," he said defiantly. "I will never go back there again."

Seizing this moment to be uncharacteristically decisive, Lloyd said, "You don't have to, Son. I'm not going back either."

Narcissa was stunned into momentary silence, then recovered long enough to shout, "Damn you both. I'm not fixing lunch. You can starve as far as I care."

Lloyd and Cloud drove over to Hasty Tasty and ate burgers and fries, while Narcissa sulked in her bedroom. At one point during the meal, Lloyd reached over and stroked the back of Cloud's head. He came close to saying he loved his boy, but couldn't quite get the words out. Instead, he said, "We should do this more often, just us guys."

Cloud beamed inwardly. This was the best meal he had ever eaten, and somehow he knew that he would remember this day for a long, long time. The sensation of his father's caress stayed with him till he fell into blissful sleep that night.

The rest of the summer passed with no more church for Lloyd and Cloud but also no more father and son lunches. Narcissa attended services alone for a few weeks, out of angry stubbornness, but finally acknowledged to herself that the control over husband and son that church had provided her was now lost, and she stopped going. After all, she reasoned, what's the point of listening to a disagreeable preacher if you can't gain leverage over your family as a result?

Three people occupied the same house, living separate lives. Narcissa tried to reengage with Cloud, but he maintained an emotional distance she could not penetrate. Lloyd did not raise the subject of divorce with his wife. There would be time for that later, when Cloud was older. He didn't want a judge to decide where Cloud should live, on the one hand feeling resentment that judges always gave custody of children to the wives, and on the other hand fearing that in this case, Cloud might insist on staying with his father and the judge would agree. The fear was that he did not know how to be a good father. And so, the status quo was better than forcing painful decisions.

Cloud brooded about his flight from DAFT. In rejecting Smith and his temple, Cloud sensed an unseen reality more potent, more beautiful, and more sublime than the church was capable of describing. Indeed, the church, via Pastor Smith, was distorting this ultimate reality, which Cloud was increasingly hesitant to call God. Whatever it was, Cloud respected it and did not want to trivialize it, as he perceived Smith was doing.

Cloud did not see Quincy at all that summer, but late in August he had another dream about him. There had been a thunderstorm that evening. A lightning strike to a power line had knocked out the electricity in the neighborhood. All the families in the area dug out candles for illumination, and with their evaporative coolers out of service, opened front, back, and side doors to invite errant breezes into their homes.

During the storm Cloud sat on the front porch basking in a wet gust. The street had become a channel for three inches of flash flood, turning his home into a temporary river front property. When the rain stopped, he drank in the ozone-scented atmosphere. He had always liked the musty smell of air pumped into his room by the rooftop cooler, but he delighted even more in the pungent odor of after-the-rain electrified oxygen.

His mother grumbled about the loss of power and stubbornly insisted on waiting in the living room for its restoration, while his father sat in the kitchen by the side door, patiently cradling a glass of ice water in his hands. Cloud accepted the seasonal storm with its inevitable lightning strike on a utility pole as an unscheduled holiday that was best celebrated outdoors. As he opened his senses to the event, he thought about Quincy and imagined him on crutches, sloshing through mud puddles, arriving soaked at Cloud's porch and demanding comic books. He laughed at that unlikely prospect.

Later, after he went to bed, the troubling dream about the bully came to him.

CHAPTER FIVE

Terp had started dance lessons when she was four, and she loved every minute of every lesson. Each Saturday morning she put on her tiny leotard and tights, ready for her mom to drive her to the studio at least half an hour before Penny was ready, and even then she usually arrived ahead of the other students. While waiting for them to arrive, Terp made faces in the wall-to-wall studio mirrors and whirled around the floor, causing her long tresses to fly across her face.

Her dance instructor, Martha Papillon, explained that her nickname, Terp, was the start of Terpsichore, the muse of dance. Her mother told her it had come from saying Terry Person fast and mixing the sounds. Terp had no idea what a muse was, but she delighted in any connection between herself and dance. She cherished the story her mother often repeated that she suffered colic as an infant. The only thing that would quiet little Terry's wailing was swaying in her father's arms while he played his recording of the new Leroy Anderson hit "Blue Tango" over and over. The notion that she craved dance music even from the crib made her happy.

One day, not long after the vacation in Arizona, Terp told her mother she was going to be a dancer on television someday. "Maybe I'll get a job as one of those Old Gold cigarette dancers on TV," she said. All the viewer could see in these commercials were the legs of the dancers, as giant cigarette packs and accompanying matchboxes covered the rest of their anatomy. "They can't see their bodies," Terp continued, "so maybe the TV station might hire a kid like me to dance." She reflected a little more on this prospect and then said, "But daddy smokes cigarettes with a different picture on the pack, so maybe they wouldn't let me do it, because daddy doesn't buy their kind."

Penny laughed and said, "You've got a long way to go, little Terp, before you find out what to do with your life. Maybe you'll marry a pilot or a doctor. Keep dreaming, honey."

At that instant, Terp remembered the floating boy and wondered if she would marry him. But she had no idea who he was or where he lived, and so she put the thought away for a later time and ran off to watch *Name That Tune* on television.

Forty-five minutes later, after Penny had kissed her goodnight and shut the door to her room, Terp lay awake musing about her encounter with Big Head. The bright memory brought her a sense of elation that argued against sleep, and in response to an inner urge, she climbed out of bed, pulled off her pajamas and danced around the dark room to a tune she composed spontaneously in her mind. Terp stepped softly so as not to make any noise that would attract her parents and swayed her arms through the air intuitively seeking contact with her invisible floating partner.

Cloud's troubling dream included not only Quincy but also his father. Burkholdt Queensbury was a Highway Patrol officer, tall and solidly built. He moved gracefully with authority whether he was in civvies or uniform. Quincy had inherited his size from his father, but his pudginess had come from his mother. There was not an ounce of softness in the frame of his father.

In the dream, Quincy was reading comic books, and his father came in and tore them up and slapped Quincy around the room. The boy seemed to bounce off the walls like a rubber ball, while the father caught him and sent him flying against another wall, faster and faster each time. The image was something Cloud had seen in a cartoon on an afternoon kids show on Channel 5. Only instead of a cat, it was Quincy who was bouncing like a huge tennis ball. Then

Quincy was lying alone on his bed crying. Cloud woke up in a heavy sweat.

Unable to get back to sleep, he decided to try floating. He pulled off his underwear and moved to the rug, where he lay flat on his back, breathing slowly and deeply. Instead of leaving his body, however, his mind wandered to a distant Eden-like place where he saw himself leaning against a soft, tropical tree. The ground was covered with velvety clover, inviting him to walk upon it barefoot so the leaves could tickle and massage his feet. Since he had not a stitch of clothing on, he not only felt his feet being tickled, but his whole body was gently massaged as he reclined, rolled around, and reveled in the warm, green world. And then a girl, also naked and as slender as he, waltzed into the scene. She had long dark hair and glowing eyes. Lowering herself into a space on his left, she nestled against him and the two fell asleep tingling and smiling.

When he awoke just before dawn, he was still on his back on the rug and dried semen was spread all over his stomach. "Shit!" he exclaimed through clenched teeth and leapt to his feet. Making his way quickly and quietly into the bathroom, he cleaned himself off with a washcloth and returned to his room.

A few nights later, he lay supine on his bedroom rug and successfully left his body, ascending to the ceiling. Narcissa had stayed up late re-reading a paperback novel, and en route to the bathroom stopped on impulse at Cloud's door, cracked it open and peeked in. Seeing her son's inert body on the floor, she stepped inside and said, "I wasn't aware that you slept on the floor, or for that matter, that you slept in the nude." Hearing no response, she sighed. "Like mother like son, I guess, at least about bedroom attire."

Assuming he was asleep, she bent down to peer into his unresponsive face. Hovering above the room, Cloud was startled by the intrusion and in panic shouted, "Don't touch me!" Narcissa heard nothing, for Cloud had no vocal chords while floating outside his body. Nevertheless, she felt something -some mental force- commanding her to step back, which she obeyed immediately, feeling momentarily fearful.

Cloud dove back into his body, and as Narcissa turned to leave, he said as casually as he could muster, "My back's sore, so I'm stretching it out."

"Oh," she said with relief. "That makes sense. Well, goodnight, Cloud."

When Cloud registered for courses at West High, he was presented with three options to meet the physical education requirement. He could take gym, marching band, or ROTC. He didn't think twice about his choice of Reserve Officers Training Corps.

Throughout grade school, the best he'd ever experienced when teams were chosen for baseball, football, soccer, or even volleyball was third to last. Usually he was second to last, just ahead of the boy with cerebral palsy. It wasn't that he lacked coordination, but he was smaller and younger than every other boy in his class. Enduring yet more rejection in gym class was not appealing.

He had taken trumpet lessons briefly in sixth grade, but the teacher had told him he would never be a musician, so joining the band was out. ROTC is what he would have chosen anyway, because it meant marching, rifle drill, and wearing khaki uniforms to school every Tuesday. And especially it meant following in his father's footsteps, on track to becoming a commissioned Army officer. This was his secret dream. Quincy opted for ROTC also, although he was in a different platoon and the two seldom spoke.

For ten days each November, the Arizona State Fair dominated the neighborhood where Cloud lived. His house at 1926 W. Villa Verde was less than a block from the fairgrounds. Many area residents, including the Morgans, charged fair-goers fifty cents to park on the yellowed grass of their front lawns. Cloud financed his own visits to the fair with the Liberty and Franklin half-dollars he had earned in this way.

One Friday in 1957, he headed for the main fairgrounds entrance on McDowell, and as he approached the gate a wounded veteran accosted him. The man, missing one leg, stood on the sidewalk, propped up by wooden crutches. In his right hand was a coffee can covered with decorative paper. "Hey kid," he called out to Cloud, "put a dollar in the can. I'll give you a poppy for your lapel."

Cloud was embarrassed. He had plenty of silver in his pocket, but a dollar was a lot of money. "I don't have a lapel," he said, blushing.

"Big deal! I don't have a leg, so I guess I won't cry over your missing lapel," said the veteran.

Cloud turned his face from the man and rushed toward the entrance.

"Hey, rich kid!" the ex-soldier shouted after him. "I hope you grow up to be a soldier and have your leg blown off too!" Cloud did not look back, but the man's words rang in his brain the rest of the day.

He interrogated himself about why he had refused charity to the disabled veteran. He probably wouldn't have spent much on the midway. He had more cash than he needed. In fact, his favorite thing to do at the fair was free.

In years past, he had stood for hours in the agriculture building fascinated with watching Navajo sand painters create intricate designs of white, blue, yellow, and black. He always tried to locate the intentional flaw the artist created, supposedly to let the evil spirits out, but he could never find one. Cloud suspected the flaw had more to do with protecting the *iikaah* from outsiders. The sand paintings were, after all, created to restore harmony and thus healing to Navajo people. This day had turned into one of great disharmony for Cloud, and he wished his equilibrium could be restored.

Yet he sensed something amiss in the veteran's approach to him, and he was reluctant, even afraid to go back and put a dollar in the can. The fair simply wasn't any fun this year, he decided. Cloud left through another gate and went home to spit shine his ROTC shoes, polish his brass, and iron his khaki shirt and pants. Ordinarily he did this task Monday night, in preparation for platoon inspection on Tuesday, but he was feeling guilty for withholding alms, and the extra diligent use of Brasso, Kiwi shoe polish, and a hot iron seemed like a good way to atone for his selfishness.

That night, Cloud floated again. This time he left his room and explored the house from the vantage point of the ceiling, although he stayed out of his parents' bedroom. He had never before left the confines of his own room but now felt a need to be more daring.

Cloud saw thick dust clinging to the top of the picture window drapes. The furniture was worn in places he had previously not noticed. His father's business journals were neatly piled on top of a world atlas on the end table by the couch, and his mother's romance novels were strewn across the stand beside her easy chair. A half-eaten box of sweet prunes rested on a pile of paperbacks on the floor next to her chair. And there on the carpet, four feet in front of the television, Cloud saw an indented area, the outline of his body in the space he had occupied for half his life, where he had watched **Rin Tin Tin**, **The Lone Ranger**, **Superman**, **Gold Dust Charlie**, **It's Wallace**, and many other shows. He saw that he'd made a mark in his home, and it was in the carpet in front of the TV.

Biology was Cloud's favorite class his freshman year. At the start of each term, the teacher, Mr. Logosaur, made disputable statements to see if anyone would challenge him. To his great disappointment, few students did. Logosaur quoted American physicist Albert Michelson: "The more important fundamental laws and facts of physical science have all been discovered," Michelson wrote in 1894. Logosaur followed this with words spoken in 1899 by Charles H. Duell, United States Commissioner of Patents. Duell said, "Everything that can be invented has been invented."

"What do you think?" the teacher asked. There was silence in the room. "If I said I think these men were right, what would you say?" he prodded. Hands went up around the room. "Yes, Mr. Logosaur," came the responses. "There is nothing new under the sun," quoted one student in defense of the pronouncements.

Cloud could not contain his frustration. His hand shot up, and when the teacher called on him, he said, "They were wrong, Mr. Logosaur. There is much more to invent. We haven't discovered everything yet."

"Then tell me what we haven't yet discovered," Logosaur countered.

"I don't know. How can I know that right now? But I'm sure we don't know everything about the universe. And besides, look at how much stuff has been invented since whats-his-name said everything has already been invented," Cloud responded. "And Einstein's discoveries came after that other physicist," he added as an afterthought.

Mr. Logosaur smiled. He had a live one. The semester would not be a total waste.

Logosaur's instruction in Darwinian evolution inspired Cloud, the concept exploding in his brain. It helped him formulate a personal understanding of the universe and his place in it. He saw himself as part of a chain of relationships extending past human existence, connecting him to all life and every atom of creation.

After class one day, a fellow student told Cloud evolution was wrong, that God created humans, and humans do not evolve. Cloud said he thought they did evolve.

"So if humans were once apes," the student said, "then you're saying someday they might become -I don't know- maybe flying monkeys or something. What a crock!"

"Not monkeys," Cloud responded seriously. "But we might evolve into *some* kind of flying creature." He then blushed, thinking of his secret out-of-body flights.

"God's gonna strike you dead for that," the student said. "You'll go to hell, but maybe Satan will let you hang out with your buddy Darwin in the hottest part of hell."

"I'll take my chances," Cloud said and walked away. He felt confident that humans were still evolving and liked the idea of being related to monkeys, birds, and grasshoppers. The notion that he was of the same substance as mountains and oceans was comforting. And at that time he had no difficulty seeing the existence of God and the process of evolution as fully compatible.

But then the nightmares began. Cloud suffered vivid dreams four or five nights a week in a recurring pattern. First was a dream that he visited Quincy to give him comic books, and when he returned home, the place was empty and his parents were gone. Nobody knew where Narcissa and Lloyd had moved. Sometimes in this nightmare he did not recognize the house when he returned home. It was now built of wood or concrete block instead of tufa stone. Sometimes the house was on a different street or in another town, but he knew it was his house and his parents were deliberately absent.

Next came a dream that he was ill with a horrible disease and his parents had to burn all his things. He saw them with their arms full of his clothes, his comic book collection, his science fiction novels, his ROTC uniform, his rock and roll records, all the things that added material accents to his identity. They carried them out to a fifty-five gallon steel barrel, threw them in and set them on fire. He lay naked and sick in his bed, unable to stop his parents from casting his life into the fire barrel.

In the third dream, he flew to Jupiter to perform a heroic deed for the people of Earth. When he got to the giant planet, he learned his task was to dynamite a wicked witch who was ruling the solar system in a very cruel manner. He managed to sneak into her room and wire explosives around her rocking chair, and once outside, he pressed the plunger and blew the witch to pieces. When he got home, anticipating a hero's reception, he discovered the body of the wicked witch in a box in his front yard. And she wasn't really dead! She was about to spring to life and pay him back for trying to kill her.

He could not stop the nightmares. To avoid them, he tried floating, but it didn't happen. No matter how hard he tried to leave his body, he was unable to do so. The dreams snuck up on him in the hours before dawn, and he shuddered through them, completely at the mercy of his unconscious mind.

One day in the spring of his freshman year, his mother told Cloud to go directly home from school, because Korricks would be delivering new furniture, and he would need to sign for it. Neither she nor Lloyd could get home from work in time to do that.

When the truck arrived, he watched the men unload two double beds along with mattresses and box springs. That evening, the three of them set up the two new beds in the master bedroom, moved the old double bed, his parents' marital bed, into Cloud's room, and put Cloud's old twin bed in the garage at the back of their property. Now everyone in the family had his or her own double bed.

Two weeks passed before Cloud realized that the three nightmares had not recurred. Was it coincidence, he wondered, that these fearful nocturnal episodes ceased when the family sleeping arrangements changed? Had he given up his childhood anxieties when he switched to a grown-up bed? He felt a strange ambivalence that his parents no longer slept in the same bed but did not allow himself to think too much about the significance of that.

The absence of nightmares provided Cloud a welcome season of deep rest, but in time the place of those tormented imaginings would be filled with other dreams, not as personally frightening but equally disquieting.

CHAPTER SIX

One student who heard Cloud's eighth grade graduation speech heeded his advice that people could change. Quincy changed his name to Quinn. The new name reminded him of the strongly masculine actor Anthony Quinn. As Quincy he had felt the need to prove he was not a sissy, hence his inclination to bully smaller boys. But as Quinn, in a new setting where only a few people knew his past, he would be able to reinvent himself as a cool cat with nothing to compensate for.

Cloud noticed the change in his nemesis and felt a tinge of affection for him. He was tempted to see if the two could be friends based on their new high school identities. Cloud had been a loner his whole life and did not have any other friends, so Quinn might be a good place to start. But he was wary. A tiger with its stripes painted over was still a tiger. So Cloud observed Quinn from a distance and did not make an overture about becoming pals.

Cloud's first high school friend turned out to be another loner and an outsider in the school's social culture. Firstlaugh Begay stood to the right of Cloud in the third squad of third platoon of Company B of the Junior ROTC Battalion at West High. The Navajo lad was so shy that Cloud felt like a raging extrovert next to him.

The cadet platoon sergeant teased Firstlaugh, calling him his injun soljer. Other cadets soon joined in, believing that it was all in good fun, but the platoon sergeant took this as affirmation and escalated to calling Firstlaugh redskin, renegade, heap good scout, and squaw-boy. Firstlaugh said nothing in reply, but Cloud was furious and went to the older student privately and told him to knock off the racist language.

He ignored Cloud and continued to use the derogatory expressions. In frustration, Cloud went back and informed the bigot the Navajo Mafia Klan would be coming after him, and this scared the credulous cadet sergeant into silence. No such group existed, of course, and Cloud never mentioned his fantasy threat to Firstlaugh.

Cloud and Firstlaugh fell into a routine of eating lunch together each Tuesday, when the ROTC cadets wore their uniforms to school. They set their trays across from one another and listened to the cafeteria jukebox pump out rock and roll.

"How did you get the name Firstlaugh?" Cloud asked his friend the first time they ate together.

"It's from a Navajo custom. The first time a baby laughs is an important event. The adult who witnesses a baby's first laugh throws a big party called **Chi Dlo Dil** to celebrate this sign that the baby's ready to be social." He paused from telling the story, but Cloud said not a word, waiting for his friend to continue. "My father was good at getting babies to laugh, and he threw a lot of parties before he went off to the war. So when I was born, my mother thought about my father making Hawaiian babies laugh, where he was stationed at the time. There was no chance for him to see my first laugh, so she honored him by naming me Firstlaugh."

"Wow," Cloud said.

"It could have been worse," Firstlaugh went on. "She thought about making it Son of First Laugh Maker, but that would have been too much to write, so she settled for one word."

"What did your father do in the war?" Cloud asked.

"I don't know. He was in the Marines and fought on Iwo Jima, but he won't talk about it. He just says he did odd jobs for Uncle Sam."

Firstlaugh had been born in Tuba City, on the Navajo Reservation. His parents had been raised as Traditional Navajos, although they had become secularized through attendance at the government school in town. After the war, his father took advantage of the GI Bill, enrolling at Arizona State College at Flagstaff. When he graduated in 1951, he began teaching at a reservation school in Chinle. After a few years, the family moved to Phoenix so that Firstlaugh's father could work on a master's degree in education at Arizona State College at Tempe. Over time, this stretched into a doctoral program, and to support the family, Mrs. Begay took a job with the U. S. Government as a clerk at the Phoenix Indian Hospital.

"My father has a lot of respect for the traditional beliefs of our people," Firstlaugh explained over lunch one Tuesday. "He doesn't practice it, and he doesn't believe it literally, but he tells me the stories have meaning, and he wants me to learn them."

"I wish I could get my dad to talk about his family stories," Cloud said. "But he always says someday he's going to tell me, but he never does."

"Well, these aren't stories about my family but about the **Dine**, our people. They're like stories in the Bible. They tell how the world came to be," Firstlaugh explained. "My father says our stories are not factually true. They're myths, but spiritually true. They point to something important about human beings. He's working on a doctorate, so he talks like that."

"I wish your dad would say that to the minister of the church I used to go to," Cloud said. "He claims that all the stories in the Bible are absolute facts. I don't see how they can be, what with evolution, fossils, and the discoveries of science."

"I believe in science too," Firstlaugh said. "But I still want to learn the ways of my people. I told my father I want to visit a *hataalii* -what the whites call a medicine man- and he said OK. A *hataalii* is a singer, one who heals by chanting songs."

"Are you sick?" Cloud asked.

"Not physically. Homesick, I guess. Seeing a singer is like going to English class where they teach you how to diagram sentences so you can understand how it all works. A *hataalii* can teach you how to diagram the world so you can see how you fit in with everything. It's important to be in balance with the creation, to walk in beauty."

"But what if the singer tells you things -and he really believes those things- that you know are not true?" Cloud asked.

"It doesn't matter if they are literally true," the Navajo

explained. "The stories and songs are reflections of what my people have lived through. You should listen to my father. He can tell you about history and myth that will make you want to jump into the past and see for yourself what made the **Dine** love the land and believe in ghosts."

As part of his campaign to reinvent himself, Quinn Queensbury decided to develop a reputation as a daredevil. An opportunity to demonstrate fearlessness came in early spring 1958. An infestation of grasshoppers swarmed across the West High campus. The ROTC field was so thick with the insects that drill practice was cancelled. While other cadets cursed and made disgusting noises in response to grasshoppers flying into their faces, Quinn acted nonchalant.

"Hey, in some countries they eat hoppers like delicacies," Quinn announced.

"Let's see you eat one then," another boy responded.

"OK. Give me two-bits for every one I chew and swallow," Quinn replied coolly.

The members of his platoon circled him as they pledged their financial support to his gustatory endeavor. At twenty-five cents per insect, Quinn went home three dollars richer that day. The esteem he earned from his peers was mixed, however. Some thought him fearless while some thought him an idiot.

The following week, though, he clearly improved his reputation among male classmates. He obtained a paperback copy of the steamy best selling novel **Peyton Place**. The Grace Metalious epic was legendary among adolescent boys, whose parents would not let them read it. As a service to his peers, Quinn took on the task of reading the entire book and underlined all the sex scenes, thereby saving others from having to wade through unwanted plot and character development.

Quinn generously passed the book from boy to boy, using the school parking lot as the transfer station. As one would return it to him, another would be waiting to pick it up. Quinn provided this wonderful service free of charge, knowing that it would reap a rich harvest of return favors.

By the time Cloud took his turn with the novel, the book's spine was broken in multiple places and pages were falling out. After reading the underlined portions, Cloud carefully removed all the pertinent pages and clipped them together in a condensed version. When he returned the remnants of the book and the now separate underlined pages, Cloud suggested that Quinn throw away the book and share only the condensed version with the still long list of eager boys. This would allow the pages to be placed inside another book, reducing the chances of getting caught.

Quinn considered this a great idea and thanked Cloud with a generous pat on the back. He was beginning to admire Cloud for the devious way his mind worked.

Cloud had lived in the same house, second from the corner, since his parents bought it in 1946. This entire time Miss Listerbaum lived next door in the house on the corner. Her given name was Jael, but no one in the neighborhood knew her by that name. She was Miss Listerbaum to everyone. Her father had owned a dairy farm west of Grand Avenue. He was a dour, dominating man who browbeat his wife and threatened to batter her, although he never did so with fists. Words were his weapons of choice. In 1890, when Esther Listerbaum gave birth to their first child, a daughter, she insisted on naming the girl.

"You can name the boys," she told her husband, "but I'll name the girls." This seemed a small matter to him, and he quickly agreed to the bargain. So the new mother gave her daughter a biblical name, Jael. She was confident that her incurious husband, who shunned church and read nothing except farming journals, would never learn that Jael was the name of a woman who drove a stake through a man's eye. This gave her secret comfort.

In later years, Miss Listerbaum came to believe her name was the reason she never found a husband. But then, perhaps she had absorbed some of her mother's suspicions about men. Jael longed for a kind and literate man, a gentleman, who would coax her out of her shell. The few who made passes at her when she worked in the office at the farm were very much like her father and not at all to Miss Listerbaum's taste.

There had been one special man, however. On February 8, 1932, a man appeared at her doorstep. She remembered the date well, because she had just heard an announcement on the radio that Winnie Ruth Judd had been convicted of murder by a jury of twelve men at the Maricopa County Superior Court. Jael was certain in her mind that the dozen righteous men had gotten it wrong.

She kept a Congo canvas water bag on a post next to her front door. The Depression was at its deepest. Herbert Hoover was still in the White House, and Franklin Roosevelt had not yet entered the scene to offer hope to the nation. Thousands of unemployed young men and even young women were riding the rails in search of better conditions somewhere else. Many were children. Jael kept the water bag filled for these hoboes. Printed across the Congo bag were the words, "A refreshing drink for man or motor."

Another water bag was stowed in the kitchen of her small house at the south end of the dairy farm. When she ran errands out to farms west of Phoenix, she hung that bag from the radiator cap of her father's doorless flatbed truck, in case the engine boiled over in the desert heat. It frequently did.

At that time, Jael lived at the terminus of 23rd Avenue, north of Christy Road, a short hike from the Southern Pacific railroad tracks that ran parallel to Grand Avenue. Just past Six Points, where Christy Road began as the westward extension of McDowell Road, the tracks angled southward toward the Union Depot on Harrison. Thus the area around her home was a frequent jumping-off place for hoboes.

On this fateful day in February, Jael heard the sound of someone taking a drink from the front door water bag. While nibbling on a cube of unsweetened baker's chocolate, she peeked through the curtains and saw a young man badly in need of a haircut. Not all the hoboes who stopped to drink knocked on her door, but when they did, she fed them. She saw something unusual in this one. His eyes radiated lively intelligence different from the hopelessness she so often observed in these travelers. Mentally, she willed him to rap his knuckles against her door, and obediently he did so.

Rather than having him sit on the back porch to eat sandwiches, as was her custom with hoboes, acting solely on intuition she invited this man into her house. His name was Wolfe Ingram, and he told her he was a recent graduate of the University of Chicago. He had been unable to find employment teaching Spanish or English or anything else that would make use of his education. He ate hungrily as he told his story to this kind woman whom he accurately judged to be twice his age.

"If you want to be a teacher," she said, "you need a decent haircut. Will you let me trim your hair?"

"I would be very grateful if you would," Wolfe said.

She bade him sit in a chair on the back porch and took brush and scissors to his unruly mane.

"Now, you need a bath," she said in motherly fashion. Never before had she allowed a hobo into her bathroom, but this day she ran a tub of hot water for Wolfe, and after he had undressed, ordered him to throw his clothes out to her. While he luxuriated in the tub, she washed, dried, and ironed his clothes. As she performed these domestic chores, she daydreamed about throwing off her own clothes and climbing in with the young man. At nearly 42, her body remained attractively slender, with firm muscle tone, and surely he would find that pleasing, she told herself. But then she acknowledged that her face was aging prematurely and that would not please him. As it happened, it was not morality or a sense of decency but decades of delayed gratification and shyness that made it easy for Jael to restrain from acting out her erotic fantasy.

Now dressed in clean clothes and properly groomed, Wolfe asked Jael for a sheet of paper. Sitting at her kitchen table, he wrote out a poem he had composed for her. While he was tending to this creative task, she wrote on the back of a farm business card the name and address of a secretary who worked for the Phoenix Union High School District. They exchanged documents and said farewell.

After he had left, she sat down to read "The Hoboes' Angel." Jael would treasure this poem her entire life, and over the years, her brief encounter with Wolfe would grow ever larger in her mind. Wolfe Ingram would become the lost love of her life and the father of her make believe son.

As events unfolded, Wolfe visited the secretary and through a series of connections was hired to teach Spanish and English at Phoenix Union High School. On November 17, 1933, he joined 4500 students and faculty members of the school on the football field where they formed the school emblem, a coyote. The formation was photographed from above, and the picture was widely distributed. Jael Listerbaum obtained a copy and put it in an envelope with her poem.

Miss Listerbaum liked Cloud and was always kind to him. On weekends, with Narcissa's permission, she invited him over for cookies and tea from time to time, during the years Cloud was in elementary school. She filled his mind with tales about growing up in Phoenix in territorial days, the big celebration downtown when Arizona became a state in 1912, and how she bought her first phonograph record that year –"Ragtime Cowboy Joe"- because she was tickled a popular song mentioned Arizona.

"I bought it at the Redewill Music Company on Washington," she said. "Years later, during World War I, I was down at the city hall bandstand and heard old Doc Redewill himself conducting the National Guard Band as they played 'Ragtime Cowboy Joe' in march time. They straightened out the syncopation, so you could hardly recognize the tune. I liked my Bob Roberts recording better."

One Saturday she told him about the city building Encanto Park in 1935. Her nephews rode their bikes in the bottom of the lagoon before it was filled with water. Another Saturday she told him about the lungers -the tuberculosis patients who moved to Phoenix in the early decades of the century, hoping to recover their health. Many of them lived in tents at the base of the sunny slopes north of the city.

Another day when she was feeling especially brazen, Miss Listerbaum told Cloud about the off-color history of radio station KTAR. "In 1929, the station was given the call letters KREP. It was supposed to stand for K-Republic, after the Arizona Republic newspaper. It soon became a laughingstock, and crude people made a point of deliberately mispronouncing it. So the next year they got it changed to KTAR. That was supposed to stand for K-The Arizona Republic, but people said it was really Keep Taking Arizona Republic."

Many times she told him about hoboes who rode into town in boxcars during the Depression, growing wistful as she spoke about them. "They called themselves sidecar Pullman passengers," she said. "I always had food for them in exchange for chores. Lots of men a single woman couldn't trust back then, but hoboes were all good men. They marked my house with the outline of a cat. That meant a kindly lady lived there."

The most lurid story, which she told repeatedly, was about Winnie Ruth Judd, the young woman who was convicted of the 1931 killing of two of her female friends. The crime was well known in local lore. The Republic reported she had hacked them up and stuffed the body parts in a large packing trunk, which she took to California by train. She became known as the trunk murderess.

Winnie Ruth was declared insane and confined to the State Mental Hospital in Phoenix. From time to time she briefly escaped, which generated rumors among the students in Cloud's school that Winnie Ruth Judd was coming to chop up stray kids. The mention of her name was enough to send chills up the spines of all but the bravest students. Simply invoking the address of the place of her confinement, 24th and Van Buren, would elicit imaginings of maniacs running wild, ready to rip the head off any child foolish enough to venture near the place.

Miss Listerbaum loved to tell this story, and happily obliged any request for it. She felt a good deal of empathy for the unfortunate Miss Judd, suspecting that she had been framed for the heinous deed. Thus she unfolded her account of the crime and its aftermath with a tinge of contempt for the authorities who prosecuted Winnie Ruth. "You can be sure there was a man behind it all," she proclaimed at the end of each recitation.

She had a tale about another notorious woman, the salty actress Mae West. "In nineteen thirty-three," she recounted, "The Orpheum Theater downtown showed a scandalous movie called *I'm No Angel*. It was starring Mae West. Now for some reason, I got it into my head that I wanted to see that movie. Well, I was forty-three years old, and it looked like I was past the time for finding a husband, so I figured I didn't have to worry about my reputation anymore.

"I took the Grand Avenue streetcar down town, and who do you think I saw in front of the Orpheum but Mae West herself. She was decked out in a fancy dress, sitting up on the back seat of a convertible. I was so bold that I walked up as close as I could get to her car and called out, 'Miss West, are you really startling like the marquee says?' And she shot right back, 'You better believe it, honey!' 'Well, I'm going to see for myself,' I said. And I did, and she was. Of course, nowadays it doesn't seem startling at all, but that was a quarter century ago."

Cloud looked forward to taking tea with Miss Listerbaum. He felt he knew her as well as he knew his own parents. What Cloud did not know was that Jael Listerbaum had been watching him his whole life through her front and back windows.

She watched him in the front yard playing in mud puddles at the edge of the street after an August rainstorm. She watched him build imaginary cities in the dirt in a bare corner of his backyard. She watched him run barefoot down the street in summer, sprinting between shady spots where he would pause in exquisite pain before continuing down the hot asphalt toward the vacant lot, where he would perch in a cottonwood tree and survey the world below, imagining it to be very different from the way it was.

She monitored him leaving for school in the morning and coming home from school to an empty house in the afternoon. She saw him racing into the house to escape Quincy and heard the bully's threats.

Silently she saw him off on summer days when he hiked over to the Encanto Park pool, dressed only in a bathing suit and flip flops, with his towel around his neck. She admired his casual tan. On Saturdays in the hot season, she watched him hang up the washing on the clothesline, a task his mother had assigned him. As soon as he had pinned the last wet garment on the line, he would go back to the start and begin folding the already dry shirts and undergarments into the basket.

Miss Listerbaum gazed into Cloud's face as he spied on the quail strutting and bobbling in his backyard, pecking at seeds in the grass, and as he shouted greetings to the roadrunners that scampered across his front lawn.

She saw so many things in Cloud's life, but never spoke a word to anyone about her observations, least of all to the boy himself. These images were her private possessions, transformed into tableaux in her mind, which she could return to and enjoy when all the lights were out and no one was around. As Cloud progressed through high school and his behavior toward her changed, she would draw more frequently on nostalgic memories of the pre-adolescent Cloud. In nighttime secret chambers of her mind she allowed herself the fantasy that he was her son.

CHAPTER SEVEN

Onan and Nissa Verrall, a childless couple in their late thirties, lived across the street from the Morgans. He was a draftsman for the Highway Department, she was a clerk at the Post Office, and together they were nudists. They spent their weekends at a naturist camp in the hilly desert north of Phoenix.

Certain teenagers in the neighborhood learned about their recreational habits in the spring of 1958, through the agency of Quinn Queensbury. Using the same arcane channels by which he had gained a copy of **Peyton Place**, he also obtained a variety of girlie magazines and a current issue of Healthy Nudist Magazine that contained a picture of the Verralls wearing only smiles. When Quinn showed the magazine to Cloud, dramatically pointing out the photograph of Onan and Nissa, Cloud did not imagine he would have the opportunity to see his neighbors thus in real life.

Nissa had grown up in a gymnosophist family and introduced her husband to social nudism after the war. In 1957 the Verralls experienced a life-changing event when they met another naturist couple who led them to Jesus. Onan and Nissa became born-again Christians. And with the enthusiasm of new converts, they felt an overwhelming desire to evangelize others. In May 1958 they decided to tell their neighbors about the church where they had found peace and joy in the Lord. First on their evangelism list was the Morgan family across the street.

Nissa telephoned Narcissa and asked Lloyd and her to dinner two weeks hence on a Friday evening in mid-June. Cloud was not included in the invitation. Narcissa assumed that as a couple without children, they wouldn't think to invite Cloud, but that was just as well, because the boy was going through a teenage rebellious phase, and who knew how he would act at the neighbors' table.

The first Wednesday of June, when school was out and his parents were at work, Cloud decided to try something adventuresome. In his backyard was a garage that opened into the alley behind the house. The garage had long since been converted into a storage room and home-office for Lloyd. In between the garage and Miss Listerbaum's property was a four feet gap of land enclosed by Miss Listerbaum's garage and a concrete block wall along the alley side. Lloyd had filled the space with sand when Cloud was small, and the boy had used it as a giant sand box. In recent years oleander bushes had overgrown the entrance to the sand pit, creating a secluded space for whatever mischief Cloud might conjure up.

This day he took a throw rug from his bedroom out to the hidden area. After smoothing out the sand, he spread the rug, took off all his clothes, and lay supine upon it. He entered into a time of slow deep breathing, trying to induce an episode of floating in the outdoors. Cloud wanted to inspect the neighborhood from the air, but he was anxious about getting caught, half expecting Miss Listerbaum to come over to find out what he was up to. As a result, he was unable to leave his body. Nervously, he dressed, shook out the rug, and walked back into the house.

Cloud need not have worried about Miss Listerbaum, however, for at the time she was involved in her own very private ritual. Jael lived simply but allowed herself one indulgence. She bought phonograph records and had an extensive collection of 78-rpm discs. In 1930 she bought a Lee Morse novelty number called "Tain't No Sin," in which the sultry vocalist crooned in suggestive syncopation that when the weather is hot there's nothing inherently sinful about disrobing. The chorus invited people to take off their skin and dance around in their bones.

If anyone had asked her, Miss Listerbaum would have said the recording was scandalous. But she secretly delighted in the idea of throwing off clothing and dancing around naked. Near the start of each summer, Jael Listerbaum pulled out that recording and played it over and over as she danced around her living room pretending to cast off her clothing. Understandably, she never told a soul about her fantasy performance.

The evening arrived for the dinner party with the Verralls. Narcissa pulled a new dress she had bought for the occasion over a full slip as she speculated about how formal the dinner might be. Nissa had not specified appropriate dress, and Narcissa didn't think the Verralls would be exacting in the social graces, but just in case, she decided upon a middle course. She would leave her pearl necklace and earrings at home. Lloyd picked out his favorite tie to accent his lightly starched white dress shirt, but in recognition of the hundred and one degree temperature outside did not wear a coat.

Onan and Nissa proved to be far more casual in dress than the Morgans. Onan wore Bermuda shorts and a polo shirt, while Nissa wore a loose fitting jersey and Capri pants. Both were barefoot.

"Welcome to our home," Nissa said. She had the urge to send them back across the street to change into more comfortable garb but restrained herself lest she insult them before she had the chance to talk about Jesus.

"We weren't sure how to dress," Narcissa said.

"No problem," Onan boomed, "But you can take off your tie, Lloyd."

Lloyd loosened it and unbuttoned the top button, but did not remove it entirely.

The dinner proceeded well, with conversation about the neighborhood and how things were going at work. All four of them were employed, so it was natural for each in turn to talk about Onan's shop at the Highway Department, Lloyd's bank, Nissa's Post Office branch, and Narcissa's metal fence plant, where she worked as office manager.

The couples had lived across the street from one another for years but had never socialized prior to this evening. Lloyd decided he liked his neighbors and would enjoy spending more time with them. Narcissa felt strangely comfortable with the unpretentious Nissa and thought about a reciprocal invitation to dinner at the Morgan house.

Of course that would include Cloud, so she must remember to have a talk with him about social manners.

"Narcissa," Onan asked, "where are you from originally?"

Feeling the glow of her second glass of wine, she responded with uncharacteristic directness to a question she usually tried to avoid. She was not fond of her roots. "I was born in Bagdad, in the company hospital," she said. "My dad was a mining engineer. He used to bring the family down to Phoenix for shopping. I loved that. It was so much cheaper here than the company store, and the variety was so much greater. I decided when I finished high school to move to Phoenix."

"Wow," said Nissa. "It must have been fun growing up in a copper mining town. All those colorful Old West prospectors and other frontier characters."

"I hated it," Narcissa responded. "It was so provincial. But the company had a movie theater, so I spent my weekends there, and between that and the radio at night, I managed to learn about the wider world. When I graduated from high school in 1940, I took a bus to Phoenix and right away got a job at my favorite department store, Korricks."

"I'm a native Arizonan too," said Nissa. "I was born right here in Phoenix and was in the second graduating class at North High in 1941. Onan's from Minnesota and came here during the war and like so many soldiers, decided to stay when it was over."

"Yeah, I was a guard at the German POW camp out in Papago Park," Onan said. "Remember when a bunch of them escaped on Christmas Eve in 1944? It made the national news. Man, we had hell to pay for that one. The Germans built a tunnel, and it took us weeks to get 'em all rounded up. Actually, some of them turned themselves in. It seems they were planning to use canoes to float down the Salt River as part of their getaway. They had maps of the area, see, and they assumed a river had water in it! Hah! They learned real fast that ain't necessarily the case in Arizona. What about you, Lloyd?" Onan continued. "Where are you from? Were you in the service?"

"Oh, I grew up in Pennsylvania. Harrisburg. I went to Penn State for a couple of years, but the war came along and I volunteered and ended up out here at Thunderbird Field." Avoiding mention of overseas service, he then shifted to talk about banking.

After dinner the women cleared the table then joined the men in the living room. As they settled into cushioned chairs, Lloyd took the opportunity to ask his hosts about something that had engaged his curiosity. "You folks seem to go out of town nearly every weekend. Do you have a cabin in the high country?"

This was the opening Onan had been waiting for. "No, not a cabin and not in the high country. That'd be too cold. We go to a church camp up the Black Canyon."

"Oh," said Narcissa. "We used to go to the DAFT church on Granada, but Lloyd and Cloud didn't like it, so we stopped."

"This is a different kind of church," offered Nissa. "And we go there from Friday evening to Sunday night."

"Do you sit in the pew that whole time?" Lloyd asked.

"Oh heavens no," Nissa answered. "The church service is an hour or so on Sunday morning. The rest of the time is for relaxation, games, socializing, Bible study. We have our own room for sleeping, like a motel."

Fumbling for the correct terminology, Narcissa asked, "What kind of church is it? I mean, what denomination?"

Onan answered, "It's called the Natural Christian Church. Actually, it's the Natural Christian Church (Born Again), because there is another group called the Natural Christian Church (Eden Rite) and they have different doctrines from us, but our social practices are the same."

A light of suspicion began to dawn in Lloyd's brain. Narcissa hadn't quite reached that point but was intrigued with the direction of the conversation. "Tell me what's so different about your church," she said.

Nissa said, "Glad to. And we have some literature about it that we want to give you. You can read up on it and see if you'd like to join us some Sunday."

"But tell me about it, first," Narcissa responded with the slightest tinge of impatience. "How would I know if I want to read it until I've heard about it?"

"Well," Onan said with a long exhalation of breath, "Natural means naturist. That is going to church the way God created us -with no clothes."

"You mean nudist?" Narcissa asked, surprised but not shocked.

"Yes," said Nissa straightforwardly.

Lloyd was bemused, and Narcissa was hooked by the direction of the conversation. She leaned forward in her chair and asked, "What's it like, going to church nude? It sounds sort of sacrilegious. I thought all churches were prudish about that stuff."

"It's a very spiritual experience," offered Nissa. "Not sacrilegious at all. You really should read our pamphlet. It tells you all about our church and what we believe."

"There are no pictures of naked people in it," added Onan.

The couples talked for another hour about various aspects of nudism and the Natural Church. Narcissa found herself strongly drawn to the idea. She had a great body and responded favorably to the idea of showing it off in a context where sex was not on the agenda. She wasn't sure how to read Lloyd's level of interest, however, and Nissa had made it clear that this was a family church, and married people were not allowed to attend services without their mates.

Lloyd had two concerns. The first was what would happen if a bank customer or employee should encounter him at a nudist colony. He quickly recognized this would not be a problem, because anyone who saw him there would obviously approve of the place. The second was Cloud. "What about our boy?" he asked. "We can't leave him by himself all weekend long."

"Oh, no," interjected Nissa. "You should bring him along. There are lots of young people there, and he can make some new friends. I've been attending nudist camps since I was a child. Kids love the freedom to run around naked, even more than adults do, I think."

This prospect did not trouble Narcissa. Over the years, prior to Cloud entering puberty, Narcissa had made a habit of walking into the bathroom in the nude while Cloud was taking a bath. She would brush her teeth, wash her face, or pee, so Cloud could see what a woman's body looked like. It was part of Narcissa's plan for Cloud's sex education. Cloud had also seen his father naked many times, so the prospect of him seeing both of them without clothes at the same time caused her no concern.

"If we were interested in visiting your church, how would we go about it?" asked Lloyd.

"The first thing you do," instructed Onan, "is practice being nude at home. Spend a Saturday or two going about your regular chores, inside the house, with no clothes on. All three of you. When you are comfortable with that -and it really shouldn't take too long- make a date to come over here for the afternoon, and we'll play cards, and fix burgers on the grill. Our backyard is completely private, so you can relax in the buff outside if you want.

"The next step is to meet with our ministers. They're a husband and wife team. They will explain the rules of the church camp and decide if you're ready to attend. The thing is, you have to come to a church service on Sunday morning first before you can have unrestricted access to the rest of the grounds."

"Sounds like you've got it all planned out for us," Lloyd said.

"Take your time and think about it," said Onan. "Read the literature and talk to Cloud about it. If you decide you don't want to do it, I'll never mention it again."

"But whether or not," said Nissa, "we want to be friends. We like you and hope you'll come over again for dinner or drinks."

"We'd like that too," said Lloyd. "And by the way, does anyone else from our neighborhood attend your church?"

"Not yet," said Nissa. "I'd really like to get Miss Listerbaum to go. I think it would be wonderful for her. We have members her age. She might think we're improper lunatics, but someday maybe I'll approach her. The Zadoks are Jewish, so they're not likely to be interested in a Christian camp."

As they stood to take their leave, Narcissa said to Nissa, "Forgive me for asking, but I've been wondering all evening. Are you wearing a bra?"

"Of course not," bubbled Nissa. She took hold of the sides of her blouse and pulled it off over her head. "See!" They saw Nissa's uninterrupted tan.

Narcissa and Lloyd went home and both read the pamphlet that night. Across their respective beds they talked late into the night about whether they should try the Natural Christian Church. Lloyd tentatively suggested that the experience might lead them back into one bed, but Narcissa thought that idea was premature. She had already decided they would attend the church, however, without acknowledging this to Lloyd.

The next morning they slept late, so that Cloud was uncustomarily the first one up. By ten all three were out of bed and going about their Saturday tasks: grocery shopping and laundry for Narcissa, weeding and watering the front yard for Lloyd, and cleaning the bathroom and homework for Cloud. Cloud thought his parents seemed unusually animated. Apparently they had enjoyed themselves at the Verralls' house. He wondered how surprised they would be if they ever found out that Onan and Nissa were nudists, and more specifically that he not only knew it but had seen a picture of them naked.

"How was the party?" Cloud asked Lloyd when he came into the kitchen from working on the front lawn.

"Oh it was fine," Lloyd answered. "Onan and Nissa are nice folks."

Cloud wanted to hear more but his dad was intent on his next chore. His mother appeared to be cheerful as she put away groceries but not in the mood for conversation.

The surprised one turned out to be Cloud. Sunday morning after breakfast, Narcissa asked her son to join mom and dad in the living room for an important talk. "Uh oh," he said to himself. This was going to be the dreaded facts of life talk. He believed he already knew more than they were likely to tell him, but he put on a stoic façade and plopped himself down on his end of the couch, mentally steeled for the inevitable halting attempt at describing sexual intercourse.

"We've been thinking about going to a different church," Narcissa announced.

Cloud was simultaneously relieved that this would not be the sex education talk and troubled at the prospect of going to any church. "Oh?" he whispered.

"It's not like DAFT," she said. "Nothing like that at all. We think you'll like it. There are lots of young people there and the pastors are very nice. It's the church the Verralls go to."

Cloud said nothing. He did not understand this at all. The Verralls? Did they go to church? His silence was soon rewarded with an explanation, as first Narcissa then Lloyd then Narcissa again then Lloyd in turn told him about the Natural Christian Church, their words flowing from them in a way Cloud had never before experienced.

Lloyd said, "We want you to read this booklet and think about it, and we'll talk some more over dinner. There's no rush. No decision has been made."

Cloud took the softbound document to his room. His first thought was if the family practiced nudism, he wouldn't have to worry as much about being caught naked while floating. It had already happened once. Late one night his mother had walked in on him while he was out of his body, but luckily he was still in the room at the time and came up with a good excuse after he quickly popped back into his skin. He hadn't needed to explain about being naked that time, he assumed, because lots of people sleep naked in hot weather.

Since then, however, he had been doubly cautious about where and when he floated, but he longed to experiment with doing it from various locations, particularly to try again from the sand pit next to the garage. Yet the prospect of discovery remained a major source of concern to him. What if his mother or father found his empty nude body in the yard during the daytime while he was exploring somewhere around the neighborhood? It struck him as gleefully ironic that a church might provide him a bit of relief from this particular anxiety.

Next he wondered whether he would meet anyone from West High at the nudist church camp. That prospect was both appealing and embarrassing, depending on whom he encountered. His imagination conjured sitting in a pew with unclothed fellow students, and he felt a pleasing conspiratorial bond with them, but with a mental jolt the vision shifted to naked teachers in that pew and his confidence faltered.

He shook his head to clear his mind and opened the pamphlet. After reading it, Cloud decided he liked the thoughtful and humble way the denomination laid out its basic doctrines. He believed very little of the theology, but they were not biblical literalists, and he sensed that unlike DAFT, his doubts would be welcomed rather than feared at the Natural Christian Church. This settled the matter for him.

Cloud found his mother loading clothes into the washing machine on the back porch. His father was in the backyard cleaning up after mowing the field of Bermuda grass punctuated by patches of bullhead stickers that served as their lawn, and Cloud waved for him to come in. When Lloyd stepped inside the screened porch, Cloud said, "I don't need to wait until dinner. I'm all in favor of trying the new church."

"Good news," said Lloyd. "I guess we should start with the approach Onan laid out for us. When would be a suitable time for us to practice nudity around the house?"

Feeling suddenly empowered by this turn of events, Cloud pulled off his tee shirt, handed it to his mother and said, "Here, Mom, this needs to be washed." Without pausing he slipped out of his jeans and underwear and handed them to her too. "I'll be in my room if you need me," he said and walked away.

CHAPTER EIGHT

Narcissa laughed and said, "Here we go." She began disrobing in the laundry room, followed in quick order by Lloyd.

"I'm grimy from yard work," he said. "I'm going to get a shower and fix myself a sandwich stark naked." He began singing "Nature Boy," badly imitating Nat King Cole.

Cloud lay on the rug in his room, trying to leave his body, but his mind was so full of the change in his family that he couldn't concentrate sufficiently. He would try another day. Floating around the neighborhood was his new goal, and guessed he didn't have to start outside to do that.

Monday morning Narcissa and Lloyd reluctantly dressed and headed for work. Cloud tried to float, first from his bedroom and then from his television watching spot in the living room, but though nothing interfered with his concentration, he did not succeed. He thus decided to give up trying and see if it might happen naturally some time when he least expected it.

The following Friday, Onan and Nissa again gave up their evening drive to the Natural Church Camp in order to continue the process of evangelizing the Morgan family. When the three from across the street stepped into their front porch alcove, Onan opened the door and ushered them in past his unclad body. Nissa came in

71

from the kitchen, wiping her hands on a dishcloth and shook hands with Cloud, Narcissa, and Lloyd in that order. "Welcome to our naturist home," the naked couple said in unison.

Cloud had had no difficulty avoiding erections around his nude mother. Although he would not have expressed it this way, he had too many troubling feelings about her to have developed any Oedipal attachments. But he felt a twinge of movement beneath his pubic hair when Nissa walked into the room. After the Morgans had disrobed, however, Cloud's general nervousness served him well, and the evening went smoothly without any embarrassing displays of erection.

After dinner, Onan poured red wine for the adults. "We use real wine for communion at church," he said. "Everyone above the age of seven partakes. It's just a small sip of the vine. Would it be OK if Cloud had a wee taste of the sacrament?"

"Would you like that, Cloud?" Narcissa asked.

He shrugged his shoulders. "Sure, I guess," he said. Onan set a wine glass before him and poured several thimblefuls of red liquid into it.

Raising her glass, Nissa prayed, "May the Lord bless us and keep us. Amen." And they emptied their cups.

The next morning, the Verralls left for the camp to prepare the way for their neighbors' first visit on Sunday. Onan had drafted elegantly detailed directions for Lloyd. The Morgans were to arrive at the gate at 9:00 a.m. The Verralls would meet them and escort them to the office of the pastors, the Reverends Adam and Evelyn Rarom. After an hour of instruction, they would be introduced to members of the church council, and worship would begin promptly at 11:00 a.m.

Everything went according to plan. Although the pastors were naked when Nissa introduced them, the Morgans were still clothed. After a few questions to Lloyd and Narcissa about their motivation for coming to the camp, Pastor Evelyn led them to an undressing room, and once the three were properly nude, the instruction began. Pastor Adam started with nudist etiquette, and Pastor Evelyn continued with a brief introduction to the tenets of the church.

Lloyd asked about the catechetical requirements for membership. Was it necessary to believe all the doctrines of the church? Pastor Adam said it would take a lifetime to learn all there was to know about faith and doctrine. They didn't need to believe much at all the first Sunday. Doubts were welcome tools for honing belief. Besides, they had read the church pamphlet, which explained their basic doctrines, so they knew enough to start with.

Adam exchanged a well-practiced glance with Evelyn. She nodded, and Adam rose and extended his hand to the three prospective members. "We are delighted to welcome you to worship at the Maricopa County Congregation of the Natural Christian Church (Born Again)."

Pastor Evelyn then invited them to meet members of the church council. After introductions and handshakes, Adam and Evelyn excused themselves to prepare for worship, and Cloud, Narcissa, and Lloyd entered into rounds of small talk over sips of lemonade. No teenagers served on the council, so Cloud was surrounded by adults. Nissa Verrall was present as the council's newest member, so she established herself as Cloud's escort, guiding him into talks with older men and women. She needn't have worried, though, because Cloud, as an only child, was already adept at adult conversation.

The sanctuary was full. More than a hundred naked men, women and children of all ages sat in the pews, and with the exception of toddlers and a few pre-adolescent boys, most assumed respectful postures. A harp and flute duet of "All Things Bright and Beautiful" was played as the prelude. The congregation loved this hymn, associating it with purple mountains, desert sunsets, and their own suntanned bodies.

As the chimes intoned eleven, the two pastors, nude except for leaf-green clerical collars, walked at a reverent pace from the narthex to the chancel. Now facing the people, Evelyn stretched her arms wide and proclaimed, "This is the day that the Lord has made."

"Let us rejoice and be glad in it," Adam countered in like manner.

After an opening hymn and prayer of confession, Adam read verses two and three of the twentieth chapter of Isaiah, in which God told the prophet to go about naked while delivering his message, and Isaiah did as he was told, walking naked and barefoot in public for three years. Evelyn read the Epistle lesson, the twelfth verse of the third chapter of Colossians.

"This is our message for today," she said. "As the letter to the Colossians so eloquently proclaims, we are to clothe ourselves with compassion, kindness, humility, meekness, and patience. These, far more than any decorative or utilitarian bolts of cloth, are what Christians truly are called to wear."

When it came time for the offering, Adam explained for the sake of the new family that since people did not bring wallets or purses to the service, there were no offering plates. Voluntary church donations and recreation fee payments were accepted at the office or monthly by mail. The offering time in church was used for members to tell how they had given of themselves, their time or energy to others or to the church.

This day's offering was testimony from an eighteen year-old young woman named Rose. She told how she had stood up for a twelve year-old boy who had been chased by a bully. She approached the bully and explained to him that Jesus expected better of him and he should apologize for threatening the youngster. The bully promised to reform, she said.

Thus was Cloud Morgan introduced to a world where he would find clarity and confusion, joy and disappointment.

Adam Rarom grew up in a Catholic family in Los Angeles, the third son among six children. For as long as he could remember, his family planned for him to become a priest. After college he entered a seminary for diocesan priests, but dropped out a year later. Drawn to spiritual things but chafing at ecclesiastical and doctrinal strictures, he enrolled in the liberal Protestant Quick Phantom Divinity School in Pennsylvania and received a Bachelor of Divinity degree in 1948.

Evelyn Seth, an only child, was raised in a Unitarian congregation in Vermont. From the time she was five, she knew she wanted to be a pastor. Evelyn met Adam at seminary and promptly fell in love with him. As their relationship blossomed, their contradistinctive spiritual journeys bent, twisted, and wound around each other, binding them together on a quest that would lead eventually into the desert wilderness of Arizona. Evelyn's search for structure wrapped around Adam's search for freedom, and something entirely new emerged. They wed in 1949 and for two years jointly served a conventional congregation in Ohio. Yearning to take the gospel into an unharvested field, however, the idealistic couple quit and set forth as apostles to the nudists, not to clothe the naked but to explore Christian spiritual life in an unveiled environment.

In 1953, Adam and Evelyn became founding members of a new American denomination, the Natural Christian Church. That first year, congregations were formed in California, Nevada, Arizona, and New Mexico. The following year, congregations were added in Colorado, Utah, and the Territory of Hawaii. When they sought incorporation in Arizona, they discovered there was an independent naturist church in Tucson using that name. To demonstrate the peaceful nature of the Christian faith, the two churches quickly agreed to add distinguishing identification in parentheses. Thus in Arizona the official name of the new denomination became the Natural Christian Church (Born Again). The Tucson congregation graciously appended (Eden Rite) to their name.

The three Morgans attended services at the camp every Sunday the rest of that summer. As often as they could, they arrived on Friday evening or Saturday morning, but sometimes other commitments precluded staying the entire weekend. All three relished the physical pleasure and comfort of running about without clothes. Cloud's initial suspicion that going to church naked would feel irreverent even to an impious skeptic like himself proved unfounded. In a remarkably short time, nude felt normal and exposed body parts were simply part of the holy and beautiful fabric of religious life.

During worship in late July, the Raroms baptized a two year-old boy. The congregation processed outside to the pool deck. Evelyn jumped into the pool and reached up for the toddler. Adam explained that in the earliest centuries of the Christian Church, people were nude when they were baptized.

"Baptism means being born again," he said. "It is by presenting oneself naked before other believers that one truly experiences the release of being born again. It is through our nakedness that we become completely honest with one another and with God. We practice total immersion baptism in this church, so that everyone who sees or feels it will know and remember the liberal grace of God symbolized by the water."

Cradling the baptismal boy in her arms, Evelyn immersed him, and as she lifted him out of the warm, clear water, Adam jumped in beside them, placed his hand on the boy's head, and gleefully recited the baptismal formula.

"Remember your baptism!" Evelyn shouted to the assembled worshipers, at which signal everyone jumped into the pool, held hands with someone and repeated to their partners, "Remember your baptism."

The following Sunday, Adam preached a sermon based on the Ten Commandments, giving particular attention to the prohibition against adultery. "Sexual intercourse is permitted only between a husband and wife," he said. "Adultery is a violation of God's plan, and so is fornication. You know what I mean, friends. Some think that a little slipping around on the side is not so bad. Some think that whatever consenting adults want to do in the privacy of the back seat of a car or a motel room is strictly between them. But God is there too, so remember that if you ever contemplate adultery. God is in the car or motel room with you.

"For you young folks here, I have a special message. These commandments make it clear that God wants you to wait for sex until you are married. Please, save yourselves for your future husband or wife. Save that precious gift for the person you will someday marry."

The next weekend, Rose, the young woman who had given a testimonial offering the first Sunday the Morgans attended the church, sought out Cloud and suggested they take a walk. She led him down Skunk Creek to a spot hidden by Mesquite and Palo Verde trees where she spread a beach towel on the dry sand.

Three months shy of his fifteenth birthday, Cloud had not yet experienced a growth spurt. His secondary sex characteristics were fully evident, but his body was more boyish than manly. His chest had not expanded and he was six inches short of the height he would attain within a year. Rose was three inches taller than Cloud, with the body of a grown woman and the uncomplicated face of a teenager.

Rose said, "I really believe what Pastor Adam preached last Sunday. I'm going to save myself for my husband and not have intercourse before I'm married."

"Why are you telling me this?" Cloud asked.

"Because I want to teach you something," she said. "Kissing and stuff like that are OK. The Bible doesn't tell you not to kiss somebody or not to massage somebody's back or legs or other places."

"Yeah?" Cloud drawled into a question.

"So I'm going to teach you how to have pleasure without having sex. Lie down here and I'll show you," Rose ordered.

Cloud lay supine on the towel, and Rose began gently massaging his face, then neck, arms, chest, working her way down his abdomen with increasingly light and teasing strokes. Not surprisingly, his penis became erect, and Rose cupped it in her right hand, massaging it in just the right way to induce ejaculation, which occurred without undue delay. She wiped her semen-drenched hand on her shoulders and neck.

"Good for the skin," she remarked. "Now it's my turn. You massage me."

"I'm not sure how to do it," he mumbled. "Your shoulders and face I can do, but I don't know how to massage down there."

"Don't worry. I'll lead you through it the first time."

So Cloud massaged Rose's face and arms and had no difficulty figuring out how to rub her breasts in a way that made her purr. When he reached her pubic area, she demonstrated with her own fingers, and he adjusted his touch in accord with her instructions of "too hard" or "a little more pressure." She soon reached orgasm, through which she held Cloud's hand in place.

After a moment in contemplation of her pleasure, she said, "We'd better get back where people can see us." As they approached the swimming pool, she said, "See you next week," and jumped into the pool. Cloud casually walked to the board and dove in gracefully, barely causing a ripple on the surface of the water.

The next Saturday Rose and Cloud repeated their secluded pleasuring, and this time Cloud added a few more flourishes with his hands. They continued the ritual a third time, but when Cloud approached Rose about a rendezvous the fourth week, she declined.

"Look, Cloud," she explained, "I'm saving myself for my future husband. If I get too involved with any one person I might want to have sex with him."

"Isn't *this* having sex?" he asked. "But I'm only fourteen, so you won't get too involved with me."

"This ain't sex, but you'll have to find somebody else for pleasure," she cooed.

Later that day Cloud saw Rose and another boy his age go for a walk. As it happened in the evolution of his life, years would pass before Cloud would find a pleasurable partner.

As August drifted to an end, Adam and Evelyn asked for a conference with Narcissa, Lloyd, and Cloud.

"We're wondering if you folks are ready to formally join our church," Adam said.

"What exactly do we have to do to become members?" Lloyd asked.

"You have to appear before the council and say that you believe in God, Jesus Christ, and the Holy Spirit, and that they are in some mysterious way one unified entity," Evelyn explained.

"And you have to be baptized by immersion," Adam added.

"I'm ready," Narcissa proclaimed with enthusiasm.

"Well, I've already been baptized," said Lloyd. "I stopped going to church when I was twelve, but I was taught you can only be baptized once."

"What denomination?" Asked Adam.

"American Calvinist," said Lloyd.

"I thought so," said Adam. "This is a stumbling block for us. We believe baptism must be by immersion and you must be naked at the time. I'll bet you were sprinkled wearing a baptismal gown in the Calvinist Church."

"Yes, and I still have it. My mother mailed it to Phoenix when Cloud was born, a not too subtle hint. Well, he's too big for it now and not likely to need it anyway. I want to be a part of this congregation," Lloyd continued, "but I don't think I can submit to another baptism. It would feel like I was second-guessing God or accusing God of not paying attention the first time around."

"We respect your convictions, Lloyd, and of course you can be a part of us without baptism, but you won't be able to vote on church matters or serve on the council," Adam explained. He then turned to Cloud. "Are you ready, Cloud?"

Cloud had been dreading this moment, for it would require him to confess something in front of his parents that would upset them. "I'm not sure about the Trinity. I have some doubts about that. And I guess if I can't say I believe in the Trinity, I shouldn't be baptized." He paused to consider whether this was sufficient to make his case and decided it was time to bare his mind as fully as he had already bared his body. "The truth is, I am an agnostic."

Narcissa gasped dramatically. "You're no such thing, young man!" she said.

Lloyd responded to Cloud's declaration by saying nothing.

Evelyn said, "It takes courage to be that honest about your doubts, Cloud. I admire that. The struggle to find faith is very hard for some people. We won't pressure you to make a decision about baptism or anything else." She then offered to spend some time with Cloud exploring theological issues, helping him to clarify what he believed and to understand the implications of those beliefs.

Lloyd said he would like to join in that conversation too. So it was arranged that Evelyn, Lloyd and Cloud would enter into a period of Socratic conversation about the nature of God and the sacraments of the church. Narcissa's baptism was scheduled for the next Sunday, pending approval by the church council.

CHAPTER NINE

Narcissa was radiant as she and the pastors led the procession to the pool for her immersion. Swimming and playing volleyball had toned her already striking body. She was tan all over, her hair was sun-bleached, and her face glowed in anticipation of sacramental attention.

Before beginning the baptismal rite, Evelyn preached a sermon, based on the second chapter of John. "The wedding at Cana," she intoned, "was more than the site of Jesus' first miracle. The vessels in which he turned water into wine were tubs for the Jewish purification rite. Water for bathing was stored in them. When Jesus invited the wedding guests to drink the wine he prepared in these tubs, he was symbolically inviting them to be baptized.

"The wedding feast is a metaphor for the joy of salvation. And baptism is a purification of our sins. Since people naturally bathe in the nude, Jesus was preparing his followers for nude immersion baptism, inviting his followers to partake in a new form of purification."

Cloud heard something in Evelyn's sermon that pleased him. If the containers that Jesus ordered filled with water were used for bathing, he reasoned, then their inner walls would be coated with the residue of soaking people. The water poured into them would mingle with accumulated oils, skin, hair, and other human by-products, making a tasty brew. This bathwater is what the inebriated wedding guests drank, proclaiming it to be the finest wine. Cloud decided that Jesus possessed a wonderful and wry sense of humor. Why was it that nobody else seemed to get the joke? No matter. The result was that Cloud began to admire Jesus as a prophet who was not afraid to use humor to get his message across. Jesus was brilliant, Cloud concluded.

While he was musing on his discovered bit of biblical humor, the baptismal service proceeded. Narcissa climbed down the ladder into the pool and waded over to the place designated for the baptism. The pastors were in the habit of jumping in, but she had spent a lot of time getting her hair just right, and she wanted to keep it immaculate as long as possible, which meant until she was immersed.

Pastor Evelyn spoke the preparatory words, noting how especially heartwarming adult baptisms were. Pastor Adam told the congregation about Narcissa's journey of faith. She liked the sound of that phrase -journey of faith. Yes, that's what it was, a journey.

"Narcissa suffered some disappointments along the way," Adam said. "She put her trust in expressions of Christianity that, though sincere, were not life sustaining. But she has blossomed through the nurture of our Natural Christian congregation, as her presence before you now attests."

Evelyn jumped into the pool, splashing water onto Narcissa's carefully coiffed hair. Narcissa flinched but quickly recovered. "Narcissa Cloud Morgan, do you desire to be baptized?" the pastor asked.

"I do," she answered.

"Do you believe in God, Jesus Christ, and the Holy Spirit as one in unity?"

"I do."

"Do you desire to drown your sins and be born again?"

"I do."

Adam then jumped into the pool and the two pastors grasped Narcissa's shoulders and lowered her backward into the water. Lifting her up a few seconds later, Adam placed his right hand on her wet hair and pronounced the baptismal formula.

"Welcome, sister in Christ," Evelyn said, and proceeded to offer a prayer of thanksgiving for Narcissa and for the blessings her presence brought to the church.

Narcissa stayed on an emotional high plane the entire day. This was the happiest day of her life. She reveled in the attention and good wishes from her new friends. There had been nothing mystical about it. She had not felt the presence of God in the midst of the sacrament. But being in front of all those people, all of them listening as both pastors said wonderful things about her, caused her heart to pulse with pride.

She was especially glad that her husband and son stood with her in the receiving line after the service as member after member offered their good wishes. They had been spending a lot of time discussing theology with Evelyn, and Narcissa couldn't help but feel a little jealous of the special attention Lloyd and Cloud were getting. But today was her day and all the attention went to her. Toward evening she found herself wondering about becoming a minister herself. She knew she would be terrific leading the congregation in Sunday processions.

Narcissa was able to extend the glow she felt from the public affirmation of her baptism through Labor Day. The church drama club mounted a play to be performed twice during the long weekend, and Narcissa auditioned and got a part. It was not a lead role, but it was enough to put her on stage in front of a crowd.

The play was a one-act drama about naturism called **Barely Proper**. The playwright, Tom Cushing, had subtitled it "An Unplayable Play," because when he wrote it in 1929, he believed the entirely nude cast would present a major impediment to it being acted in the flesh. Cushing was wrong about its viability, however, because it had been staged as early as 1933 at a naturist camp in Upstate New York and in other such venues over the years since.

The plot centers on a young German woman named Frieda who is engaged to Derek, a proper and naïve Englishman. Derek visits the suburban Berlin estate of his fiancée's parents to meet his in-laws-to-be. However, Frieda has not yet told Derek that her family practices naturism. The fully dressed couple converse in the drawing room and then Frieda excuses herself to change. As Derek awaits, her brothers, Ajax and Agamemnon, enter the room naked, followed by the maid wearing only a cap. Next, two family friends, Mitzi and Heinrich, also naked, come in. And then Frieda returns without her clothing.

Derek is, of course, stunned. An argument ensues in which Frieda breaks off the engagement, but Derek is unwilling to let her go. Reluctantly, he agrees to try naturism. Then Frieda's naked parents enter. As the play unfolds, cast members engage in sight gags and participate in a conversation full of philosophy and puns about the cult of gymnosophy. The play closes with Derek proclaiming that Frieda's naturist principles mean more to him than his own clothes. "I'll just grin and bare it," he says.

Narcissa was cast as Frau Schmidt, Frieda's mother. She felt a thrill at landing a part, but this was immediately tempered by the reality that her role would be the parent of a grown woman. She quickly calculated that apart from Herr Schmidt she was the oldest person in the story.

During try-outs, Narcissa had secretly hoped she would be chosen to play Frieda. Though she was thirty-six, she was certain she could easily portray a woman in her early twenties. When a teenager named Rose had been announced for the role of Frieda, Narcissa was momentarily deflated but held her breath for a part as one of Frieda's sisters or perhaps the maid. When her name was called out for Frau Schmidt, she felt simultaneously elated to get a role, any role, and yet gut-punched for the particular character she was judged by the director to embody.

"Narcissa, you're a trouper," she repeated silently to herself. "Act like a trouper. You can do it."

During rehearsals, a resilient Narcissa decided that being called upon to portray a person older than her actual age was a matter of art for the sake of art. All the best actresses did this and received great praise for doing so. She would be emulating the best of the best in the acting tradition.

When she came on stage for the first performance before an audience, all doubts about her role disappeared. At the sound of her first laugh, she experienced a flow of energy narcotic in intensity.

At the curtain call, Narcissa held hands with the actor who played Herr Schmidt and strode grandly to center stage. Her ears clearly perceived an increase in the volume of applause as she bowed and recognized the voices of Lloyd and Cloud cheering louder than the rest, which caused her to weep with happiness.

Backstage, as she removed her makeup, she carried on a

conversation in her mind. "Well, Mom and Dad, your daughter is now a successful actress. What do you think about that?"

Two weeks later, the fellowship time after church included a comedy talent show, and Lloyd worked up a skit for him and Narcissa. He sauntered on stage wearing an oversized pair of jeans held up by kite string in a large bow. Carrying a guitar, he lip-synched the Johnny Cash hit "I Walk the Line." Narcissa moved about the stage with a giant piece of chalk making a twisting line that Lloyd tried unsuccessfully to follow.

When the song ended, he put the guitar aside, stood rigid facing the audience, and sang his own words to the Cash tune:

"I keep my pants up with a piece of twine,

But I don't like them chafing my behind.

My butt could use some bright and warm sunshine..."

Now standing beside him, Narcissa tugged on the end of a string in the bow, causing his pants to fall to the floor, while finishing the verse:

"For no tan line, just pull the twine."

The audience roared with approval, and Narcissa beamed. Nevertheless, on the way home Sunday evening, she glowered silently that she was the better performer but Lloyd got the bigger part.

School had resumed for Cloud after Labor Day, but the Morgans continued to visit the camp every Sunday morning, returning home after dark. In late September during a worship service, Cloud fell into a deeply meditative state and saw auras around the two pastors. Adam's was yellow and Evelyn's was turquoise. Cloud did not know what, if anything, the colors meant but sensed they were benevolent auras.

While enjoying the displays of tinted light, he fell deeper into a trance, and during the sermon, without intending to, he left his body and floated to the ceiling of the sanctuary. Looking down, he saw his body sitting perfectly still as if listening intently to the preacher. He noted the tops of heads, some balding, some unruly mops, some beautifully groomed. In the back of the sanctuary, an entire row of people seemed to be sleeping.

His floating episode continued into the narthex and through the closed doors out into the early autumn sunshine. Cloud rose up into the sky, like a hawk, circling around, taking in everything. "Wow!" he said to himself. "Magnificent!" He looked at the church building in the center of the camp and next to it the pool. Surrounding these were bungalows, the dormitory, the volleyball and tennis courts, and in the far corner, the small cemetery. Beyond that was open desert, covered with barrel, cholla, and saguaro cactuses and strewn with hard boulders. It was breathtakingly beautiful in its way, but outside the camp was a harsh environment for people without clothing.

Cloud remembered a song from his grade school music class and sang it to himself: "Deep river, Lord. I want to cross over into campground." He laughed to himself at the irony. He hadn't known what campground was, and now he was floating over a beautiful campground. The only problem, he brooded to himself, was that he did not believe what the good people of this camp believed, so he was something of a party crasher in their promised land, guilty about it but wanting to be here anyway. Sensing the sermon was about to end, Cloud headed back to his body. As he entered it, his body twitched, and his father leaned over and whispered, "Fell asleep, huh? I won't tell."

One late October Saturday, over dinner at home, Lloyd talked with more energy than usual about the theology discussions he and Cloud were having with Evelyn Rarom. "She has really influenced my thinking," he said. "I may end up changing my mind about being baptized again. She makes a lot of sense, but she's not pressuring me or Cloud. She doesn't try to talk me out of my beliefs, but helps me see them more clearly. She's really a delightful person."

Lloyd failed to see Narcissa stiffen when he made this last remark. Early the next morning, Narcissa climbed into bed with her husband and snuggled up to him. "We haven't been intimate for a long time, dear. Let's spend the morning here and see what happens." She proceeded to do something that made him stiffen. They did not go to church that day.

Cloud was disappointed, but he had not finished his homework on Saturday, as was his practice, so he used the time to catch up on school assignments. He was disappointed because despite his doctrinal non-belief, he enjoyed the worship services. He found the sermons challenging, giving him something solid against which to reflect. And he especially valued the theological discussions with

Evelyn. But it was only one Sunday they would miss. Next week for sure he and his dad would sit in Evelyn's office again and discuss metaphysical ideas and their implications.

The following weekend, Narcissa had a cold, so they missed church again. The week after that, Cloud's ROTC unit participated in a Veterans Day parade on Saturday, and Narcissa decided he needed Sunday for homework. He was stirred by the parade, because the band played Sousa's "Washington Post March" as he passed in review. But the next week Narcissa was behind in her chores and needed Sunday to catch up.

Nissa Verrall called to say they were missed and wondered if anything was wrong. Narcissa assured Nissa that things were fine but their lives were complicated at the moment. She wrote a letter to Adam and Evelyn the next day, in which she explained their absences and promised that the Morgan family would be back in regular attendance in the spring. This was a promise that Narcissa did not intend to keep.

Cloud had not spent much time with Miss Listerbaum while he was attending the Natural Christian Church. With that activity out of his schedule, he resumed visiting her on occasional Saturday afternoons. She was curious about where the Morgans had been going every weekend for months but was too polite to ask directly. Sensing this, Cloud volunteered a vague comment about renting a cabin in the mountains.

He also began to act differently in her presence. Her house was familiar and comfortable to him, but she was beginning to get on his nerves a little. She didn't seem quite as knowledgeable as he remembered from years past. She told the same old stories. He was changing rapidly and she was not. He was gaining a measure of what he thought of as literate sophistication while she remained a frontier spinster.

In a moment of whimsical impatience, he invented a story to tease her. "I have some neighborhood news," he said, feigning excitement. "You know the Zadoks across the street?" He was referring to a Jewish family that had moved into the neighborhood several years earlier. The husband and wife were Polish, having escaped Nazi persecution in the early 1940s. In a circuitous and at times heroic journey they had made their way to America near the end of the war. Their daughter Darla had been born in the United States within a week of their undocumented arrival in America in 1945.

"Yes." she said, "They seem like nice people."

"Well, I heard Mr. Zadok talking to a man in front of Larry's Market, and this man was wearing a dark suit and talked with a foreign accent. Mr. Zadok handed him a roll of film and the man gave him a wad of twenty dollar bills."

"That's odd," Miss Listerbaum said.

"It's more than odd," Cloud continued. "The man in the suit was Russian. I think Mr. Zadok must be a Soviet spy."

"Now you don't know that, Cloud. Surely there is a perfectly good explanation for what you saw."

"But what if he is a spy? What should we do? Maybe we should call the FBI."

"I don't think it would be proper to call the FBI because of a suspicion based on someone's foreign accent," she said. "People's lives could be hurt by false suspicions."

"We can't be too careful these days," Cloud countered. "Of course the FBI wouldn't listen to a kid like me, but if a grown-up called they might investigate. Would you call them, please? If only so I won't be worrying about it all night."

She sighed. "Alright, Cloud, I'll do what I can. Get me the phone book."

Miss Listerbaum dialed the number and after two rings a gruff voice answered, "Phoenix Field Office. May I help you?"

"This is Miss Jael..." Cloud pressed the button in the phone's cradle to terminate the call. "Cloud, what are you doing?"

"I've been thinking. What if I'm wrong? I wouldn't want to get Mr. Zadok in trouble. You're right. The government's a bit paranoid these days. I'll just keep my eyes and ears open and if I find out anything more, I'll let you know."

"You just made up that story, didn't you, Cloud?"

"Not exactly," he hedged, "It's partly true, but I exaggerated a little." He had indeed seen Mr. Zadok in front of Larry's Market, and he did see him give Larry the roll of film to send in for processing. But there had been no foreign man in a suit and no wad of twenty-dollar bills.

Jael Listerbaum was hurt that Cloud had used her for his practical joke, but she felt she would lose him for good if she scolded him, so she dropped the subject and poured him another cup of tea. "I'll read your tealeaves when you've finished," she said.

Though Cloud had not advanced to the castes of the most popular or the brainiest students at West High (and never would), in his sophomore year he established himself as a likeable member of a secondary order in the school's social hierarchy. This was the caste of the bright individualists. They generally made good grades but not consistently, for they tended to pay less attention to subjects they lacked interest in. In some ways they were better described by what they were not. These bright individualists were neither alienated nor angry. They were not driven to succeed through high grades or to gain attention through sports or social activities. They did not feel the need to conform to the values and whims of the larger school society, although they felt no compulsion to challenge them. Seemingly oblivious to current styles and campus customs, they pursued ideas and activities they cared about.

The peculiar interests of the members of this caste varied widely, but a few characteristic themes developed in the late 1950s, the closing years of the Eisenhower era. Literature and the arts were important. Most of the boys and some of the girls read science fiction novels. Most of the girls and some of the boys wrote poetry or short stories, while a few wrote songs. Some experimented with ham radio and audio-visual equipment. Virtually all of them, boys and girls together, liked folk music.

The Kingston Trio introduced Cloud to two new friends, although the popular folk trio did not make this introduction in person. It happened during a lunch break one fall afternoon. Aldous Askeladd and Odie Wolf were sitting on the grass in the middle of the quad singing, "Hang down your head, Tom Dooley..."

Cloud, walking by, said, "You need a trio to sing that properly."

"Join us," said Aldous. "Maybe we can get a record deal."

"I can't sing," Cloud said. "But I really like the Kingston Trio's music."

"Do you know 'Scotch and Soda'?" Odie asked.

"Yeah, but I like 'They Call the Wind Maria' better," Cloud replied.

"Hey, sit down and sing a few bars with us," Aldous entreated. "We won't complain if your technique is bad."

Feeling a sense of spontaneous comfort, Cloud joined them, surprising himself by half singing half speaking a decent rendition of "They Call the Wind Maria."

Odie Wolf's given name was Odolf. Like Cloud, he was an only child. Odie had already gone through his growth spurt, raising him up to five feet, five inches, which stature he would maintain for the rest of his life. His parents were very well off financially, and although he was neither smug about his family's affluence nor vain about his extraordinarily attractive face, his doting mother still pampered him.

Aldous Askeladd was the middle of three children. He had been named for the novelist Aldous Huxley. His father owned a first edition of **Brave New World**, of which he was enormously proud and protective. He would show it to selected friends, but would not let anyone touch its cover or pages.

Aldous grew up with a book in his hand and had the glasses wrapped around his face to prove it. By the time he was ten he had graduated from **Tom Swift** and **The Hardy Boys** to books by Isaac Asimov, Arthur C. Clarke, and Ray Bradbury. Though he was nearly six feet tall and well muscled, Aldous was indifferent to sports, preferring to exercise his hands instead by strumming an old banjo.

The three bright individualists quickly formed a strong triad based on mutual affection for science fiction novels and folk music. Cloud still ate lunch with Firstlaugh, but that relationship continued in compartmentalized form, as Firstlaugh eschewed socializing with Cloud's new friends. The Navajo felt that Aldous and Odie were nice guys, but they came from a world alien to him, and it was easier to maintain a friendship with one **bilagaana** -Cloud- than to socialize with a whole pack of them.

On a Monday afternoon in November, Cloud met Aldous and Odie in the quad and said, "I had a strange dream last night. I was flying a small plane, trying to keep up with three singers in the plane ahead. They were going someplace cold to do a concert, and I was trying to tell them to turn around but their plane went down and disappeared in the snow." He did not tell the dream exactly as it had unfolded in his mind. In the dream he had not been flying a plane but had been soaring out of his body, but he decided to edit this particular detail.

"Who were they?" Aldous asked.

"I don't know. In the dream I knew that I knew them, but they wouldn't tell me their names. I called to them but they wouldn't answer. I'm worried they may be the Kingston Trio."

"There's nothing to be worried about. It was just a dream," Odie said.

"Yeah, I guess you're right," Cloud said. He dropped the subject but remained troubled by the residue of the crash imagery still in his brain. He had not told his friends about his previous prescient dreams and did not think this was a good time to raise the subject. They might think he was a weirdo and not want him around anymore. Cloud held to the hope that this was simply a strange dream and nothing more.

CHAPTER TEN

KRUX radio broke the news to Cloud the morning of February 3, 1959, that it had been more than a strange dream. At one in the morning that day a chartered plane had crashed into the snow near Clear Lake, Iowa, killing three singers: Buddy Holly, Ritchie Valens, and J. P. Richardson, better known as The Big Bopper.

The news deeply grieved Cloud. They had not been a trio as he had assumed but three individual performers, who had flown together for the first time in their lives straight to their deaths. Though he was sorry for the loss of life, most of Cloud's grief was directed at himself, for the burden his prescient mind placed on him. Aldous and Odie remembered that Cloud had told them about his dream, and they commented on how eerie it was. But they did not know the larger context of Cloud's history of such dreams, nor did they know anything about his out-of-body experiences, so they shrugged it off as a coincidence.

Aldous wanted to talk about **Brave New World**. "You guys should really read it," he enthused, as he had many times before.

"I'll read it if you lend me your dad's copy," Cloud said.

"You know better than that," Aldous answered. "He would kill me if I so much as took it outside the house. But there's a copy of it in the school library. I saw it in the card catalog."

"Well then, I'll check it out right now," said Cloud. He walked to the south side of the quad, entered the library, and headed for the fiction stacks. The book was not there. He went to the circulation desk and asked if someone had checked it out.

"No, it's here," the librarian said. "But you can't borrow it. It's on the teachers' shelf."

"What does that mean?" Cloud asked.

"The teachers' shelf contains books reserved for faculty members. The only way I could let you borrow a book on the teachers' shelf is if you had a note signed by your parents and a teacher giving you permission to read a specific book. If you managed to produce such a note, you would be the first student in the history of this school to do so."

Cloud was not willing to press the case any further. The following weekend he rode his bike to a bookstore, bought a Modern Library edition of the Huxley book, and read it through, stopping only for food and calls of nature. He then lent it to Odie, with strict instructions that he return it as soon as he was finished reading, for Cloud had decided that he wanted to keep the book for his growing library.

Out of this exchange of reading material came a catchword for the trio of sophomore boys: viviparous. It sounded upbeat and slightly risqué to their ears. Characters in the book used the word in a negative sense, but ignoring the literary context, the boys used it as an all-purpose term to describe things they liked, especially attractive girls. For a time they spoke of the current year as 51 AF, After Ford, mimicking the dating system used in **Brave New World**, counting the years since the introduction of the Model T automobile. They soon grew tired of this conceit, however, and concentrated on identifying viviparous coeds walking through the quad.

On a moonless night in February, Lloyd and Narcissa attended a dinner party hosted by the president of Lloyd's bank. Jael Listerbaum took advantage of the event to invite Cloud to dinner at her home. She hadn't seen much of him in recent months and wanted to reconnect.

After the meal of roast beef, boiled potatoes and boiled carrots, followed by rice pudding, they adjourned to her back porch to sit in metal lawn chairs and talk. Cloud enjoyed the conversation, once again appreciating her recollections about Phoenix in the old days. He had missed her stories, he thought. And then, a bolt of mischief struck him, and he jumped out of his chair and pointed into the night sky. "There! Did you see it?" he asked.

In those days, on clear nights with a new moon, it was still possible to see an awe-inspiring array of stars from vantages within the city of Phoenix.

"That's the Milky Way, Cloud," Miss Listerbaum said.

"I know that," he replied. "I saw a flying saucer. I'm sure it was from outer space."

"You saw nothing of the kind, young man," she said.

"Yes, yes. There it is again. Look how fast it's going. Do you see it?"

"My eyes are getting old, Cloud. I don't see anything but stars," she answered.

"Look, now it's idling." He pointed to an especially bright star, which he identified as the spacecraft.

She saw the star and said, "I don't see any flying saucer, Cloud. All I see is a twinkling star."

"I've got really good eyes," he said. "I think I see a dome and windows on the top of the ship. Do you have binoculars?"

She went back into the house and returned within a minute with the binoculars.

"Wow!" said Cloud, while adjusting the eyepieces so that the view was blurry. "I was right. The dome and windows are there. Here, take a look for yourself, Miss Listerbaum."

She looked for herself and saw an obscured field of sky. She tried adjusting the focus but Cloud had twisted the eyepieces so far that she had difficulty with the task and gave up. "I don't see anything, Cloud."

"I didn't see anything, either, Miss Listerbaum. I'm sorry. I don't know why I do things like that."

"Your apology is accepted, Cloud. Now, did I ever tell you about Phoenix before we had evaporative coolers?" She had, but Cloud allowed her to continue without interruption. "Some of the swanky hotels downtown got coolers in the 1920s but most folks didn't have them in their houses till after the war. Mostly we just put up with the heat, but summer nights were so hot I used to sleep out on the screened porch. A lot of folks did. Houses had porches in the back in those days, for privacy on summer nights. I'd soak a cotton sheet in water then wrap it around me and lie down on a canvas cot for the night. Some fools did that and then put the fan on them to cool off even more. Half of them came down with pneumonia. Sort of self-inflicted lungers."

In the spring, Lloyd raised the subject of returning to the Natural Christian Church on weekends. Narcissa said firmly she did not want to go. When Lloyd pressed for a reason, she said, "I'm embarrassed by Cloud's behavior. When he told the pastors he's an agnostic, I wanted to crawl under the table. I was just mortified. Here we are baptized Christians and he refused to be baptized. It's going to take me a long time to get over that social embarrassment."

"Why didn't you say something about it at the time?" Lloyd asked.

"Oh, don't get me started on that," she dodged. "You're embarrassed too."

"No I'm not, and if you won't go, Cloud and I can't go. Husbands and wives must go together. That's the rule," he offered.

"I'm sorry, but I can't do anything about that," she said. "I have an errand I need to do. I'll be back in a couple of hours." She left the house and drove to the Phoenix Public Library at Central and McDowell. She was not sorry, of course, but relished the control she had acquired in the situation. And if she were to tell the truth, Cloud was not the reason she did not want to return to the camp. She had discovered something else to fill her weekends, her imagination, and her ego for some time to come, something that did not involve an attractive female pastor to distract her husband: the Arizona Past Lives Association.

Narcissa had seen an ad in the Phoenix Gazette about regression therapy. A person could discover her past lives through a special hypnotic technique offered by the APLA. She had called the number and made an appointment for a consultation at a small, tidy suite in a whitewashed two-story office building at Central and Encanto.

After two sessions, she had been deemed ready to be hypnotized by Dr. Dante Kherbet.

Her first regression had occurred a few days earlier, before Lloyd had broached the subject of a return to the naturist church. She would tell him about the experience in a few days, but she didn't want to say anything about her previous-life exploration just now. Before she talked with Lloyd about her past life work, she needed to do some research about utopian societies in nineteenth century Pennsylvania.

After the first regression session, Dr. Kherbet had told her she was a natural subject. He was very impressed with the ease at which she connected with the most recent of her previous lives. Many more sessions would be needed, of course, but his notes revealed key words and phrases she had spoken while under hypnosis. The results were so promising that he would use a tape recorder the next time, so she could hear herself afterward. Of course, taped sessions carried a somewhat higher fee, but he promised her that the additional cost was well worth the investment.

The handsome and charismatic doctor gave Narcissa a typed sheet containing her key words and phrases. "Go to the library and see if you can discover anything about these," he told her. The paper contained the following words: "Enlightened Kinship, Father Le Fay, Voltaire, Susquehanna, 1842, the Farm."

After consulting with a staff librarian and getting a brief lesson in how to use the card catalog, Narcissa received several potentially useful leads. One was a recently donated volume entitled *Communistic Societies in South-Central Pennsylvania, 1800-1850*. Paging through this tome, she came upon the following report:

"The Susquehanna Enlightened Kinship Society is yet another example of the secular communal society typology, which, as noted above, has more in common with the specifically religious utopian societies than would at first appear to be the case." She scanned down the page and read: "The founder, Voltaire Le Fay, was so committed to his vision of complex marriage, that in 1842, he gave his own daughter, sixteen year old Narcissa, to be the spouse of every man in the commune."

Narcissa leaped up, knocking over her chair, and shouted, "Oh no!"

"Shhh," came a chorus of replies. But she ignored them. She had found what she needed. Dr. Kherbet would be very pleased indeed.

At thirteen, Xuan was beginning to assume the shape of a woman, but her features still retained a youthful innocence. On a day in late June 1959, she was walking home from an errand, mentally rehearsing the bamboo folk dance, which she had been learning at school. Along Tu Do Street in front of the Majestic Hotel, she passed an American Army officer, a major, Xuan thought. She did not look directly at him, of course. That would be rude, but she glanced sideways at his kind face.

The American appeared to be in his late thirties, a decade younger than her father. The teenager perceived that the officer smiled at her in an avuncular greeting as their paths crossed. And then time stopped for Xuan.

Her mind shivered in a state of suspended animation, and she saw a tent where soldiers were eating and watching a film. Vietnamese and American soldiers sat together in the place. Suddenly the scene was filled with angry Viet Minh guerrillas, who were spraying the tent with machine gun fire, killing the soldiers who were watching the movie.

Then, just as suddenly, she was standing stock still in front of the hotel, shaking visibly from the vision she had seen. She looked behind her and the American officer was nowhere in sight. Xuan hurried home to her room. Sitting on the floor in the lotus position, she tried to meditate in order to calm her wildly beating heart.

Six years earlier, she had seen a disturbing vision of an Army truck crushing a basket of figs, she reminded herself, and nothing had come of that. So why should she worry about this vision? Xuan relaxed a little and focused her mind on a gecko on the wall. She stared at the lizard, thinking good thoughts about the diminutive reptile that ate mosquitoes.

As she watched, the gecko scurried up to the ceiling and transformed itself into a boy, a Caucasian boy, perhaps her age or a little older. She couldn't tell. It was hard to guess the ages of white people. He was dressed in khaki, and he hovered around her ceiling, visually examining the things in her room, then gazed directly at Xuan. Americans are so impolite, she thought, looking into people's eyes.

The floating boy smiled at her, a gentle, affectionate smile, and she blushed. Without meaning to, she smiled back, and in that instant, the boy dissolved into a gecko on the wall. Xuan felt somehow calmed by the gecko episode, and she put the violent vision out of her mind.

On July 8, 1959, two American military advisers, Major Dale Buis and Master Sergeant Chester Ovnand, along with a group of Vietnamese soldiers, were watching a movie in a mess tent at the Bien Hoa Air Base, when a band of Viet Minh fighters attacked the tent and killed them. These men were the first Americans to die by enemy fire in what years later would become known in the United States as the Viet Nam War and in Viet Nam as the American War.

When Xuan heard the news report about the incident, she became very upset, more so than her parents could fathom. She did not tell them about either of her visions, but from that day forward, she assumed the habit of scanning the streets for fig baskets wherever she walked in Saigon.

When Narcissa told Lloyd about her past life regression sessions, he was simultaneously relieved and angry. As was his custom, he expressed his anger in a subdued manner, speaking in measured tones about the folly of spending too much money on a questionable enterprise. "You don't want me to invest money in a tangible asset like land, but you think it's OK to fritter it away on hypnotism," he said.

"Listen, Lloyd, I put bread on the table here too. I can spend the money I earn any way I want to," she retorted. Before he could offer a rejoinder, she added, "And what about the money we spent on recreational fees at the nature camp last year?"

Lloyd sighed and went to the backyard in search of a chore to do while he pondered the sad state of his life.

The relief he had felt from hearing Narcissa's news was related to his suspicions about her unexplained absences. While she had been visiting Dr. Kherbet and going to the library for research, Lloyd had been wondering if she was having an affair with some other man. But the more he reflected on that possibility, the less he was able to imagine what other man that might be.

Though they did not return to worship at the NCC, the

Morgans continued to engage in casual nudity around the house. Attempting to compensate for not returning to church, Narcissa invited the Verralls for dinner, drinks and canasta in the buff, and this led to further intermittent exchanges of neighborhood naturist hospitality.

One day while his parents were at work, Cloud lay nude on the living room carpet, meditating in order to leave his body. Outside, the noontime temperature had reached 110 degrees in the shade, but Cloud sprawled in front of the cooler vent so that cold damp air flowed directly on him. Instead of floating, however, he developed a shuddering chill. Instinctively he rose to his feet and went out into the backyard.

A blanket of hot dry air immediately surrounded his body, and this felt so sensually pleasant that he spread his arms wide and danced in circles across the grass, gingerly avoiding patches of stickers that might pierce his bare feet. Cloud gloried in the blissful sensation of sun-baked air massaging his bare skin.

Miss Listerbaum watched the dance from her bedroom window, adding this scene to her inventory of treasured but never spoken memories.

The Morgans managed to get away from Phoenix for a week that summer. Lloyd insisted on going somewhere on vacation and threatened that he and Cloud would go by themselves if Narcissa decided to stay in town. She did not like the prospects of the two of them off on their own and agreed to go for one week. He rented a cabin in Oak Creek Canyon, a few miles from the sleepy village of Sedona.

Heading north on the Black Canyon Highway, Lloyd concentrated on the driving, while Narcissa meditated, hoping to induce more memories of the life of Narcissa Le Fay. Cloud spread out in the back seat reading *The Catcher in the Rye*. He felt an affinity for the idiosyncrasies of Holden Caulfield, and thoroughly enjoyed J. D. Salinger's idiomatic style. From time to time, Cloud burst out laughing at some incident or wry Caulfield comment and then tried to suppress it lest his parents ask him what was so funny. He would not be able tell them without considerable embarrassment. But he need not have worried about them prying into his literary adventure. Narcissa was fully intent upon retrieving a past life, and

Lloyd was entranced by the road ahead and had become lost in a fantasy about leaving his wife. Billy Grammer's recent hit "Gotta Travel On" came on the car radio, and Lloyd turned up the volume and lip-synched the peripatetic number as if it were confirmation of his wish to get away from Narcissa.

After cruising through a wonderland of wind-sculpted and rusted stone formations, Lloyd passed the junction of State Route 179 and US Highway 89A and motored into Sedona, home to five hundred or so independent minded souls residing in rustic dwellings hidden among evergreens and red-hued rocks. Downtown Sedona, perched at the rim of Oak Creek Canyon, consisted of little more than a motel, a gas station, the post office, and the Oak Creek Tavern, which served also as grocery store, pool hall, and community center for the locals. Tourists who stayed in the lodges and cabins along Oak Creek below also patronized the tavern in hopes of spying a movie star or two during the frequent filming of Hollywood westerns.

The cabin in the canyon was a modest, wood frame unit with attached bathroom and shower stall accessed from the outdoors only. Living, sleeping, and eating areas, including three Army bunks, a small couch, a rocking chair, a refrigerator, stove, and sink, were all in one room. Narcissa was not impressed, but Lloyd thought it would do just fine. He had rented it from a bank customer who offered a very attractive price.

Cloud decided it was going to be a painfully long week if he had to be cooped up with his parents all the time and determined to go exploring alone in the canyon as much of each day as he could.

However, the vacation did offer an opportunity for Cloud to spend significant time with his father. He had recently gotten his learner's permit, a prelude to acquiring a driver's license in the fall. Lloyd promised to let Cloud practice driving on some of the rural roadways in the area. This was one activity Narcissa was quite willing to let the two males do by themselves. True to his word, Lloyd took Cloud out every morning after breakfast for an hour or so of driving, north on the winding climb toward Flagstaff or southwest toward Cottonwood. By the end of the first lesson, Lloyd knew that he could relax at least a little, because Cloud's driving instincts were good. Father and son didn't talk much about anything except driving technique during these training sessions, but an unacknowledged bond of affectionate respect grew between them.

Spending most his days hiking along the creek and up the sides of the canyon, Cloud found the time passing quickly and pleasantly. Then on the next to last day of the vacation, he encountered something unexpected. While exploring Ponderosa pines, Gambel oaks, and bigtooth maples southwest of Slide Rock, he paused to watch a red-tailed hawk coasting on thermals and unconsciously walked in the direction of the bird's flight. As a result, Cloud happened upon a switch-backed trail that led to a mountain pass out of Oak Creek Canyon into a wilderness area that beckoned irresistibly.

CHAPTER ELEVEN

Cloud climbed the steep canyon slope until he reached Sterling Pass and then hiked downward between red rock walls toward Vultee Arch. Along the way, thick vegetation scraped his legs, and he narrowly missed a patch of poison ivy, making him glad he had worn Levis instead of shorts. However, he went much farther than he had intended, because the land entranced him, luring him over one more rise and around one more curve, until he lost track of time. Intrigued by a shaft of dusty sunlight playing on the side of a ledge, he navigated over boulders and around brush to trace its path, thereby discovering a passage through the rock.

Bending and creeping two yards through the fissure, he found a small valley with a clear, shallow pool seemingly carved by an artist from the surrounding rock. Cloud sat to rest and eat. Stretching out on the basin's rim, he took off his sneakers and socks, and waved his bare feet through the cold water. The sensation was reminiscent of running barefoot over hot asphalt before plunging his feet into a clump of shaded grass. In this case it was the cold rather than the heat that throbbed through his soles.

The color of the ledge he rested upon was a subdued gold. He was so taken with the place that he wondered if he might be able to leave his body and explore it from the air. Making a 360-degree survey of the area, he focused his eyes on distant points and saw no indications of human activity. Satisfied that he was safe, he stripped off his clothes, made a bed of his pants and tee shirt and lay down to begin deep breathing.

Before he could draw the first long and slow draft of air into his lungs, he heard a low growl in front of him. He raised his head, and peering into a grotto on the other side of the pool, saw the tawny visage of a mountain lion.

Cloud knew that any sudden movement on his part might cause the lion to attack, but he had no interest in remaining supine with the six-foot long creature forty feet away. Acting on intuition, he spoke to the animal. In a quiet and surprisingly steady voice, Cloud told the mountain lion that the human was going to stand, and in graceful slow motion, he sat up, and while continuing the stream of consciousness conversation, maneuvered his legs and arms into position to raise his torso, pulled his legs under him, and stood in what was surely a ***tour de force*** of muscular coordination.

"Well, Mr. Mountain Lion," Cloud crooned, "here I am standing before you as naked as you are. You can see I mean you no harm, and I would be most honored if you would consider joining me for lunch. I brought extra food, and you are welcome to share in the repast. But to be honest, I'm not a very good cook. Of course, I didn't actually cook the meat I put into my sandwich, so technically, my cooking ability is a moot point. And on the other hand, you are probably not much of a gourmet anyway. Now I mean no offense by that last remark. Maybe you are indeed a mountain bred gourmet and would appreciate the finer culinary creations which, sadly, I am unable to provide."

The lion's ears, which had been upright, relaxed. Cloud thought he saw a smile form on the feline face, but dismissed it as a hallucination born of adrenaline. He kept talking and backed slowly up the slope. The lion made its way out of the cave in a lazy, almost indifferent manner, stepping along the far side of the basin, and disappeared into a crop of dense vegetation.

Quickly Cloud retrieved his clothes and backpack and, still naked, crawled back through the fissure, scraping his knees in the process and encountering a swarm of bees on the other side of the rock wall. Only a few stingers made it into his exposed flesh as Cloud thrashed and climbed his way back to the trail. There he dressed and began the climb toward Sterling pass, where he stopped to eat lunch. "It's lucky the wind was blowing away from the cave," he said to himself out loud, "or that lion would have smelled this roast beef sandwich. Well, I would have gladly shared it with him." He laughed at his own preposterous conversation, rose to his feet and headed for an appointment with exhaustion on an old Army bunk bed.

The taped regression sessions, Narcissa felt, were bearing fruit. She was disappointed at the brevity of the initial recordings, which extended between forty and fifty-five seconds each. Dr. Kherbet explained that he had to delete the long sequences of preparatory regression for two good reasons.

First, the process information contained in them was proprietary, and although he personally had no problem revealing the information to someone as intelligent and trustworthy as Narcissa, the attorney who handled the incorporation of APLA advised him in the strongest terms not to share such material with any member who did not possess certain professional and educational requirements. His hands were tied on that score. There were serious liability issues involved, he explained.

However, if Narcissa completed a series of courses, which involved two or three years of study on average, she would be eligible for the inner circle and would not only be privy to the process information, but she could also assist in regressing other members.

The second reason for editing the tapes had to do with the effects of the information on Narcissa herself. She might hear something that would influence her conscious mind that would interfere with or distort her past life memories. An authentic past life experience might be tainted or confused by her journey back through this life. A trained person was needed to filter out the static of her present life, and of course, that was Dr. Kherbet's job.

The tapes contained only Narcissa's voice. What she heard herself say (in three installments) was this:

"My name is Narcissa Le Fay [pause]. I was born in November of 1825 on a farm in York County, Pennsylvania [pause]. I do not know the day in November. No one ever told me the day [pause]. I do not remember having a mother. She probably died when I was a baby [pause].

"It is a communal farm, run by my father, Voltaire Le Fay. He's in charge of everything. He is mean to me [pause]. The name is the Susquehanna Enlightened Kinship Society [pause]. When I was sixteen, my father gave me in marriage to all the men in the commune [pause]. I don't know how many men -dozens. They all had sex with me [pause]. I was quite a prize when I was sixteen [pause]. They all lusted after me. After all, I am very beautiful, and they all want me. Even some of the women want me [pause]. I hate it, of course. I hate them, all of them. Most of all I hate my father [pause].

"It's beautiful here. The land is so green [pause]. The more beautiful the setting, the nastier the people."

Darla Zadok begged her mother to let her invite some of the neighborhood teenagers to her fourteenth birthday party in November.

"The young people from Temple aren't good enough?" Mrs. Zadok asked.

"They're fine, Mom, but I'd like a few non-Jewish friends too."

"So, who would you invite from the neighborhood?"

Darla named three girls and one boy from her freshman class at West High and Cloud Morgan, who lived one house over across Villa Verde Street.

"The girls, OK," said Mrs. Zadok. "And the freshman boy...OK. But that Cloud is maybe too old. He's a junior already, is he not?"

"Yes, Ma, he's a junior. He just turned sixteen last week. That's only two years older than me. For high school kids that's no big deal." It dawned on Darla that her mother's concern was not specifically Cloud's age, since she had encouraged Darla to make friends with Jewish boys who were sixteen and seventeen. "I'm not going on a date with him, Ma. He's a nice boy who lives in the neighborhood. It would look bad if I invited other kids from the block and not him. That's all."

"OK, invite Cloud," said Mrs. Zadok.

That wasn't exactly all, Darla acknowledged to herself. She liked Cloud and thought he was cute. Her parents would not approve of her dating a *goy*, of course, but if she were ever inclined to go against their wishes by going out with a non-Jewish boy, Cloud would be her first choice. All of this was conjecture on her part, however, because he had shown no special interest in her.

As it happened, Cloud was very pleased to receive Darla's invitation. He thought she was pretty. Darla's almost black hair framed a smooth skinned olive complexion and large brown eyes, and he found this combination attractive. He had not yet begun to date, but if some time he were to ask a girl to go to a movie with him, the first one he would invite would be Darla.

The party went well. Late in the afternoon, one of the boys from the Temple asked Darla to dance. "Put a record on and let's rock," he said.

"OK," she answered. "Let's go out in the back yard where we can have some room." She picked up her portable record player -a birthday gift- and a stack of 45-rpm records and led the group outside. After plugging the cord into a porch outlet, she put on a disc. The boy who had asked her to dance approached with a grin and arms open, but she brushed past him, saying, "Not yet."

The rhythmic sounds of the Barry Sisters singing "Hava Nagila" resounded through the yard, as Darla began to dance the hora alone. She made her own circle in the grass, stepping and whirling with lively grace. Cloud was entranced. If he had thought she was pretty before he saw her dance, now he thought she was hypnotically beautiful.

Then Darla invited others into the circle, beginning with the boy who had asked her to dance. Soon all of them formed a rag tag ring, including Cloud, dancing with various levels of competence. Klutz and ballerina alike joined in with glee.

When the record stopped, someone shouted, "Again!" And Darla ran onto the porch and reset the needle to the beginning. The circle of teens resumed amidst boisterous laughter.

In the end, the party represented a high and a low for Cloud's emotional health. The high was seeing Darla dance with skill and joy. The low was the same. Cloud came to the conclusion that Darla was so attractive, outgoing, and talented that she would never be interested in a skinny, quiet kid like him.

On a particularly hot evening in late June 1960, Narcissa drew a bubble bath after dinner and settled in to relax in the tub for several hours, re-reading a favorite romance novel.

Cloud was inclined to honor her need for solitude, but following an extended time of patient waiting, he desperately needed to relieve himself. He considered going in the backyard, but it was still light out and he was nude, so before trying this option he opened the door to the only bathroom in the house and said, "Sorry to interrupt, Mom, but I really have to pee. Do you mind?"

"I don't mind a bit, as long as you use the toilet and not the trash can," she said.

"That's a weird thing to say," Cloud responded.

"You don't remember, do you? When you were about six you walked into the kitchen and peed in the trash can right in front of your father and me," she said, neglecting to mention that she and Lloyd had been arguing at the time.

"I must have been in one of my altered states of consciousness," Cloud said. "Or maybe subconsciously I was acting out a comment about my life."

"Honestly," huffed Narcissa, "I don't know where you get your strange ideas."

At that moment, Lloyd walked into the room. "Get on with it, Cloud. I'm about to wet my pants."

"You're not wearing any pants, dear," Narcissa noted dryly.

"Oh right," he laughed. "I'm about to wet the floor. Let's cross swords, Cloud."

The two males stood astride the toilet and in glorious relief sent crossing yellow streams into the bowl.

Narcissa stood and began to towel off. "Let me know when you boys are finished playing with your weenies," she said. "I have to go too, so don't bother to flush."

"We're done," said Lloyd with a quick shake. "It's all yours."

"No," said Cloud. "It's all urine."

In July, Miss Listerbaum invited Cloud over to watch television. The Democratic and Republican presidential conventions were being broadcast, and she liked company as she observed and commented on the hoopla.

"Naturally, I'm a life-long Democrat," she told Cloud. "So you can expect me to point out the Republican shenanigans."

She had never before spoken with Cloud about politics, and this side of her surprised him. "I would have guessed you were a Republican," he said.

"Nothing of the kind," she retorted. "Native Arizonans are nearly all Democrats. In 1910, when Arizona wanted to become a state, President Taft and his Republican cronies blocked it. He tried again two years later. Our constitution -the Arizona constitution-allowed for the recall of elected officials, and Taft wouldn't sign the statehood bill, because we could recall judges. But we fixed that rascal. The Territorial Legislature took recall out and Taft signed the bill. Then after we became a state in 1912, the legislature sent out an amendment to put it back in the constitution, and naturally it passed." She smiled triumphantly. "And then, we got old Taft good. We passed an amendment to the state constitution that allowed women to vote, even in national elections. That was eight years before the whole country allowed women to vote."

"Yeah, I learned that in eighth grade history," said Cloud.

"I've voted in every election since statehood," she said. "And I voted straight Democrat all but two times."

"What were the exceptions?" Cloud asked.

"In fifty-two I voted for General Eisenhower for president, who I think would have made a fine Democrat," she explained. "But I couldn't bring myself to vote for him twice, so in fifty-six I voted for Stevenson. I voted for Barry Goldwater once for senator. Of course, the Goldwaters are all Democrats, except Barry, so I gave him the benefit of the doubt, but only that one time.

"If you don't watch 'em like a hawk, Republicans will misbehave every time. Some are brazen enough to do it when you're looking. Like the way they stole Boulder Dam's name. The Boulder Dam project started under Harding and got funded under Coolidge but work on it didn't start until Hoover. Old Hoobert Herver got it renamed for himself before it was done but while he was still in office -a damned slimy thing to do.

"Franklin Roosevelt had the good sense to change it back to Boulder Dam, but after the war, those shameless Republicans changed it yet again to *Hoover* Dam. Some *California* Republican's idea. Cloud, there are two things you can never trust,

Republicans and Californians. But I refuse to call it anything but its proper name, **Boulder** Dam. It's too grand to be named after the father of Hoovervilles."

The seventy year-old woman and the sixteen year-old boy settled in to watch the Democratic convention unfold. On the day the state delegations voted to nominate a candidate, both were caught up in the drama. When it became clear that Senator Kennedy was heading for nomination on the first ballot, Jael Listerbaum began to cheer. "He's gonna make it!" she yelled. "He's a real charmer, a real war hero -and smart too."

Out of politeness, Cloud had kept quiet about his Republican leanings, but now he couldn't stop himself from puncturing her elation. On the spur of the moment he said, "They've made a fatal mistake. Some of the delegations have nominated John Kennedy and some of them have nominated his brother Jack."

"What are you talking about, Cloud?" Miss Listerbaum said.

"Haven't you been listening?" he said with all the seriousness he could muster in his voice. "That bald-headed guy just cast all his state's ballots for Jack Kennedy. That's the senator's younger brother."

"No, it couldn't be. Jack is a nickname for John...Isn't it?"

"I think it's going to be thrown out on a technicality. They're going to have to start all over," Cloud persisted.

"Cloud, you're crazy," she said. "They know who they're talking about."

"OK," Cloud conceded. "Maybe so. Yeah, you're probably right."

But he had planted a seed of doubt in the septuagenarian's mind. She fretted for a few minutes and then stood up and announced, "I'm going to find out about this." She went to the telephone stand, looked up the number for the Arizona Republic information desk and dialed it. When a cheerful voice answered, she said, "I'm watching the convention on TV right now, and I noticed that some delegations are voting for John Kennedy and some are for **Jack** Kennedy, and I..."

Cloud heard muffled laughter at the other end of the line. "No disrespect intended, ma'am, but Jack and John are different forms of the same name. That's his nickname."

"Thank you for your assistance," Miss Listerbaum said and put the receiver in its cradle. "That was very embarrassing, Cloud."

"I'm sorry," he said, now feeling like the scum of the earth. "Please forgive me. I don't know what came over me."

Two weeks later, when the Republicans were on the verge of nominating Richard Nixon, she turned to Cloud and said, "They're going to have to start all over. Some of them have nominated Richard and some his tricky brother Dick."

"Maybe I should call the Arizona Republic and get it all straightened out," he replied, and they both laughed.

On the night of September 26, 1960, Terp sat on the couch with her parents and watched the televised debate between Senator John F. Kennedy and Vice President Richard M. Nixon, each trying to make a better case for voters to elect him president. She did not follow all their arguments, especially about missile gaps and international tensions. But she did not like Nixon's dark beard and gruff way of explaining things, while she did appreciate Kennedy's smile and lilting voice. And she knew even before the first words had been exchanged between the candidates that her parents wanted Senator Kennedy to win the debate.

"Daddy, why are you voting for Kennedy?" she asked when the debate had ended.

"Well," he said, "Kennedy stands for change, and we need some fresh air in Washington. All Nixon is interested in is finding Communists under every rock. Meanwhile the country is being torn apart by segregationists."

All Terp had heard about Communists was that they came from Russia and they were very cruel to their own people. She knew more about segregation, because she had heard adults talk about it, mostly saying that it was wrong. But she had also listened as children her own age said hateful things about Negroes, and she could not conceive why the color of people's skin automatically made them bad.

Over the years, her father had been in the habit of singing around the house as he tended to various chores. Mostly he sang topical and novelty songs. He liked Spike Jones numbers such as his World War II favorite, "Leave the Dishes in the Sink, Ma." But Tom also had a taste for serious message songs. Penny teased him once that he never sang love songs anymore the way he had when they were courting, and he responded by breaking into a terribly off-key and melodramatic performance of the Perry Como hit, "No Other Love." Terp grimaced and put her hands over her ears, and that was his last foray into love ballads.

A song Terp recalled vividly from his repertoire was "You've Got to Be Carefully Taught" from the musical play **South Pacific.** She remembered it not only because her dad sang it but also because he talked to her about what the song meant: Hating people because of their race is not natural. It's something children are taught when young, and they carry that hate into their older years. The Persons made a point of raising their children to be respectful of people regardless of race or creed.

Tom tried to think of a better way to explain to his eight-year old daughter the difference between the presidential candidates. After a pause he said, "Terp, do you remember when you were small I used to sing a song about soldiers?"

"The Jerk Song?" she asked. "That's really funny."

"Yes, that's the one. It came from a Broadway musical, **Call Me Mister.** I took your mother to see it long before you were born. There was a song in the show about two soldiers. One was a jerk before he was drafted, but he went through all the terrible things that happen in a war. The other was about a man who was a slob before the war. At the end of the war, the jerk was still a jerk and the slob was still a slob.

"Both Senator Kennedy and Vice President Nixon served in the war. Nixon piled up a decent record as a bureaucrat, while Kennedy was a leader in combat and a hero, saving the lives of his crew when his PT boat was shot up. Kennedy was a bright and talented man before the war and a great man as a result of it. Nixon was an angry and devious man before the war and was still that way afterward. Some people grow up in hard times and some people don't change at all."

He was not confident his explanation had helped his older daughter understand presidential politics any better, but as it happened, Terp had clearly absorbed his sentiments, and she determined to do something in response. If her father supported

John Kennedy for president, then she supported Kennedy with all her heart and soul.

Over the next few days, Terp gathered garden fence stakes from the basement and attached them to pieces of cardboard she had cut out of grocery boxes to make campaign posters. Every weekend she marched around the neighborhood carrying a series of hand-made Kennedy for president signs.

A month later, the Person family settled onto their couch to watch a broadcast of the Disney *Zorro* television program. As usual, Penny and Tom sat together with Mary snuggled into her mom's side and Terp into her dad's side.

As the story of the swashbuckling Spaniard in Old California unfolded, Terp suddenly shouted out, "Oh, I get it!"

"What's that, punkin?" Tom asked.

"Zorro's family is rich, and he doesn't have to work. He can do anything he wants to, but what he wants to do is help the poor people. Senator Kennedy's family is rich too, so he doesn't have to work, but he wants the job of president to help the poor people."

"What a great insight, Terp. I'm very impressed," said Tom.

A week later, after John Kennedy had been elected president, Terp ran around the neighborhood singing the Zorro theme song and slashing a K into the air with an imaginary sword in imitation of the slashing Z for Zorro that punctuated the television hero's salvific triumphs. "Kennedy, Kennedy, Kennedy," she sang with glee.

During the time Terp was carrying out her neighborhood campaign for John Kennedy, Cloud was deep into his first semester as a high school senior. For his American government class he read George Orwell's *Animal Farm*, which led him further into a deepening distrust of collectivist societies. It was easy to accept that the Soviet Union and Red China were enslaving their people through totalitarian rule, but he also considered the ways the United States government constrained the freedom of its citizens.

In particular, he believed the military draft was patently unconstitutional because it amounted to involuntary servitude. He was still enrolled in ROTC and intended eventually to serve in the US Army, but that was his free choice, not coercion. The subject of conscription was not in the curriculum, however, and he hesitated to raise his view of it in class, because he felt the teacher would question his patriotism.

Nevertheless, ROTC proved to be a disappointment for Cloud. Both he and Firstlaugh had been passed over for promotion to cadet officer. Sergeant Frogger, instructor for the Junior ROTC program, distrusted introverts and dismissed Cloud's ability because of his baby face and Firstlaugh's because he was an Indian.

"I think Frogger favors boys for cadet officer who would only make enlisted rank in the real Army," Cloud told Firstlaugh as they commiserated with one another over lunch one day. "He only appointed a few college-bound students as cadet officers."

"Almost all the cadet officers are brawny and muscular types," said Firstlaugh. "None of us skinny ones made it."

Cadet second lieutenant Quinn Queensbury was now Cloud's platoon leader, although he treated Cloud with respect after Cloud privately explained to him the proper sequence for relaying commands, thus saving Quinn from making a fool of himself.

In October, a cadet company commander quit school to marry his pregnant girlfriend and get a job. After shuffling officers to fill the vacancy, a platoon leader slot was now open. Cloud went to Sergeant Frogger and said that as the senior NCO, he should be next in line for the platoon leader position. Frogger said he would think about it but instead appointed a junior boy. Exasperated, Cloud then dropped ROTC in favor of a study hall and vowed to prove Frogger wrong when he got into ROTC in college.

When it came to politics, Cloud was influenced by the conservative credo that the government that governs best governs least. This was as true for him in regard to matters of personal behavior as it was for economics and defense. The words that best described Cloud's developing social philosophy were *laissez faire* and libertarian.

The criterion Cloud used to test the limits of his live and let live ethic was his mother. There was no doubt Narcissa would do whatever she wanted, and the test for Cloud was to determine at what point her personal freedom did harm to his. That would be the point beyond which he would be obliged to take self-protective action.

Cloud believed his mother was a fool to spend time and money on past life regressions, but it made her happy, and although it was frustrating to listen to her babble about her experiences, it did him no harm. So he tried as much as possible to ignore her prating about Narcissa Le Fay.

Still, it proved hard to tune her out completely. As time passed, Cloud's mother dominated dinner table conversations with evolving insights about this poor creature who had been so badly abused by her father that a century later the memory of her life at the SEKS Farm affected the ability of Narcissa Morgan to trust men. For differing reasons, Cloud and Lloyd felt embarrassed to hear this subject in front of the other. But there was no hushing Narcissa when she wanted to bare the soul of her previous incarnation.

Cloud did not believe his mother found it difficult to trust men. She had trusted T. C. Smith and Adam Rarom, he thought. And she invests inordinate trust in Dante Kherbet. But challenging her brought more misery than it was worth, so he stayed mum. He also thought Kherbet was a quack and con artist and that his mother's hypnotically induced memories were confabulations. He had discovered the term while doing his own research at the library. Confabulations, he learned, are fantasies that lodge in people's minds that they believe to be actually true.

October unfolded with no new words about the nineteenth century Narcissa. Perhaps his mother was getting bored with the subject, Cloud thought. By All Saints' Day, which was Cloud's seventeenth birthday, he was beginning to hope that this phase of his mother's quest was over. He dreaded to think what she would pursue next, but with any luck, he and his dad would not have to listen to any more stories about the wonderful and truly gifted Dr. Kherbet.

Her silence about the Arizona Past Lives Association lasted until mid-December, when Narcissa, over a meal of macaroni and cheese, announced to her husband and son that she had received an early Christmas present. Her mentor had led her to a breakthrough in which she recaptured memories of an earlier past life. "Dr. Kherbet and I have worked so hard for the past two months," she enthused, "and finally we shattered that barrier of mental resistance and out poured Penelope Waxfork. Well, no one was more surprised than I. I mean I was on the verge of giving up and spending the rest of my days contemplating Narcissa Le Fay, and then Penelope came to me. Isn't it wonderful?"

Cloud and Lloyd did not share Narcissa's joy, but they sat quietly and pretended to listen to the story of a brave young woman who lived in Metuchen, New Jersey during the American Revolution. Her husband had been captured by the British at the Battle of Short Hills in June 1777. And Penelope heroically executed a plan for her husband's escape. It was uncanny, Narcissa averred. Penelope's behavior was so completely congruent with the way Narcissa herself would act if circumstances ever required. The account went on at length until Lloyd volunteered to wash the dishes and Cloud remembered he had a lot of homework to do. Narcissa promised she would tell them more the next evening, which the two Morgan men did not doubt.

CHAPTER TWELVE

Firstlaugh came to Cloud's house one afternoon so they could study together for their first semester final exams. The door to the master bedroom was open, and as Cloud escorted his friend into his adjacent bedroom, Firstlaugh noticed a painting of a young woman wearing a war bonnet on the wall above a dresser.

"Who's that supposed to be?" Firstlaugh asked in a surprised voice.

Approaching the boys from the living room, Narcissa commented coolly, "That's a Canadian Indian maiden, Cree, I think. The piece is rather valuable, painted years ago by a famous Old West artist."

"I don't think she's Indian," said Firstlaugh. "Look at her features. That has to be a white woman dressed up to look like an Indian."

"Well, young man," said Narcissa, "you might want to have your eyes checked. Except for headdress and moccasins, she's not dressed up in anything at all."

Firstlaugh's face flushed in embarrassment and he said nothing.

Narcissa continued, "This painting is an idealization of Indianhood." Silently she congratulated herself at this clever turn of phrase that she had made up on the spot. "The artist is simply showing what a proper Indian maiden ought to look like."

"I don't think so, Mother," said Cloud. "He's only showing his own fantasy. I've always thought of her as mixed race, though. I like to think the painter was experimenting with genetic speculation. That's kind of appealing to me. Like the Mexicans of Spanish and Indian ancestry. The combination of the two races produces beautiful results."

"I don't know where you get such strange ideas, Cloud," Narcissa said huffily. "Most certainly not from me."

"The lady in this painting looks like she might be a quarter Indian at most," said Cloud, hoping this would mollify his mother and end the conversation.

Regaining his voice, Firstlaugh said, "I like the way Indians **really** look."

"So do I," said Cloud. The boys ducked into Cloud's room and closed the door.

After two hours of diligent study, the students relocated to the back yard for a little sun and fresh air. Cloud spied Miss Listerbaum tending her grape vines in the next yard and brought Firstlaugh to the fence to introduce him to his neighbor.

"Why don't you two lads come over for tea?" she said. "I'll read the leaves and tell you how you'll make out on your final examinations."

Ten minutes later they were seated around Miss Listerbaum's kitchen table as she steeped a pot of tea. When she served the beverage, she put two teaspoons of sugar and a generous amount of milk in her cup, and since she had taught him the art of tea drinking, Cloud followed her example. Firstlaugh, however, took his straight.

"It must be lonesome for you with so few Indians at West High. Why didn't you go to the Phoenix Indian School?" Miss Listerbaum asked Firstlaugh with an innocent tone of voice.

"Too many bad family memories," said Firstlaugh.

"I think I know about that," she said. "Back in the twenties and thirties, I used to go over there to pick up students to work on the farm. I think they still called it the Industrial Indian School back then, and it was out in the country, way north of town at Central and Indian School Road." Miss Listerbaum's eyes rolled upward as she retrieved a memory that also caused her lips to smile.

"Some of my clan kin went there," explained Firstlaugh. "They were supposed to have permission of the parents to enroll reservation kids at the boarding school in Phoenix, but sometimes they faked the papers and kidnapped the children."

"I know about that," Miss Listerbaum said. "Shameful. I remember one girl who was being trained to be a hotel maid. Not that that required a lot of training. She was smart enough to be a hotel manager. Anyway, for a couple of years in the late twenties, when I picked up boys to work at the dairy farm, I would pick up Mazie supposedly to learn domestic arts by working in my house. There wasn't a whole lot to do around the place, but she was a fine companion, and she watched over things while I was out running errands for my father."

Firstlaugh said, "I had a…I think you would say great aunt, who sometimes went by the name Mazie, and she went to the Indian School."

"Well, this girl's real name was Silver Bead, **Yoo nimazi** in Navajo. They decided to rename her Mazie because that was an American name. She had to wear a uniform at school -no Indian dress allowed- and was required to go to a Christian church service on Sundays. I felt sorry for the girl. She was so lonely and unhappy."

"I remember her," said Firstlaugh. "She was related to my father's family."

"You said *was*," Miss Listerbaum noted. "Is she gone?"

"She went young," said Firstlaugh. "Alcohol. She couldn't cope with trying to live in two worlds."

"I am so sorry," said Miss Listerbaum, feeling genuine grief. She paused for a moment of silent respect, and then said, "Would you like to know a secret about your great aunt?"

"Sure," said Firstlaugh. "I always want to hear family stories."

"Well, Silver Bead, as I called her once I learned what her Navajo name was, came dressed in a domestic maid's costume to work at my house. One day I asked her if she liked the outfit. I think she must have trusted me, because she told me she hated it and she hated the student's uniform she wore the rest of the time. She missed her traditional clothing, but they wouldn't allow that at the boarding school. And she hated going to white man's church too. She didn't mind the stories about Jesus but the church service made her feel nauseous.

"So I conspired with her to remedy the situation. I arranged for her family to send a package of clothing and a pouch of corn pollen to my address. After that, whenever she was at my house, Silver Bead wore her own clothes."

Tears formed in Firstlaugh's eyes. "To a Navajo, a pouch of corn pollen represents church and Bible and more," he said.

"Well, I have it on good authority, that a certain Navajo young lady smuggled corn pollen into Christian church services in Phoenix in the late twenties," said Miss Listerbaum. "She believed anyone as holy as Jesus would recognize the sacred quality of corn pollen."

"And she was right about that," said Firstlaugh.

"And if you'll allow me a political plug," she continued, "I am so proud of President Franklin Roosevelt for his treatment of Indians. In the mid-thirties, his administration created the Indian New Deal."

"I know about that," said Firstlaugh. "It was the Indian Reorganization Act of 1934. It recognized the value of Indian culture and language. Some of the tribes thought it didn't go far enough, but it was a major step forward."

"One of my friends over at the Indian School told me they had to stop forcing students to attend Christian church services," Miss Listerbaum said. "A Federal directive guaranteed freedom of religion for Indians. The government couldn't interfere anymore with their ceremonial practices."

"That's the best thing I've ever heard about FDR," said Cloud.

Miss Listerbaum sighed, in touch with an errant thought. "In the old days, before the war, the Indian School played my alma mater, Phoenix Union, in the big Thanksgiving football game. Being a much bigger school, PU usually won, but I always rooted secretly for the Indians." She reddened at this impromptu confession and covered her unease with, "Oh my! It seems your tea is all gone. Time for me to read the leaves."

Upon examining the residue in the cups of the two boys, she paused to meditate on her observations. After an interval of silence, she pronounced, "See here, Firstlaugh, over in the corner of your cup, the leaves look like a cloud. And in your cup, Cloud, this large leaf looks like the silhouette of a man laughing. This tells me that you two will be lifelong friends. But," and again she paused for dramatic affect, "the positions of these significant leaves reveal that there may be a time, perhaps years, when your paths through life will lead in separate directions. But have no fear. In due course they will join again."

"Yes, but what about our final exams?" asked Cloud.

"Sorry, lads, I don't see anything about them. I'm sure you'll do fine."

The combined music and drama departments at West High mounted a musical every spring. This year it was *South Pacific*. Cloud went with Odie to the Friday evening performance to provide moral support for Aldous, who sang and danced in the chorus to "There Is Nothing Like a Dame." Cloud was so enamored of the play that he returned alone to see the Saturday performance.

The part that touched him most deeply was the tragic interracial love affair between Lieutenant Joe Cable and the Tonkinese maiden Liat. The role of Liat was played by Katy Chen, a freshman girl of Chinese ancestry, and Cloud became smitten by Katy as Joe Cable sang "Younger Than Springtime" to her.

At home, he looked up Tonkin in the encyclopedia and found that it was a region of Viet Nam. A sense of *déjà vu* fell over him as he read about French colonialism in Indochina and the South Pacific. Vietnamese peasants were sent to work on plantations in the islands.

On Monday after school, Cloud bought the *South Pacific* movie soundtrack album and in the solitude of his room played it over and again every evening for weeks. Emotional and romantic webs began to grow in his mind spun out of *South Pacific*, the suffering people of Viet Nam, and dreams about his own intended military future.

Arising from this musing, he decided to evaluate his social life and found it deficient. He had come within two months of graduation from high school without once taking a girl out on a date. Of course, neither had Aldous. Odie had gone to a few dances at the Phoenix Country Club, but those had been arranged by his father to escort the daughters of other club members. It was not that

Cloud felt the need to have a steady girlfriend, but he was on the verge of missing a major component in his rite of passage through high school. He envisioned a big red mark stamped on his diploma that proclaimed INCOMPLETE. And this was a grade he could never make up.

The solution was obvious to Cloud. He would find a date for the prom. His first thought was Katy Chen, but before he could approach her, he saw Katy in the quad holding hands with the boy who had sung to her in the school musical. After another minute of reflection, he settled on his neighbor, Darla Zadok. At the end of school he deliberately altered his routine so he would just happen to overtake Darla about halfway through their respective walks home. And everything worked perfectly until he reached her side and said hello.

"Mind if I walk home with you?" he said.

"Sure," she said.

Cloud's brain demanded clarification. "Sure you mind or sure you don't mind?"

"Please, walk with me," she said.

Cloud wondered what to say next. Should he just blurt it out or work up to it slowly? He figured he would get tongue tied if he tried to create an elaborate prelude to his question, so he opted for the direct route. "I was wondering if you would consider going to the prom with me," he said without prelude but with sufficient diplomatic wiggle room to allow her a gracious exit if she needed one.

"Oh!" she said. "That's a bolt out of the blue. Oh, uh, thank you for asking me."

Cloud guessed that the thank you would prove to be thanks but no thanks, so he sought to keep the subject open by saying, "Don't tell me now. Just think about it and let me know in a day or two."

"Yes," Darla said.

"Yes you'll think about it, or yes you'll go with me?" Cloud asked.

"Yes, I'll go with you, that is if my parents let me," she answered.

"Great! I hope they say yes," he responded. Though he tried to look cool, he wore an insuppressible silly grin the rest of the way home.

When he announced to his parents that he was planning to go to the prom, Narcissa was pleased and excited. "Who will you be taking?" she asked.

"I've asked Darla Zadok," he said. "But she has to get her parents' permission."

Narcissa's enthusiasm diminished noticeably. "Do you think that's wise? Don't you think Darla should go out with... someone of her own people?" she asked.

"What's wrong with Darla?" Cloud asked.

"Oh, nothing, I suppose," Narcissa responded, clearly not believing her own words. "It's just...well, her parents are foreigners, and uh..."

Lloyd intervened. "Darla is a fine young lady, Cloud, and I hope the two of you have a wonderful time at the prom. You've got very good taste in females." Lloyd winked at Cloud.

Narcissa abruptly changed the subject to the latest news in her past life search. "Dr. Kherbet has determined that I have a karmic savings account. I am one of those rare spiritually advanced people with an excess of good karma from the actions of my previous selves. So I have a sort of eternal savings account I can draw on in this incarnation. I don't have to wait for salvation in the next life but can gain it now. Most people have karmic debts, but I am karmically wealthy. He promised to guide me in accessing that wealth."

"I'll bet," said Lloyd. "I can hardly wait for the money to roll in."

Several days passed before Cloud received a final answer from Darla. Her parents were wary about their daughter going to an important event with a non-Jew. She begged them to say yes, and in the end they agreed to let her go. "But one thing," her father added, "only to the prom. No more dates with Cloud. No steady. Is that what they call it?" Darla didn't like the stipulation but ultimately agreed to it in order to clear the way for the dance.

Odie's parents gave him an early graduation present, a 1959 Triumph TR3 roadster. He drove it to school with the top down and made a ritual show of putting up the top or snapping on the tonneau cover before shuffling off to his first class. The attention he received as a result of this graduation present emboldened him to ask a cheerleader to go to the prom with him, and she said yes. Aldous asked a quiet girl who had worked on the **South Pacific** stage crew, receiving a prompt yes. Only Firstlaugh, among Cloud's close friends, decided against the event. Even Quinn Queensbury found a date.

Senior ditch day was an unofficial tradition at West High. The Friday before the Saturday night prom was set aside for massive senior truancy, and the principal relaxed his usual strict standards of accountability.

Odie, Aldous and Cloud decided to use the day for exploring in the mountains west of Phoenix. Cloud had heard there were petroglyphs in the White Tanks, made by the mysterious and long departed Hohokam Indians, and he wanted to see if he could locate them.

Since Odie was the only one with a car, they traveled in his roadster, with Cloud in the passenger seat and Aldous scrunched sideways into the small storage space behind the seats. The car stirred up a generous amount of dust on the dirt road they followed, and with the top down, it poured in upon them, so they wore goggles and tied bandanas around their faces, covering their noses and mouths. Odie found a spot to park the car, where a ring of mature palo verde trees would provide continual shade as the sun shifted across the sky. They girded themselves with Army surplus web-belts and hooked on canteens, lunch packs, and small tools then set off hiking.

After several hours of peripatetic search, Cloud climbed a pile of boulders to get a view of the broad desert valley to the south and east. Odie and Aldous were busy exploring a cave nearby. He sat cross-legged on the top rock and pulled out one of his canteens. After taking a moderate swig, he poured water on his bandana, which he had long since taken from his lower face and tied around the top of his head.

A sight in the distance, several miles away, caught his attention. Something was shining out there, like a mirror in the desert. It was too bright to be a mirage. Probably the windshield of a car, Cloud thought. Yet he continued to gaze at it, unable to turn away. Within seconds, Cloud entered a trance and saw himself as a child lying naked in his old twin bed. He was thrashing around in a fevered state, and four teenage boys, whom he did not recognize, stood around his bed laughing and drinking beer. Suddenly they were silent and turned and ran from the scene.

Cloud left his body and floated off the rock, hovering above the scree below. Surprised at this development, he turned and examined himself seated securely on the large, flat boulder. So, he mused, nakedness was **not** a prerequisite for inducing an out-of-body experience. But he had never before done it wearing clothes. In his earliest conscious memory of floating he had been naked and had assumed that was a necessary part of the technique for inducing it. Now he pirouetted his non-corporeal self to the southeast and floated toward the reflection in the desert, curious about what it might be.

As he sailed across the sky, he thought more about the first time he had experienced leaving his body and realized he had just seen a vision of that occasion, except there were no other boys present when it actually happened. The only other person around at the time was his friend, who conversed with him inside his head. "Oh my God," Cloud said to himself. He had forgotten about the mental friend who was with him when he was six. By the time he was thirteen, he had decided that friend was simply his overactive imagination. What was going on back then, he wondered?

Cloud wafted through the air closer to the reflection, getting near enough to see that no car was in the area, but there was a depression in the land where something was gleaming in the sun. Some kind of prismatic effect was occurring. He thought again about his childhood imaginary friend. A faint recollection about a promise of some kind came to him, but he could not quite grasp it. The only connection he could make was that this friend, or whatever brain phenomenon this friend represented, was the means for how he learned to float.

Before he could get close enough to the shiny spot to see clearly what was causing the reflection, Cloud heard Aldous yell, and he soared back to his body as fast as he could. Aldous was kneeling in front of Cloud, waving a hand before his face. "Yoo hoo? Where are you, Cloud?" he called.

Cloud's body jerked. "I'm right here -meditating. Do you mind?" Cloud said with a trace of irritation in his voice.

"Oh, sorry," said Aldous. "I didn't know you did stuff like that. I was worried when you didn't answer me when I yelled."

The rest of the day was productive and fun. They found dozens of pottery shards and petroglyphs, all of which they left untouched. The boys were tired and encrusted with dirt when they arrived at their homes that evening, but with sleep and a thorough scrubbing tomorrow, they would look presentable in their tuxedos.

Cloud lay in bed mentally dissecting the vision he had seen earlier in the day. Who were those four boys? What did they have to do with his imaginary friend? No answers came, but a deep and dreamless sleep did.

Narcissa insisted that Cloud bring Darla to the house so she could take pictures of her son and his date in their formal attire. Darla's pale blue gown was modestly cut, but the flow of the fabric revealed the shape of a woman. Her hair was done up in such fashion and her makeup applied with such skill that she looked much older than her fifteen years. Cloud, on the other hand, looked handsome in his tuxedo, but his boyish face betrayed any hopes he might have of passing for a college man.

Before borrowing the keys to his father's Buick, Cloud escorted Darla next door so that Miss Listerbaum could also photograph the pair. She was thrilled to see Cloud and Darla in their finery and used an entire roll of film before they were able to get out the door and on their way to the dance at the Mountain Shadows Resort.

Cloud had briefly entertained the idea of taking Darla across to the Verralls so that Nissa also could see them dressed up in formal garb. He enjoyed the nurturing attention Nissa had given him through the years and anticipated she would be delighted by the visit. Ultimately, he decided against it. His parents' relationship with the Verralls had waned over time. Cloud suspected this was due to his mother's discomfort at hearing Nissa's inevitable accounts about how well things were going at the Natural Christian congregation. Narcissa didn't appreciate reminders she had disappointed her husband and son.

Aldous, Odie, and Cloud and their dates stayed together the first half of the evening, providing a level of comfort for the socially inexperienced young men. But after a while the cheerleader wanted to mix with her friends and took Odie in tow. Darla wanted to introduce Cloud to her friends from the classes at synagogue, and perhaps show off the good-looking *goy* she was with.

This left Aldous sitting with his shy date at a little round table where they talked about the work of Arthur C. Clarke and Isaac Asimov. He had brought along his banjo, which he strummed quietly as they talked. When there was a slow dance they shuffled to the floor and held each other awkwardly while shifting to the melody.

Despite only a few waltz and fox trot lessons in grade school, Cloud was a good dancer within limits, and Darla was excellent. So they spent more time on their feet than Cloud had anticipated. When the deejay spun slow ballads like the Everly Brothers harmonizing on "All I Have to Do Is Dream" and Jackie Wilson's plaintive "Night," Cloud responded with natural grace, feeling united with Darla, unable to distinguish where his body ended and hers began. But when he tried to keep up with the pulsing rhythms of fast songs, like U. S. Bonds' "Quarter to Three" and Del Shannon's new smash hit "Runaway" he was less adept, feeling self-conscious and awkward. As much as he liked the up-tempo music, his muscles seemed unable to coordinate comfortably with the demands of the beat.

Nevertheless, he was having a very good time and was disappointed when the deejay announced the last dance. He took Darla's hand as they walked to the floor, where she fell into his arms and they swayed as one to the voice of Ray Peterson crooning "Goodnight, My Love."

They held hands on the way to the car, and when Cloud opened the door for Darla, he turned to her and gently kissed her lips. She responded by wrapping her arms around him and kissing him with a great deal more intensity than his tentative kiss had produced.

When at last he fell into bed, after delivering Darla safely into the arms of her waiting mother, Cloud was happier than he ever remembered being. He had never felt anything like the glow that pulsed through his body. Was he in love? He didn't know how to answer that question, but he was certainly in something beyond friendship.

The following Monday, Cloud asked Darla to go with him to the Kingston Trio concert at the Encanto Bandshell on Friday. She really wanted to go, she said, but it was the Sabbath and she had to go to Temple. Besides that, her parents did not want her to date until she was older, and they had made a one-time exception for the prom. This news hit Cloud like a punch in the stomach. He couldn't speak, and the look of disappointment on his face was so pronounced that Darla kissed him lightly on the lips and said, "I'm sorry, Cloud. I wish we could be... wish we could spend time together."

Having reveled in the sensate splendor of slow-dancing with Darla to the sound of Ray Peterson crooning "Goodnight My Love" only a few days earlier, Cloud now grieved her absence to the strains of Peterson whimpering his latest hit, "I Could Have Loved You So Well."

Aldous became Cloud's companion for the concert, and both of them thoroughly enjoyed the music, reclining on the sculpted grass steps in front of the open-air bandshell. Cloud brooded about the loss of Darla and how great it would have been to cuddle next to her rather than sit next to Aldous, but the bright folk music brought him out of his funk and provided a measure of healing to his wounded youthful spirit.

For her ninth birthday late in May, Terp's parents took her to see the Broadway musical **Camelot**. Her eager mind soaked up the music and dancing and dazzling sets as the story of King Arthur, Queen Guenevere, and Sir Lancelot unfolded on stage. She was enchanted with the idealism of the mythical kingdom and grieved at its demise.

Late that night, when she finally fell into exhausted sleep in her own bed, images from the play filled Terp's head. Her mind wrestled with the flow of the story, how it had been witty and lighthearted until the scene where Lancelot resurrected a knight he had killed, and suddenly after that everything seemed to be so serious and even gloomy. Toward dawn, she dreamed about the tragedy of King Arthur, but in her mind she saw not Richard Burton but President John Kennedy. In place of Julie Andrews as Guenevere was the First Lady, Jackie Kennedy. And standing in for Robert Goulet as Lancelot was a short, roguish man she did not recognize. As the dream unfolded, the president faded from the scene and Jackie married the unknown Lancelot who was dressed now as a pirate. No, she mentally protested. That's not how the story goes!

Terp awoke shaking from the nightmare and could not get back to sleep. The next night the same troubling images returned. She tossed in her bed trying to escape them, without success. Eventually she sought to dispel them by conjuring other, more comforting images. Thus at her urging Big Head came into her mind. The Old One smiled wistfully at Terp and whispered, "Someday you will understand, but tonight, sleep without dreams." Immediately she dropped into deep slumber.

In the weeks following her visit to Broadway, Terp forgot about Arthur, Lancelot, and Guenevere, musing instead about the nymph Nimue who beguiled and seduced Merlin with her song "Follow Me." Something about the older man falling hopelessly in love with the enchanting maiden resonated pleasantly in her developing psyche and made her feel strong. A mystical current tingled through her limbs as she imagined being Nimue. Yet a faint premonitory sense that Merlin might also possess some power to captivate Nimue whispered in her mind.

CHAPTER THIRTEEN

Lloyd's graduation present helped Cloud recover from his first disappointment in love. A competing bank had repossessed a 1955 Ford Fairlane with only 18,000 miles on the odometer. It was, in the parlance of used car salesmen, a cream puff, and through his connections Lloyd managed to buy it for an exceptionally good price. He put four new whitewall tires on the tan over white two-door sedan and stored it at his assistant manager's house until graduation day.

For Narcissa, the commencement ceremony was distinguished only by the tiny asterisk in the program indicating that Cloud was graduating *cum laude*. This provided her with something to drop casually into coffee break conversation at work. Aldous had two asterisks, showing that he had achieved *magna cum laude* status. Firstlaugh rated one asterisk also, but Odie's grade point average fell short of any honor.

The students processed to a droning chorus of Elgar's "Pomp and Circumstance" that Cloud replaced in his mind with the sprightly and irreverent Adrian Kimberly version, a current Top Forty hit. After the distribution of diplomas, the handshakes from the principal, and the all-school choir's ritual singing of "You'll Never Walk Alone," Cloud found his parents in the parking lot and told them not to wait up for him, as he was heading to an all-night graduation party at the Camelback Inn.

Riding in Odie's roadster en route to the party, Cloud hummed "You'll Never Walk Alone."

"I never liked that song," said Odie. "It seems like a threat."

"A threat? How so?" asked Cloud in astonishment.

"Well, if you're stupid enough to go out walking in a storm, you're bound to get injured, and then you'll never be able to walk without assistance," Odie explained.

"You're either pulling my leg or completely nuts," said Cloud.

"No, really," Odie responded. "My dad owns an insurance agency. That's the way insurance people have to look at the world. It's good for business."

"Then you should like the song," Cloud noted. "Threats are why people buy insurance."

"Yeah, you're right. Now that you say it that way, the song sort of grows on me," Odie said with a leer. He began to whistle the tune.

At the Camelback Inn, toward two in the morning, Odie cannonballed into the pool while fully dressed, rejoicing in the laughs and attention the deed gave him. Conveniently, he had a change of clothes in the boot of his Triumph.

Around four, Odie, still pumped on adrenaline, delivered a very sleepy Cloud to Villa Verde Street.

The Fairlane was parked in the driveway, and Cloud wondered who was visiting at that hour. When he found the keys to the car taped to his bedroom door, he realized it was a graduation present. In case he needed further confirmation, an ornate greeting card lay on his pillow, offering a pre-printed sentimental congratulatory message and signed "Mom and Dad." Printed beneath was a note from Lloyd, that read, "Enjoy the car, Son." No longer drowsy, he tore outside and made an hour-long pre-dawn test-drive, grinning all the way.

June proved to be a lonely month for Cloud. Aldous got a summer job scooping ice cream at Mary Coyle, Odie accompanied his parents on a trip to Europe, and Firstlaugh went to the reservation to visit relatives. Cloud decided to treat himself to a tour of Arizona in his new car. It would be more fun with a friend along, but he knew how to be content by himself. He had lived his entire life in the Grand Canyon state and had never seen the canyon, so that would be his first stop.

Having packed hiking gear, food, and sleeping bag, he set off for the South Rim. There he filled his canteens, pulled on his backpack and set off down the Bright Angel Trail. The trail was a switchbacked brook of dust, rocks, patches of mule dung, and occasional reservoirs of mule piss. Though he descended rapidly the five miles to Indian Gardens, his feet and knees ached for a non-existent level stretch of trail. At the gardens he replenished his water supply in Garden Creek. Resuming his journey, he briefly followed a gently sloping path that soon plunged into a twisting route. He noted that it would not be easy going back up. This was the opposite of mountain climbing where the hard upward work comes first.

Nine miles into the canyon, he reached the silver suspension bridge that led to Phantom Ranch across the river. Rather than cross, he detoured westward, along the riverbank. After a mile hiking through scrub brush, climbing over rocks, and splashing through shallow water, Cloud decided to rest.

Shrugging off his backpack, he removed his hiking boots and socks and put them on a rock to dry in the sun. Without conscious thought, in one continuous motion he disrobed and stepped naked into the brown, sluggish river and sat in a patch of mud, skimming his hands across the surface of the water, as if they were seaplanes practicing take offs and landings. Then he moved into a deeper area and swam with a leisurely backstroke. Refreshed, he climbed out of the water and stretched out on a rock.

With the sun licking the wetness from his skin and feeling a slight breeze nipping at his body, he fell into a deep reverie of peace and contentment. All is well with the world, he thought. He half expected to float out of his body and considered that it would be nice to sail above the water, exploring nooks and crannies in the canyon. But it would be as equally enjoyable simply to lie on this rock.

All his senses and mind opened to the elements of the universe, and Cloud felt a mystic oneness with all that exists. No words were available to him, no human language could describe the experience, the understanding, and kinship with every particle of existence that sifted through his being during the eon that passed as he lay there.

A dragonfly buzzing around his eyes ended his reverie. He reached up to shoo it away and the spell was broken. The memory was gone. Only the residual aftermath of awe told him that for an instant he had seen the solution to the universal puzzle, but it was gone from his consciousness, with no promises for a second look.

Cloud dressed, pulled his backpack onto his shoulders, and hiked back to the suspension bridge. As darkness enveloped the bottom of the canyon, he found a tiny clearing in the forest near Phantom Ranch, where he spread his sleeping bag and curled up for the night.

Deep, dark waters swirled through his dreams. He was swimming in a muddy pool, and decided to explore beneath the surface. He saw very little but sensed treasure was hidden in the fathoms below. Surely treacherous things lurked there also, but Cloud was not concerned with them. What was he searching for? Something he would be able to feel but not touch? He felt the press of water against his face as he propelled himself through the murk, and then a faint glow spread through the water, and Cloud saw intimations of witches, tornados, yellow brick roads, and wizards. These were images from **The Wizard of Oz**, which had been seared into his brain when he was eight. How strange, he thought, to watch an underwater movie.

The toasting sunlight on his face brought him out of the dream. As he stretched his arms and legs to greet the new day, Cloud experienced a pleasant muscular ache, reminding him of what he had done the day before. He was also very hungry.

After eating a peanut butter and cheese sandwich and a banana chased by water, Cloud began his trek out of the canyon, working his way in a leisurely manner uphill to Indian Gardens. There he refilled his canteens and lolled around, watching the other hikers track by in both directions. They were an odd lot, he mused, and there were too many of them. He resented the clamor made by packs of extroverted hikers and wanted to enjoy the Grand Canyon in silent solitude.

Late in the afternoon, he looked around for a spot to spread his sleeping bag among the cottonwoods, but no place seemed good to him. A competing thought was influencing his search for a place to sleep, leaving him dissatisfied with every option. The dream of swimming in dark waters had transformed into a wish to climb out of the canyon at night. He decided not to stay at the gardens but to head for the South Rim, knowing that most of the uphill trek would be after nightfall. The prospect of being alone, of having the Bright Angel all to himself, was the most appealing element in his plan.

Soon after starting out, however, he noticed a particularly large raven circling ahead of him gliding on thermals, acting like a hawk. Thinking of Edgar Allan Poe's poem, Cloud spoke to the bird. "You're going to croak 'Nevermore' at me, aren't you? But I don't want to hear it." For a moment he wondered if this raven might be an omen about something that awaited him on the trail above. Then he threw off that idea as silly.

Night came with sudden finality, and Cloud had to stop to allow his eyes to adjust to the darkness. He sat in the middle of the deserted trail and finished off one of his canteens. He still had another full one. The idea of hiking in the dark didn't seem as intriguing as it had when he was resting at Indian Gardens, but he was determined to reach his goal.

Stars and a sliver of moon provided some illumination, but shapes and shadows confused his eyes. His steps grew ever slower as he groped his way around switchbacks where no external light penetrated. His knees grew increasingly resentful of bending against the upward slope of the trail. Cloud kept going. After a while he fell into a droning rhythm, shuffling one foot in front of the other, higher and higher toward the rim.

He lost his balance when the trail suddenly rose an inch higher than his right foot anticipated, and he tumbled into the dirt, cutting his lip. He lay there bleeding, knowing full well where he was but not caring. Perhaps he would set out his sleeping bag in the middle of the trail and spend the night here.

No! Get up Cloud, he told himself. A few minutes later he rammed his left elbow into an unseen outcrop of rock, causing him to wince and curse. Now it wasn't stars overhead that guided him but stars of pain circling his face. Pausing only long enough to clear his head, he continued the journey, promptly stepping into a puddle of mule piss. After an interval of careful progress, he rammed his left foot into a stone and fell, bruising and cutting his right forearm in the process. With his arm wrapped in a handkerchief, Cloud rose and staggered forward.

Passing through the second tunnel, he knew he was nearing the rim and lumbered on. When he reached the first tunnel he sighed, "Only three hundred paces to the trailhead!" Summoning a burst of energy, he tramped to the rim, and hobbled the remaining half-mile to his car. He threw his gear in the trunk and wiped the coagulated blood from his face and arm with a wet cloth.

A mile down at the bottom of the canyon it had been hot, but the night air was chilly against his sweaty body here at the top, and he started to shiver. He was glad he'd brought an Army blanket. Wrapping himself snugly in the blanket, he curled up in the backseat and dropped quickly into a deep, dreamless sleep.

While washing himself in the public restroom next morning, Cloud wondered where to visit next. Tuba City is not far, he thought. Maybe he could find Firstlaugh. After a breakfast of beef jerky and potato chips, he drove east on Route 64 toward the Navajo Reservation. Turning north onto US 89, he stopped at the Cameron Trading Post for a pee break and bought a bag of licorice and more chips. Fifteen minutes later, he proceeded eastward into the sandstone depths of Navajo Land. Along the way he saw an outcrop of rock that looked like a pulpit overlooking a vast high mesa nave. A vision of himself preaching from a real pulpit flashed in his mind and he laughed out loud at the preposterous image.

On Main Street in Tuba City, Cloud stopped at the Tuba Trading Post and asked a clerk where he could find the Begay family. She laughed, saying there were thousands of Begays. He refined his question by specifying Firstlaugh, and she suggested he try the Calvinist Church a block north on the cottonwood-lined lane, opposite the government boarding school.

This seemed an unlikely venue for his friend, but with nothing to lose he drove to the church and walked past the stone turret bell tower through the open sanctuary doors right into Firstlaugh. Actually, Firstlaugh backed into Cloud while demonstrating to the children the best way to finish a vacation Bible school craft project.

"Pardon me," he said, before turning around. "Cloud! What are you doing here?"

"Looking for you," Cloud said. "What are *you* doing here? I didn't know you were a Calvinist."

"I'm not, really," Firstlaugh said. "Some of my clan family are members here, and since I'm staying with them, I volunteered to help out with the kids. It gives me something to do. We're about to have lunch. Would you like to join us?"

Cloud was very hungry and quickly agreed. They sat outside on little chairs at little tables and enjoyed a feast of mutton soup, fry bread, and Kool-aid. The cook was one of Firstlaugh's aunts, who said to Cloud, "So, you're Freddy's school chum from Phoenix, huh?"

Cloud started to ask who Freddy was, but Firstlaugh bent over and whispered, "I'll explain later."

After the meal the children were sent home, and Cloud told Firstlaugh about his hike in the Grand Canyon. "By the way, what's this stuff about Freddy?"

"The Christians in my family don't like my first name. Because it's from tribal culture, they think it's not compatible with Christianity. So they gave me a Christian name," Firstlaugh explained.

"But Freddy's not a Christian name," Cloud responded.

"I know, but it's a white European name, so it's just as good," Firstlaugh said.

"You mentioned clan family. What clan are you?" Cloud asked.

"I was born to the Crystal Rock Clan, my mother's clan, and born for my father's Black Sheep Clan. If I ever get married, it can't be to a Crystal Rock woman or with some exceptions a Black Sheep. It would be considered incest if I did. The Navajo Nation marriage license has spaces to list the maternal and paternal clans of bride and groom."

"Sounds complicated," Cloud responded. "By the way, I'm thinking about heading east through the reservation. Any complications there I need to know about?"

"I don't know," Firstlaugh answered. "Just be careful crossing the Hopi Reservation. Tempers are running high over there, because so many Navajos claim land the feds gave to the Hopis eighty years ago. The Hopis have taken us to court. They say the **Dine** are squatters, but our people say they've lived in those places for generations."

The Hopi Reservation formed a large rectangle surrounded on all sides by the much larger and irregularly shaped Navajo Nation.

"But the Hopis are the most peaceful tribe in the country. And I'm not Navajo, so why should I worry?" Cloud countered. "And I'm not sure generations count for very much when the Hopi measure their time there in centuries."

"Yeah, you'll probably be alright. Just don't stop and take pictures. They don't like cameras," the Navajo said. "They'll yell at you for taking photographs. And don't go sneaking around any kivas. Their religion is very private. They don't like their sanctuaries violated."

"Nobody does," Cloud said. "I'd like to visit a kiva, though. I read somewhere they're set up the opposite of Christian sanctuaries. Instead of showing off with a steeple -a phallic symbol if there ever was one- a kiva is hidden underground, like a womb. A Christian minister, wearing his Sunday best, preaches from a high pulpit, but the barefoot Hopi priest leads worship from an altar in the lowest part of the room." Cloud paused, wondering silently about the image of an altar in the bottom of a sanctuary. He had encountered this bit of information in Arizona history and cultures class four years earlier, and it had remained a compelling concept to him, although he had no sense why. "I don't have a camera with me," he added.

Cloud thanked Firstlaugh and said farewell. After refueling the Ford, he picked up Route 264, a back road that snaked its way into the Hopi Reservation. Cloud drove across Third Mesa and stopped to look around in Oraibi, the oldest continuously inhabited village in North America.

He reflected that the land at the center of Hopi culture seemed bleak compared with the land of the surrounding Navajos. The desert outside Phoenix was lush in comparison with the aridity of this place. Yet, people have seen fit to live here for a thousand years, so they must know something the rest of us don't, he mused.

When he reached the junction with Route 87, he headed south toward Winslow and Route 66, and upon arrival at the main highway between Chicago and Los Angeles, he turned eastward toward Holbrook, his final destination for the day. In town he decided to splurge with some of the graduation gift money his grandparents in Bagdad had sent him. Rather than find a place to stretch out his sleeping bag, he rented a motel room shaped like a teepee. After registering, he asked the clerk why the motel owner chose to imitate Plains Indians, when Arizona Indians didn't live in teepees.

"Aw, the tourists don't know the difference, and a hogan would only confuse 'em," he said.

Once in his room, Cloud reflected on the gift of five new twenty-dollar bills his grandparents had sent him. He had seen them only twice in his life, even though they lived less than two hundred miles away. He had sent them an invitation and would have liked for them to attend his graduation ceremony, but they sent money instead. His other grandparents, on his father's side, didn't make the trip out from Pennsylvania, but Cloud hadn't expected them to. They had sent a fancy card with a check for $25.00 inside.

Cloud spread his Arizona map on the bed to plot the next leg of his journey. He considered going west on Route 66, which would provide several options for a turn to the south toward Prescott. And if he got to Prescott, he could swing over to Bagdad and visit his grandparents. The more he thought about reconnecting with his roots in this manner, the more certain he became that he would not be welcome there. He had no idea why this was so, but he felt it deeply, and he was learning to trust his intuition.

Well then, he decided, he would go east to see the Painted Desert and the Petrified Forest. This he did the next morning, and he found that although the dancing colors of the Painted Desert had a hypnotic effect on him, nothing unusual happened. He simply enjoyed the spectacular scenery without any inclination to leave his body.

He made his way south to Show Low and on through the equally scenic and serpentine Salt River Canyon, before stopping in Globe for the night. The following day he drove through the Queen Creek Tunnel to Superior, looking at mountains of slag from the copper mines along the way. Making a side run down Route 177, he parked at an overlook and stared into the huge open pit copper mine at Ray. The workers seemed like elves next to the giant earthmovers that lifted tons of dirt for the mostly copper but also silver and gold hidden in it.

The words of his father the banker came to his mind. Arizona's economy is built on the Five Cs: copper first, followed by cotton, cattle, citrus, and climate. Climate was a code word for tourism. Of course, Cloud thought, Four Cs and a T didn't have the same ring to it as Five Cs. And if you added lettuce, alfalfa, electronics and air conditioning the whole scheme would be ruined.

The thought of ruining a mnemonic device led Cloud to consider the pit in front of him. He was not opposed to big business and heartily approved of profit-making enterprises, but something about the gaping hole below bothered him. It was certainly safer than underground mines, and yet, would vegetation ever bloom here again? He returned to Phoenix with the first stirrings of an environmentalist conscience.

Odie came back from Europe in July. On evenings when Aldous was not scheduled to work at the ice cream parlor, Cloud and Aldous would take turns riding behind the bucket seats in Odie's Triumph sports car as the three of them cruised up and down Central Avenue. A few blocks north of McDowell was a retail store parking lot where sports car enthusiasts congregated to talk, and this became the trio's summer headquarters.

The store closed at five, and the owner was himself a sports car buff, proudly driving a Morgan. He gave the boys permission to use the lot as a base for cruising Central, on the condition that they allow no "Detroit iron" to park there. That meant no Corvettes or Thunderbirds were welcome. Only European sports cars were considered worthy. So every evening during the summer of 1961, that parking lot was full of Austin-Healys, Alpines, MGs, Triumphs, Porsches, and an occasional Karman-Ghia. A Jaguar XKE pulled in one evening, but its driver did not feel at home with all the lesser vehicles, and he never returned.

As Odie, Cloud, and Aldous traveled the circuit up and down the avenue, teenage girls in big sedans would wave and giggle, and clipped conversations would be carried on from vehicle to vehicle. Every once in a while, one of the boys managed to convince a carload of girls to pull over on a side street or follow them to Encanto Park, where they could talk in a more leisurely manner.

One such occasion led to five girls stuffing themselves into Odie's two seat roadster, along with Aldous and Cloud sitting on the boot with only their lower legs in the space behind the seats. Odie drove thusly overloaded, slowly to be sure, the six blocks to their special parking lot. Unfortunately, a police car followed them into the lot and issued Odie a citation for the offense. It took three trips to get the girls back to their car, but it seemed worthwhile to Odie, because on the last trip he was alone with the one among the five he fancied, and she agreed to a date with him.

Late in August, on a day when Aldous was working, Odie and Cloud cruised far south on Central, reaching the entrance to South

Mountain Park. "Let's go to the summit lookout," Odie said.

"That's the kind of thing you should be saying to a girlfriend," said Cloud.

"Yeah, but I want to see what this baby can do on ess curves," Odie answered.

"OK," Cloud said.

Odie accelerated through the flats and turned onto the winding road to the top of the mountain. "Hey, this is fun," he yelled as he raced up the curving roadway, increasing speed with every turn.

"Be careful!" Cloud shouted. "You're on the wrong side of the road!" At that moment, Cloud saw two beams of light, headlights from a vehicle descending the mountain, shining into the darkness beyond the road. Cloud could see those rays shifting direction as the car they were attached to followed the curve of the mountain. In a few seconds they would be shining directly at an off-white Triumph roadster moving much too fast in the wrong lane.

The young man driving the Buick headed toward Odie's car was somewhat distracted from his task. He was a careful driver in ordinary circumstances, but at this moment, his date was nibbling at his ear and making a lewd suggestion, and while he wanted to drive his father's car in a safe manner, he did not want to say anything that might dampen the mood of his girl, for he knew a secluded place to park below. All he could think to do to resolve the delicate situation was slow down.

As the Buick rounded the curve directly into the path of the Triumph, the driver of the larger car slammed on the brakes. Odie did likewise, but instead of turning back into his proper lane, he swerved to the left. The small car crashed through the guardrail and down the embankment.

The other driver stopped long enough to see what happened to the sports car, then continued down the mountain, lest a car coming around the blind curve from the summit would crash into him. In the event, Odie and Cloud were exceptionally lucky. Had he described the event to her, Nissa Verrall would have told Cloud he was providentially blessed. But he would have dismissed her words of heavenly protection with an unspoken denial. Years would pass before either boy would tell anyone about this incident.

The embankment the Triumph crested across gave way to an

eight feet wide shelf that sloped downward in a gentle grade then rose slightly. A pile of large boulders stood at the end of the shelf, and had the car continued forward at the rate of speed Odie had attained on the roadway, the two boys would have been killed upon impact. But Odie brought the vehicle to a stop a yard from the rocks, and a brief inspection revealed only minor damage to the front bumper. With the aid of a flashlight, Cloud directed Odie in turning the car around so that he could drive it back onto the roadway. They decided to skip the summit and went straight home.

That night, Cloud dreamed about being driven into a head-on collision. He wasn't in Odie's car but riding in the back of a dark truck. And he wasn't alone but surrounded by a crowd of young men he did not recognize. The crash would not stop but continued on and on in slow motion, threatening to kill him when the crunching physics of the event ultimately came to an end. More and more vehicles -all kinds of them: cars, tanks, motor scooters, and rickshaws- entered into the chain reaction, and the collision kept growing in seemingly endless procession. He awoke in a panic and could not get back to sleep.

Three days later, Cloud registered as a freshman at Arizona State University in Tempe. He chose history as his major subject and anthropology as his minor. Rather than incur the cost of a dormitory and a food plan, Lloyd decided it would be better for Cloud to live at home and commute to classes, making good use of the automobile he had given to his son. The distance to campus, via Grand Avenue, Van Buren, and the Mill Avenue Bridge was thirteen miles one way, but with gasoline less than two bits a gallon, it was the financially prudent thing to do. Lloyd gave Cloud a check for $85.00 to cover his first semester's tuition and cash to pay for his books.

Odie enrolled at ASU also. Aldous, recipient of a generous scholarship, flew off to New England to study at Middlebury College in Vermont. Firstlaugh chose Arizona State College at Flagstaff, so he could be close to the reservation.

During orientation week, Cloud received several noteworthy pieces of clothing. The first was a freshman beanie, which he dutifully wore while he and hundreds of other freshmen carried buckets of gold paint up the side of Tempe Butte for the annual repainting of the giant stone A laid out on the side of the steep hill.

The other items were parts of his ROTC uniform: khaki trousers, a long sleeved khaki shirt, cloth belt with brass buckle, and a garrison cap. As a school with many Federal government contracts, Arizona State was obliged to require able-bodied male students of military age to participate in ROTC for two years. Most of the young men bitched about it, but Cloud was pleased to continue studying military science, and at his first drill he was made a squad leader and given sergeant stripes. Despite another outbreak of pimples, which made him feel more adolescent than college man, his self-confidence greatly increased as he fixed the stripes onto his military shirt.

CHAPTER FOURTEEN

Cloud had become good friends with the boy who stood next to him in his high school ROTC squad. Something akin to that would happen in college, but in this case, Cloud was the squad leader, and the friendship developed with the student in his squad who was least happy about being there.

Theophilus Gynt let Cloud know at the second drill that he was researching conscientious objector laws to find a way to get out of what he forthrightly described as "Mickey Mouse toy soldier bullshit." Gynt followed this assertion by waving his arms in the air and whistling the "Mickey Mouse Club March."

Cloud, who was torn between pride in the uniform and his conviction that forcing men to serve in the military was morally and constitutionally wrong, was drawn to Theo immediately.

Theophilus had received his Christian name from his father, a minister of the Scandinavian Protestant Church, in honor of the anonymous most excellent Theophilus, the addressee of the Gospel according to Luke. Theo liked it, for he did indeed love God, as the name signified. However, as with so many other PKs -preachers' kids- he held considerably less affection for the Church, particularly the one his father served.

Theo knew more minister, priest and rabbi jokes than anyone

Cloud had ever met, yet he never invoked Jesus or God in conjunction with his large vocabulary of scatological terms and curses, which he used prodigally. He liked to brag that he had broken every one of the Ten Commandments by the time he was thirteen, and when someone would express doubt about that accomplishment, he would explain that according to the doctrine of his church, hating someone is the same as murder, lustful thoughts are the same as adultery, thinking about taking something that belongs to someone else is the same as stealing, and so on. Yet for all this antichurch bravado, Theo knew in the depths of his being that a benevolent God lived at the center of existence.

One might wonder how the agnostic soldier Cloud and the God loving conscientious objector Theo would form a fast friendship, but life is full of wonders, and bond they did. As it happened, they were both history majors and shared a number of the same classes. This made it convenient for the two to study together, and Cloud became an unofficial third resident in Theo's dorm room, often staying late into the evening before driving the thirteen miles home.

In February 1962, Terp's family took another vacation trip to Arizona. Though it meant Terp would miss a week of school, Tom and Penny felt a strong need for a break from the bleakness of the New Jersey winter. Business was going well, and they felt they could afford the indulgence. This time it was not a grand tour by automobile but via TWA Constellation from New York to Phoenix. The season was auspicious, because Arizonans were celebrating fifty years of statehood that month. The Persons luxuriated in gentle sunshine at the Jokake Inn in Scottsdale.

Though Terp had no idea how far they were from the place she had met the Old One five years earlier, she yearned to meet again this mysterious being with the big head. The problem, however, was that she could not tell her parents this was her intention. So she casually said, "Remember that time we went for a picnic and Mary bumped into a jumping cactus? Let's do that again. Let's go back to that place for old times sake."

As much as he enjoyed making his older daughter happy, Tom said, "Punkin, our schedule of activities is already too full. I just don't think we can fit that in. Besides, that was way over somewhere northwest of Goodyear, and I don't think I could even find it."

Terp bravely tried to have fun on the trip, but privately she was deeply disappointed at this lost opportunity and became determined to find this compelling creature some day.

When the Persons returned from their winter vacation, Terp's neighborhood friend and classmate, Michelle, asked if she'd like to go to church with her. Michelle's parents went every Sunday, and Michelle, whose older brother refused to attend, wanted someone her own age to sit with. Michelle chose not to tell Terp that Bring-a-Friend Sunday was coming up and she was following her pastor's urging to do so, because that wasn't her primary motivation. Michelle wanted Terp along to ameliorate her boredom with the services.

Though the church was not in Edison but in neighboring Metuchen, Tom and Penny gave half-hearted blessings, while clearly stating they were not interested in going themselves. Thus, Terp began attending Second Calvinist Church of Metuchen and quickly developed considerable fondness for the place and its pastor, the Reverend Mr. Argyle Watts. Unlike Michelle, Terp never became bored with the services.

In 1858, forty-three members of the First Calvinist Church of Metuchen came to the conclusion that the congregation had become dangerously infected with the liberal New School nonsense. This new movement in the denomination was abolitionist in inclination, which was fair enough as a philosophy but problematic insofar as it interfered in real life with sister Calvinist churches in the South and with certain economic interests of prominent church members.

But this was a minor concern compared with the real problem. Diminished support for the **Westminster Confession of Faith** and the concomitant flirting with the anything goes doctrinal inclinations of the New England Congregationalists really galled these two score and three men of sound doctrine.

Now, these loyal Old School conservatives were not so radical as to split off into another Calvinist denomination, as did some of their fellow religionists in other communities, but they did vote to form another Calvinist congregation as a sanctuary for those who desired sober and orthodox worship and did not want to meddle in political issues. Being orderly people, they named the new congregation the Second Calvinist Church of Metuchen.

In one of the frequent ironies of church life, over the course of the next century, pastoral search committees from that congregation selected pastors who were incrementally less conservative than their predecessors. Functioning in reaction to the perceived deficiencies of their long-tenured pastors, the committees looked for new shepherds who were a little more easy-going than the departing ones. And in time, the make up of the congregation came to reflect that liberalizing evolution.

By the 1950s, when mainline churches all over the nation were growing rapidly, the congregation at Second Calvinist was fully involved in denominational efforts to reform the liturgy, encourage greater sacramental participation, and embrace the arts. This last subject is one that their Calvinist ancestors had held in grave suspicion. The church also strongly supported the ordination of women, and rejoiced in the middle of the decade when the American Calvinist Church General Assembly approved that reform.

In the 1960s, the congregation was so committed to the civil rights movement that a contingent of members and Rev. Watts traveled to Alabama to meddle in racial politics, which is exactly what the founding members of the church did not want to do.

The fifteen hundred member Second Calvinist Church on Amboy Avenue was large enough that ten year-old Terp Person, who had never before been to a church service, might be swallowed up in the crowd and go unnoticed for years. But that did not happen. Rev. Watts saw something very appealing in her naïve and expectant face, and he made a decision to befriend her.

Terp loved church. As Sunday succeeded Sunday, she fell in thrall to the large choir and its soaring anthems. When the sopranos let loose their descants, her skin would tingle with joy. The processionals, with the young beadle leading the way, carrying the Bible into the sanctuary, often moved her to tears, and she determined that she would one day become a beadle. The high drama of the liturgy flowed into her mind where she made it her own answer to whatever the world may offer. She gloried in the stately hymns booming forth from the congregation and echoing off the stone walls of the sanctuary. When they sang "Guide Me O Thou Great Jehovah," she didn't want the hymn to end. But it did, and then they sang "For the beauty of the earth, for the beauty of the skies," and she didn't want that to end either.

And then there was Rev. Watts. His full yet kindly voice overflowed in her ears as he preached words of comfort and inspiration that touched her soul. He was an ordinary looking man in his mid forties, married to Ruth, a woman of comfortable appearance, and father of a daughter who was away at Amherst College in Massachusetts.

Many parishioners would characterize him as stodgy but approachable. He was not comfortable with the college group's coffee house ministry in the basement of the church but he knew he needed to bend a little with the times. Argyle Watts was a liberal traditionalist, with all the emotional bumps and intellectual bruises that came with being such a person.

On Good Friday that first year of Terp's involvement with Second Church, she asked her mother to take her to the sanctuary for the tenebrae service, as Michelle's parents were not going to attend. After some haggling, Penny agreed to drop her off and pick her up an hour later.

Terp sat by herself in the huge sanctuary as various texts relating to the trial and crucifixion of Jesus were read, each followed by a tolling of bells and extinguishing of candles. Terp did not move as her mind absorbed the terrible passion drama. The sanctuary was draped in shadows when Argyle Watts read the John 19 account of the soldiers placing a crown of thorns on Jesus' head and wrapping him in a purple robe, saying, "Hail, King of the Jews!"

The room was dark, but a light flashed in Terp's brain. Purple...robe...king, she thought. An image of the Old One formed in her mind. There was no thought that Big Head was Jesus. That much was clear in her mind. But royalty for certain. For a few minutes, she was buoyed up in joy in the midst of the tragedy of crucifixion. The memory of standing in the presence of goodness and grace five years earlier sustained her until she felt the need to return her attention to the tenebrae service, and she let go of the image of that shack in the desert.

The sanctuary was now completely dark as the congregation sat in silence, waiting for a signal that Jesus had died. Minutes ticked by and Terp closed her eyes to pray. Suddenly a loud, jarring clang of metal on metal filled the sanctuary and she jumped to her feet and opened her mouth to shout, when the pastor intoned, "It is over."

Ushers led the congregants into the narthex, maintaining silence. Once outside, Terp saw her mother and ran to the car. "Are you alright, honey?" Penny asked. Terp's face showed tears and lines of grief, but something more was there, an aura of strength and hope not often seen in the countenance of one so young.

"Sunday is such a long time away," she said. "I'll be sad all day tomorrow."

Penny did not know how to interpret her daughter's words but thought she needed corrective advice. "Terp, you're not going to be sad," she declared. "You'll feel just fine. And you don't need to go back to this church on Sunday if you don't feel like it."

"I have to go on Sunday," Terp said. "It's the most important day."

If importance were measured solely on the basis of attendance, Terp's superlative description of the day was accurate. The sanctuary overflowed with people at the eleven o'clock service, as it had for the three earlier services. Terp, Michelle, and her parents squeezed into pew space where three might sit comfortably. Michelle's father grumbled about C and E Christians, and Terp asked what that meant.

"Christmas and Easter," Michelle whispered. "They're the people who only come at Christmas and Easter. Dad doesn't like them, but Reverend Watts always makes a point of welcoming them."

Michelle's father leaned over to the girls and said as quietly as he could, "The minister's a canny Scot who figures two Sundays a year are better than none."

"Don't you believe it, girls. He's just gracious, that's all," countered Michelle's mother.

Terp felt a lingering sadness from the dark experience of the Good Friday service. Then the processional began with the beadle leading the choir into the sanctuary. The worshippers rose to their feet as the sopranos, tenors, altos, and basses streamed toward their places on the chancel, followed by the pastor and associate pastors, gowned not in their usual black but in shimmering white robes. Half a thousand voices resounded with "Jesus Christ is risen today, Al - - le - lu - ia!" And Terp wept at the beauty and joy of it. She tried to sing, but the words stuck in her throat, not because she didn't believe them, but because they overwhelmed her. She would have to let the others sing for her this day, her first Easter.

Why he started reading an unassigned novel of nearly twelve hundred pages three weeks into the first semester of his sophomore year, Cloud could not explain. He had been browsing through the fiction stacks in the library and his eyes had come to rest on *Atlas Shrugged*. He pulled the Ayn Rand tome from the shelf and read the opening question, "Who is John Galt?" and did not stop. He was quickly caught up in the mystery of the plot and drawn in even more by the philosophical ideas woven into the story.

The book was a paean to capitalism that also assumed the non-existence of God. Cloud chuckled at the irony. It was the Communists who were supposed to be godless, he thought, but Rand is arguing that there is no place for God in a rational capitalist system. There is no transcendent magic, the novel claimed. Value is the result of human effort and thought.

He neglected his other studies while reading the novel, and by the time he finished he had revised his understanding of himself as an agnostic. An agnostic is an atheist without the courage to say so, he decided. Henceforth when asked he would tell people that he did not believe in God.

What *Atlas Shrugged* provided him was a framework from which to make sense of the contradictory elements and experiences of his life. Only objective reality exists. Facts are facts and do not change in response to feelings. There is a rational explanation for everything, Cloud learned, and this meant scientific reasons existed for his prescient dreams and out-of-body experiences. The human mind is the key to everything. It is capable of much more than the human race has thus far discovered. The supreme value is a mind devoted to reason.

Cloud soon discovered that a small group of students gathered monthly on campus to discuss the philosophy of Ayn Rand. Joining them one evening, he learned about "The Objectivist Newsletter," a journal published by Rand and Nathaniel Branden, and he subscribed to it. This led him to a taped lecture series offered at a motel on East Van Buren. The group leader played a tape-recorded lecture given by Nathaniel Branden, discussing various implications of objectivist philosophy, one of which was enlightened self-interest.

That, decided Cloud, was why he wanted to become an Army officer. It was in his own self-interest to protect the United States from rapacious communistic nations. He would join the military not because the nation had a pre-existing claim upon his life, but because he could do an important job well and be paid for it.

One night, after a long day at school, followed by a taped lecture at the motel, Cloud headed toward home along Van Buren. It was late enough on this weeknight that few other cars were on the road. As he approached Five Points, where Grand Avenue began its northwesterly track from the intersection of 7th Avenue and Van Buren, he saw that the light was green, so he could continue right onto Grand without having to wait at the long traffic signal. He hit the accelerator to insure that he reached the intersection before the amber light appeared, and as he did so, a silent command entered his brain.

Cloud heard nothing and saw nothing. Nevertheless some form of communication imprinted the message "STOP!" in his mind. It came with such insistent authority that he took his foot off the accelerator, pressed in the brake pedal and clutch and brought his car to a stop in front of the still green light. Immediately a pickup truck barreled north on 7th Avenue through the intersection where Cloud's car would have been if he had not stopped. Two seconds later a police car with lights flashing let its siren wail as it sped through the intersection in pursuit of the truck.

Cloud sat at the intersection through two complete light sequences before pulling out onto Grand Avenue and finishing his journey home. He knew there was a scientific explanation for what had happened, as was the case with his other unusual experiences, and he intended someday to find out the how and why of these things.

The following week, Cloud invited Theo to go with him to the objectivism lecture. Afterward, they headed for Woody's El Nido at Central and McDowell for a late meal and conversation about the concepts that Cloud found so attractive.

"It's a religion, Cloud," said Theo.

"What do you mean religion?" Cloud protested. "They don't believe in God."

"God has nothing to do with most religion," Theo said. "Look, you pay a fee to get in. That's the offering. The congregation, followers of the infallible Rand, gather in their pews, which in this case are folding chairs, and the priest, the one set aside to operate the tape recorder, welcomes the people with the ritual of friendship."

"Come on!" said Cloud, "You're way off base." But he was beginning to enjoy Theo's analysis in spite of his devotion to objectivist philosophy.

"Then there is the creed," Theo continued. "Something about swearing by my life not to live for anybody else's sake. The reading of scripture comes when Branden, the revered disciple of the infallible one, quotes from Ayn Rand's sacred writings. And, of course, the lecture is actually a sermon, based on these texts."

Cloud chewed on his fried red chili burro and took a swig of milk, using the time his mouth was occupied with food and drink to think of a response. Theo had a brilliant mind, and he could analyze human behavior better than anyone he had known. "OK," Cloud said. "I'll grant you there is a ritual to the lectures, but a religion requires a divine being of some sort, and neither Ayn Rand nor Nathaniel Branden claim to be divine. In fact they claim exactly the opposite."

"Buddhism and Taoism do not require God, and they are clearly religions," Theo said. "But that's not the point. The point is just about any human activity, given enough loyalty or devotion, can become a religion."

"Yeah, the Soviets have made Marxism into a religion," Cloud said.

"Hey, it's gonna be late by the time you get me back to my dorm," Theo said. "Why don't you stretch out on the rug in my room? You've got an early morning class tomorrow, don't you?"

"Thanks, Theo. I've got a sleeping bag in my trunk. Let me call home so they don't alert the Highway Patrol when I don't show up." Cloud found a dime in his pocket and made the call.

As the year unfolded, Cloud fell into the habit of staying in Theo's room once or twice a week. He stored a change of clothes and a few cosmetic items in Theo's closet and kept his sleeping bag rolled up in a corner of the room. If Theo's roommate, a quiet engineering major, objected to the extra person in the small room, he never mentioned it. And he seemed not to mind that Theo and Cloud never invited him along when they went out to movies or other activities.

The only person who expressed misgivings about the arrangement was Narcissa. One rare Saturday evening when Cloud was home for dinner, she registered her complaint. "Your father and I have some concerns about this Theo you stay with at school," she began. She had not met Theo, and in fact, she had not discussed what was on her mind with Lloyd but found it useful to invoke him as an ally.

"What about him?" Cloud asked.

"Well, you spend the night with him a lot," she said. "And we don't know what kind of person he is. There's no one else around, and maybe he wants to lead you into trouble."

"Someone else is around, Theo's roommate," Cloud explained, but he sensed that this information was irrelevant to his mother.

"Well, I'll just come out and say it," Narcissa continued. "We want to know if this Theo is— uh— a homosexual."

"What?" Cloud cried.

"Well, you know, Cloud, spending all those nights with another young man is a little peculiar, don't you think? What's the attraction of sleeping in a dorm room?"

"Mom, you're crazy!" Cloud shouted.

"Don't you talk to me that way, Cloud," she shouted back. "And let me tell you this. If you turn out to be a queer, you can move your junk out of this house tonight and never come back!" Her face was red with rage.

Cloud was stunned. Where had that come from? Neither of his parents had ever spoken about homosexuality in his presence, so he had no idea that his mother felt this way. He knew some homosexuals but was personally indifferent to the existential reality of that orientation. Based on the content of his sexual fantasies, he was fully confident that he was hopelessly heterosexual. But what did it matter? What other people did with their bodies was their own business, he believed. It had never occurred to him that anyone would suspect he might be involved sexually with Theo. He looked over at his father, and Lloyd, looking abashed, shrugged his shoulders and said nothing.

"Let me assure you, mother," Cloud said with a bitterness so deep that it surprised him, "I am not homosexual. But even if I were, it would be none of your damned business!" His voice rose as he continued, "You don't know me. You don't know anything about me. You– you– " He started to say witch but held his tongue, recognizing that this would open a door he did not want to go through.

"I know you a lot more than you think," Narcissa retorted. "I know that Quincy Queensbury called you a queer. I heard him say it at your eighth grade graduation."

"Quinn didn't know what the hell he was talking about," said Cloud. "Back then kids used that term as synonymous with jerk or jackass. And it's crystal clear you don't know what you're talking about either."

Narcissa sputtered, "I know you've had lots of boyfriends but I've yet to see a single girlfriend, except for that Jewish girl you took to the prom. But that was a one shot deal. Was that all for show, Cloud? You're good looking, Cloud. So where are the girls? Maybe you're *too* good looking for girls. Is that it?"

"You have absolutely no idea who I am, so just shut the hell up!" Cloud shouted.

Lloyd at last spoke with a deep, muted voice. "Now everybody just calm down. Nobody's accusing anybody of anything."

Narcissa burst into tears, and Cloud stormed out.

In the sanctuary of his room, Cloud stretched across his bed fully clothed and recalled scenes from his childhood. He decided that although he had a mother and father, they had not raised him. He had raised himself in spite of them. The notion that anyone would suspect him of being homosexual surprised him but was no cause for concern. One way or the other, it didn't matter to him.

That night he endured a nightmare, one he had suffered years earlier, about a witch he needed to kill for the sake of the planet.

The next morning, Narcissa was sweet and cheerful, acting as if nothing had happened the evening before. No one in the family referred to the words Narcissa and Cloud had exchanged over dinner. Cloud was feeling resentful, however, and needed to get out for a while. He donned hiking boots and announced he was going out for air.

Driving across town to Paradise Valley, he parked in Echo

Canyon on the north side of Camelback Mountain. From a spot below the Praying Monk, a sandstone outcrop on the camel's head, he hiked -without stopping to rest- an ascending course covering more than a mile that took him to the granite summit of the camel's hump, sixteen hundred feet above the eleven hundred feet elevation of the Valley floor. A breeze at the top mingled with the sweat oozing from his face and neck, causing him a distinctly sensual pleasure. He poured half the water in his canteen over his head and drank the rest, intensifying the feeling of physical satisfaction.

From this highest perch in the Phoenix Mountains, Cloud felt a mystical kinship with the desert community below and with its frontier hospitality. But he remained angry and embarrassed by his mother's prejudice and his father's passivity. I wonder if I'll ever understand how they got that way, he thought.

On his descent, a jackrabbit jumped in front of Cloud, preceding him along the trail for a hundred yards, as if showing the way. The long-eared creature momentarily slowed, matching Cloud's pace, then bolted from the path. "I'd have to float to follow you, Jack," Cloud announced with a smile. "But not today. Another time, perhaps."

On a pleasant day in the spring of 1963, toward the end of the dry season, Xuan visited the **Cho Ben Thanh**, the Ben Thanh Market, for perhaps the thousandth time in her seventeen years. Nothing unusual had happened to her there, except for that vision ten years earlier when she imagined seeing a basket of figs crushed by a truck. This day the young woman would see another vision, more frightening in its specificity than anything her extra-sensory perception had uncovered thus far.

She strolled gracefully among the booths, in search of vegetables for soup and French magazines for entertainment. Xuan's straight black hair, which fell to the middle of her back, swayed slightly as she walked. The back panel of her white *ao dai* caught a snippet of breeze and puffed out behind her, showing off white silk slacks. The traditional dress she wore was a long-sleeved tunic divided at the waist into front and back panels that extended to her feet.

As she reached for a French fashion magazine, her eyes fastened on a newspaper displaying a photo of an armored personnel carrier under a headline about President Diem's latest crackdown on

Communist rebels. Xuan went into a trance, which was not something she welcomed. The last time this had happened she had seen a preview of grisly death.

This time she saw South Vietnamese President Ngo Dinh Diem inside the tank-like vehicle in the photograph. He lay there, bloody and beaten, surrounded by his own Republican soldiers. She was quite sure he was dead. When the trance ended, she found herself clutching the magazine with a very stylishly dressed blonde woman on the cover. She let it slip out of her hand and hurried off to her home.

Xuan considered saying nothing to her parents. The first vision she had seen never came to pass, but it did not involve anyone dying. The second vision had unfolded as she had seen it, and many people were killed. As far back as she could remember she had been taught to honor family and respect human life. This was too important and too frightening to keep secret. Perhaps if she revealed it to someone else, the spell would be broken and nothing would happen.

Xuan decided her father was the safest person to tell what she had seen in the market. He was a wise and stoic man, who would understand her experience and would know how to relieve her anxiety. When he heard his daughter's words, however, he reacted with extreme nervousness and ordered her to tell no one else. She must never mention this again, even to her mother. Xuan had never seen her father in such a state of agitation, and his response did not reassure her. Rather, it caused her to become even more troubled. Instead of breaking the spell, she believed she had only strengthened it by revealing this vision to another human being. She would be reluctant to do so again.

What she did not know but would learn later in a painful way was that her devoutly Buddhist father, a minor official in the national government, was clandestinely involved in an anti-Diem organization. He wished the subject of his daughter's vision would be true but feared premature exposure of these activities aimed at bringing about such an eventuality. And he immediately perceived that Xuan being the vehicle for such foreknowledge sealed his own fate. That she was the bearer of such imagery signified to him that the secret desires of his own heart had been transmitted to the world, and the karma thus created would result in his death as well.

CHAPTER FIFTEEN

While Xuan was in a trance in the Saigon market place seeing her president lying dead in an armored personnel carrier, on the other side of the planet Cloud was in bed on the verge of awakening from another nightmare. In this dream, he found himself in a large city, watching what seemed to be a Veterans Day parade, and the President of the United States came riding by in an open convertible. Cloud, standing on the sidelines in uniform, raised his right hand in a sharp salute for his Commander-in-Chief, and as the tips of his fingers reached the brim of his hat, gunshots pealed through the air. Cloud thought this was the start of a 21-gun salute, but then the president tumbled over in the car.

For days he brooded about the dream. Surely this wasn't like the one about Quincy that later came true. It must be symbolic of something related to his own aspirations, he told himself. Ultimately he chose to interpret the dream as a parable about military service. As his sophomore year approached an end, Cloud had to decide whether to apply for Advanced ROTC. If accepted, the Army would pay him a stipend, and he would be obligated to enter the service as an enlisted man if he failed to complete the requirements for commissioning. Except for the dream, he would not have wasted a moment contemplating what to do. As long as he could remember, Cloud had wanted to be an Army officer.

Was this dream some kind of warning to follow another course? Did the president's fall somehow represent his own failure at ever becoming an officer? Was commissioning a dream that would be taken away from him?

He came to the conclusion that if he did not pursue commissioning he would spend the rest of his life wondering if he had made the wrong decision. Better a life of failure than a life of regret, he thought. His application for the advanced military science program was quickly approved. The die was cast.

The previous fall, Cloud had become distracted from his studies by reading *Atlas Shrugged*. This May he stole time away from preparation for final exams by opening another novel, one considerably shorter than the Ayn Rand epic but just as engrossing.

Theo, who ordinarily was not a fan of science fiction, recommended a work of that genre to Cloud, Robert A. Heinlein's *Stranger in a Strange Land*. The novel told the story of a man who had been born and raised on Mars, though his parents were human. He returned to Earth with a human body but a Martian intellect. Theo was intrigued by the author's analyses of various religions juxtaposed against the new religion the protagonist, Valentine Michael Smith, developed in the course of adjusting to life on Earth.

Cloud thought Theo saw religions everywhere, just as right wing politicians saw Communists everywhere, and left wing politicians saw robber barons everywhere. But Theo had good taste in literature, so Cloud borrowed the volume from his friend and entered a world of fantasy that serenaded his deepest desires as enticingly as had the very different fantasy world of *Atlas Shrugged*.

Theo did not know about Cloud's exposure to nudism and participation in the Natural Christian Church. Cloud was surprised, therefore, to discover that this book Theo recommended described nudity as an important aspect of the new faith the Man from Mars developed. In his science fiction epic, Heinlein posited that clothes are barriers that keep people isolated and hinder development of mutually enhancing relationships. Nudity is essential to sacramental living, and sex is an integral part of such a life.

Cloud laughed as he read about the ritual of water-sharing in *Stranger in a Strange Land*. It evoked remembrances of the baptisms he had seen Adam and Evelyn conduct in the NCC swimming pool. Apart from the particular historical doctrines of Christianity as compared with paganism, the central difference between the Natural Christian Church and the fictional Church of All Worlds, Cloud thought, was sex. The Natural Christian Church was puritanical about sexual relations, while the Church of All Worlds actively encouraged free and open sex. Cloud believed the ideal of sexual morality lay somewhere between these extremes, although as a nineteen year-old virgin, the sexual imagery in the book powerfully affected parts of his body and lingered pleasantly in his memory.

Where Cloud found himself critical of the novel was its apparent promotion of communal living and non-monetary economics. He was a staunch **laissez faire** capitalist, influenced most recently by Ayn Rand's philosophy, and he was not going to fall for any pipe dream of a socialist utopia. Thus he resonated with the curmudgeonly father figure and author's alter-ego character Jubal Harshaw, who spouted anti-altruistic truisms that would cause Ayn Rand's John Galt to smile. As an only child growing up in solitude, however, the prospect of living with a nest-full of bright people fueled Cloud's romantic desire for a large, spontaneously intimate family. The world Heinlein created in this novel was an enchanted place for Cloud to dwell for a season of contemplation.

Heinlein's depiction of the Old Ones on Mars triggered a fond memory. Cloud thought of his imaginary friend from the time when he was six and had the measles. He decided that Old One was an apt name for the ideal being he had created in his mind at a time of dire illness. Upon reflection, he reasoned that he must have possessed a precocious sense of antiquity to conjure such a friend, and this thought bolstered his self-esteem.

As time passed, the part of **Stranger** that influenced Cloud the most related to mental powers. Valentine Michael Smith knew how to use his mind to control his body. This captured Cloud's attention, because his own mind had been doing unusual things with his body for most of his life, and he had come to the conclusion that this was perfectly normal and scientifically demonstrable. Heinlein's fanciful novel provided Cloud with affirmation that this was so. There was nothing mystical about his out-of-body experiences or prescient dreams. Anyone could have those experiences.

— ☉ —

That spring, Terp developed an unusual habit for an eleven year-old, faithfully watching the fifteen-minute CBS Evening News broadcast. She was enamored of Walter Cronkite, who delivered even terrible news with reassurance in his voice. On the eleventh day of June 1963, Cronkite reported, a Buddhist monk in Saigon, in protest of the Diem regime's repression of Buddhist religion, bade two other monks to douse him with gasoline and then calmly set himself on fire. A news photographer captured the self-immolation of the Venerable Thich Quang-Duc on Phan-dinh-Phung Street, and within three days the fiery image had been spread across America for Terp and everyone else to see.

Even Uncle Walter's reassuring tone could not prevent Terp from bursting into tears at the story, and she brooded over it for days. The following Sunday, Terp hoped the incident would be mentioned in the church service to help her better understand it. Rev. Watts was good at weaving important news into his prayers and sermons. She was therefore disappointed that no mention was made of the traumatic event.

The sermon text that day was John 2:1-11, the story of Jesus turning water into wine. "This passage is a metaphor for our deepest longings," Watts said. "Its setting is the dearest form of human celebration, the wedding feast. Everyone was invited to the feast at Cana, which Jesus attended and at which he made water into wine. This, of course, prefigures the Last Supper and Holy Communion which Jesus prepares ever anew.

"Yet there abides a mystery amidst this call to celebration. About water becoming wine, the seventeenth century metaphysical poet, Richard Crashaw, perhaps best captured the essence of the mystery when he said, 'the water saw its God and blushed.' The water saw Jesus and blushed. How wonderful an image for us to contemplate!

"Crashaw's contemporary, poet Henry Vaughn, also took note of this mystery with these words: 'So some strange thoughts transcend our wonted themes, and into glory peep.' The miracle at Cana is for us a peep into the glory that awaits. Not knowing that it was Jesus he should be addressing, the steward of the wedding feast said to the groom, 'You have kept the good wine until now.' Friends, it is Jesus Christ who keeps the good wine until we most need it. Let all here assembled find joy in the mysterious feast of our Lord!"

Terp found the sermon stirring and intriguing, but she needed to hear some word about the monk in Saigon. After the service, she asked her pastor why a religious person would do such a thing. He was startled by her question, in part because he did not expect children her age to keep up with international news. But the greater surprise came from the nature of the question itself. Why indeed would a man who had devoted his life to a religious quest engage in an act of self-immolation?

Watts had read the story in the New York Times but had not asked himself Terp's question. He saw the event in the context of a war between North and South Viet Nam, but did not pretend to know much about the complexities of Vietnamese society. He knew that South Viet Nam's president, Ngo Dinh Diem, was Roman Catholic, while a strong majority of the country's population was Buddhist. He simply accepted the monk's protest as another inscrutable element of the Asian world.

"Gosh, Terp, I need to think about that for a while," the pastor said. "What motivates the human heart to such awful ends?" She had waited to be the last person in line to greet him, so he had a little time before the next service. "Let's go to my office and talk," he suggested. This was exactly what she hoped would happen.

"It was the most terrible thing I've ever seen," Terp said, when she was comfortably ensconced in a large stuffed chair opposite Argyle Watts' desk.

The pastor sat behind the desk, affecting a mien of prayerful contemplation. "Buddhists don't think about the world the same way Christians do," he explained. He paused to consider that he was speaking with a little girl and not a mature parishioner. But this was no ordinary little girl, he thought, and proceeded to converse with her as if she were an adult. This proved to be a wise decision, for Terp recognized that he was treating her seriously, and thus her admiration for Watts grew.

"Buddhists, especially monks," he continued, "try to become detached from the world, whereas Christians, or most Christians anyway, seek to become involved with the world."

"You mean Christians try to fix what's wrong and Buddhists try to ignore it?" Terp responded.

"Very well put," Watts said. "Of course it's more complicated than that, really. There are nuances of meaning and practice that come into play. But basically, if a Christian gives up his life for a cause, he is giving up something that he values. If a Buddhist does the same thing..." He paused to consider the train of thought he was following and did not like it. "No, that's not right. Let me try a different tack. Christians sometimes become martyrs, offering up their lives for some greater good. What this monk did was different. He took his own life rather than give it for someone else."

"I don't understand," Terp said.

"Frankly, Terp, neither do I," Watts admitted. "Let me think further about this, and we can talk again. But now I've got to get ready for the next service."

As she left the pastor's office, Terp saw Michelle at the end of the hall, prompting her to remember ruefully that Michelle's parents were providing her transportation home.

"Where were you?" Michelle gasped. "We've been looking all over for you. We were worried about you."

"I'm sorry," Terp offered. "I was talking with Rev. Watts and I lost track of time."

The following week, at Watts' invitation, Terp convinced her mother to drop her off for the last service, after which the pastor and his wife took Terp to their home for lunch. The conversation about the monk continued over chicken salad sandwiches and bean with bacon soup.

"Where have you come to in your thinking, Terp?" the pastor asked.

"It's not right to take your own life, especially in such a brutal way," she said. "But I can't help but think there's something about this we don't know."

"Go on," Watts said, impressed with her reasoning.

"Well, what I can't understand is why a person who was mad at the government would kill himself. Why wouldn't he try to kill the president or something like that? Why commit suicide?" she continued.

"Hmmm?" Watts responded.

"I mean it's not right to kill someone else. I don't mean to say the monk should kill the president of Viet Nam or anything like that. But it just seems more natural to want to hurt someone who's hurting you rather than adding to your suffering by hurting yourself."

"So," the pastor said, "you've been doing some deep thinking. Let me ask you a question. What should a Christian do in a situation like this? How should a Christian properly protest an evil done against him?"

"Let me have a week to think about it," Terp said. "That's what you said about my question." They both laughed.

It did not dawn on Terp until long after Argyle Watts had dropped her off at home that he had not answered her question. She decided that next week she would ask him what *he* thought about his question as well as hers. She daydreamed about having Sunday lunch around the kitchen table at the Watts house every week from then on.

Her dream did not come to pass. The following Sunday, Watts announced to the congregation that he would be leaving on vacation right after church and would not be back in the pulpit until mid-August. The Watts family owned a cabin in Vermont, to which the minister retreated for six weeks every summer. Terp was deeply disappointed but vowed to wait and press him for answers to both questions at her earliest opportunity.

The chance came in late August, when her pastor once again invited her to Sunday lunch. He was delighted that she turned his question back on him and responded at length about the responsibility of Christians to support the civil rights movement. "In fact," he announced, "this coming Wednesday, I will be participating in a march on Washington led by Dr. Martin Luther King. A group of Negro pastors in Newark honored me with an invitation to accompany them. Terrible things have been done to Negroes in this country, Terp, and Dr. King has the right answer to address those injustices. Peaceful protest is how Christians should respond when evil is done against them.

"Martin," Watts continued, falling into the familiar mode of address that clergy use with affection among one another, "has no desire to set himself on fire but wants to smother the fires of hate with insistent love." He paused to reflect on his turn of phrase. "It's odd that I used the word desire in this context, because it is the absence of desire that allowed that Buddhist monk to set himself on fire."

Terp, who had been following her pastor's remarks up to this point, did not understand what the absence of desire had to do with self-immolation, but she was so in awe of the Reverend Argyle Watts that she nodded approvingly, waiting for more wisdom to pour from his mouth. She felt invited into the inner circle of something very important. Next Sunday couldn't come soon enough, when he would tell her all about the march and what Martin Luther King, Jr. was like in person.

This would prove to be Terp's last lunch meeting in the Watts home, however. The Sunday of the Labor Day weekend was invariably the most poorly attended Sunday of the year at Second Church, and Watts traditionally appointed an associate pastor to preach to the sparse congregation that day, while he took study leave. This year in particular he was not going to waste his sermon about the March on Washington on the faithful remnant who celebrated the end of summer by coming to church. He waited a week for Rally Day, when the sanctuary overflowed with people, to tell them about his proximity to the civil rights leader as Dr. Martin Luther King, Jr. intoned the words "I have a dream..."

Thereafter on Sunday afternoons, Watts taught the confirmation class, preparing a score of fourteen year-olds for church membership. He was not surprised when Terp asked to join the class, and though he thought she was intellectually ready, he worried about the precedent this would set by allowing a pre-teen into the class. If he did so, undoubtedly many parents who wanted their children to go through the process at more convenient times would request exceptions, and he didn't relish that prospect. Confirmation class was disorderly enough without making age optional. So he told Terp she had to wait for three years.

A disappointed Terp Person clung ever more tenaciously to the words, the sermons, and prayers of Argyle Watts.

On All Saints Day in 1963, Cloud's twentieth birthday, events unfolded west of the International Date Line that would shape his future in profound ways. At 1:30 in the afternoon, Saigon time, elements of the Army of the Republic of Viet Nam surrounded the presidential palace and sent in demands that President Diem surrender. The coup attempt, in which Xuan's father played a minor role, was led by a group of generals, who enjoyed the tacit support of the United States government.

Diem refused to give himself up, but that night he fled in secret to a Catholic church in the Chinese suburb of Cho Lon. On the morning of November 2, he surrendered to the generals, and while being transported in an armored personnel carrier, was murdered by ARVN soldiers. The *coup d'etat* was now *fait accompli.*

News of the assassination spread quickly through Saigon, and Xuan was an early recipient of the information. She wept. This was not because she cared about Diem. She despised his oppressive regime. The tears came in response to another prophetic vision coming to reality, and this burden felt too heavy for a girl of seventeen to bear.

"*Choi oi,*" she prayed. "Oh, let me never again see the future." Yet as the words passed from her lips she knew intuitively that this prayer would not be answered. Then in a flash of understanding she saw that her father was involved in the conspiracy against the dead president, and she resumed weeping with abandon.

On November 22, after a lunchtime sandwich at the Memorial Union, Cloud strolled across campus to Old Main to hang out in the military science lounge until the start of his favorite class, American frontier history. He settled into a comfortable chair and listened to KRUX broadcasting hit songs through a pre-war Philco radio console that stood against the north wall of the room. He grinned as the disc jockey announced that "Washington Square" by the Village Stompers was coming up next.

"A cool song. I'd like to see Greenwich Village," he said to the assembled cadets.

Cloud would one day get his wish but would not hear the song that day or any of the next four days, because at that moment a news announcer broke in to report that President Kennedy had been shot while riding in a motorcade through Dallas. There was no report on the extent of the president's injuries. Everyone in the room immediately formed a half-circle around the radio, as if thus arranged they could command more information from its old speaker.

Apart from a scattered chorus of "Oh no!" and "Oh my God!" the students listened in silence. Ten minutes passed before Cloud remembered the dream in which he had heard gunshots and saw the president slump down in his car. His body went cold at the thought but he said nothing to anyone. Half an hour later the announcer, in his most solemn voice, reported that officials at Parkland Memorial Hospital had confirmed that President John Fitzgerald Kennedy was dead.

When the time came for his class, Cloud dutifully walked to the room. A handful of students had summoned the strength of mind to gather there according to schedule, but no one spoke or looked at anyone else. Cloud sensed that looking into the eyes of another student would be like trespassing into a private region of sorrow. It was something only a voyeur would do. He stared at his desk instead.

After some interval of time -no one was keeping track- professor Otis Young arrived, his face broken with grief, and without saying a word wrote "CLASS CANCELLED" on the board and fled before anyone could ask for a word of wisdom.

Cloud shuffled out and headed for the parking lot, in possession of an early start to the weekend, which neither he nor anyone else he knew would enjoy. The traffic was light for a Friday afternoon, and drivers who in other circumstances would have competed aggressively for position at traffic lights drove with uncharacteristic patience, even politeness.

Cloud did not venture far from a radio or television set the next four days. The military rituals captured his attention far more than the speculations about the shooting. Shadows were clear in the bright sunlight of the cold day as the president's body was delivered by caisson to the Capitol, where it would lie in state until the funeral service. Pallbearers in dress uniforms then returned the casket to the caisson as the cortege continued to St. Matthews, and thence to Arlington Cemetery. Six matched gray horses drew the caisson up Pennsylvania Avenue to the church and across the Arlington Memorial Bridge to the cemetery.

Strains of the Navy hymn, "Eternal Father, Strong to Save," echoed in Cloud's mind. At a conscious level, he did not believe that an eternal Father existed to save anybody, as the killing of the president demonstrated, but he was nevertheless moved by the hymn, and at some dark place inside him, its notes resonated with an unconfessed hope for transcendent authority.

A student monitor entered Terp's sixth grade homeroom class at 2:40 that afternoon. Apprehensively he approached the teacher and handed him a note. Mr. Pulaski unfolded it and scanned the message, which read: "President Kennedy has been shot while campaigning in Dallas, Texas. No word on his present condition."

Edward Pulaski, a combat veteran of World War II, looked at the monitor and growled, "This is a joke, right?"

"No, sir," the student responded. Nervously he fingered the remaining messages he needed to give to teachers down the hallway.

"You can go, Son. Deliver the rest of your messages," he said, suddenly subdued. Pulaski looked up and saw that all eyes were focused intently on the piece of paper in his hands. "Class," he whispered, then raised his voice only a little, "this note says that President Kennedy..." He paused for the right words and continued with, "has been... wounded somewhere in Texas." The students gasped, none louder than Terp. "We don't know how seriously," he went on, speaking strongly now, "but I'm sure word will come soon about how he is doing. Please put your heads down on your desks and silently pray for our president."

Terp did as she was instructed, praying harder than she had ever prayed in her life. "Please let him be safe," she whispered. "O God, heal his wound. Make him get well. Please, God, please, please, please!"

The lesson plan was forgotten as teacher and students prayed and waited for further information. The minute hand on the clock seemed stuck, as if each minute that passed had to be wrenched from it. Terp's prayer grew into an intense repetition of simple supplications for the president's recovery.

The news came, borne by the same monitor with a fresh bundle of messages in his hand, at ten past three. As soon as Pulaski saw the boy's frightened face, he knew the news was not good.

"Oh my God!" he cried, and then calling upon the inner strength that saw him safely through combat in France and Germany, he read the note aloud: "President John F. Kennedy died at Parkland Memorial Hospital in Dallas. He was fatally shot by an assassin while riding in an open car with Texas Governor John

Connolly, who was also wounded but is expected to survive." There was an addendum that he did not read aloud: "Parents are already beginning to assemble at school to pick up their children. The buses will operate at normal schedule for those students whose parents are not able to pick them up. Please escort your class to the auditorium and remain with them until all students have been released to their parents or placed on the proper bus."

The halls will be crowded with teachers and students pushing toward the auditorium, he thought. He decided to talk to his class for a while before leading them down the corridor. "I remember when President Roosevelt died," he said without preamble. "April 12, 1945. I was in Germany, fighting the remnant of the army of the Third Reich, and when the president's death was announced I cried, because the man who had led this nation through the Depression and a terrible World War, who had inspired us all to give the best we had in us for a greater good, died when we were on the verge of victory. What were we going to do? He had been president since before I was a teenager. It was hard to imagine anyone else as president." Painful, unwelcome memories of the war flooded into Pulaski's mind.

"I thought it was the most tragic thing I'd ever experienced," he went on, "until the next day when my unit liberated Buchenwald. Do you know about Buchenwald, class? Have you ever heard of it? It was the most horrible place you could imagine. It was a concentration camp where the Nazis tortured and starved and murdered people simply because they were Jewish." He paused to consider the harmful effect his stream of remembrances might have on the children in his charge. They're traumatized enough, he thought, without hearing my war stories.

"Forgive me for wandering," he said. "The point I want to make is that President Truman stepped in and led the country well after President Roosevelt died, and I'm sure that Vice President Johnson...uh...President Johnson will be the leader we need in this terrible time."

Former Sergeant First Class Edward Pulaski then rose and led his platoon of sixth graders safely to the auditorium.

Terp was reeling. How could this be? Hadn't she prayed hard enough? She had done the best she knew how. But maybe God didn't listen to the prayers of little girls. Her young psyche was doubly pierced, first by the grievous fact that the president she campaigned for three years earlier was dead and then by the suspicion that her prayers on his behalf had been inadequate.

When she learned, later that evening, that the president was already dead at the time she began praying for him, a little of the suspicion of inadequacy lifted from her mind. But not all of it. A residual belief that she was somehow spiritually deficient taunted her from time to time.

Two days later, something new happened in the community, in response to the presidential assassination. Protestants attended Catholic masses and Catholics attended Protestant services. Terp was part of a delegation from Second Calvinist that worshiped at the neighborhood Catholic church, where she solemnly shook hands with her homeroom teacher. A sliver of her grief had begun to dissipate, but a great deal remained throbbing in her brain.

When she returned home from the mass, Terp remembered that the Buddhist monk who had set himself on fire in June had been protesting the actions of a Catholic president. Her comment to Rev. Watts about the monk killing President Diem instead of himself rushed to consciousness, and a wave of shame broke over her. How could she have said such a thing? She prayed that God would forgive her for those evil words, as if they were in some effectual way connected with Lee Harvey Oswald's decision to kill President Kennedy. Someday, she thought, she would ask her pastor if spoken words could kill.

Xuan's father was deeply troubled when news of the Kennedy assassination reached him. "I know nothing of this new American president *Gion Xon*," he said in the privacy of their apartment, "but I fear he is not a man of subtlety. I have a premonition of many deaths in our land."

"Premonitions of death are nothing new for you," said his wife.

"Yes, but today I see many more dying than in the past," he answered.

As was her habit, Xuan quickly assumed her father's worry as her own. She went to the roof to brood alone, convinced now that she would lose her father to the war. Tears fell from her eyes. Though it was the dry season, the sky was overcast, and a heavy cloud directly above her suddenly burst. Xuan stood still as rain poured upon her, soaking her to the skin. For a reason she did not understand, the deluge, though chilling, buoyed her spirits. Perhaps all shall be well, she thought.

CHAPTER SIXTEEN

Anchored securely within his body as he soared through the air, for the first time in his life Cloud traveled by plane in June 1964. He flew to Seattle to report to ROTC Summer Camp at Fort Lewis, Washington. The six-week boot camp was required for the advanced officers training program.

Theo had taken him to Sky Harbor Airport, waiting with him until he boarded. Before Cloud stepped into the sunlight to cross the tarmac to the waiting DC-8 passenger jet, Theo patted him on the back and joked, "I expect to see a trained killer when you get back. Study hard, cadet!"

Cloud turned and said, "I'm not doing this to kill people but to protect them."

"Yeah, I know," Theo admitted, "but it breaks my heart to see a gentle man like you pursue such a violent career."

As the plane lifted off the runway, Cloud wondered if his friendship with Theo would survive the career choices each was intent on making. In the wake of the Kennedy assassination, Theo had started attending a liberal Quaker meeting in Phoenix, and in the spring he decided that after graduation he would enroll in a theological seminary to study Christian pacifism.

As the plane plowed its way through the atmosphere, Cloud

turned away from painful thoughts about Theo and reflected instead on the pleasant physical phenomenon of breaking the sound barrier. He was now sitting still inside an object moving through space faster than sound. A cartoon image spread across his brain. He visualized the whining sound of the engines, panting and gasping for breath, catching up with and reattaching to the aircraft as it slowed for landing. The mental picture of sound gasping for air made him laugh. What did sound look like, anyway?

In what felt like a natural progression of thought, he then considered out-of-body experiences. What effect would moving faster than the speed of sound have on him if he left his body? Probably none, he decided, as long as he stayed inside the cabin. He gazed out the window at the white blanket of clouds below and his mind leapt ahead. What if, rather than floating around the cabin, he went outside and floated in the clouds? This was an enticing thought. Cloud among the clouds. But would he be able to keep up with the plane? Would the jet abandon him in water vapor and thin air?

After the experience of sailing through pristine ether above cumulus castles, the maculate and sour smell of coal furnaces greeted Cloud when he reported in at Fort Lewis. He had never considered that odors accompanied the production of warmth for human comfort. At home a single electric heater supplied all the warmth necessary for his entire house. He considered the carbon-scented atmosphere a symptom of decadence, feeling that inhaling the ubiquitous dust from the Arizona desert was somehow healthier than the particles of soot permeating the late spring atmosphere around the base.

He was assigned to second platoon of F Company, which he soon learned was known among the other companies as Funny Company. That was fine with Cloud. It didn't matter where he was assigned as long as it was not H Company -Hell Company- the experimental unit where the cadre practiced sadistic forms of discipline to test how well it might work with smart-ass college students. According to instant camp lore, H Company would produce a high drop out rate.

The students lined up for standard Army white-side-wall haircuts. Each one, upon stepping out of the barber chair, instinctively ran a hand through the stubble remaining on top. But there was no time to mourn the shearing, for uniforms and field gear had to be issued and stowed neatly in footlockers. Bunks had to be made so tightly that the captain could bounce a quarter off the blankets.

The World War II vintage wooden barracks the cadets were assigned to were grimy and sprinkled with hidden trash. Cloud concluded this was by design, because as soon as gear had been stowed and bunks made they were all set to scrubbing and cleaning their temporary homes. Cloud drew latrine duty.

Summer camp became a blur of physical training -push-ups beyond number, pull-ups, stretches, and long runs wearing combat boots. The second day, Cloud developed shin splints that ached the entire six weeks.

Close order drill went exceedingly well. Cloud was accustomed to drilling rag-tag college students whose sole motivation was the Federal law mandating two years of ROTC. At school, the marching formations were far from crisp, but the units at Fort Lewis were all advanced ROTC cadets motivated to stay in step. Cloud reveled in well-executed columns, obliques, and flanks.

When it came time for the Army physical fitness test, Cloud encountered his first taste of failure. He scored in the acceptable range on the overhead ladder, low crawl, and dodge-run-jump, but did not pass the hand-grenade throw. For some reason, he could not develop sufficient thrust to propel the weapon the required distance. Perhaps the problem was poor technique, but he blamed his long, thin arms for the deficiency. His score was so low on this event that he feared it would bring the average of his other scores below the failing mark. If he could not pass, he would be sent home, and his dream of becoming an Army officer would be over.

The final part of the fitness test was a timed mile run. Cloud had never before run against time and had no idea how he might do. The cadets lined up, the gun sounded, and they began running the measured course. Cloud put his head down and raced as fast as he could, oblivious to everyone around him. As he entered the final leg he heard voices seemingly addressed to him. Members of the faculty lined up along the course were shouting, "Go, Mr. Morgan, go!"

To his astonishment, he was the first cadet to finish the run, clocking in at 5:27, which was thirty-three seconds faster than needed for the 100 point maximum score. This more than compensated for his lack of skill with a hand-grenade and provided insurance against washing out. No one was more surprised or elated at this turn of events than Cloud.

Halfway through camp, Cloud's platoon stumbled in from a three-day field exercise to the news that if they cleaned their gear and made the barracks shine, they could have the entire next day off. As they cleaned, swept and mopped, they speculated about how they would spend a whole day without orders. Precisely at 10:00 p.m., the platoon sergeant declared their work up to his inspection standards, and the cadets fell exhausted into their bunks. Cloud fully intended to stay in bed till noon.

The relief he felt about the absence of reveille must have released a signal in his brain, because three weeks of dreamless nights gave way and dreams poured forth one after another. Most of the imagery reflected experiences of summer camp. He relived mosquito attacks in the field, setting up defensive perimeters in the forest, eyes stinging in the tear gas tent, and washing endless piles of dishes from the mess hall. Toward dawn, however, a dream of a different character flowed from the inner recesses of his mind.

A young woman danced before him. As she whirled to ethereal music, her long dark hair flowed in response, hiding her face from recognition. Her hands and fingers moved in precise and elegant patterns while her bare feet pointed and lifted and turned with airy grace. She swooped and rose, bowed and spun with such ease that Cloud longed to be with her, to let her lead him in the dance and to teach her how to float.

Old buildings surrounded the field where she danced, but they were whitewashed by the brilliant light enveloping her slender body in an extended aura. Palm trees stretched above the rooftops and white blossoms wafted in the breezy wake of her whirling movements.

"Who are you?" he asked, without speaking aloud but willing his question to reach her telepathically.

The response came not from the dancer but from an old friend, the one who had conversed with him through feelings when he was six years old and floated for the first time, the one he believed was a mysterious part of his own mind. "She cannot answer yet. She was born in the East. It is possible, even likely, that your paths will cross one day."

"Where? When?" Cloud demanded.

"Do not search for her. Only be mindful that she may appear in dark times," the Old One instructed.

Cloud awoke, full of regret at leaving the dream world of his Eastern dancer. He looked around the barracks, filled with cots of soldiers-to-be, each man for the moment lost in slumber, some dreaming, some oblivious. As he settled his head back into the pillow, intent on abandoning temporary wakefulness, he vowed not to let go of his beguiling revelation. The vow was not needed, however, for so vividly had the dancer's image been etched into the tissue of his brain that she returned to him as soon as his eyes closed. She stood facing him, her arms spread wide, her palms open to his view. He rejoiced in pleasant recognition, but no matter how hard he focused his interior attention, Cloud could not see her face.

Three days later, the cadet in the bunk next to Cloud washed out in dramatic fashion. Trig Ironfield was an engineering major from Northern California, and from the beginning he had found it difficult to accept the highly controlled but often irrational system of instruction and discipline within which the camp functioned. Cloud had told him to pretend that this was Wonderland and like Alice just do whatever he was told. The fact that it did not track with reality was irrelevant, he told his troubled friend. Then remembering that Alice fought back against the idiocy, he sought another example.

"Think of summer camp as an opera," Cloud explained. "Opera plots are typically outlandish and inconsistent. What you have to do, Trig, is suspend belief, accept the conventions of the medium, wait through the droning recitatives and sit back and enjoy the beautiful arias when they come."

Cloud had recently finished a music appreciation course for a humanities credit, but no matter how fitting his advice may have been for a liberal arts major, it did not register with his companion, and one morning soon thereafter, Trig awoke with an overpowering vision of how he had been blind to the true reality. The Army was absolutely correct in all its pronouncements!

"Look," he explained to Cloud, "we see mindless bullshit, but the Army knows better. The brass are brilliant in devising the system. We expect complex interrelationships and solutions built on careful calculations and well-balanced reflections. We expect performance based on the laws of physics and the neutral law of reasoned men. But war is not like that."

Cloud was silent, encouraging Trig to continue.

"The Army bases everything on two principles. First that war is irrational."

Cloud nodded in agreement.

"And second, that everything, and I mean absolutely everything, must be fitted to the needs of the least common denominator. All instruction, all methods, all procedures must be understandable for the dumbest son of a bitch in the service."

That night, the visionary cadet did not go to bed at lights out. Instead, Trig wandered through the barracks placing tags on every moving part he could find. He used string and paper to attach to every doorknob instructions for how to open the door. He wrote an explanation of how to use a key to open a lock, carefully using words of no more than five letters, that he hung on the lock on the weapons storage closet. He placed instructions on how to use a urinal on each porcelain receptacle in the latrine, and similar instructions on the toilets, including proper instructions for wiping.

The next morning Trig continued his crusade to help the Army reach its goal of preparing every last soldier to understand how to do every task. The platoon was taken to the rifle range, and while the range master lectured the group on safety procedures, he wandered off to place instructions on the targets, so the bullets would know what to do when they got there.

A few minutes later, an ambulance arrived and Trig Ironfield was taken for a ride in it, providing him the opportunity to compose the proper way to enter such a vehicle. The young man was never seen again, and nothing was ever said to the platoon about his departure. When Cloud asked the faculty platoon leader about the fate of his friend, he was told his curiosity would be noted and recorded. The tone of the captain's voice led Cloud to infer that his question fell into an uncommendable category.

At mid course, this officer had told Cloud that he ranked in the top five among the cadets in second Platoon. When the ratings came out at the end, Cloud ranked fourteenth. The narrative portion of his evaluation stated that Cloud had great potential, but he relied too much on his knowledge and he questioned authority. Cloud asked the officer to explain what this meant and was told that his asking that question proved the platoon leader's point.

Cloud returned to his final year at ASU more confident than ever in his physical capabilities but uncertain about his place in the Army system. He believed he had comported himself exceptionally well and felt betrayed by his platoon leader who knocked him down in the rankings only because he knew more than some other cadets and asked uncomfortable questions. Was this the way the Army treated its officers? He spoke with his military science advisor about the experience, and the advisor told him, using as much tact as he could muster and still be truthful, that Cloud's summer camp platoon leader was a marginal officer who was assigned to ROTC because no competent field commander would take him. For some reason, this reassured Cloud, and he returned to his military science studies energetically.

At any rate, Cloud's summer camp ranking apparently meant little to the ROTC faculty at ASU, for he was promoted from platoon leader to cadet major, serving as intelligence officer on the brigade staff. For a time, he nursed the idea of visiting the West High campus in uniform and stopping by to see Sergeant Frogger who had not considered him officer material. That rejection still stung, but upon reflection, he dismissed the idea as premature. Better to wait until he was a real commissioned officer, he decided.

A short time later, an attractive invitation from his military science advisor led Cloud into unexpected trouble with his father. The advisor suggested he apply for the flight-training program, and Cloud responded with an excited yes. Having excellent eyesight, he easily passed the physical. After receiving a student pilot's license, he began once-a-week flying lessons at Deer Valley Airport, north of Phoenix.

Lloyd was not happy about the flight program and tried to talk Cloud out of pursuing it.

"But you were a pilot, so what's wrong with me being one?" Cloud asked. "I want to follow in your footsteps. I'd think you would be proud of me for that."

"I'm more proud of you than you could ever know, but it's dangerous work, Son, and your mother and I would worry about you."

This made no sense to Cloud, yet as much as he tried to elicit more information, Lloyd would not say more. He would not confess to Cloud his true concern. Lloyd suffered an intense dread that his only son would be killed in combat in order to atone for his father's mistake.

Quinn Queensbury did not return to ASU that fall. In truth, he had flunked out at the end of his sophomore year but had continued to hang out on campus the following year, sitting in on a few large lectures and pretending to be a part-time student while he worked as an inventory clerk at a nearby auto parts store.

As a state institution supported by taxes, the university had to admit marginal students who were Arizona residents. But once accepted it did not have to retain them. Thus a sink or swim academic environment prevailed for freshmen and sophomores, in which the bright ones survived and moved on to upper level classes while the dull ones flushed out of the pond.

Quinn was smart enough but not sufficiently motivated to keep up with the academic work, and he drowned in a sea of incomplete homework and unread assignments. However, his absence from campus in the fall of 1964 had nothing to do with abandoning the pretence of being a student.

Quinn was no longer in town because he had received a draft notice, and with never a thought to the contrary, reported dutifully for induction. He was sent to Fort Ord, California for basic training. Camp Pneumonia they called it, and three of his platoon mates ended up in the base hospital with respiratory illnesses. The luckiest of them received a medical discharge, but the other two were reassigned to a later class. Quinn had no such luck, and after basic was sent to advanced infantry training at Fort Benning, Georgia.

The other men in his training company who had attended college had been sent to specialized schools after basic. They were told that for every soldier in the infantry, the Army needed ten in support roles, and so the college elite among the draftees peeled off for training with the Signal Corps, Chemical Corps, Quartermaster Corps, Army Intelligence and Security, Adjutant General Corps, and the Military Police. A few high school graduates followed them, but the rest, along with the high school dropouts were funneled into the combat branches, Infantry, Artillery and Armor.

Quinn didn't care about technical training or rear echelon assignments. He knew that the only way his father would ever grant him an ounce of respect was if he served in a combat unit. And though the war in Viet Nam was consuming only a small portion of Army troops at the time, he had no doubt that he would be assigned there.

For recreation on occasional weekend evenings, the Senior ROTC cadets conducted tactical maneuvers in the dry bed of the Salt River north of campus. Mostly they practiced reconnaissance missions, splitting into opposing teams, one to try to reach the objective and the other to try to ambush their attempt. To make the game more interesting, the defensive team did not know the offensive team's objective. As darkness enveloped them, the cadets formulated plans for maneuvering undetected through brush and sand to reach particular landmarks.

One such night, Cloud was assigned to the offensive team, and their mission was to locate a column under the Mill Avenue Bridge with a message painted on it in blue. They were to read the message and return with that information without coming to the attention of the defensive team.

The six members of his unit decided they would have better odds of bringing the message back if they split into three two-man teams. Even if two of them were detected, the third could get through. Cloud paired up with a cadet named Murry, a junior who had not yet been to summer camp. They blackened their faces with charcoal, covered their heads with black caps, rolled around in the sand to knock the shine off their fatigues, and set out in silence.

After half an hour of crouching and crawling through the riverbed, Cloud and Murry heard loud voices a hundred yards north. "Halt! Who goes there?" a cadet on the defense team shouted theatrically. His question went unanswered, but shortly another defensive team member bellowed, "Get up, you two! You've been nailed."

Cloud decided to take advantage of the temporary shift of attention to the captured cadets and move quickly ahead. He signaled Murry to follow, circling around to the south bank of the river, westward under the bridge and then turning east to survey the structure. They could make out the concrete columns supporting the bridge, but the night was too dark to see blue lettering.

"We've got to get closer," Cloud mouthed. Following his intuition, he selected columns in the middle section to inspect first. They crawled forward until they were close enough for Cloud to signal that Murry inspect the west column and he would check the east one. He crouched by the inside of its base, raised his right arm upward and swept the surface with his hand, feeling for smooth places that would indicate paint. His intuition proved reliable, for on the opposite side he detected lettering. But he would need light to read the words.

Having found nothing, Murry joined Cloud. As they had planned at the start, Cloud signaled Murry to spread open his poncho to create a shield so Cloud could use a flashlight to read the message. As soon as the light flooded the blue letters, Cloud said (louder than he had intended), "Son of a bitch!"

"What is it?" Murry whispered.

"It says," Cloud responded in a much softer voice, "John Galt shrugged."

"What does that mean?" Murry asked.

"I'll explain later," Cloud said. "First let's get out of here."

They retraced their earlier course and found the rendezvous point without difficulty. One team had been captured, and one was still out there somewhere.

Cloud wrote the message on a piece of paper and handed it to the umpire.

"What the hell does that mean?" Murry demanded.

"Beats me," the umpire said. "This is not the right message."

"Well it was painted in big blue letters on the column," said Cloud with a note of indignation in his voice.

At that point, the missing team appeared and delivered the message they had located. It read: "Kilroy was here."

"That's right," the umpire said. "Well done."

"Whew!" the cadet responded. "We were worried, because it was painted with green letters."

"The message we found was definitely painted with blue letters," Cloud shouted. "What gives?"

"It was toward the north end of the bridge, right?" the umpire asked.

"Yes," said the other team.

"No, the middle," said Cloud and Murry.

When everyone regrouped, the umpire assigned victory to the defense. When the offense complained, he explained his logic. "The offense had six members. Two were captured. Two brought me a message painted in blue, but it was not the message I painted. Two brought me the right message, the one I painted, but it was green, and your instructions were to find a blue message. So you all screwed up."

"Hey, that doesn't make sense," Murry complained. "Nobody could have completed the mission the way you set it up."

"Well, I thought I was using blue paint, but that's immaterial," the umpire said. "The lesson here is that the enemy is unpredictable, so you have to follow orders exactly in order to defeat him."

Cloud shook his head and decided the umpire must be related to his platoon leader at summer camp. Hiking back to his car, he murmured to himself, "John Galt shrugged." Discovering the allusion to **Atlas Shrugged** painted on a support for the Mill Avenue Bridge led him to further reflection upon the proper role of the military in American society, and in particular on the rhetoric of the presidential candidates. Since he planned to be a career Army officer, this issue was very important to him.

In less than a month, the nation would go to the polls to vote for either Lyndon Johnson to serve a full term as President of the United States or Barry Goldwater to succeed him. Cloud mentally compared the two. Senator Goldwater supported increased military intervention in Viet Nam, while President Johnson soft-pedaled the matter. Everything Cloud had learned in military science classes led him to conclude that the people of South Viet Nam desperately needed American help to get rid of the Communists from the North. So the cause was just. But some of his classmates, including Theo, said that Goldwater was reckless and would drop atomic bombs on North Viet Nam. Cloud believed that nuclear weapons should never again be used in war.

He thought Johnson was absolutely correct on civil rights but wrong on economic policy. He respected Goldwater's honesty and conservative economic principles, but was troubled by the support he was getting from Southern segregationists. Ayn Rand tipped the balance for Cloud when she endorsed Goldwater. Cloud would turn twenty-one two days before the election and thus would be able to vote for the first time in his life. He planned to cast his ballot for Barry Goldwater.

Narcissa and Lloyd also decided to vote for Goldwater, although for different reasons. Lloyd had met the senator and liked him immensely. His policies would be good for business. He didn't think the Republican candidate had a chance of defeating President Johnson, but it seemed right to support a favorite son.

Narcissa's boss had invited her to an organizational meeting of campaign volunteers, and she had fallen in love with Barry Goldwater. The first time she met him she told him that her husband also had been a pilot in World War II. As she later savored the moment, recalling the senator's warm smile and handshake, she couldn't help comparing the two pilots in her life. Barry was a tad more handsome than Lloyd, with a rugged, boyish charm that overly serious Lloyd lacked, and she suspected from the electricity she felt when the senator's palm covered hers, that it had been more than an ordinary handshake. She decided that Barry was interested in her.

Narcissa Morgan became a Goldwater Girl. She wore a straw bonnet with a blue and white Goldwater banner around it, even to work, with encouragement from her boss. Every bit of her spare time was spent at the campaign headquarters or running errands for the campaign. She forgot about the Arizona Past Lives Association. Politics was more important and far more exciting than digging through her musty past, and the money she no longer spent at APLA she donated to the presidential campaign. Her dinner conversations were replete with Barry said this and Barry said that.

And all the while she held safe in her heart the glowing knowledge that a man who would soon become President of the United States of America was interested in her. The news broadcasters reported that President Johnson was far ahead in the polls, but she was certain that come Election Day, a great outpouring of Goldwater supporters would surprise the world. People might tell pollsters they planned to vote for Johnson, but when they found themselves in the privacy of that booth, they would know in their hearts that Barry was right. She knew that a silent majority would turn the tide in favor of the man of her dreams.

And fill her dreams he did. Every time he was in town he made a point of saying hello and thank you to her. Of course, he said that to the other girls too, but she was sure that was for cover, so that no one would suspect he had a special interest in her. Once the election was over, his wife Peggy would move to the White House, but he would come back to Arizona often, and when he did, Narcissa knew that he wanted her available. Soon after the election, she convinced herself, Barry Goldwater would ask her to become his mistress, and she would say yes.

Terp and her father developed a Friday night ritual in the fall of 1964. ABC Television began broadcasting "Twelve O'clock High," a drama series based on the exploits of the Eighth Air Force in England during World War II. This provided Tom an opportunity to tell his older daughter some of the war stories Penny did not want to hear any more. Terp loved it. It gave her a sense of being special, that she and her dad were developing a private bond of understanding.

They would sit together on the couch, and every episode provoked memories that led to more stories about the war. During a commercial break one Friday Tom said, "We were coming back from a mission over Germany and the oxygen system failed. We all started to black out, but luckily the pilot had just taken a deep breath before it conked, and he held his breath long enough to dive to an altitude where we could breathe. But that meant we were flying low over enemy territory. It was a genuine nervous-in-the-service time, I can tell you, but we made it home in one piece."

Terp snuggled into his side, feeling deep pride in her father, whose service was so important that a television network would produce a show about it. One evening, at the end of the program she said, "Tell me about the guys in your crew."

"Actually, I flew with several crews," he said. "The first one I joined because the bombardier had been killed. I can't remember the name of the pilot, but I think he was from Pennsylvania. The story I heard was that on the way home from a bomb run, the plane came under antiaircraft attack, and the pilot took evasive action. The bombardier was returning from using the relief tube when the plane banked hard and he tripped and fell into the bomb bay doors. Naturally they gave way. As he fell, he hit his head on one of the doors and this must have stunned him, because his chute never opened."

"Oh, how awful," Terp said.

"Being a bombardier, I'd have to agree with you. It was tragic, Terp, but lots of things happened like that. War is not as glorious as they show it on TV. Anyway, I flew one mission with this crew, and everything went smoothly. No gremlins and no flak. I dropped our load on the Krau...uh, on the target, and we hightailed it to England. The next mission the pilot didn't show up, and the co-pilot took over and they threw in some other guy as co-pilot. The pilot was supposed to be sick or something, but they wouldn't tell us what was wrong. After that they broke us up and dispersed us among other crews that were short."

"Did you ever find out what happened?" Terp asked.

"No, we never did." Tom answered. "It was all very hush hush. There was a rumor that pilot got out on a Section 8, but I doubt it. I saw him on base once or twice."

"What's a Section 8?" Terp wanted to know.

"Oh, it's when someone is released from the service for mental reasons. But I don't believe that it actually happened. They weren't letting anybody out in those days, whether they were crazy or not."

After another episode, Terp said, "Dad, did you ever think about the people you dropped bombs on?"

"Oh, punkin, I couldn't allow myself to think about that during a mission. I had to concentrate on my job, and there wasn't any time to wonder about anything else. I had factories and marshaling yards in my sight, anyway, not people."

He would not reveal the truth to her, that he avoided imagining what effect the bombs he released would have on humans by mentally composing comic dialogue for a play he wanted to write after the war.

"What about afterward?"

"Well, Terp, I had a job to do and I did it. Hitler was an incredibly evil and powerful man, and he had to be stopped. I couldn't allow myself to think about how the German people were suffering, because they were following orders from him." His voice choked, and silence reigned for some seconds, and then he said, "The war was terrible, but we had no choice except to fight it as hard as we could."

Terp wanted to know if he had thought about the people under the bombs he had dropped after he returned home from the war, but she could see that the subject was painful to him, so she kept quiet. On one hand, she was troubled about the human suffering from the war in Viet Nam that she had been watching on television and wondered if World War II had been like that. There was something inhumanly violent about the reports of this new war. On the other hand, she loved her father and knew that he was a kind and gentle man. There was no doubt in her mind that her dad was a brave, decent, and compassionate human being. Anything he did in the war must have been absolutely necessary.

She also knew that after these Friday evenings watching "12 O'clock High" with him she loved her dad more dearly than at any time in her life.

CHAPTER SEVENTEEN

Red-faced and stern, the instructor sat in the tandem seat behind Cloud. Preflight procedures had been completed and the yellow Aeronca Champion taxied down the runway with Cloud at the controls. He felt the plane lift off the ground and grinned in response. The flight instructor, Old Man Bocker, who also owned the plane, did not smile.

"Steady," he told Cloud. "Do it in a smooth motion. You don't need to jerk the craft into the air."

"Yes, sir," Cloud answered. It had felt smooth enough to him, but he didn't own the plane, which he and the other flight students called the air knocker -more precisely Bocker's air knocker.

Following instructions, Cloud took the aircraft through a series of maneuvers. When he banked left, Cloud leaned his body to the left, following the movement of the plane. Bocker hit him on the left shoulder and shouted, "Don't lean!"

"Yes, sir!" Cloud responded.

Cloud then banked the plane to the right and leaned right. Bocker hit him on the right shoulder. "Don't lean!"

"Yes, sir!"

It happened three more times during the lesson, and his shoulders were sore, for each time he leaned with the banking plane,

Bocker hit him harder. Eventually Cloud stopped leaning, but he didn't like it. When he leaned into a turn, he felt as if he were one with the machine. He did that with his car also. When he sat straight he felt like a remote commander. That's what Bocker wanted him to be, but Cloud preferred his way.

When I solo, he thought, I'm going to lean and Bocker can hit his own damned shoulders for all I care. And that's how it came to pass. His first solo flight was a joyous experience. The take-off was smooth, and once airborne alone, Cloud felt at home in a familiar environment. The first few times he banked the plane, he deliberately leaned into the turns, but after a while, he became so intent on his task that he forgot to lean and sat straight in his seat.

He was full of himself as he brought the Champion in for a landing. He slowed on approach, nose up, perfect attitude. What beautiful technique, he told himself. The only glitch was that the wheels were still three feet above the field at the point when he expected to touch down. The plane stalled and dropped to the tarmac and bounced with no grace at all. Cloud was able to keep the machine from tipping as it hit the ground again, and ultimately no damage was done. Cloud, however, was embarrassed and Old Man Bocker's face was redder than usual.

Bocker stood in front of Cloud with his arms across his chest, nervously tapping himself on his shoulders. "You're bound and determined that the US Army is gonna buy me a new aircraft, aren't you, Morgan?" he growled.

"Sorry, sir. I misjudged the distance," Cloud said. He realized he had been guilty of premature reflection on his first solo flight before properly finishing it. On his next solo flight he paid greater attention to landing procedure.

When the presidential election returns came in and it was clear that President Johnson had won in a landslide, the three Morgans responded in widely different ways, which each, following tacit family rules, refrained from revealing to the other two.

Cloud was unsurprised that the great majority of voters had misunderstood Barry Goldwater's principled stand on matters of individual freedom, and he stoically accepted the challenge of remedying this general ignorance. He was mortified, however, that apart from Arizona, the only states polling a majority for Goldwater were southern states with segregationist agendas. It seemed completely illogical to Cloud that segregationists would vote for the man responsible for racially integrating the Arizona Air National Guard in 1946. This only confirmed his suspicion that the great masses were stupid. His greater fear, however, was that the rest of the nation would misinterpret the election results as proof that the senator was a bigot.

Lloyd was disappointed that Arizona would not be benefiting from the elevation of a native son to the White House. A torrent of economic benefits would have come to the state in a Goldwater administration. But at a deeper level, he was secretly relieved, because he believed that Lyndon Johnson would find a way to stop the war in Indochina before it got any bigger. Since Cloud had begun the ROTC flight program, Lloyd had been worrying that his son would be drawn inevitably toward that war. After the election, he slept a little more soundly.

Feeling as though she had been kicked in the stomach, Narcissa went to bed and salved her pain with silent tears. Her beautiful senator was not going to enfold her in his arms. She knew how men behaved. The stinging defeat would send Barry all the more firmly into the arms of his wife. For weeks following the election she mourned the loss of her fantasy affair.

Then in early December she received a letter that interrupted her season of grief. "Mrs. Lloyd Morgan" was hand written in red letters on the face of the off-white envelope and her address appeared in blue. The edges of the heavy stock envelope were bordered in tiny American flags. Inside was an invitation from the wife of the owner of the company where Narcissa worked as office manager.

Narcissa was being summoned to a party at her employer's home the following Friday evening. Lloyd was not invited, as this was a women only event. At the bottom of the invitation was an intriguing note: "Come prepared for fun and to hear exclusive news of national importance." That evening, she phoned Marybelle to confirm her acceptance of the invitation.

The ten women who came to the event learned that they had been carefully selected based on their suitability for rising to positions of prominence among the social elite of the community. Narcissa recognized five of the other women as volunteers from the

Goldwater campaign, and in her mind, this lent credence to Marybelle's words.

That night, Narcissa was introduced to the Ladies' Patriotic Beauty Society. The party was carefully scripted, beginning with an icebreaking game that allowed each woman to identify herself and brag a little bit, then the reading of a poem extolling the glories of love of country.

The news of national importance turned out to be an account of how nobly Peggy Goldwater was conducting herself, as well as speculative tidbits masquerading as inside information about Republican strategy for 1968. Narcissa blanched at the first mention of the senator's wife, but as the praise for Peggy poured forth, she came to enjoy being in a place where she could gather intelligence about her rival in love. Eventually, Narcissa thought, there would be some dirt, and she wanted to be there when it was spread around.

The climax of the evening came when Marybelle unveiled an array of cosmetics and perfumes, each in elegant packaging bearing patriotic motifs. The ladies laughed and told unflattering stories about their husbands as they sampled the various scents and applied make-up to their arms and faces.

All of the women placed orders for patriotic beauty products, and Narcissa's order was the largest. As the guests in turn said their farewells, the hostess silently signaled for Narcissa to tarry. When the others had gone, Marybelle said, "I think you're a natural for this kind of work, Narcissa. You have the looks and the brains, and you have the...uh, let's say right political instincts. The Society has an opening for another beauty hostess in Phoenix, and I'd like to recommend you for the post."

"I'm flattered, Marybelle," Narcissa said, "but where would I get insider news?"

"You leave that to me," her boss's wife said in a conspiratorial tone.

And so it came to pass that Narcissa Cloud Morgan invested all her spare time and creative energy into hosting patriotic parties for selected women who showed promise for becoming prominent members of the Phoenix social scene. Marybelle fed her a stream of personal gossip and political speculation, some of which Narcissa used in her parties and some of which she kept to herself.

The affair she had anticipated having with Barry Goldwater soon faded from consciousness as her sales commissions grew. Pain retreated from her heart into a quiet and seldom used corner of her mind. Ever vigilant for new opportunities, Narcissa became the first beauty hostess in the society's Arizona territory to branch out into selling undergarments emblazoned with stars and stripes designs. See-through panties (except for a strategically placed American flag) became her best selling item.

Over the Christmas break, Cloud continued his holiday pattern of non-engagement with his parents by escaping into novels, the longer the better. This time he began with Thomas Wolfe's **Look Homeward, Angel**. He was captured from the start by Wolfe's description of Oliver Gant wanting above all else to carve an angel's head out of stone. Why this should attract him he did not understand, but something about the desire to define the shape of a heavenly being resonated deep within him. It was as if Cloud himself had seen an angel but was as incapable as Oliver Gant of capturing that vision in tangible form.

He waded through the prolix narrative, sometimes frustrated by the thousands of unnecessary words Wolfe piled into his novel, yet Cloud could not stop. Something about the tumultuous Gant family drew him further into their fictional lives. They were nothing like his own family. Where the Gants had many children, he was an only child. Where the Gants lived in chaos, his home life was orderly and free from physical abuse.

The only connection Cloud could make between **Look Homeward, Angel** and his own life was an ironic reversal. In the novel, it was the protagonist Eugene Gant's mother Eliza who was hungry to buy land, and his father Oliver who was opposed. In the Morgan family, the reverse was true.

Lloyd never seemed to speak to Narcissa about buying land, but he often told Cloud what a good investment it was. Cloud guessed his parents had argued over real estate investments at some time in the past, because occasionally Narcissa would make snide remarks about her husband's desire to speculate with acreage no sane person would want. She dismissed Lloyd's judgment by saying he wanted to be king over dirt.

As his journey through ***Angel*** progressed, Cloud developed great affection for Eugene Gant. Early on he concluded that no matter how many angel statues Oliver Gant accumulated, Eugene was the real angel Oliver produced without knowing it. Why anyone would prefer a stone cold angel to a flesh and blood one baffled him. Images of Narcissa and Lloyd filled his mind when he asked this question. Ah, but that was a different matter, he thought. He knew he was no angel, metaphorical or otherwise.

Long after reading its last page, the novel reverberated in Cloud's mind. He did not believe angels existed, and the cherubic, sentimental images of angels on Christmas cards turned his stomach. Yet a longing for a transcendent form of existence grew in Cloud's psyche, and he let the possibilities of Wolfe's "age of myth and miracle" rest there without molestation.

Cloud's skill as a pilot had improved markedly, and Bocker no longer supervised his take-offs and landings. One bright, cloudless day he coaxed the air knocker into the sky and reckoned a course north from the Deer Valley Airport that would take him directly over the Natural Christian Church camp at New River. Once upon a time he had surveyed the camp from above while floating out of his body, and a bout of nostalgia prompted a desire to see it again from on high.

Now as he looked down at the place from this higher vantage, Cloud felt a pang of loss. He wasn't close enough to recognize any people on the ground, though he guessed he knew some of them.

A soliloquy played silently in his head. "I don't believe in God, and yet I believe in these naturists who believe in God. But I don't belong with them because I don't believe in God." A sense of sad resignation took hold of him, informing him that religious belief was the arbiter of community membership, properly determining who could be in and who must stay out.

A deep urge to resume his theological discussions with Evelyn Rarom filled his mind, creating momentary elation. No one at the NCC had ever excluded him because of his doubts or disbelief. Maybe he should give her a call and see if he could visit the church camp. His superego quickly quashed this notion, reminding him that he had voluntarily exiled himself from this Christian community by rationally choosing atheism. This yearning for transcendence was seductive, dangerous, and not compatible with his reasoned rejection of the supernatural. There was nothing left for him in Eden.

In high school Cloud had studied Latin and German, and in college he continued in German and then added Russian. This proved to be significant when Army officials decided which branch Cloud would serve in when commissioned. The previous fall he had filled out a preference form, and when branch selections were announced in March, he had been assigned to his first choice: Army Intelligence and Security.

"Don't worry," his advisor said. "We'll get it switched to Transportation Corps."

"Why would you do that?" Cloud asked. "I want to be commissioned into AIS."

"Oh no, you can't do that," the advisor explained. "You're in the flight program, and Army regs don't allow intelligence officers to fly planes."

Cloud was stunned. "I think it would be an asset to have an intelligence officer who could fly places without having to involve pilots without the proper clearances."

"Well, Cloud, what you think doesn't matter, and questioning the regs will not advance your Army career. I'm afraid you'll have to switch to another branch."

"Give me a day to think about it, sir," Cloud said, and his advisor graciously agreed to this request.

That night Cloud weighed his dream of being a pilot against his equally strong desire to do intelligence work. He was only a few hours away from a private pilot's license. The lessons had not gone well at the beginning, but he was doing fine now. But his greatest satisfactions came from using his skills in analyzing people and situations, and he loved languages.

At least some Army officials wanted to make use of his intellectual abilities, he reasoned, as evidenced by selecting him for AIS. But others preferred to ignore those abilities and confine him exclusively to flying. He knew he could do both.

By morning he had decided to follow his head rather than his heart, and at least in part to send a message to the misguided Army bureaucrat who had decreed that intelligence and aviation were mutually exclusive, he told his advisor that he was dropping out of the flight program. He would accept a commission into the Army Intelligence and Security branch.

When he learned about Cloud's decision, Lloyd felt tremendous relief.

Cloud brooded for a few days, grumbling about organizational stupidity, but when he realized that he was angrier about the rule than about giving up the flight program, he decided to invest no more energy in the matter, which was providential, for that week he found something else to brood about.

For a course in twentieth century novels, Cloud read D. H. Lawrence's **Lady Chatterley's Lover**. The paper he wrote for the class focused on what Cloud regarded as Lawrence's naïve ideas about industrialization and economics. Though he failed to mention this in his report, he found the sex scenes lyrically beautiful.

What haunted him, however, was the relational premise of the novel. Clifford Chatterley had been badly wounded in World War I, returning an invalid. The baronet's chronic medical condition led his healthy and sexually unfulfilled wife Connie to take a lover. Cloud could not get the wheelchair bound Clifford out of his mind. Lord Chatterley's image metastasized throughout his brain.

He remembered the veteran with a missing leg who accosted him at the state fair when he was a freshman in high school. Had that man been cuckolded too? Was Clifford Chatterley's fate common among men whose bodies had been mutilated in combat? Would something like that happen to him? A wave of depression descended through Cloud's body as in his mind he heard the soldier propped up on crutches shouting the hope that Cloud would someday suffer as he had. And now he was less than three months from becoming a commissioned officer and called to active duty.

These dark thoughts did not linger, however, because they were shortly overwhelmed by a wonderful epiphany in Cloud's cultural anthropology class. The April afternoon was warm as he sat in the last row doodling while listening to the professor lecture with clinical dispassion about Bronislav Malinowski's work among the artlessly unprudish Trobriand Islanders, who encouraged their children to explore sexual activity among their peers. Cloud sketched a mythical South Pacific island; a palm graced Eden with a lagoon where children safely gamboled and played sex games.

Cloud was making notations about his island in his usual meditative manner of writing backwards when an explosion of understanding hit him. The clear and brilliant knowledge saturated his brain cells. In his mind he saw that all the myriad aspects of his college curriculum for the past four years were interrelated.

Anthropology was part of English literature. He recognized them as facets of the same reality. It was easy to make out the connections among Russian and German and English, but biology and geology and even military science were organically part of a grand design that included music appreciation, Asian architecture, accounting, statistics, and ancient history. Studying the Battle of Little Big Horn and the massacre at Wounded Knee in American frontier history and dissecting a cat in biology lab were using different lenses to look at the same subject. Not a single course he had taken was a discrete experience but everything was integral to a seamless educational experience, with every discipline touching every other. The rainbow tissue holding it together was so obvious. Why had he not noticed it before? His entire education could be reproduced from a single grain of sand on a Trobriand Island beach, because that grain of sand was related to all existing thoughts and things. For good or ill, whether rational or mystical, concrete or intangible, all existence was physically interconnected and intellectually inseparable.

Adrenaline coursed through his system and his body hummed in pleasure. Over the next few hours, details blurred. The momentarily lucid pathway linking that grain of sand and Russian verbs faded. But this was no evanescent insight over and forgotten in a flash. Cloud's discovery stayed with him, large and memorable. It changed how he absorbed and processed information. And he would recall it often during the next two years as he sat in US Army classrooms learning all sorts of arcane material.

The night Cloud graduated from Arizona State University, he stopped at a convenience store to buy a couple of six-packs of beer to contribute to a party that Theo had organized. He was not surprised that the clerk asked for proof of age, for he had a boyish face and was only seven months past the legal drinking age of 21. However, after producing his draft card, his driver's license with picture on it, and his ASU student ID card with picture on it, the clerk refused to sell him the beer. The man behind the counter said he would never believe that the boy standing in front of him was over 21.

He ran out to his car and returned with his commencement program. "Look, right here," he said. "See, I just graduated from ASU tonight, so surely, given the corroborating documents I've already shown you, this confirms that I am of legal age."

But the clerk wouldn't budge, and so Cloud went to the party empty handed. And as it happened, nobody noticed.

The next day at a campus ceremony in Old Main, along with ten of his ROTC classmates, Cloud was commissioned Second Lieutenant in the United States Army. He promptly handed a silver dollar to the first enlisted man who rushed forward to salute him. Cloud noted wryly that his first salute came from the man who had given faulty instructions in the Salt River maneuvers and then disqualified his team for completing the mission despite his error. Cloud was instructed to go home and wait for active duty orders that would arrive in a few weeks.

When he pulled into the driveway, his mother rushed out to meet him, saying in a breathless voice that Miss Listerbaum had been taken to the hospital and was apparently in bad condition. Cloud peeled out of the driveway and sped to Good Samaritan Hospital, where he found his neighbor in a private room.

Her face brightened when he entered the room. "I'm so glad you came, Cloud."

"Well, I just heard." He saw she was gaunt but feared asking what was wrong.

"I'm not very strong, and I don't think I have much longer in this world."

"Oh, don't say that. Of course, you're going to be fine," Cloud fired back.

"There's something I want to tell you, Cloud. Sit by me on the bed."

He did, and as she spoke he took hold of her right hand.

"I know you've behaved like a scamp, teasing me and all that, and since you went off to college, you haven't visited very much. But I want you to know that I love you as the son I never had."

Cloud's eyes filled with tears. "I love you, Miss Listerbaum,"

Cloud said, surprising himself at his words, because he had never consciously entertained them before this moment. "And I wish you were my real mother."

"Bless you, Cloud," she said. "But you mustn't say things like that. Your mother loves you as much as she knows how." Though she shucked off his words, she was immensely pleased to hear them.

"I love you, Miss Listerbaum," Cloud said again.

She smiled at him and then closed her eyes and drifted off into another realm. For a few minutes, silence filled the room, and then she spoke again, although not to Cloud. "Yes, I'll tell him," she said in a clear, strong voice.

Jael Listerbaum opened her eyes and peered into Cloud's eyes. "I'm going to die soon," she said. He started to protest but she gripped his hand more tightly and said, "Hush now, and listen to me. I want to tell you my dreams. I dreamed about you many times over the years. In the most vivid one you were hovering in the air, flying around inspecting the neighborhood. Isn't that odd? But that's how I saw you, floating on air."

"How did you know?" he whispered.

But she ignored the question. "I have a message for you, Cloud, from an old friend. When everything turns upside down, dance on the ceiling."

Before he could respond, she lapsed into a coma, and as he sat with her, holding her hand, she died. When he realized that she was gone, he summoned the duty nurse and slipped out of the room. This was his first encounter with the death of someone he loved, and he felt numb, but as he walked through the hospital corridors, no tears came. In the parking lot, he climbed into his car and tried to put the key in the ignition but found his hand was shaking uncontrollably. Then, without prelude, he burst into sobs of heaving grief that continued for half an hour.

While Cloud was thus engaged with tears, several thousand miles to the east and north, Terp lay supine in bed with her head dangling backward over the mattress edge staring at the ceiling. From this perspective, Terp perceived the ceiling as the floor and vice versa. She enjoyed observing this peculiar world and let her imagination romp through the room where the floor was made of swirl-patterned plaster. The top of the door brushed the carpeted ceiling, and its bottom swung two and a half feet above ground level. In her mind, she executed a ballet leap over the high threshold of her room out into the hall. This was a fantasy exercise she engaged in from time to time for physical relaxation and mental stimulation.

At that same moment, thousands of miles to the west and south, Xuan was finishing her daily yoga routine by standing on her head on a bamboo mat, with her palms cupped around her head and her forearms flared out to brace her stance. As was her whimsical custom, she envisioned herself dangling from the ceiling, and fancied that soon she would descend featherlike to the stucco floor and begin to dance.

Three days later, during her funeral service in the mortuary chapel, Cloud remembered Miss Listerbaum's last words. What did she mean? Dance on the ceiling? And what did it mean that she had dreams about him floating? His mind was fatigued from so many transitions all at once, so he let go of the matter.

After the service, one of Miss Listerbaum's nephews approached Cloud. "My aunt left a note that she wanted you to have some of her things," he said. "Come over to her house and I'll give them to you."

The legacy she gave to Cloud consisted of a box of old books on Arizona history, a folder of newspaper clippings about Winnie Ruth Judd, and a large manila envelope containing many photos of Cloud at various ages, including Cloud and Darla before the prom. There was also a single photograph of Jael Listerbaum, taken when she was sixteen, and a picture of Phoenix Union High School students and teachers arranged into the shape of a coyote. Behind this was a handwritten poem on yellowed paper. In addition to these items, she had given him her entire phonograph record collection.

She was a beautiful young woman, Cloud thought as he studied her picture. It's too bad no one ever fell in love with her. The record collection was fantastic in his estimation and he was grateful to receive it. But the pleasure of cataloging the 78-rpm discs would have to wait for another time. He didn't know what to make of the coyote photograph. The poem was a sentimental piece about the beauty and kindness of a woman who feeds and cares for hoboes. Cloud decided it must have been written by one of the hoboes Miss Listerbaum repeatedly told him stories about. He smiled to think there might have been a touch of romance between her and a rail-rider.

Exhausted as he was, from final exams, graduation from college, commissioning, awaiting active duty orders, and the death of his surrogate mother, another stressful transition would soon be added to Cloud's life.

Narcissa was doing very well selling patriotic cosmetics, so well in fact, that she decided to resign her position as office manager and devote full time to marketing. She now fancied herself an entrepreneur, finally emancipated from the ignominy of being merely an employee. This decision led to a huge argument between the owner of the fence company and his wife, who had recruited Narcissa for the Ladies Patriotic Beauty Society. Narcissa had managed the office with great skill, but she was indifferent to her boss's pleas for her to stay with the firm as well as his marital difficulties. She did make a point of profusely thanking Marybelle for leading her to what she described as her true vocation, but that was only to protect her source of inside political gossip.

However, Narcissa was no longer satisfied using her attractive but modestly sized home for the sales parties. She wanted a house with more floor space, multiple bathrooms, and the most important detail, it needed to be in a more prestigious neighborhood. Over dinner one evening she broached the subject of moving. Lloyd was immediately receptive to the idea. He was now working in the corporate office of the bank, and it was time he started inviting other executives to his home for cocktails. A nicer house would be a business asset.

The next day, Lloyd did a survey of foreclosures made by other banks, and found a beautiful three-bedroom home on Monte Vista Road in the upscale Palmcroft neighborhood. A tall redwood fence enclosed the back yard, shielding the kidney shaped pool from public view. They bought the house in July and made plans to move into it, and thus out of the only house Cloud had ever known, in August, a week before Cloud would be leaving for his first assignment at Fort Benning, Georgia.

While supervising packing for the move, Narcissa knocked over a stack of Cloud's 45-rpm records that he had carefully placed on his bedside table. A dozen discs fell to the floor. When picking up and restacking them, she missed one, Bobby Darin's "Dream Lover," which she thereupon stepped on and cracked. Cloud howled when he discovered this.

"Well I don't see the tragedy," Narcissa huffed. "Here's a dollar. Go buy another one."

"It's five years too late for that," he yelled. Cloud's emotional response might have been less if she had destroyed a different record, but he now associated this song with the dancer from the East. In a flash of intuition, he saw that his mother would not approve of his dream lover when he ultimately found her, which he was certain of doing.

With three bedrooms in the new house, Narcissa decreed that she and Lloyd would have separate rooms, and the third bedroom would serve as a combination guest room and a place for Cloud to stay when he came home on leave. Since the house on Villa Verde was paid off, Lloyd decided to keep it for rental income.

During dinner, the day after moving in to the new house, Lloyd said casually, "Now that we have a pool and a privacy fence, we should invite the Verralls over for skinny-dipping. We haven't seen them in ages."

"Oh sure. Let's do that someday," Narcissa said in a neutral tone while at the same time slowly shaking her head no. The idea of showing off their improved social status to their former neighbors held some appeal, she thought, but Nissa and Onan were not the sort of people who were impressed with elegant living. The proof of this was that Nissa had repeatedly declined invitations to patriotic beauty supply parties.

"If you had patriotic sunscreen lotion, I might be interested," Nissa quipped on one occasion.

Narcissa did not find this amusing. Nevertheless, she had already decided that she would sunbathe nude beside their pool when Lloyd was at work.

CHAPTER EIGHTEEN

Packed into his decade old Ford was every important possession Cloud thought he might need for the next two or three years of active duty, including many books and all the components of his stereo system. The Fairlane had served him well during his college commute, and now it would carry him across the country from the red rocks of Arizona to the red hills of Georgia.

Driving east on US 70, Cloud approached the New Mexico state line with a sense of elation, because traveling eastward was a new experience for him. New Mexico didn't qualify as the East, he knew, but as a boy he had thought of places like Kansas City and Des Moines as exemplars of the storied region his father referred to as back east. It wouldn't really be the East, he now decided, until he crossed the Mississippi River. In Cloud's mind, the small geographic area known as the East Coast began at St. Louis.

Near the border with New Mexico, he saw a large sign in front of a service station: "LAST GAS AT ARIZONA PRICES!" Instinctively, Cloud moved his foot to the brake pedal, but emotional inertia urged him onward, and he lifted his foot, deciding in an instant that he did not want to stop until he had crossed into a place he had never been before. For interest's sake, he noted the price, and when he pulled into Lordsburg, he discovered that the sign was technically correct, but it failed to disclose that the price of gasoline was cheaper in New Mexico.

After a dreadfully long day that began with three hours of driving into the fiercely rising sun over the plains of Texas and another day of bestial humidity in Louisiana, Cloud crossed the Mississippi River at Vicksburg. Mentally, he scratched this achievement from a list of life goals. From this point he continued on US 80 to Columbus, Georgia.

On Sunday morning, he searched in vain for a pleasant radio station to serenade him as he traversed the southern highway. All he could pick up, however, were religious services broadcast by preachers who sounded to Cloud like drawling imitators of T. C. Smith. In frustration, he clicked off the car radio and drove in silence. Unable to turn off his brain, however, he debated in his head with the radio preachers.

When he pulled into a gas station in Selma, the attendant stepped behind Cloud's car to check the license plate before ascertaining Cloud's refueling wishes. "Outta state folks gotta be mighty careful round here, boy. Now, Arizona, that's Goldwater country, ain't it?" the pudgy white-faced clerk said.

"Yes, that's right. Could you fill the tank with regular, please?" Cloud replied.

"Now, don't be in such a rush, boy. You're not one of them smart-ass demonstrators are you?"

"I'm on my way to report for active duty at Fort Benning," Cloud said, trying to keep his voice at a conversational level, but feeling ill at ease.

"Naw, I guess Arizona's a long way from Jew York City." The clerk laughed at his joke and proceeded to pump gas into the Ford's tank. When he came to collect payment, he added, "We don't sell gas to people from up north that stick their necks inta other folks' binness." Cloud drove away feeling he had narrowly escaped being set on by attack dogs.

The assignment to Fort Benning had come because all new intelligence officers were required to complete the Infantry Officers Basic Course before starting specialized intelligence training. This made sense to Cloud, because intelligence officers would need elemental understanding of military operations. Thus, he was highly motivated to learn as much as he could. In retrospect, he would be disappointed to have learned more about idiosyncrasies in the Army system than about subjects to help him be a better intelligence analyst.

His first lesson was in correct nomenclature. Members of his IOBC class filled out forms for issuance of dog tags, and in the space for religion Cloud wrote atheist. A few days later when the steel identification tags were distributed, Cloud discovered his religion had been changed to "No Preference." He asked around to see if anyone else had suffered a bureaucratic change of faith, but no one had. He considered requesting that his dog tags be reissued to reflect his stated belief, but dropped the idea when he remembered he was deep in the Bible Belt and it would not be good to start his military career with an unpopular quarrel over religion.

Much of the training was a repeat of ROTC summer camp. Cloud had anticipated that he would be treated like the officer and gentleman he now was by act of Congress, but in this he was disappointed. Although his dorm room in Infantry Hall, with another Second Lieutenant as roommate, was an improvement over the open barracks at summer camp, all the young officers were subjected to nitpicking room inspections and sophomoric bed checks, conducted with a similar level of reasonableness as fraternity hazing.

The item that got Cloud in trouble was his stereo system. No one else on the third floor had brought one along, and he thus became popular among compatriots from the North and West, who could not find their kind of music on local radio stations. The problem, Cloud was told in sternest fashion by an unsmiling first lieutenant, was that such equipment was not authorized, and it had to be removed from the room.

Cloud suspected the real problem was the Peter Paul and Mary album he left on the turntable during the day. The inspecting officer considered the folk trio dangerously subversive. To avoid trouble, Cloud unhooked the tuner, turntable, and speakers each night before going to bed and stowed them in his locker. On evenings when he returned to his room early enough to care about music, he brought them out, hooked them up, and played records, including discs other officers brought over.

This is how he met Second Lieutenant Mercury Zared, a University of New Mexico ROTC graduate who loved the leftist folk anthem "If I Had a Hammer." Like Cloud, Mercury would be assigned to the Army Intelligence School at Fort Holabird, Maryland when IOBC was finished. He was an Army brat, the oldest son of a career Quartermaster Corps officer. And in the same way that Theo, the preacher's kid, talked irreverently about the institutional church, Mercury spoke about military life from the point of view of a cynical insider who knows all the flaws and the best ways to get around the system.

In the storied annals of the Infantry School at Fort Benning, Cloud's class would not be recorded as one of the sharpest. Half of the members were intelligence and security officers, while a significant contingent were Reserve and National Guard soldiers on active duty for training, and a few were allied soldiers from Iraq. As a result, the serious minded Infantry branch junior officers were greatly outnumbered by those who were simply punching their tickets on their ways to other careers.

Cloud did well with class work and was successful in the field with the map reading and compass courses, but one part of the curriculum he was unable to master -bayonet training.

Members of the training detachment fixed bayonets to their rifles and prepared for the exercise through repetition of a response chant. "What is the spirit of the bayonet?" the instructor shouted.

"To kill!" the young officers yelled back.

"Louder!"

"TO KILL!"

This exchange continued until the instructor perceived a sufficient level of fervor had been reached and then sent them charging down the course in succeeding waves to attack straw dummies while screaming with as much fury as their lungs could force through their vocal chords.

Cloud dutifully stabbed his bayonet into the first dummy, pulled it out and continued on to the next, but he could not force his mind to accept the targets as menacing. He felt somewhat silly about what he was doing. He could not get the spirit of the bayonet. Reflecting on it later, intellectually he recognized the need to break down the natural resistance to slashing another human being to death, but as much as he had tried to release his fury into those straw dummies, nothing clicked. Some of his classmates had been successful, however, achieving a level of bayonet spirit that rendered them temporarily unable to speak in complete sentences and filled their eyes with maniacal gleams.

Having failed this particular test of manhood, Cloud considered redeeming himself through another physical challenge. Southwest of the Infantry Hall stood the 34 feet high mock towers used for airborne training, and to the north were the 250 feet high parachute drop towers. Cloud would apply for the three-week airborne class. Although this would delay the start of intelligence school, it would be a boon to his career and mark him as an elite officer.

That night, he had a nightmare about bailing out of a plane. Before his parachute could open, the drop through the air caused him inadvertently to float out of his body, and he watched in horror as his uncontrolled physical shell splattered on the ground below. Now he was an orphan with no body to return to. He interpreted this not as a prescient warning but as sound advice against applying for jump school. As with his decision to quit the flight program, Cloud sensed that foregoing airborne training was another decisive turning point inexorably maneuvering him away from childhood dreams and toward his destiny.

Two days later, his sense of humanity rather than his sense of manliness was tested. Representatives from Fort Holabird came to Georgia to administer the Army Language Aptitude Test to all AIS officers. Cloud found it fun, like a challenging crossword puzzle. The examination provided words and phrases in the artificial language Esperanto, which were then to be translated. When the results were announced, Cloud had missed a perfect score by one point, and he was encouraged to apply for foreign language training. He would think about that option during the six-month intelligence research course he would begin in a few weeks.

Near the end of the eight-week infantry course, Cloud received a letter from his father. Lloyd filled several pages with his small and efficient penmanship, telling Cloud about life at the bank and the roads through the Salt River bed that had been washed out in the recent thunderstorm. On the last page, Lloyd wrote: "We heard yesterday that Quincy Queensbury was injured in Viet Nam. He is in an Army hospital in California and is expected to be confined to a wheelchair the rest of his life. It is a terrible thing to be wounded in battle. When I get more news about him, I'll let you know. Some of his training was at Fort Benning, so you may run into someone there who remembers him."

Cloud went cold when he read about Quinn. He remembered his dreams about the former bully breaking his leg and being beaten by his father. What an ugly irony this is, he thought.

Early in November, Cloud drove north to Baltimore without stopping to sleep, reported in at Fort Holabird, visited the Provost Marshal's office for a parking sticker, left his car in the officers' lot, dumped his gear in a BOQ room, donned his dress greens, took a cab to Friendship Airport, and flew to LaGuardia Airport. Taking advantage of his unused allotment of travel time plus a few days leave, he was doing something he had wanted to do as a result of years of movie watching. He was going to see New York City, and in particular, Broadway.

The instructor at the Hoi Viet My English Language School in Saigon was trying to explain idiomatic uses of the word float. "You can make a root beer float or watch a Rose Bowl Parade float," he said. "In both cases the word float is a noun, but with different meanings. With regard to root beer, the noun float refers to the action of the verb float. The ice cream floats in the beverage. Boats float on the surface of the ocean. That's a pure verb usage. But we also call borrowing money floating a loan."

Various stares greeted the instructor, some blank and some bored. One student was fully engaged in the presentation, however. Acting on a sudden impulse she did not understand, Xuan asked, "Please sir, how about to say a person float?"

"Yes, Miss Xuan. We would say a person floats in a swimming pool. That's a good example," the instructor said encouragingly.

"I think maybe a person float in air," responded Xuan.

"No. We would say a person, such as an acrobat...or an airplane...flies through the air. A very graceful person might glide across the room." The instructor used his hands and arms to illustrate flying followed by a clumsy attempt at gliding across the concrete classroom floor.

"I think some person must float in air," Xuan continued. She had never before contradicted any teacher, but she was filled with a strong conviction that her English in this special case was correct. A moment later, realizing her disrespectful behavior, she apologized to the American instructor. But the idea took root in her mind. A person -she imagined a male person- could indeed float.

CHAPTER NINETEEN

While Cloud was flying to New York, a creature of comforting presence meditated seventy-seven feet above the street, sitting cross-legged atop the arch at the southern terminus of Fifth Avenue. The monument marked the north entrance to Washington Square Park in Greenwich Village. The Old One was covered from neck to feet by a coarsely woven black gabardine cloak. Anyone gazing up Fifth Avenue from the other side of the park could easily see the Old One silhouetted against the skyline, but the tourists who might do that had gone back to Midtown, and no one else looked up. In the cold approach of evening people stared straight-ahead, planning routes to their warm city apartments or suburban homes. Nevertheless, those walking by the base of the arch felt a momentary lift of energy as they passed on their ways beneath the unseen Old One.

Within the park, however, some distance from the arch, a young man new to New York wrapped himself in an Army blanket and squeezed into a hollow at the base of a large tree. He had arrived in the city that morning, November ninth, and made his way to the East Village to meet folk singers. Clutched to his chest as an extra layer of protection from the wind was a manila folder full of songs he had written. He had better plans for that folder, for he was going to haunt Fourth Street with complete confidence that eventually he would run into Bob Dylan or some other noteworthy folkie and show off his melodic work. The songwriter had spent all his money getting from Albuquerque to New York, and now he was very hungry and very cold, and his cough was getting worse.

Among a host of other matters, the Old One was aware of this young man's needs and was waiting patiently for an opportune time to insert a suggestion into his mind. And then the lights of the city began to flicker.

Cloud took a cab from LaGuardia into Manhattan to the Edison Hotel, west of Broadway on 47th Street. Entering the art deco lobby he felt he was stepping into a world he had seen in a movie, and he smiled broadly for the sheer joy of being there. With room key in hand he got into the elevator en route to the fourteenth floor. Standing next to Cloud were a trim man about his father's age dressed in a three-piece suit redolent of cigarette smoke and a pretty girl in her early teens wearing glasses and an elegant blue dress with white gloves. He assumed they were father and daughter, and they, too, were going to his floor.

"Where's home, lieutenant?" Tom Person asked Cloud.

"Arizona, sir. Phoenix," Cloud answered.

"Great place," Tom said. "We've been there a couple of times on vacation. Let me guess; you're stationed in New Jersey. Fort Dix?"

"Sorry, sir, Maryland," Cloud said. "Fort Holabird."

Terp said nothing, but at the mention of Arizona, her eyes widened and the top of her head tingled.

At that moment, the elevator doors opened and the passengers walked down the hall to their respective rooms, which by chance were situated next to each other.

Strange sounds emanated from radio station WABC in New York. Si Zentner's sprightly arrangement of "Up a Lazy River" grew lethargic, as if someone were pressing on the turntable, slowing the record down. Disc Jockey Dan Ingram said, "I don't know what's happening. Lights are getting dim all over the city." The 5:25 evening news broadcast went out over the airwaves in surreal, deep bass voices, which faded to a distant whisper until at 5:28 all was silent.

The electricity grid throughout the Northeastern United States had gone down, and along with those of many other lesser-known places, the lights of New York City disappeared. Yet the natural order of the universe provided partial redemption as a full moon beamed brightly across the dark cityscape. However, people trapped in subway tunnels and elevators were not able to enjoy the lunar display.

Early in 1965, Tom Person had promised Terp that he would take her to dinner and a Broadway show for her thirteenth birthday in May. The day passed, however, without specific plans for the father and daughter event, and the press of business delayed possible dates in the summer. But in the fall a client gave Tom two third row tickets for **Fiddler on the Roof.** The performance would be a Tuesday night, and Tom decided to make up for the delay by proposing that they stay over in the city and go shopping the next morning. Terp would have to miss a day of school, but as much as she loved her classes, she was thrilled at the prospect of an early holiday outing with her dad.

Now the day had come. They had checked into their room at the Edison and were resting before dinner, but unforeseen circumstances now threatened their plans. The power went out in their room, and apparently her favorite radio station, WABC, was off the air, because Terp's transistor radio hissed but could not pick up a signal.

As the songwriter, Colin Glee, shivered in his improvised nest, a strong suggestion entered his brain. Get up now! Walk along Fourth Street! With the thought came a mild boost of energy, and so he rose, trembling but intuitively confident that Bob Dylan was on Fourth Street that very minute.

Colin stumbled along the sidewalk, anxiously looking for the shape of a guitar case silhouetted against the moonlight, and while looking far ahead he collided with a young man about his age. "Excuse me," he mumbled distractedly but then glanced at the man and saw a Lobos baseball cap. "Hey, are you from New Mexico?"

"Yeah," the man said warily.

"Me too," the songwriter said before bursting into spasms of coughing and falling to the concrete.

Fifteen minutes later, Colin was lying on a couch in his fellow New Mexican's tiny East Village apartment. The man who rescued him from the cold night, Asher Shepherd, poured chicken noodle soup ingredients from a paper packet into a pan of boiling water on his gas stove.

Illumined by candles, the two men shared a loaf of French bread and steaming soup. As they ate, the providential nature of their collision on the sidewalk became clear to the songwriter. His savior was a law student at NYU.

"My old man was a small time musician," Asher explained. "He had a dance band and played gigs all over Texas, Oklahoma and the Rocky Mountain States. He was cheated so many times by club owners that I think it finally killed him. He died of a heart attack when I was fifteen. So I'm studying entertainment law. I want to be able to protect people like my dad, and singers who get ripped off by record companies, and writers who get their ideas stolen by big studios."

The songwriter, who had long since learned to trust his intuition, knew as the hot soup funneled down his esophagus radiating warmth throughout his body, that he and this budding entertainment lawyer would be close friends for many years to come.

Meanwhile back in the park, people gathering around the Washington Square Arch felt calm and safe amidst the confusion of the blackout. They expected that all would be well. Some went off into the surrounding area and herded strangers to the base of the arch. Gather over here, they said. It's safe under the arch.

Cloud sat in the quiet darkness for a quarter hour before restless curiosity motivated him to go out into the hall to see if anyone had news of the situation. At that moment, WABC returned to the air via emergency generator, and Terp's transistor radio filled her room with a voice explaining the blackout. Tom suggested they go to the door and pass the news to anyone in the hallway. Terp swung the heavy door wide and it banged into the wall, momentarily startling her.

"Yoo-hoo? Anyone there?" Terp called.

"I'm here, your next door neighbor," said Cloud. "What's happening?"

"I have a transistor radio," said Terp "The whole city has lost power."

Cloud felt his way along the wall until he stood beside Terp. It seemed a disembodied dream to him as they listened to her radio in the pitch-black corridor.

"No ***Fiddler on the Roof*** tonight," she sighed.

"I'm really sorry, Terp," came Tom's voice from inside.

"Me too," said Cloud. "I hope you'll be able to see it soon." A wave of fatigue that had been chasing him since he had raced northward through Atlanta caught up with him at that moment and he said, "I'm going to my room, but if there's any important news, will you knock on my door and let me know?"

"Sure," said Terp. Talking in the dark to this lieutenant from Arizona gave her an odd sense of levitating weightlessly out of her body.

Back in his room, Cloud fell into bed. His next conscious thought was that the room pulsed with light. Electric power had been restored more than three hours earlier. He looked at his watch and saw that he had slept fourteen hours. Switching on the radio, he was serenaded with "A Wonderful Dream," a three-year old doo-wop ditty. He sang along remembering the pleasant illusion of dreaming in the hallway the previous night.

After shaving and showering, Cloud changed into civilian clothes and went in search of breakfast. Once sustained with bagels and cream cheese and coffee, he set out to hike the streets of Midtown Manhattan. At a theater memorabilia shop on Forty-fifth Street, he thought he saw his fourteenth floor neighbors from the Edison Hotel but wasn't fully confident about it. He had only seen them briefly in the elevator and they had been dressed formally. These folks in the store were clad in jeans and wool sweaters. When he had spoken with the girl they were in total darkness. Fearing he might be mistaken and deferring to his general shyness, he did not greet them.

Terp saw Cloud across the room, wearing civilian clothes. She felt certain this was the lieutenant who listened to the news with her the previous night. Experiencing a sudden adolescent discomposure, however, she did not wave to him.

Tom, intent on salvaging as much as possible from the event, found a souvenir publication about ***Fiddler on the Roof*** and handed it to Terp to peruse. "Hold it up and smile," he said and snapped a picture of her with the book. He was unaware that when developed the photograph would reveal in the background an image of Army Second Lieutenant Cloud Morgan in mufti.

Later in the day, Cloud rode the subway to Greenwich Village, where he found a comfortable spot in Washington Square Park to enjoy a chilidog for his midday meal. When he ambled over to inspect the arch, he felt a strange sensation that he had been there before, but that was impossible. As he reflected on the *déjà vu* experience he refined it in his mind. It was not that he had been in this place in the past but rather he knew someone connected with it. However, he couldn't remember who that might be.

Apparently the chilidog had restored his energy, he thought, because he began to feel buoyant and confident standing in front of the arch. Presently, loaded with curiosity, he resumed his exploration of the city. Two men brushed by him, deep in conversation about music copyrights, and Cloud gained a momentary thought that he knew them, but they were strangers, and in truth he had never met them. The ties among these three men existed only in the consciousness of the being on top of the Washington Square Arch.

Fort Holabird seemed more like a college to Cloud than an Army base. Indeed, its 96-acre campus in the southeast corner of Baltimore was known among military insiders as the College on the Colgate, referring to the creek that meandered through the fort. Officially, Fort Holabird was home to USAINTS, the United States Army Intelligence School.

Shortly after arriving at the base, Mercury Zared queried Cloud, "How do soldiers at Fort Holabird get to class?"

"Walk, I guess," Cloud said.

"No," Mercury explained. "USAINTS go marching in." He hummed the spiritual.

Housing at Holabird was tight, so junior officers were encouraged to find off-base quarters. Cloud and Mercury found a two-bedroom apartment in Dundalk, six blocks east of the post. They soon fell into an 8 to 5 routine of classes, with evenings and weekends free. Gone were room inspections and shouting field instructors.

The faculty at "the Bird" were experts in a myriad of specialized fields, all of which required intellectual capabilities. The most physically demanding part of the course work was surveillance training on foot in downtown Baltimore, but for an inveterate hiker like Cloud, this was not enough exertion to break a sweat. The surveillance by automobile course offered a few dangerous moments, but all of these came about because the drivers had seen too many movie chase scenes.

Cloud loved the grand sweep of intelligence disciplines. Most of the curriculum was classified secret, but there was one unclassified course Cloud found uninteresting but useful. A civilian woman, Astrid Flicker, known deferentially to everyone on post as General Flicker, taught typing. In a classroom filled with lieutenants and captains, each behind a typewriter, Astrid Flicker was clearly in command. Patiently yet sternly she instructed officers with advanced degrees to keep their fingers on the home keys. She began the course by demonstrating what level of competence she expected by the end.

Sitting confidently behind her machine, which no one else must ever touch, Flicker scrolled in a blank piece of bond paper and typed a hundred words a minute to the recognizable rhythm of Rossini's William Tell Overture. She then passed around the full sheet, which contained not a single error. None of her students ever matched her skill, but that was not her motivation for the demonstration. No one challenged her authority to teach typing, and that was what she wanted.

"Gentlemen, your typewriter is a weapon, and you must treat it with the same respect and provide it with as much care as you would a rifle, a howitzer, or a tank," she told every class. She was rigorous in requiring that the covers be properly replaced over the machines at the end of each session. Cloud loved the concept of the typewriter as a weapon. "The typewriter is mightier than the bazooka," he told Mercury over lunch.

During the next typing class, Cloud twisted the roller rapidly to get the paper out and General Flicker glared at him and said, "Stop, Lieutenant Morgan!" He stopped, and she explained yet again to the entire class the proper way to remove paper from a typewriter.

The school employed professional actors for teaching students how to conduct interviews. If the right questions were asked in the proper way, the actors provided the information needed for completion of the scenario, but if not, they volunteered nothing, and they were adept at addling novice investigators and twisting their words into rhetorical knots.

Cloud quickly realized that interviewing was like working on a puzzle, trying to gather as many pieces of the picture as possible, recognizing that no such picture is ever complete. He did very well in this course.

The courses on Communist infrastructure in Viet Nam and the organization of Viet Cong cells came right after lunch, and the major who taught the class had a deep, droning voice, which lulled Cloud into drowsiness. Cloud expected that this information would one day be important to him but nevertheless had difficulty staying attentive enough to absorb it. The class felt to him like a frustration dream in which he knew there was something important for him to discover but recurring obstacles kept him from finding it.

In February, members of the class submitted location preferences for duty assignments. In two months, school would be over and the real work would begin. Cloud, however, requested further education at the Defense Language Institute in Monterey, California in order to study Vietnamese. This required an additional year of active duty, from the two year commitment for Reserve Officers to three, but this was not a problem for Cloud, who anticipated becoming a Regular Officer and remaining on active duty for two or three decades.

The Army's answer to Cloud was yes. After graduation in April, he would take accrued leave and then report to Monterey in May. Mercury was assigned to a plain clothes position in a field office of a Military Intelligence Battalion headquartered in Southern California. The field office was in Phoenix.

CHAPTER TWENTY

Home on leave, Cloud felt like a stranger in a strange house. Narcissa had donated most of her son's furniture, including his double bed, to Goodwill. She had been inclined to trash the lot, but Lloyd wanted the charitable tax deduction. The guest bedroom was now furnished in a feminine patriotic décor.

In January she had moved Cloud's personal possessions into the detached garage, including his 45 and 33-rpm records and the 78-rpms he had gotten from Miss Listerbaum. This discovery caused him a momentary tantrum. Fortunately it was only April, so they had not yet been exposed to the warping summer heat. Narcissa relented and allowed Cloud to move his records and photos into a back corner of the guest room closet, but his extensive library, games, model antique cars, and clothes remained banished from the house.

While sorting through his things in the garage, Cloud found his father's old combat boots unceremoniously shoved between a box of books and a milk crate. He mentioned this discovery to Lloyd, who told Cloud that he could have the boots if he wanted them. He did want them, or at least he felt the need to protect them for some deep-seated reason he could not articulate. Cloud wrapped the boots in a towel and placed them in an A. J. Bayless grocery bag, which he folded and stapled shut and set inside a cardboard box on which he wrote his name in large block letters.

The new place on Monte Vista was larger than the Villa Verde house, and as far as one can argue architectural tastes, more pleasant to look at. Its design was a combination of Spanish and Territorial, with a red tile roof and white stucco walls. The Palmcroft neighborhood clearly reflected a higher socioeconomic status, but to Cloud this was not home and never would be.

He called the Askeladds to find out where Aldous might be. He was in Iowa City, working on a master's degree in creative writing at the University of Iowa.

He called the Wolfs to see if Odie were around town and learned that Odie was working in his father's insurance agency. With one more call, he arranged to meet Odie for lunch at Macayo's on Central Avenue. Over cheese enchiladas and refried beans the high school chums caught up on their lives.

Odie had scraped through ASU with a degree in business administration and had immediately found employment in the family firm. "It turns out I'm really good at selling life insurance," he said. "Tell you what, if you buy me a margarita I promise **not** to give you a sales spiel."

"My sales resistance is pretty high," Cloud said. "But I'll buy you a margarita anyway." By the time lunch was over, Cloud had bought three margaritas for Odie while nursing one himself, and Odie had tried to sell him a life insurance policy anyway. He returned to the agency with no sale, however.

On the short trip back to his home guest room, Cloud decided to cut short his leave and make a leisurely drive to Monterey. Aldous was in Iowa, Theo was at a seminary in Chicago, and spending more time with Odie held no appeal. Miss Listerbaum was dead. Mercury wouldn't be in town till next month, and he had no idea where Firstlaugh might be. There was nothing for him in Phoenix. The next day he packed his car and set out for California.

The campus of the Defense Language Institute West spread over an idyllic setting on a bluff overlooking Monterey Bay. While students diligently studied Russian, Chinese, Arabic, Vietnamese, and other tongues above the bay, sea lions below produced their own barking language to compete with the polyglot human efforts. Cloud recognized the place as home the moment he arrived. It would be his joyful retreat for the next forty-seven weeks.

Five days a week, Cloud attended class from eight to noon and two to four, speaking, translating, reading, and savoring the Vietnamese language as taught by instructors who had been born and raised in Viet Nam. Interspersed with the language study were anecdotes about Vietnamese peculiarities and stories about their culture. In the evenings Cloud did homework, using a reel-to-reel tape recorder in his room. He loved every minute of it.

Weekends were free, and at first he was content to stay in his BOQ reading novels and listening to the radio. He started with James A. Michener's 930-page novel *Hawaii*. As he entered into the world woven by Michener, Cloud found that he did not appreciate the customs of early Hawaiians and positively detested nineteenth century Protestant missionaries, but he resonated with the struggles of the Chinese and Japanese characters. Perhaps this related to his current context of mental immersion into an Asian language. In any case, Michener's tales of the bravery of Japanese-American soldiers during World War II profoundly moved Cloud. The land hunger of the Chinese Kee family matriarch reminded him of Thomas Wolfe's Gant family matriarch in *Look Homeward, Angel*, and also of his father's quiet capitulation to the land anathemas of his mother.

What settled into his long-term imagination, however, was Michener's depiction of the golden man, who is a product of the meeting ground of world cultures. Cloud decided he wanted to be such a man, comfortable with the ideas and ideals of many civilizations.

After a few walled-in weekends, he became restless with living vicariously through the written word and decided to explore the world outside the base.

Pentecost fell on May twenty-ninth, and this was the day set aside for reception of the confirmation class at Second Calvinist Church. Terp, who would celebrate her fourteenth birthday the following day, was the star in this year's group and also the only one who had not yet received the sacrament of baptism. The other teenagers in the class, including her best friend Michelle, had been baptized as infants. Thus Terp alone would feel the liberal three-fold sprinkling of water on her head when the newest members were presented to the congregation.

Argyle Watts' sermon text was Isaiah chapter 60, verse 8: "Who are these that fly as a cloud, and as doves to their windows?" He likened these confirmands to innocent doves and expressed hope that they would be spared from the ravages of the war that was growing more savage in Southeast Asia. He used an image of a peaceful cloud as a recurring motif in the sermon, and drew mental pictures of these innocent young Christians looking out their windows into worlds that offered the possibilities of peace and war. He prayed that these boys and girls would know peace in their lifetimes. It was very effective, and afterward, the parents in the congregation, all of whom had vivid memories of World War II, lauded him for his fine words.

As she listened to her pastor's elevated rhetoric, Terp imagined flying through the air, enfolded in the safe cushions of a cloud, looking down at the benign land below. Then it was time to leave her reverie and come forward for the membership ritual.

After answering the baptismal questions in a clear and confident voice, Terp knelt on the chancel steps and shivered in joy as the Rev. Argyle Watts intoned, "Terry Person, child of God, I baptize you in the name of the Father," and he scooped water from the font and poured it on her brown hair, "and of the Son," and he applied more water, "and of the Holy Ghost," and he added yet more water, letting his hand rest lightly on her head. He began to pray for her, and while his words of thanksgiving for Terp's life flowed into the sanctuary, Terp saw herself enveloped in a dazzling white light that radiated a great sensation of love. Her entire mind basked naked and unashamed in the glow. She began to weep for the sheer joy of it all.

When she stood to join her classmates for the formal welcome into full church membership, her face glowed and her mouth stretched into a wide grin. After the service, Terp asked her parents, who had come to church just this once to see her confirmed, if they had seen the white light.

"No," said Penny, "but we saw your beaming smile."

During the cookies and punch reception, she asked Watts if he had seen it, and he had not. However, he did have a message for her. "Terp, I'd like you to think about someday going to seminary and becoming a minister."

"Me?" she said in a shocked voice.

"Yes, you, young lady. You still have high school and college ahead of you, but it's not too early to think about what God may be calling you to do with your life."

The suggestion excited Terp, but she had never met a female pastor and had no idea how likely such a pathway would be for her. Still, if Rev. Watts thought it was possible, it must be.

Three weeks later, Terp stood in the receiving line after church, waiting her turn to shake hands with the pastor. A disheveled, agitated man entered the narthex from the street and stumbled toward Watts. Unknown to anyone there, the man suffered paranoid schizophrenia and believed someone with a gun was following him with plans to kill him. He mumbled words to this effect as he approached the pastor, turning several times to look over his shoulder for the would-be assailant.

At the moment Terp reached out to shake hands with Watts, the disturbed man brushed by her extended right arm, intent on grabbing the pastor and clinging to him for protection. Immediately upon touching Terp, he calmed down and begged pardon for interrupting and politely asked for a few minutes of the pastor's time when he was available.

To that point, Argyle Watts had been unaware of this man's approach, since he was concentrating on greeting parishioners, and thus did not notice the change in behavior. Terp saw the transformation of demeanor but attributed it to the godly qualities of her pastor. She told her parents that afternoon that Rev. Watts had calmed a disturbed man just by looking into his eyes.

On a humid Saturday morning in June, Terp and Mary were at the dance studio awaiting the start of their regular lessons. Terp was pirouetting around the room, fantasizing about becoming a minister some day. She wondered if ministers ever danced in church and laughed at the provocative silliness of the thought.

Suddenly a sharp pain stabbed her chest, and she fell to her knees. The pain eased, leaving a residual dull ache. Intuitively she knew nothing was wrong with her. Something has happened to someone in my family, she thought. She hurried over to Penny, who was reading a magazine in the corner, and said, "Mom, we need to go home now!"

"Are you alright, dear?" Penny asked.

"I don't know. We just need to go home right now!" Terp said urgently.

When mother and daughters arrived at the house, they found Tom Person crumpled on the living room floor, dead from a heart attack. All thoughts of seminary or becoming a minister disappeared from Terp's consciousness at that moment.

Before the sun set that day she came to doubt the providence of God, for how could a caring God let such a good man die? As she lay in her bed in the darkness of that first night with her father gone, her body ached as if she had been physically beaten. After several hours of conscious grieving and periodically pounding the mattress with her fists, Terp fell into an exhausted sleep.

Toward dawn, she woke with a start, remembering her encounter with the Old One. When all seems lost, look for the floating boy Big Head had told her. Well, all was lost now, she told herself, so where was this boy? Though she took pains to be alert to his appearance, no such entity, incarnate or metaphorical appeared to her in the days ahead, and she fell into depression.

One day the thought occurred to her that since she had met Big Head in Arizona, perhaps the floating boy was there also. She would probably have to make a trip out west to find him. Where was that place in the desert? Her father had said it was somewhere northwest of Goodyear. At the library, Terp consulted a map of Arizona and found Goodyear west of Phoenix. Tracing a finger northwestward, she ran into the White Tank Mountains. Yes, she vaguely remembered mountains in the distance, but the possible locations covered a big area. She would need help in searching it out. The greater problem, she realized, was convincing her mother to make another trip to Phoenix. The dim prospects of this happening deepened her depression.

Terp skipped church three Sundays in a row after the memorial service Argyle Watts conducted for her father. Then she began to miss the liturgy and returned to regular worship. But it wasn't the same spiritual high it had been before. She went to church out of neurotic habit and a sense of ritual obligation but no longer gave her heart unreservedly to the worship.

In time she would admit to herself that her father's quarter century of smoking two packs of cigarettes a day trumped God's desire for him to live well and long. She was nevertheless angry that God allowed humans the free will to kill themselves by degrees through their bad habits. Tom had tried to quit many times and several years earlier had contemplated a radical cessation program at a health ranch in Santa Fe, but he was embarrassed about it and did not follow through. Penny and the girls never knew.

Cloud lay still on his bed, breathing deeply and focusing his thoughts on leaving his body. Soon he floated above the bed and then flew through the wall into the air outside. Once in the open, he directed himself to the top of the bluff and down to the choppy waters of the bay.

As he approached a pod of sea lions, they sensed his invisible presence and began barking vigorously. Cloud thought he could detect a note of fear in their voices. His intention was to listen to them at close quarters to find out if he could discern meaning in their noises. If he could learn to translate human languages, might he also learn to translate the languages of other mammals? The possibility intrigued him.

"Be still so I can converse with you," he thought, for he had no voice when out of his body. "I won't hurt you. I am your friend." The animals quieted somewhat but did not cease barking. After a few minutes hovering over the sea lions, Cloud tired of the experiment and decided to move on and see more of the bay. He sailed upward and swooped down almost to the surface of the water and then up again, like a bird searching for food.

For more than an hour he gamboled in the air currents over the water, a longer time than he had been out of his body before. It felt good to him, as if he were stretching his extra-sensory muscles, building mental endurance. When he returned to his body, he vowed to do this more often. As he did calisthenics and ran laps to keep his physical body in shape, he must also actively exercise his mind beyond academic study.

After this, Cloud set aside time on weekends for exploring the region. On Saturdays he traveled hither and yon by car, and on Sunday mornings he left his body in his BOQ and floated above the bay. He came to think of this latter activity, glorying in the splendors of the natural world, as a ritual of worship for an unbeliever.

It wasn't long before the sea lions accepted his unseen presence as benign, and though he never cracked their language, he felt able to communicate a sense of affection to them through proximity. He dove under the water with them, discovering in the process a new realm to explore. There was much beneath the surface to examine. This reminded him of his dream while sleeping at the bottom of the Grand Canyon. Treasure lay hidden in the fathoms below. But instead of scenes from *The Wizard of Oz*, as in his canyon dream, he witnessed a fantasy-scape of weird sand and rock shapes and funny fish.

His self-confidence grew, for now he was able to experience the realms of air and sea by floating out of his body and the realm of land by using his body to drive and hike. Cloud's mental and physical muscles grew strong during his tenure at the Monterey language school.

Still, he always traveled alone, so his social skills were not developing. His fellow officers were either married or not interested in Cloud's Saturday itineraries, and he was not allowed to fraternize with enlisted personnel. The year at Monterey was evolving into a time of solitary pursuits, but this suited Cloud well enough. He was used to making his way alone.

Once, while walking uphill in Chinatown in San Francisco, he saw a young woman across the street who looked like Darla Zadok, but he knew it was not she. Darla was studying at Kenyon College in Ohio. The sighting reminded him how lonely he was, however. For the next few nights his dreams were filled with images of unrequited love. Darla became for him the ideal of unobtainable womanhood.

He sat quietly on the steep beach at Carmel, staring out to sea, letting the movement of the waves hypnotize him, begging the waves to wash away his longing for love. The image of the dancing girl returned to him, and he ached with desire that was far more spiritual than physical. This was not a good time to fall in love, he told himself, but he needed someone to care for and someone who would know and cherish him. Apart from these periodic pangs of longing, however, Cloud felt stronger and more satisfied with his life than ever before.

On a Saturday trip to Marin County, Cloud happened upon San Francisco Theological Seminary, which caused him to think about Theo. He wondered how Theo was doing with his pacifism studies.

Hiking about the campus, Cloud found the library at the top of the hill in Geneva Hall. That's where a library ought to be, Cloud thought -at the top of a hill. For as long as he could remember he had found it difficult to pass by libraries and bookstores without entering, and this one proved no exception.

CHAPTER TWENTY-ONE

Tempted by the waiting trove of books, Cloud went into the library. A man about his age greeted him from behind the circulation desk. "You look lost, brother. Need help?"

"I'm just looking around. Is that OK?" Cloud stammered.

"Sure thing, soldier," the student said. "Enjoy the window shopping."

"How did you know I'm a soldier?" the civvy clad Cloud asked.

"Haircut's a dead giveaway," the longhaired student responded.

"I'm studying at the Defense Language Institute in Monterey," Cloud said. "Do you have any books on Vietnamese culture or religion?"

"Wow, this is a first. A soldier who wants to learn about the culture of a place before blowing it up!"

"I don't want to blow it up. I want to help protect the people," Cloud explained with a defensive edge in his voice and feeling that he had already had this conversation with Theo.

"Ah yes. Erasmus was indeed right when he wrote, 'Sweet is war to those who do not know it.' By the way, my name's Gunnar Bishop," the student said, and he thrust his hand across the counter toward Cloud. He was as tall as Cloud, just short of six feet, medium build. His face was framed by shoulder length blond hair and hidden by a full beard, which intensified the effect of his piercing blue eyes.

"I'm Cloud Morgan," he said, taking Gunnar's extended hand.

After a few minutes of desultory conversation, Gunnar sent Cloud into the stacks, where he found a book on the Cao Dai religion of Viet Nam. He was not allowed to take anything out of the library, but Gunnar said he could use an unoccupied study carrel and when he was ready to go just leave in the carrel any items he had taken from the shelves.

Cloud soon learned that Cao Dai was a new religion that developed in the southern part of Viet Nam in the 1920s. It incorporated elements of Buddhism, Taoism, Confucianism, animism, and Christianity, attempting to bring them into harmony. Cloud considered the language in Gabriel Gobron's book overly reverent claptrap, but the concept of distilling something of value from all these ancient belief systems, searching for a consistent nugget of truth among them, intrigued him. Viet Nam is a place where the great cultures of East and West have collided, he mused. Therefore it must offer intellectual riches to anyone who looks for them.

Gunnar Bishop stopped by Cloud's carrel curious about what the soldier had found.

"*History and Philosophy of Caodaism*," Cloud said. "Fascinating stuff."

"Hey, I'm off duty in a few minutes. You wanna go get some coffee?" Gunnar asked. He was not a popular student and was eager for companionship.

"Sure, why not."

They drove to a small café in San Anselmo, where over lukewarm coffee and croissants Gunnar told Cloud that he was a pacifist.

"My best friend Theo is a pacifist," Cloud responded. "He's at a seminary in Chicago right now."

"Does he believe in God?" Gunnar asked.

"Of course, he does! He's in seminary isn't he?"

"Not everyone in seminary believes in God," Gunnar proclaimed. "I don't."

"Neither do I," Cloud said.

"Now that really surprises me," Gunnar responded. "I perceive you as more deeply spiritual than most of the students here. A lot of them are pious frauds."

"I really doubt that," Cloud said. "But, tell me how a person who does not believe in God can go to a school that trains people to be Christian ministers."

"Most of the students here do believe in God in some form or another. I'm the exception. But a lot of my classmates, me included, are here because studying for the ministry insures exemption from the draft," Gunnar explained. "The seminary is in an ethical bind. If it refuses to accept students who are conscientious objectors to the war in Viet Nam, but whose religious credentials are, shall we say, less than impressive, it may become the agency of those persons getting drafted and sent off to war. But if it accepts students who have no intention of being ordained but who are simply trying to duck the draft, it taints the pure purpose of the school. Ultimately, I think, the seminary faculty would rather protect a life than maintain purity."

"You're rather brazen to be telling this to an Army Military Intelligence officer," Cloud said. "You don't know me. What if I should report you to your draft board?"

"I do know you, Cloud. My intuition tells me that you not only understand my position but that you can be trusted with not only my secrets but anybody's secrets."

"Well, you're right about that," Cloud confessed.

Thus began a series of weekend treks to San Francisco Theological Seminary where Cloud explored the stacks for material on Southeast Asia, as well as anything else that beckoned to his fancy. He and Gunnar walked and talked and ate lunch together. The common bond of atheism combined with strong attraction to religion transcended their very different views about the nature and necessity of war.

One Saturday afternoon Gunnar said, "Don't come here next week. I want you to meet Irene. She lives in Salinas. We'll pick you up at the main gate and go for a picnic."

And so it happened that Cloud was escorted from the military facility in Gunnar's blue Volkswagen bus with "Thou shalt not kill!" emblazoned in red on both sides. As he climbed into the passenger seat, a freckled hand reached toward him from the back. "Hi. I'm Irene Castle. I've heard a lot about you."

"I'm Cloud Morgan. And I've heard a lot about you too. When are you lovebirds getting married?"

Irene had straight red hair that cascaded to the middle of her back on one side and fell in neat bangs over her forehead on the other. She ignored his question. "I've packed wine and cheese and bread and avocados." She said. "And I know a spot over in Carmel Valley that's just perfect for a picnic."

On the drive into the valley, Gunnar said, "Hey Cloud, I heard a new song you might find amusing." He affected a country twang and lustily sang, "I don't care if it rains or freezes, long as I got my plastic Jesus, riding on the dashboard of my car, yee hah!" He paused to survey Cloud's reaction. "What do you think? Let's make up some more verses about the superstitious dodos with the little statues in their cars."

Cloud said, "Maybe some other time, Gunnar. I'd rather satirize the errant shepherds than the simple sheep who follow them."

"I don't think it's funny at all," piped in Irene. "Having religious doubts is a good thing, but making fun of people's faith is mean."

"It was a priest who taught it to me," Gunnar retorted.

"Just don't sing it around me," Irene pronounced, ending the conversation.

A few minutes later, they reached a grassy meadow where Irene spread blankets on the grass, kicked off her sandals, and began to distribute the food. Gunnar opened the first bottle of Lambrusco and filled three paper cups with the red wine. They soon finished off the French bread, Dutch cheese and California avocados, washed down with two bottles of Italian wine. All they had left were chocolate mints and another bottle of wine, which they felt duty bound to consume.

Cloud, who seldom drank alcoholic beverages and then only in small quantities, was glad he did not have to drive back to the base. As he relaxed into tipsiness, he thought he saw Irene's nipples pressing erectly against her white cotton blouse. He looked away, but the direction his eyes chose to follow was downward to the place where her denim-clad legs formed a vee. A physical response rose inside his jeans. No one seemed to notice his impolite focus, and he quickly regained control by changing the sensual subject that had invaded his consciousness.

"Irene, do you believe in God?" Cloud asked.

"Of course I do. I'm a devout Catholic," she replied. "Well, maybe not devout, but I go to mass more Sundays than I skip."

Cloud continued his probe with tender curiosity. "So how does it work that you're engaged to an atheist?"

"Oh, Gunnar claims to be an atheist, but that's for show. He can't study with the Presbyterians for years without some belief rubbing off on him."

"She's very optimistic," Gunnar interjected. "She's also a Socialist. Why don't you tell Cloud about that, babe? Cloud's a Republican."

Thereupon followed a spirited if not incisive discussion of Socialist saints and Republican heroes. Irene spoke glowingly of Norman Thomas and Henry Wallace, while Cloud invoked Theodore Roosevelt, Barry Goldwater and Ayn Rand. Gunnar considered himself apolitical and offered anathemas upon them all. Amidst the partisan rhetoric the paper cups were dispensed with and the wine bottle passed from mouth to mouth. Laughter rather than rancor characterized their discourse.

Weaving as she went, Irene disappeared into the van, emerging with a guitar. "Let's have a hootenanny!" she proclaimed. She strummed a few chords and stopped. "Wait, let's get dressed first." Irene giggled as she gathered wildflowers that she gently installed behind Gunnar's and Cloud's ears. The sensation of her fingers on his skin caused Cloud's physical yearning to return. When she bent over to pick more and then flirtingly laced them into her hair, he blushed with desire.

Now properly adorned, Irene launched into "Where Have All the Flowers Gone?" Gunnar and Cloud quickly joined in the song.

In the cold soberness of his BOQ the next morning, Cloud wondered if consorting with a Socialist would be considered a subversive activity. He thought back on his security indoctrination at Fort Holabird. Would the Army pull his security clearance if they knew he had been drinking and singing anti-war songs with a draft dodging pacifist and a card carrying Socialist? No, he decided. He did nothing illegal and the authorities were not that stupid.

This conclusion proved to be mistaken, however, because Cloud's travels already had come to the attention of the Army Counter Intelligence unit in San Francisco. Captain Fisgon Beaton, an avid agent in that office, opened a blue border investigation on Lieutenant Evan C. Morgan. Cases involving one of their own required special handling, so such files were identified by a blue border around the cover sheet.

Captain Beaton's inquiry failed to discover Cloud's involvement with Irene Castle, whose anti-war activities had been well documented by the FBI. Nevertheless, he reported that Cloud had been spending a great deal of time at the notoriously subversive San Francisco Theological Seminary. Beaton concluded that Cloud was naïve about Communist infiltration at the pseudo-Christian school. On the plus side, in response to thorough questioning (done at Beaton's own initiative), no one had given any indication that Cloud was homosexual. But since he had claimed no religious preference upon entering the service, Morgan should be watched for signs of un-American behavior. This report filtered up through the chain of command and was ultimately preserved in a basement vault at an Army records repository, never to be seen again.

Cloud continued visiting San Francisco Seminary, haunting the library, and breaking bread with Gunnar. Six weeks passed before he saw Irene again. She stopped by Gunnar's apartment, and since Cloud was already there, the seminarian offered to make dinner for the three of them.

Water was the only beverage imbibed with the food, while the conversation grew sharp and laden with puns pouring forth from each of them. Relaxing with sips of Sherry after the meal, Cloud acknowledged to himself that he really liked Irene. More than liked, he thought. He had fond feelings for her. She was smart as a whip, even if she did have crazy ideas about economics. And her eager, intelligent face presided over a body of classic proportions that Cloud found appealing.

Abruptly changing the subject from the failures of the Johnson administration, Cloud asked, "Irene, do you dance?" He had no idea where the question had come from and was as surprised as she that it had passed his lips.

"No," she said. "I have two left feet. What prompted you to ask?"

"I don't know. I was just remembering the senior prom, a long time ago. I took a girl who reminds me a lot of you, only she was Jewish. She's back east in college right now." Cloud knew he was lying, because the only thing about Irene that reminded Cloud of Darla was sexual attractiveness. The political conversation resumed.

Cloud brooded about Irene for weeks after that dinner. He wanted to go somewhere alone with her, but his ethical standards would not allow him to do that with a woman who was engaged to his friend. By the time he next saw her, at Gunnar's apartment, Cloud had decided he was in love with Irene. He would never tell her how he felt, of course, for she would very likely reject his profession of love. And if by some wild happenstance she expressed reciprocal feelings, this would constitute a major betrayal of his friendship with Gunnar.

At dinner that night, Irene said, "Let's have some music." She rummaged through Gunnar's record collection and pulled out a Ray Charles Album, **Modern Sounds in Country and Western Music**. As the needle hit the groove and Ray's plaintive voice filled the room Cloud felt lonely in the presence of two dear friends. He was working his way through the salad when a song grabbed his attention. It was one of Cloud's favorites, a paean to unrequited love, "You Don't Know Me." Though he had listened to this recording a hundred times, the lyrics now hit him hard. Ray Charles assailed him with the existential reality of his sharing dinner with a woman he loved who did not know how he felt, and he could never tell her. A piece of lettuce caught in his throat and he excused himself to go to the bathroom.

In the privacy of the privy, Cloud let tears roll down his face, being careful to let no sound emanate from his voice. Then he wiped his face with a wet washcloth and returned to dinner. He left soon thereafter, claiming an excess of tape-recorded homework as an excuse for his early departure.

He continued to visit the seminary now and again, but not every weekend, and although he continued to see Gunnar, he avoided situations where he might encounter Irene.

In October, Cloud received a promotion to first lieutenant.

The advent of December undid all the progress Terp had made

toward accepting her father's death. How could she get through Christmas without him? He had always handed out the presents. She lay in bed at night with a dull ache in her chest. Life wasn't fair, she thought. And to make the situation worse, her mother was becoming oppressive. Every time Terp wanted to do something or go somewhere, Penny gave her an intense grilling. Every time Terp tried to talk about how much anger she felt about her father's fatal heart attack, Penny would tell her that she didn't really feel that way.

"You're not angry, dear. You're too sweet to be angry. We're all sad that Tom has gone away, but we'll muddle through," Penny said.

"But I really am angry," Terp retorted. "I'm angry at Dad for smoking and I'm angry at God for letting this happen."

"No, you're not!" Penny snapped. "Don't you ever say anything bad about your father. It's not right to speak ill of the dead. And, I know I'm not one to speak of religious things, but I don't ever want to hear you blaspheme God."

Tom had left his business affairs in such order that his family did not need to worry about financial matters. Penny had sold the business, and with the proceeds from the sale plus Tom's life insurance policies, she was quite well off. The mortgage on the house was fully paid. At least in that dimension of life, Terp and Mary were fortunate they did not have to move from the home they loved, and they did not need to fret about the costs of their future college educations. In addition, each of the girls would receive substantial income from a trust when they reached age twenty-one.

Terp forced herself to attend the Christmas Eve service at Second Calvinist. In the past she had gloried in the music and pageantry, but this year she experienced no sublime joy at the liturgical anticipation of the birth of Christ. Yet she felt intuitively that not going to the service would create a lapse in her life that would make it more difficult to get beyond her grief.

For a time, as the worship unfolded, Terp forgot her loss. As the rising notes of "O Holy Night" sailed through the sanctuary, she allowed herself to be lifted briefly from sadness and inhaled the beauty of the moment.

Penny and Mary went to church with her that night, and afterward, Penny found herself surrounded by neighbors who wanted to express once again their condolences at Tom's passing. Terp took the opportunity to slip outside by herself. The night was cold and clear, and she pulled her coat tight around her chest as she wandered into the far parking lot, away from the crowds of people piling into family sedans where fathers impatiently revved their engines for the journeys home to living rooms full of decorated trees and wrapped packages.

She stared into the sky, wondering about the ironies of existence and sensing the death of Jesus implicit in the celebration of his birth. The good die young, and I wonder if I'm good enough to die young too, she thought. Each day of life is that much closer to inevitable death, her musing continued, but also to the ultimate release from grief. Addressing the stars, she spoke out loud, "This world is such a cruel place. Does God really care about us fragile human beings living here?"

For a moment, her existential cry was greeted with silence, but then a warm sensation developed within her mind that soon spread throughout her body. The stars seemed to double then triple in size, lighting the sky with more intensity than a full moon. Words flashed in her brain. All shall be well. That was it. No exegesis. No elaboration. Simply this: All shall be well.

As if sleepwalking, Terp ambled toward the car, where Penny and Mary were opening the doors.

"What are you doing waiting out here, Terp? You must be frozen," Penny said.

"I'm actually quite warm," Terp responded in a meditative voice.

Mary gazed at her older sister with a look that simultaneously registered disbelief and puzzled awe, but she refrained from making any comment.

Terp said nothing to her mother about the burgeoning of the stars or the message she had received. Penny would not believe the former and would not understand the latter. This was in the same private category as her encounter in the desert with Big Head. And yet, she thought, this mystical experience seemed of a higher order than her meeting with that strange creature in the desert. If Big Head's omen had any substance to it, the floating boy was definitely a truant. This radiant reassurance, however, went beyond flesh and blood advice.

A large portion of Terp's grief lifted that night, and in the coming months, she found it much easier to live with what she perceived as her mother's controlling ways.

Even so, she experienced a deep emptiness whenever she remembered that she and her dad had never found a time to see **Fiddler on the Roof**. She could never see it now, she thought, for every minute of the show her heart would ache at his absence.

III

XUAN

Thou art the gold and the crystal of heaven.
Ngo van Chieu
Founder of Caodaism

Imagine a lotus blooming in a fire.
Dao Hue

Everything in the world follows the path of war:
I sit on my bed and meditate through the long night.
Tu Fu

CHAPTER TWENTY-TWO

Cloud did not take leave over the Christmas holiday but holed up in his room, reading novels. He had a stash of books to escape into, and so on Christmas day, he opened to the Prologue of James Hilton's *Lost Horizon*. Escape into the book he did, reading straight through to the end and then immediately starting a second reading, which he completed in meditative fashion. His only criticism was the book's brevity. Cloud craved much more information about the people in the mysterious place of its setting.

Still, there was much for him to contemplate in the 1933 novel about a group of people whose plane crashed in the mountains of Tibet near the utopia of Shangri-La. He was taken with the thematic conflation of Christianity and Buddhism, particularly in light of his study of the syncretistic Cao Dai religion of Viet Nam.

He chuckled knowingly when he compared *Lost Horizon* with *Atlas Shrugged*. In Rand's novel, the heroine Dagny Taggart crashed her plane in an inaccessible section of the Rocky Mountains of Colorado, finding herself in the utopian valley called Galt's Gulch. In Hilton's earlier novel, the plane carrying protagonist Hugh Conway crashed in an inaccessible area of the Himalayas in Tibet, with Conway and three other passengers soon escorted into the utopian valley of Shangri-La. Once the similarities had been set in Cloud's mind, he rushed to fill in the contrasting blanks.

Galt's Gulch was an ideological Eden, operating according to the philosophical laws of Objectivism. Shangri-La was a non-ideological paradise where study and contemplation of opposites were encouraged. The religion of Shangri-La was a moderate combination of Buddhism and Christianity, with a dose of respectful doubt about each. The religion of Galt's Gulch was an atheocratic insistence on the primacy of reason.

Both utopias built economies based on a gold standard, and in both bureaucratic government was not welcome. The ideal in Shangri-La was to govern as little as possible, and in Galt's Gulch the ideal was no government at all. Galt's Gulch was a refuge for the greatest minds of the nation, who were on strike against supporting the collectivist rabble. Shangri-La was a sanctuary for those who wished to contemplate, understand, and appreciate the world and all its contradictions, without hurry. Any who found their ways to the valley were welcomed, regardless of their beliefs or values.

Cloud found himself drawn toward the moderate beliefs of Shangri-La, with its gracious acceptance of human foibles, and away from the less forgiving certainties of Galt's Gulch. He also resonated with Hilton's lamas, who practiced techniques of body control, levitation and extended life spans. This reminded him of *Stranger in a Strange Land*, which he had liked for the same reason. Both books -*Stranger* and *Horizon*- offered him assurance of his own normality.

As the year 1967 dawned, Cloud eagerly anticipated the coming of spring, when he expected to travel outside the United States for the first time. Graduation from language school would come in March, and so in January he submitted a request for assignment to the Republic of Viet Nam. He harbored no doubt about the request being approved. It would be absurd to invest eleven months studying the language of that nation only to be sent to Panama or Germany. However, he was uncertain as to the kind of unit he would be serving in. His preference was a slot in the southern part of the country, so he would be close to Cao Dai temples.

First Lieutenant Evan Cloud Morgan graduated with high commendation, and when he received overseas orders, he was not disappointed. In April he would report to Travis Air Force Base for transportation to Ton Son Nhut Air Base. He was assigned to a Military Intelligence Battalion headquartered in Cholon, the Chinese suburb of Saigon, where he would serve as section leader of a translation and analysis unit.

First, however, he needed to go home for a few weeks. He realized he wanted to see his parents before departing for the other side of the world. Now that he was older and more independent, he reasoned, he could reconnect with them as an adult and establish a better relationship with each of them, so that he would not be alienated from his family while serving in a war zone.

In early April, Terp's English teacher decided to prove a point about language. "Now that you're nearing the end of your first year of high school English," she said to the class, "it's time you were exposed to Chaucer. But as plainly as Chaucer wrote, this is difficult for you to do, because the English he used -Middle English- is a different language from the Modern American English we read and write today. To read Chaucer is to read a foreign language. You might think you understand it because the words look similar, but the *meanings* of many of those familiar looking words have changed. So you'd only be fooling yourself."

The teacher produced a typewritten page and as was her annual habit handed it to the brightest student in the class. She reasoned that when the class brain stumbled over Middle English vocabulary and syntax, the rest of the students would laugh and then relax and not be self-conscious when she called on them to scan strange verses aloud.

"This is the Prologue to *The Canterbury Tales*, Terp. In Middle English. Please read a few lines to the class."

Terp had never seen a text of Chaucer's great poem in any language. She adjusted her glasses and without rehearsal began to read:

> *Whan that Aprill with his shoures soote*
> *The droghte of March hath perced the roote*
> *And bathed every veyne in swich licour*
> *Of which vertu engendered is the flour.*

The words flowed familiarly from her lips as if she had often spoken this archaic tongue. Her stress and syllable pronunciation were authentic. The language resonated in the depths of her universal memory.

Stunned at Terp's unexpected fluency, the teacher quickly fell back to another task designed to demonstrate the problems of translation. "Excellent, Terp. Now please translate what you have just read into Modern English."

"Let me think a moment," said Terp. Silently she scanned the lines a second time, sensing they would open to her, and then she said, "How about this? 'When in April with his -I suppose we would say ***its***- sweet showers, the dryness of March has pierced to the root and bathed every vein in such liquor, by virtue of which the flower is engendered.' Is that about right?"

"That's exactly right," said the teacher. "How did you...when did you learn this? Did one of my last year's students tip you off?"

"No, ma'am," said Terp. "I've never read Chaucer before this moment. It just seemed natural. Apart from spelling, it's not much different from Modern English."

"If you weren't such an able student, Terp, I might suspect you of cheating," the teacher said.

The words stung, burrowing into Terp's superego, creating a sensation of physical pain in her forehead. Ordinarily, when embarrassed, Terp blushed. Now she paled in anger. "I've never cheated in my life," she said defiantly.

"I'm sure you haven't," responded the teacher. But she resented Terp's linguistic gift and avoided calling on Terp the rest of the term.

While in Phoenix, Cloud signed his car over to Lloyd, who promised to sell it and put the money in a savings account for Cloud to retrieve when he returned from the war. He would miss that Ford. It had taken him to many interesting places, but it was time to let go of it.

Cloud discovered that his relationship with his parents had indeed changed during his absence. Lloyd now treated him with deference, taking him for a walk over to Jordan's on Central Avenue, for man-to-man talk about war over a couple of Olympia beers. Cloud learned nothing specifically new from Lloyd about his overseas service in World War II, but he did feel that his father now respected him.

"There is just one thing I want you to know, Cloud," said Lloyd in a voice approximating a whisper. "I love you, Son."

"I love you too, Dad, and I'm sure that I will come home from the war just fine."

"I pray so, Cloud. I'll pray every day for your safety."

Narcissa seemed to have no doubts about Cloud's invincibility and talked him into making an appearance in uniform at one of her Ladies' Patriotic Beauty Society sessions. "Ladies, the inside news today is that my son, First Lieutenant Cloud Morgan, will soon take up his post in a super-secret unit in South Viet Nam." She beamed adoringly at the handsome fruit of her womb. "Cloud, tell the ladies as much as you can about your work without, of course, revealing any classified information."

Cloud was embarrassed, but did not want to create a scene, so he said, "I'm sorry that I can't tell you anything about my assignment, other than I will be stationed in a safe city, doing boring administrative tasks."

"He's so terribly modest," Narcissa interjected.

Cloud left, feeling angry his mother had used him to sell flag-draped underwear.

Near the end of his leave, he visited the Military Intelligence field office in Phoenix looking for Mercury and learned his friend had been posted to an intelligence unit in Viet Nam. Perhaps he would see him in-country. Cloud considered visiting his high school ROTC advisor to force a salute out of him but dismissed the idea as petty.

As the Pan American jet carrying Cloud to war rose over the Pacific, the voice of Bobby Darin singing "Beyond the Sea" echoed in his mind, and he sensed with eagerness something prophetic in the lyrics.

The first thing Cloud noticed was the humidity. Raised in the arid heat of Arizona, where summer highs routinely reach 115 degrees in the shade and occasionally 120, the prospect of the high nineties in Saigon did not concern him, but he had never experienced the drenching moist air found midway between the Tropic of Cancer and the equator. It was near the end of the dry season, and he would soon learn that daily rain was something to be ignored. Unlike the sparse annual rainfall over Phoenix that comes in sudden downpours and then disappears entirely for parching months, Cloud discovered that rain in Viet Nam is prodigal. More rain fell on Saigon in the month of May than fell on Phoenix in a year, and May was the driest month of the wet season. He accepted in stoic fashion that dampness would accompany him always in this tropic country.

When he deplaned at Ton Son Nhut, north of the city, Cloud was shuffled into a waiting area at the end of a large wooden barracks. He observed newly arrived soldiers being herded into buses and two-and-a-half-ton trucks and assumed that he would soon be joining some such vehicle.

Through wooden window slats he watched a canvas-top jeep pull up to the front door and saw a small man with what looked to Cloud like Middle Eastern features step out and enter the barracks.

"I'm here to pick up First Lieutenant Evan C. Morgan," the man announced. "Is the lieutenant present?"

"I'm Morgan," Cloud said.

"Good afternoon, sir. I'm Spec 5 Arquimedes Shapiro. Colonel Melita has sent me to get you. We're anxious to have you start work as soon as possible."

"Good to meet you, Shapiro. Which way do we go?"

"Follow me, sir."

Cloud reached for his duffel bag but Shapiro ducked in and took it from him. "Allow me, sir," he said.

"I don't mind carrying my own bag," Cloud said.

"Well, sir, I'd like to carry it for you just this time, as a welcoming gesture, but as this is a war zone, this will probably be the last time anyone does anything for you simply because you're an officer," Arquimedes said. He lifted the flap and tossed the duffel bag into the back of the jeep.

As they careened down the crowded road, heading for Cholon south of the city, Cloud said, "Tell me about the unit I've been assigned to."

"The Ten-0-Seventh Military Intelligence Battalion, sir, is an exceptionally fine outfit, where military intelligence is not an oxymoron. We're professionals who do our jobs without a lot of

Army bullshit. You'll soon learn the specifics of handling captured documents. I'm part of the team you'll be leading."

"You have an unusual name. How did you come by it?" Cloud enquired.

"My father is Jewish, originally from Germany, and there's a long story about how he got to the States. I'll tell it to you sometime. My mother is Mexican, and she also has an interesting story about migrating to the US. They met in San Diego, where I was born. I'm 100% American."

"Wow," said Cloud. "That's quite a heritage. Do you mind if I ask you a personal question...about religion?"

"Not at all, sir. And I'll answer it before you can ask it. My mother was Catholic when she came north, but she got hooked up with a group of Christian Scientists and converted before she met my father. Papa was not observant in those days, and when I came along, he was satisfied for Mama to take me to Christian Science services. Later, Mama became upset with the uniform lessons in the church. She wanted something more spontaneous, and so she left and joined a splinter group called the Church of Motherly Healing. The CMH allows people of other faiths to be part of the fellowship without converting, so Papa started coming to Sunday service with us and also resumed attendance at synagogue on Friday evenings."

"Wow again," Cloud said.

"Not what you were expecting, was it, sir?"

"Indeed not," Cloud answered. "I'm glad we'll be working together, Arquimedes, because I'm going to want to pick your brain about your religious experience."

As the jeep neared to within a block of the 1007th MI Battalion office, Shapiro suddenly pulled the vehicle to the right and off the roadway.

"What's going on?" Cloud asked.

"Look there, sir! A caravan of deuce-and-a-halfs heading toward the Delta. We have to get out of the way or they'll ram us. They hate us chairborne types."

Cloud saw the chain of utility trucks forcing traffic off the street. Each truck carried a squad of infantrymen in its open bed. The soldiers, in steel helmets and jungle fatigues and clutching M-16 rifles, were singing above the roar of the engines. Cloud thought he heard strains of an old Coasters song, "Poison Ivy." He climbed out of the jeep to watch the parade.

A Vietnamese teenager on a Lambretta motor scooter swerved out of the path of the lead truck, and at that moment, the thick twine wrapped around a basket of figs on the back of the scooter snapped and the basket fell into the roadway. An olive drab truck, with its cargo of American soldiers singing old rock and roll songs, rolled right over the basket of fruit, crushing it under heavy tires.

Cloud sensed this represented a minor loss for the family of the Lambretta driver and was about to put the incident out of his mind when he turned and looked at a young woman standing ten feet away. She was the most beautiful woman he had ever seen. Objectively speaking and using Western criteria for beauty, this was not so. But something in her posture and long black hair and the fragile lines of her face formed an image in Cloud's mind of ideal loveliness.

She had witnessed the same scene but seemed to react to it with deeper emotion than Cloud. She gasped and immediately covered her mouth with her hands, appearing to be shaken by the event. Instinctually, Cloud moved toward her to offer help, but Arquimedes touched his sleeve.

"Come on, lieutenant. We've got to get going."

The young woman rushed up the street and disappeared into an office. Cloud delayed returning to the jeep long enough to step into the road and retrieve the sole surviving fig that had rolled into a rut and thus escaped destruction. He had no conscious reason for salvaging the piece of fruit, and the driver of the Lambretta had left the scene with his life and vehicle intact, so Cloud could not give it back to its owner. Nevertheless, some whimsical intuition led him to pick it up and wrap it in his handkerchief.

"I think I'll save this for a snack," he said to Arquimedes. "And by the way, do you by any chance know that woman who was standing near us?"

"Yes, sir. That's *Co* Xuan. She works for MACV down the way from us."

"I wonder why Miss Xuan was so upset about that deuce-and-a-half smashing a basket of fruit?" Cloud mused.

Arquimedes did not answer, for at that moment, he turned the jeep into a blind alley that led to a dilapidated warehouse that would be Cloud's place of employment for months to come.

Xuan sat at her desk doubly agitated by what had just happened on the street. Normally a very efficient administrator, she was unable to concentrate on the stack of papers in front of her. Seeing the Army truck drive over the basket of figs had completed a vision she had experienced in 1953, so long ago that she had begun to believe it would never happen. The event was unnerving, but a second shock accompanied it. In 1959 she had seen a gecko turn into a Caucasian boy who looked at her and smiled, and that vision returned to mind today when she looked at that American lieutenant who had also seen the truck crush the figs. How were these two visions connected? Why did she think of the smiling boy on the ceiling of her room at the very time the earlier vision came true?

She moved papers from one stack to another, pretending to make assessments of procurement needs for special units, but in reality, the words on the papers were meaningless blurs. After a few minutes she stopped the charade and placed her hands palm down on two piles of documents and closed her eyes. Attempting to calm her pounding heart and quiet her racing brain, she focused on breathing slowly and deeply, inhaling and exhaling in a deliberate rhythm.

The technique achieved its goal, and as her mind calmed, Xuan became mindful that the two earlier visions were simply facets of the same experience. For some as yet unknown reason, she and that lieutenant were destined to share the observation of this event.

Many American soldiers, officers and enlisted men, had asked her for dates, and she had said no to all of them. She did not want to become entangled emotionally with men of another race from another country. But after today, she knew that if this particular American soldier should invite her to dinner -and she felt certain he would- she would say yes.

Xuan's reverie was broken by a co-worker. *Ong* Mut's position was no higher than Xuan's, but being the only male Vietnamese employee in the section, he pretended to be the supervisor. The long fingernail on his right pinky announced he was from the elite social class who eschewed physical labor. Mut smacked his swagger stick on her desk. "Wake up, *Co* Xuan! We are at war. You must work hard."

Xuan glanced up at the would-be martinet and said, "You slept at your desk yesterday. Maybe some day, someone will clip your fingernail while you are dozing."

Mr. Mut snorted and walked away.

After reporting to Colonel Melita, Cloud had been given two hours to stow his gear in the BOQ, get a shower, grab a sandwich and report back to the unit for orientation. At the officers' mess, he ate something that was called a cheeseburger but tasted like fermented cardboard between slices of dry sponge.

Spec 5 Shapiro led him to his desk in the Document Exploitation Unit. It was covered with stacks of typed and handwritten papers waiting his disposition. "We're way behind, sir, because of the time it took to get you here as a replacement."

"Well, what on earth do I do with all this stuff?" Cloud asked.

"This pile here, sir, is documents that have no tactical value but might be helpful for our strategic understanding of the situation. This next pile is material of tactical importance, but not urgent." He pointed to a gap on the desk and said, "If there were anything here, sir, it would be for immediate transfer to the highest priority analysis unit. But, of course, all those documents were taken care of because we didn't want to miss something important while waiting for you to get here."

"What's this?" Cloud asked, pointing to a pile of paper at the back of his desk.

"Oh, that's stuff that's really interesting but of no particular intelligence value. Personal letters and things like that. Your predecessor, Lieutenant Kennan, wanted us to give him these things so he could improve his vernacular skills during the lulls."

Cloud's team read captured documents and provided preliminary analyses of the intelligence value, if any, of the material. Over the coming months, Cloud would observe soldiers with muddy boots and rumpled fatigues coming in from the field to deliver boxes filled with papers, paraphernalia, books, magazines, and letters they had retrieved from tunnels, pulled out of rice barrels, and snatched from the hands of captured Viet Cong guerrillas. They also brought in things they had taken from houses, huts, and pagodas. Anything that had Vietnamese words on it was scooped up by infantrymen on their sweeps and raids, and in the tens of thousands, these documents would appear with prodigal regularity on the desks of the men in Cloud's unit.

Within a few weeks, Cloud became expert in the nomenclature of VC unit rosters, order of battle documents, and after action reports. He examined fake ID cards, cadre instructions, propaganda leaflets, onionskin lists of cell members, personal diaries, and family photographs.

As the months passed, reading these documents and viewing these photos produced in his mind a sense of a large community somewhere out in the bush. He experienced the members of this community only on paper, but he knew their names. He knew who had been killed and who had done heroic deeds. He knew how many meals they missed, how lonely they were hiding in tunnels, and how disciplined they were. And all the people of this community were enemies of his country.

Saigon, the city of America's Republican allies, shone in maculate contrast to this ascetic Viet Cong culture. Cloud observed street children selling sex photos to soldiers and watched French women in bikinis water-ski on the Saigon River. Thousands of refugees continued to push into the city, he noted, where of necessity they bathed and relieved themselves in crowded public lanes.

"Hey, Lieutenant Morgan, take a look at this." Arquimedes handed him a small, handmade envelope.

Cloud read the address aloud, translating by sight. "From Minh Huu, cell 756 to Mai Huu Phong, cell 656 -examined and approved 30-3-67 at cell 856." He unfolded the envelope and read the message inside. "I, your loving brother, hope to hear from you soon, my Yellow River maiden."

"What do you make of it, sir?" Arquimedes asked.

"It's **nhan tin**, a love letter," he said. He had learned in Monterey that lovers in Viet Nam referred to themselves affectionately as brother and sister. "But it's unusual. It's been censored by a VC cadre official. How'd you like me to censor your love letters, Shapiro? It also has direct intelligence value due to the coded cell numbers. Of course it's more than a month old. Run the cell numbers and see if these match anything else."

The letter was not an important document, but it captured Cloud's imagination and caused him to reflect on the persistence of love in the midst of ideological struggles and guerrilla warfare. He wondered where these Viet Cong lovers were at that moment. How old were they? What work did they do for the VC? What did this Yellow River maiden look like? Were either or both of the lovers even alive?

This led him to remembrance of the beautiful woman he had seen on the sidewalk his first day in Saigon. Her name was Xuan - Springtime- and according to Arquimedes, **Co** Xuan, so she was not married. He wanted to find her and take her to dinner, perhaps, he thought, at the **Champs Elysees** in the Caravelle Hotel. Then maybe they would go dancing. He would certainly want to find out if she were a dancer.

In the distance he heard a temple bell resound deeply, calling the people within earshot to mindfulness, to pause and be content and aware in the present moment. Cloud paused to think about the life of the monk who had purposefully rammed the sounding pole into the bell. Words of one of his instructors at Monterey returned to mind. She had gently explained to her American students that a Vietnamese monk would never say he had struck a bell but rather he had simply invited it to toll.

The circuitry in his brain then leaped to the fig he had retrieved from the street, which was still in his room. He decided to discover where **Co** Xuan worked and go there with the fig and give it to her as a mindful demonstration that they had, in a sense, already met.

CHAPTER TWENTY-THREE

Finding Xuan's office proved easy. Cloud strolled the two blocks from his office and entered the MACV annex, where he was directed down the hall to a large room with a dozen desks, occupied by eleven Vietnamese women and one scowling man. He saw her immediately and nervously stepped to the front of her desk.

"*Chao Co. Co manh gioi, phai khong?*" he said in her language.

"Hello, lieutenant. I am well. How are you?" she replied in English using a calm, neutral tone. She was not surprised he had found her and was happy he had, but propriety demanded showing no sign of eagerness.

"You speak English very well. Where did you study?" he asked.

"I attended *Hoi Viet My* English language school in Saigon. Have you heard about it?"

"Yes, it's an American school. Very good, I'm told." Cloud had rehearsed how this conversation would go, what he would say, but now that he was standing in front of her, he couldn't remember the words he had planned to say. "Er...uh... *toi ten* Cloud Morgan. We've met before, sort of, when that convoy came through and ran over that basket of figs."

"Yes, I remember," she said.

245

"You do?"

"*Toi ten* Nguyen thi Xuan. And pardon me; I've been rude. Please sit down," she said.

He sat in the folding chair next to her desk and said, "I've brought you a small gift." He reached into his overseas cap and pulled out the fig. "I don't know why, but my intuition told me this would mean something to you." He placed the fruit on her desk. "I rescued it from the street that day."

Tears fell from her eyes. She cradled the fig in her hands but did not speak.

"Oh, I'm so sorry," he said. "I've made a terrible mistake. Please forgive me. I did not intend to hurt you."

"You did not hurt me, lieutenant," she said. "This is the most beautiful gift I have ever received. You see, it was not crushed. It survived. This is a good...what is the word...?"

"Omen, a sign of a future event," he said. "In English we say something is either a good or bad omen."

She held the now dried piece of fruit before her face, inspecting it as if it were a small *objet d'art*. "Yes, a good omen, I think."

"I think we need to talk some more about this fig," he said. "Would you do me the honor of having dinner with me tonight?"

"*Phai*," she said. "Yes."

The restaurant on the ninth floor of the Caravelle Hotel offered a panoramic view of the city, but it was wasted on Cloud and Xuan, for they were so intent on listening to one another they were oblivious to the world around them. Their conversation drifted in and out of English and Vietnamese as they revealed the basics of their lives -where they were born, where they went to school, what their parents were like.

"I have an older brother," she said. "He was in the Army, I think somewhere in Can Tho Province, but I heard that he deserted. I have not seen him in more than a year. He did not come home for Tet, and that is a bad omen."

"Do you live with your parents?" he asked.

"They are dead. My father acted in the coup against Diem, and for a long time he feared revenge. But nothing happened, so he let himself believe he was safe. That was when secret Diem loyalists found out and killed him two years ago. My mother mourned for him until she died of a breaking heart."

"I'm sorry," Cloud said.

"For holidays I visit my older sister and her husband in My Tho, and I play with my nephews and nieces," she continued in matter-of-fact fashion.

"Forgive me for prying," he said, "but why were you so upset when the deuce-and-a-half ran over that basket?"

Xuan had never told anyone about her vision in the Ben Thanh Market, and she was not sure she wanted to let the story escape now. Telling her father the Diem vision had resulted only in more suffering. If Cloud had not brought her the surviving fig, she would not have revealed the secret, at least not this first night. But it seemed as if she had known Cloud for years, and despite her natural reticence, she trusted him.

"When I was seven," she began, "I saw a vision in the marketplace. That was fourteen years ago." She described the experience. "After so many years, nothing like the vision happened, so I believed that it was imagination only. But you saw it too, so you know it was not my imagination. It was only delayed."

"Why would you expect the vision you saw when you were seven to actually occur?" he asked.

"Ah. There were other visions that did...how do Americans say it?...come true," she confessed.

In the spirit of the moment Cloud felt an overwhelming need to confess also, at least some of his secrets. "I understand. Months before it happened, I had a dream that President Kennedy would be shot."

"I saw also in a vision the president being killed," she said.

"President Kennedy?"

"No, President Diem. I had a vision of his death and it happened that way."

It soon developed that their respective prescient experiences of presidential assassinations had occurred at the same time. Confessions of other dreams and visions tumbled from their mouths, joyful in the rare atmosphere of understanding and acceptance. But Xuan held back her vision of the boy in khaki floating on her ceiling, and Cloud did not reveal his out-of-body experiences. These revelations would have to wait for another more intimate time.

As Cloud escorted Xuan to her apartment, he asked casually, "By the way, do you dance?"

"I studied Vietnamese folk dance in school, but not American style," she said.

Following Vietnamese custom, he did not try to hold her hand as they rode together in the cyclo, nor did he kiss her at her door. He did, however, make another date for dinner at the end of the week. Whatever vestiges of longing for Darla or Irene that may have clung to the cells of Cloud's brain were washed away in a torrent of interest in Xuan. Her face, her eyes, her voice filled his mind that sleepless night. He was smitten and could not wait to see her again.

Xuan's feelings were similar to Cloud's, except for an element of fear that he lacked. She was afraid a romantic relationship with an American would lead inevitably to tragedy. Even kindly and polite Americans lacked a certain depth of civilization. They were manifestly simple, without awareness of subtlety. All the women she knew from the office who had become involved with American men reported these things. It was bad enough for a Vietnamese woman to go out with a Chinese, but an American could fly away in a year and ruin one's reputation forever. Some of her co-workers had been abandoned by American soldiers without even a word of farewell.

Of course, Lieutenant Cloud Morgan was different. There was something spiritual about him. But could she trust her belief that he truly was different, the exception to the rule about boorish Americans? Her parents would not approve, but they were dead. Her brother wouldn't care, but her sister might shun her for dating an American. Xuan was strongly attracted to Cloud, but determined to guard against falling in love with him.

One thought, however, trumped all her fears. She was certain that Cloud was the now grown up boy she had seen in a vision years before. Whether for good or ill, her Buddhist sense of karma informed her that Cloud was a necessary and inevitable part of her life, and she must not run away from her fate.

In the village of Can Giouc, ten kilometers south of Saigon, the Old One sat deep in meditation in a shack made of aluminum beer can sheet metal. At the edge of a nearby hamlet, seven year-old Tran Huu Den had become curious about a string and metal contraption beside the path to the rice paddies. He walked toward the apparatus, curious if it was something he could play with. The Old One was intent on distracting the boy, thus causing a flock of birds to dart in unison from a Bo tree. Den turned to follow the flight of the birds, and at that moment, a message appeared in his mind. Your mother is looking for you, it said. The message happened to be true, but his mother had not been its source, since she was not at that particular time worried about his safety. The Old One had conveyed that thought to him.

I'd better get home, Den thought, and forgot about the potential toy. Five minutes later, a squad of American soldiers tramped through the hamlet, and the point man spotted and destroyed the explosive device that was packed with feces-coated nails.

As these events were unfolding, the Viet Cong sapper who had set this booby trap slipped into Can Giouc and crept into an apparently deserted beer logo emblazoned shack behind the local elementary school. In actuality, the Old One, clad from neck to feet in a fine saffron robe, occupied the shack, but in the darkness the VC could see no one.

As the guerrilla crawled across the floor in search of a comfortable spot to curl up and sleep, his shoulder bumped into something unseen and he swore a reactive oath. But he could see nothing there, so he dismissed his clumsiness and crawled under a piece of canvas and closed his eyes. Sleep, however, eluded him.

Instead of rest, his mind filled with bright images of violent deeds he had performed -setting booby traps, executing village leaders, mutilating dozens of corpses. A sense of remorse enveloped him. The pain of recognition grew intense, causing him to shudder uncontrollably. So focused was he on the atrocities for which he bore responsibility that he was unable to perceive the wave of compassion that also surrounded him. The VC threw off the canvas, scrambled out of the shack and ran off into the countryside.

The Old One continued mentally surveying the region. For an instant before moving on to other concerns, the venerable being took note of Xuan and Cloud sitting together in a restaurant, the recognition of which produced a brief otherworldly smile.

In the dim light of the Chinese restaurant on Tan Da Street in Cholon, Cloud reached across the table and gently scooped Xuan's right hand into his left. She did not pull away.

"Hands tell a lot about a person," he said and began to trace her palm with his right index finger.

"What can you tell about me from my hands?" she asked.

Cloud lightly massaged the palm and fingers of her right then her left hand. "They reveal that you are beautiful, gentle yet determined, and very intelligent," he pronounced.

"How do they reveal that?"

"I don't know," he confessed, "but my words are true, and it gave me an excuse simply to touch your hands." He paused, allowing time for a response, but she said nothing. He continued to caress her hands, and broke the silence by saying, "What I really want to do is to touch your hair, your face, your cheeks and lips with the tips of my fingers, but I know that would not be respectful in public."

"No, it would not," she confirmed.

"Don't worry, Xuan. You're perfectly safe with me. I'm not the high-pressure type. I'll be the perfect gentleman just for the sheer pleasure of being in the same room with you."

"I believe you are a fine gentleman," she said. "And sometime I would like you to touch my face and maybe kiss me. But not here."

The food arrived and the conversation turned to other matters.

"I'd like to visit some pagodas and temples sometime. Would you be able to give me a guided tour?" Cloud said. "I'm particularly interested in the Cao Dai Temple in Tay Ninh."

"We will find time to visit temples," she answered. "That will be my honor to show you."

That night there was no good night kiss. Cloud sensed that Xuan was not ready, and he did not want to spoil a beautiful relationship with a display of American impatience. He returned to his BOQ pulsing with happiness merely from touching her hand. The next morning, after a night of deep and dreamless sleep, Cloud found his desk piled high with new documents. The real reason for his presence in Viet Nam once again claimed his attention. But in occasional moments of reflection, Cloud entertained the notion that the real reason he had come to the Paris of the Orient had more to do with Xuan than with the captured documents on his desk.

— ⊖ —

Looking up from piles of document clutter, Cloud saw Arquimedes approaching with more papers. "Hey, Shapiro," he said, "on my first day here you told me there was a space on my desk for high priority urgent documents, but that you'd already taken care of them. I've been here nearly three months and nothing new has been added to that space. What gives?"

"Well, sir, that's a just-in-case space. Lieutenant Kennan handled one of those urgent documents about three months before you came. You never know. We might get another one any day now."

Cloud invited Arquimedes to sit in the chair next to his desk. "I've been wondering about this Church of Motherly Healing you belong to. You don't have to talk about your religion if you don't want to, but if you'd like to, I have a few questions."

"What would you like to know, sir?"

"I know a little bit about Christian Science. How is your church different?"

Arquimedes squirmed in his chair as if he were settling in for a long story. "To begin with, sir, they are a lot alike. We use Mary Baker Eddy's *Science and Health* and believe in spiritual healing. Where we're different is that each CMH congregation is independent. We have no Mother Church to tell us what to do. And we've incorporated some of the Alcoholics Anonymous practices into our healing services. We don't have Readers, like the CS Church, and we don't have pastors like the Protestants. Instead, each CMH congregation is led by a Spiritual Nurse, who can be male or female."

"What I'm interested in," Cloud said, "is what you believe about the material world. Do you believe that it doesn't exist?"

"Oh, we believe that God exists. God is real, and that which we perceive as material is illusion. We are only real as spiritual incarnations of God, but what you would call flesh and blood are not the true reality," Arquimedes explained.

"OK," said Cloud, "I met a man who had a leg blown off in World War II, and he was angry about it. But if I understand correctly, you would say that his leg wasn't real to begin with, so he has no reason to be angry at losing it. Is that right?"

"Well, he believes that it's real, so that's the problem. If he would recognize that in the mind of God -that is, in reality- he is perfectly whole, he wouldn't have to be angry about the illusion of injury."

"Fascinating," said Cloud. "I've been doing some reading on Buddhism, which also focuses on the role of worldly illusion. Thanks for sharing with me, Arquimedes. I'd like to talk again sometime about the existence or nonexistence of evil."

"And what better place to discuss it than in a war zone, sir."

"Sometimes I think the war is an illusion," Cloud sighed. "It's like a novel unfolding on these papers that pass in and out of this place. Intellectually I know there's violent stuff going on out there in the field, but the field seems to be in another world far away."

"Don't kid yourself, lieutenant. It's a lot closer than you think. It's when you start to think these papers are not important that you miss something that will save somebody's life."

"Coming from one who believes I'm an illusion, that's quite an admonition," Cloud responded.

"Well, sir, I'm not very advanced in my spiritual practice, and I feel the need to look out for people I care about." Arquimedes stood up to return to his desk. "And if I may say, sir, being in love creates another whole set of illusions."

Cloud laughed. "Get back to work, Arquimedes. We'll have no talk about the illusions of love."

Xuan took Cloud to see two Buddhist pagodas not far from each other on Lac Long Quan Street. The first, Giac Lam, was built in the middle of the eighteenth century. Remembering his class in Oriental architecture at ASU, Cloud looked at the square layers of roof with corners rising into hooks and thought it seemed more Khmer than Vietnamese.

"You are partly right," said Xuan. "This is the oldest pagoda in Saigon, and it shows influences from China, India, and Cambodia, home of the Khmer civilization. This place is very important for Vietnamese Buddhists. When we fought the French, many people hid here."

After a respectful period of meditative observation of the old temple, Xuan said, "Come with me now. I want to show you another pagoda." She led him down the street to the Phat Bao Temple. "This one was built two years ago," she said.

"It's completely different," Cloud said. "The lines are rounded and gentle while the lines of Giac Lam are angular and piercing."

"Buddhism is like both," Xuan said. "Many differences living together on the same street."

"My impression is that Buddhism is a tolerant religion," Cloud said.

"Yes, much more tolerant than Christianity. One can be a Buddhist and a Taoist and a Confucian at the same time," she explained. "Some monks even teach that one can be a Christian and Buddhist at the same time, but the Christians don't accept this."

"No, I don't suppose they would," Cloud offered.

Xuan said, "When Diem was president, many Buddhists were forced to become Christian. They were killed if they refused to be baptized."

"Any religion that resorts to force to get people to accept it is morally bankrupt," Cloud declared. "Coercion is a sign of fear and a tacit admission of the failure of one's ideas. If a religion cannot attract believers solely by the content of its message, it is a truly sad religion."

"But not all Christians behave that way," she said, coming to the defense of an alien faith. "Most Christians I know are respectful of other religions."

"Speaking of being killed for one's beliefs, I remember those news reports about monks setting themselves on fire. And I heard that Madame Nhu, Diem's sister-in-law, publicly announced she would applaud at what she called another monk barbecue show. Did you ever see that happen?"

"No, I never saw it, but I know about it. The monks believe life is eternal in one form or another. It is certainly not confined to one's body. A body dies but life goes on. The monks who burned themselves were stressing the importance of what they had to say. It is a brave thing to do, feeling the pain of the fire to draw attention to truth."

"I'm going to have to think about that for a while," Cloud said. "I am too attached to my body to destroy it in such a hellish way."

"You're not a monk," she said, "and I do not want you to destroy your body."

"I can't imagine living like a monk," Cloud said, oblivious to the irony that much of his life had been lived in monkish fashion.

Xuan suggested an open-air restaurant for lunch. They sat under an awning to ward off the occasional drizzle while enjoying **Cha Gio**, Vietnamese spring rolls, along with the ubiquitous Mekong Delta rice. Cloud ordered a **Ba-Muoi-Ba** beer and Xuan drank a **Con-cop** soda.

"I've been thinking about the fact that we both have certain abilities that most other people don't seem to have," Cloud said.

"The dreams and visions?" she asked.

"Yes. How did we happen to develop these psychic abilities? And what on earth do they mean?"

Xuan flicked a piece of mushroom covered with rice paper into her mouth and chewed it while considering Cloud's questions. "I think we did not develop them. They are gifts that we did not ask for or desire."

"Gifts from whom?" Cloud asked.

"God," said Xuan.

"Well, that's where I run smack into a brick wall," he responded. "I don't believe in God. I need a scientific explanation for extra sensory phenomena."

"You would make a good Buddhist," she said. "It is not necessary to believe in God to practice Buddhism."

"But you do believe in God, is that right?" Cloud asked.

"Yes. And I believe God gave me the visions to use for good or bad in fulfillment of my karma."

"You're ahead of me then," he said. "I believe there's a logical explanation for my prescient dreams and..." He started to mention floating out of his body but checked himself. "...things, but I haven't figured it out yet."

"So, you have faith in science," she said.

"Yes. That's a funny way to say it, but yes, I have faith in science," he replied.

"I have faith in science also, but I have left room in my imagination for something mysterious past understanding. Some things about the world -the universe- are beyond the limits of the brain," Xuan explained.

Cloud resonated with Xuan's words. He found her statements compelling, for in the depths of his mind, there abided a desire to return to his youthful belief in a transcendent reality. Part of him wanted to believe in God, but his ego strongly controlled the subject and stubbornly resisted any attempts to consider God in any way except through scholarly examination and critique of religion.

"Tell me more about your type of Buddhism," Cloud said, in order to avoid saying more about what he believed.

"I practice Thien Buddhism," she said. "It is better known in the West by its Japanese name, Zen. This is the largest school of Buddhism in Viet Nam, followed by Pure Land Buddhism. Thien is a method for discerning right action, with the aim to see reality as truly as humanly possible."

"What are the principle doctrines?" Cloud asked.

"No doctrines. Doctrines keep people from gaining knowledge. Thien cultivates attitudes that contribute to loss of illusions. Right concentration, right breathing, right speech, right eating, right drinking, and ethical treatment of others and oneself."

"The eight-fold path. What about the Four Noble Truths?" Cloud asked.

"Oh, yes, the Four Noble Truths of Buddhism guide us. Life is filled with suffering. Greed and desire are the causes of suffering. Suffering ends when one removes craving and desire from one's mind. Following the Path of Noble Truth leads to the end of suffering. But these are not doctrines about God. They are..." She paused to find the right word. "They are *insights* into the nature of human reality that the Buddha discovered. They are found in the **Dharmacakra Pravartana Sutra** and other writings."

"I noticed the kiosks are loaded with books about Buddhist thought," Cloud said.

Xuan laughed. "There will never be an end to writing about the many different...what is the word?...thinkings of Buddhism."

"Different denominations, or schools, or perhaps differing implications," said Cloud, offering Xuan new vocabulary words.

"Yes, but the different schools cooperate together in Viet Nam," she added. "I am fond of the Pure Land vision of...of...the place beyond."

"Heaven?" asked Cloud.

"Maybe something like that," Xuan said. "But not like the Christian heaven."

"So, no pearly gates and angels playing harps in the clouds," Cloud said.

"Yes, no angels on clouds," she affirmed. "They believe meditation can bring one to Western Paradise, a pure land of bliss where it is easy to enter Nirvana. This is what I wish for too."

That evening, Xuan cooked dinner for Cloud in her apartment. After the meal, he helped her clean up. This was a new experience for her, and she was not entirely comfortable with a man washing the dishes, but he seemed at ease with the procedure. She had a great deal to learn about American customs, she thought.

"I have an idea," he said. "You told me you knew Vietnamese folk dancing but not American style. I'm going to teach you to dance the American way." He snapped on her radio and turned the dial to tune in AFVN, the Armed Forces network. "We'll wait for a slow song to start with."

The Army DJ announced, "Coming up next, the new hit version of 'Ebb Tide' by the Righteous Brothers, but first this reminder about taking your malaria pills..."

"Perfect," said Cloud. "Stand here in front of me, and put your left hand on my shoulder. Good." He took her right hand in his left and held it close to her shoulder then placed his right hand around her slender waist. "This is called slow dancing. Basically, when the music starts, follow my lead. Mostly you'll step back and forth sideways and occasionally backwards."

When the lush arrangement began, Cloud and Xuan joined in leisurely swaying and shuffling movements with their bodies slightly apart. Xuan had no trouble following Cloud's lead. Halfway through the song, she closed her eyes and nestled her head in his shoulder. Each hoped the song would last a long time. As the music reached crescendo, their bodies were pressed tightly together and his face caressed her shiny black hair. Before the last powerful notes faded from the air, Xuan and Cloud were locked in the most powerful kiss either of them had ever experienced.

Eventually their mouths uncoupled so they could resume right breathing. Each stared into the other's eyes, enjoying a silent interval of mutual admiration. Their bodies remained together, exchanging electrical impulses.

"*Anh yeu em*," he whispered.

"*Em yeu anh*," she softly replied.

The words of love had at last been spoken. What was supposed to happen now? Cloud thought that in America a real man would pick up the woman and carry her into the bedroom. But this was not America. On the other hand, it didn't really matter what the custom was in America or in Viet Nam either. What did Xuan want? What did she expect? He was aroused and ready for sexual intimacy any time, but he did not want his period of virginity to end with a one-sided experience. It would not be joyful for him unless it was joyful for her.

Xuan was filled with mixed emotions. She wanted to stay with this man as long as she drew breath. Her words of love were real. But he was from a different country to which he would one day return, and she had no wish to go to America. She loved her own country. She was faced with a Thien dilemma, for she knew that her love for Cloud was true and good and not illusion, but her desire to be with him would lead ultimately to more suffering. The question of sexual relations did not trouble her. It was not time yet, but when it was, she would give herself to him without reservation.

Xuan finally broke the silence. "Maybe we can sit on the couch?"

They nestled close together, and Cloud took her hand. "I really love you," he said, breaking into a broad grin.

"I love you too," she said. "And I want to ask you for something."

"Anything," he said.

"Don't promise what you can't give," Xuan chided. "What I want is something simple you can do for me."

CHAPTER TWENTY-FOUR

Xuan gently inquired, "Do you remember what you did in the restaurant on Tan Da Street?"

"I held your hand," he said.

"Yes, and you gently rubbed my palms with your fingers. Please do that again." She held out her palms. "I want to enjoy the sensation now, because we love each other."

"The truth is, I loved you then," he said.

"But this is a different time. We have said deep feelings now that we did not speak before."

Cloud understood her words as a signal she was not ready to invite him to her bed, and he relaxed into appreciation of what was enjoyable and real in the present moment. With his fingers, he began tracing words of love, in English and Vietnamese, on Xuan's outstretched hands. He found the activity sensual and satisfying, and when she insisted on reciprocating, the touch of her fingers on his palms as she crooned "*Muoi Thuong*," a Vietnamese love song, filled him with sensate pleasure beyond anything he had ever known.

Too soon it was time for Cloud to return to his BOQ, but not before more kisses and verbal expressions of love were exchanged.

Narcissa handed Cloud's letter to Lloyd. "What do you make of this?" she asked with a note of disapproval in her voice.

He unfolded the single page and read:

Dear Mom and Dad,

Things are going well with my work here. My language proficiency grows greater every day. I really like the people I work with, and I'm developing a fondness for Vietnamese food. Dad, I think you would like Vietnamese beer. It's called Ba-Muoi-Ba, which means 33.

I have become close friends with a Vietnamese woman who works in an office nearby and have learned a lot about the history and culture of the country from her. Her name is Nguyen thi Xuan. As you probably know, the Vietnamese place the family name first and the given name last. I hope things are going well in Phoenix.

Love,
Cloud

"Well," said Lloyd, "it looks like he has a girlfriend. It's about time."

"How can you say that?" Narcissa snapped. "It looks to me like he's shacked up with some slant-eyed hussy who'll be sure to give him a venereal disease."

"I don't think you know your son very well, Narcissa. He wouldn't write home about someone he was just screwing," Lloyd said.

"No, Lloyd. You're the one who doesn't know your son. He's an innocent boy who's just gullible enough to let some prostitute pick his pockets and leave him with an itchy dose of clap."

"Now, don't over-react, Narcissa. Whatever the relationship may be, it's not likely to last. These war-time romances seldom do," Lloyd said.

"And what would you know about war-time romances? Were you involved with some English bitch that you never told me about?"

"Absolutely not!" Lloyd spat out indignantly. "You know what it was like for me over there, and it was not conducive to clandestine affairs. But some of the guys I knew did get involved with local women."

Narcissa simmered for a minute then said, "If Cloud brings home an Oriental war bride, I'll...I'll never speak to him again. My God, what would the Beauty Society think if their top representative had a son who was married to a chink?"

"I think you'll find there are distinct differences between the Chinese and the Vietnamese," Lloyd said sarcastically, knowing that his words would make his wife even angrier than she already was.

"You bastard! You know what I'm talking about," Narcissa screamed.

"I'm not sure I do," Lloyd retorted. "Would your Beauty Society approve if he dated of one of the Chen girls who show up on the society page of the paper from time to time? They're Chinese, you know, and one family of the Chen clan lives in our so-called prestigious Palmcroft neighborhood not three blocks from this house. I believe they have an attractive daughter close to Cloud's age. Would she be suitable?"

"The Beauty Society aims for women who have not yet made the society page," Narcissa said to avoid directly answering.

"But would you object to Cloud dating Katy Chen?" Lloyd pressed her.

"I'm not a segregationist, Lloyd! It's a free country, and it's perfectly OK for Orientals to live in this neighborhood or anywhere else they like," Narcissa said. "That is, as long as they're educated and Americanized like the Chens. They may be wealthy, which qualifies them for social status. That's the American way. But as far as dating or marriage is concerned, they're still chinks, and I believe they should stay with their own kind. And your self-righteous bleeding heart, Lloyd, really pisses me off."

"I'm well aware of that, but I'd rather have you mad at me than at Cloud. Our son happens to be living in a war zone, Narcissa. Please don't write anything upsetting to him. That can be dangerous," Lloyd said, shifting the conversation in a direction he hoped would bring the argument to a close.

"Alright," she said with a theatrical sigh. "*You* write him and just say I said hello and wish him a safe return home."

In her sophomore year, Terp joined the Debate Club, and quickly proved she could be rhetorically persuasive. Thus in the fall of 1967, she found herself in front of the entire student body at an all-school assembly. The purpose of the assembly was to edify students through exposure to a debate pro and con on the subject of the United States military involvement in Viet Nam.

Terp's team drew the con position and had to marshal a series of reasonable arguments against the war. She was relieved to be on this side, because the task of putting forth pro-war rationales would have required her to say things she did not believe simply to win the debate. As much as she found doing this an easy academic exercise with subjects in which she had little interest, Terp could not bring herself to manufacture arguments in support of the war.

Increasingly since her father's death, Terp had grown more pacifistic in her thinking, and while not opposed to all wars on religious or philosophical grounds, she felt that the escalating war in Viet Nam was completely unjustified.

She spoke last for her side, after the alternating voices had presented an array of dry facts and figures to support their arguments. Terp decided to get personal. Stepping to the microphone she said, "Four years ago I sat in front of my television and watched in horror as the evening news broadcast a story about a Buddhist monk who was doused with gasoline and set himself on fire. Does anyone here know the name of that man?

"Recently I did a survey at the Acme Market on Old Post Road. I asked people going into the store if they remembered the event, and most adults did. To those who remembered I asked about the reason the monk had killed himself this way, and some couldn't think of any motive, but a few thought the monk was protesting against the government. Some thought he was protesting the Communists and some thought he was protesting the South Vietnamese government. Then I asked if they remembered the monk's name and not one single person did.

"I've done a little research into the matter. The man who killed himself by fire was Thich Quang-Duc. He was a beloved spiritual leader, a grandfatherly presence in his community. He was not a Communist and he was not interested in gaining power for himself or for his friends. He committed suicide to call attention to the corrupt and violent government of South Vietnamese President Ngo Dinh Diem.

"This same President Diem was a dear friend and ally of the United States of America. This same President Diem proved how much he valued American ideals by appointing his family members to high paying government posts, stealing from the poor, and by using physical force to make people convert from their religion to his.

"President Diem is gone now, but the government in South Viet Nam is no less corrupt. As liberty loving Americans, we cannot continue to support tyrants while the people continue to suffer. The people of Viet Nam must solve their problems themselves, but they cannot do it as long as our military forces protect corrupt officials.

"Did Grandfather Thich Quang-Duc die in vain? For the sake of this gentle old man who gave his life so that people like you and me would pay attention and know what was going on, we must quit this war."

Adrenaline pulsed through her body as she sat down, and she could not relax. Her body twitched, while her mind sternly evaluated her performance. She decided she had done poorly and let her team down.

Based on his knowledge of general sentiments in the community, Ethan Aaron, the school principal, assumed the pro side would win the debate by a sizeable margin, regardless of how well or poorly they presented their case. When the votes were counted, the anti side won by a margin of one vote. This upset victory Aaron attributed entirely to Terp's well-prepared emotional appeal.

— ☉ —

Cloud wondered if his letter to his parents would be received as a bombshell. He expected his mother to read between the lines and guess that he was in love with Xuan. He also assumed she would not be happy about the development. As to his father, Cloud had no idea how he would respond to the news. Although he felt himself liberated from his parents, Cloud was nonetheless anxious about the inevitable return letter from Phoenix. Would their response sever forever his ties to the place of his birth?

When the letter from Lloyd arrived, Cloud laid it on his desk and did not open it right away. Arquimedes was deeply engaged in reading a letter from home, but Cloud simply stared at his letter, contemplating throwing it away unread. Ultimately, he decided he was being needlessly dramatic, giving the epistle far more power over him than it deserved, and so he opened it and read his father's words.

Dear Cloud,

It was good to get your recent letter. Your mother and I are relieved that you are doing so well. She sends her love and hopes for your safe return home. Your friend sounds like a nice person, and I hope you will write to me about her in more detail. We are very proud of you, Cloud. They ask about you at my office and want me to convey their support for you and your fellow soldiers. There's not much news to report from the home front. Same old routine.

Love, Dad

P.S. I heard that Quincy is being transferred to the VA Hospital in Phoenix. Burkhardt told me Quincy received a Silver Star for gallantry in action.

That wasn't so bad, Cloud thought. Better than he had expected. But what did the underlined words mean? Cloud quickly deduced that Lloyd was suggesting he send a letter about Xuan to his office address rather than home. This meant his mother had thrown a fit but his father felt fine about the relationship. Cloud's interpretation of his father's intention was confirmed when he glanced at the return address, which was the bank and not Monte Vista. Setting the letter aside, he wondered what Quinn had done to earn a Silver Star.

Cloud wrote his dad with a glowing confession of his love for a very beautiful woman. As it happened, Lloyd neglected to tell his wife that he had received that letter, and it remained safe in a locked drawer of his office desk.

"I have a question for you, Arquimedes," said Cloud. "How can there be a good God when there is so much evil in this world that was supposedly created by God?"

"Well, sir, my church would say your question is faulty. It assumes that evil exists." Arquimedes settled into the chair next to Cloud's desk. "I believe, as a child of the CMH, that the only truly real thing is God, and God is pure love and goodness. Therefore, evil cannot exist. Nothing exists apart from God. There is only the false belief or delusion that evil exists. Likewise, suffering is simply the belief in suffering, and death is not a fact but a belief in the illusion of death. That about sums it up for me, sir. Any questions?"

"Yes. If God is the only thing that exists, and God is totally good, then how come so many people *think* they experience suffering and either see or do evil? How can God permit such painful illusions to exist if God is good?" Cloud asked.

"Error," said Arquimedes. "They have accepted error."

"Whose error? God's error?" asked Cloud. "How can a totally good God permit even the *illusion* of suffering or evil among those God has created?"

"Oh no, sir. Not God's error. God is perfect and does not err. We humans are prone to error."

"But we're only prone to error because God made us that way, right?" Cloud continued. "Therefore, God deliberately created us to be deluded and to experience the illusion of suffering. That seems like a perverse thing to do."

"I wouldn't say it that way," Arquimedes responded. "I would say that God in her wisdom -God is both Mother and Father, so we use pronouns interchangeably- created us as incarnations of God with the same free will that God has. God is free to do evil, but because she is pure goodness does not choose to do so. We humans, as incarnations of God, are free to fall into error, and often do."

"Let me see if I understand your belief," Cloud said. "God is capable of doing evil, but if God chose to do that, then evil would exist. And according to CMH doctrine, it does not exist. Because God's essential nature is goodness, God does not do evil. Is that about right?"

"Close enough," Arquimedes answered.

"I'm really tied up in a knot about this one, Arquimedes," Cloud confessed. "It seems to me that if God is wholly good by nature, then God is incapable of doing evil, and therefore, God does not have free will. How can a God that does not have free will grant free will to humans?"

"I'll have to think about that one, sir."

Cloud sighed. "I tell you, Arquimedes, life would be so much simpler if I could believe in a just and loving God. Actually, I think I'm getting there, but I have a few intellectual hoops to jump through first. Of course, I wouldn't be even this close to believing if it weren't for Xuan. You once said to me that being in love creates it own illusions. But my love for Xuan is the most real experience I've ever known."

"I'm not sure you should be telling me these things, Lieutenant Morgan."

"Maybe so, Arquimedes, but I'm a pretty good judge of character, and I trust you with information about my personal life. Hell, I trust you with my life period."

"Thank you, sir," the young specialist said, and he returned to his desk to inspect a new box of documents. He was still looking for a highest priority discovery to rush over to Lieutenant Morgan for immediate action.

Colonel Melita summoned Cloud to his office. "You wanted to see me, sir?" Cloud asked.

"You're doing a good job, Morgan. I appreciate your clear thinking and devotion to duty. You're a damn fine linguist," the Commanding Officer said.

"Thank you, sir," Cloud responded.

"You've been here nearly seven months now, and it's about time to give you a break. I've got a couple of slots for R and R next week, and you can have one of them. Japan and Australia. Which one would you like?"

"Wow, sir. They are both places I'd like to see."

"Well, Son, you'll probably get another chance for R and R in a few months, so pick one now and plan for the other next year," the Colonel offered, as a way to shorten Cloud's decision making time.

"I'll take Japan, sir," Cloud said. His first thought was that he could find books on Zen Buddhism in Tokyo that would enlighten his study of Vietnamese Thien.

When he told Xuan that he would be going to Japan for a week, she said, "I wish we could go together. **Nhat ban** is a place I have dreamed to visit."

"I wish we could go together too," Cloud said. "And someday we will. Someday, when this war is behind us, we'll travel the world arm in arm. We'll be Cloud and Xuan, citizens of the world."

"What a beautiful vision," she said. Tears formed in her eyes as she thought of Cloud boarding a plane for Tokyo without her. "Please be safe and come home to me."

"Nothing can keep me away from you, dearest Xuan," he declared.

The stonework in front of Tokyo's Imperial Hotel reminded Cloud of the tufa stone in his old home on Villa Verde. Frank Lloyd Wright, who designed the Imperial, also designed noteworthy buildings in Arizona, including the Grady Gammage Auditorium on the campus of ASU. Cloud had participated in the groundbreaking ceremony for construction of the Gammage edifice, and so he felt a kinship between this Asian landmark and his native soil.

No rooms were available in the original section of the hotel, the part that had withstood the devastating 1923 earthquake, so Cloud was given a room in the newer wing built in 1964 for the Olympics. The next morning he reverted to old habits and began hiking around the city.

He walked the crowded Ginza but found the modern stores with glittery expensive jewelry and perfume not to his liking. He hiked three times around the Emperor's Palace, admiring the royal carp in the moat and delighting in the meditative aura of the place. The next day, the concierge suggested the Tokyo Tower, a source of local pride, because it rose higher than the Eiffel Tower in Paris. He put Cloud into a cab to the tower, and Cloud found the excursion worthwhile.

It was fun to scan the entire city from the heights, and Cloud quickly found his hotel in the distance. When he saw how short that distance was, relative to his propensity for hiking, he decided to return to the hotel on foot and explore the non-tourist neighborhoods in between. As he did so, construction workers, housewives, and deliverymen tracked his movements. The tall Occidental was clearly out of place.

"Look!" a shopkeeper said with a note of wonder. "An American walking."

"Americans don't walk!" his assistant said. "He must be European."

That evening he found a small art theater that showed foreign films. Cloud was the only non-Japanese in the house, which provided him a unique perspective on the event. The film was not foreign to him. It was the Richard Burton-Elizabeth Taylor feature *Who's Afraid of Virginia Woolf?* The soundtrack was in English, with side titles in Japanese. Cloud noticed that the audience laughed at the saddest parts of the movie and remained silent during the ironically humorous episodes.

This caused him to reflect on the inherent dangers in translating from dissimilar languages words laden with cultural assumptions. That's what he was doing in Saigon. How much of what he produced for American intelligence use was distorted by not understanding the full meanings of simple words or contexts? He shuddered to think that the entire American war strategy was based on our inability to get the joke.

Cloud spent his last two days in Japan in a very American pastime -shopping. He found a street with many small bookshops and art print stores and fell under the inevitable spell of such places. His purchases included books on Buddhism, a book of Haiku poetry, a dozen wood block prints, and a wooden statue of the Buddha for Xuan. He also bought her a bolt of pale blue silk and a turquoise necklace. Although he was not much interested in jewelry, the necklace reminded him of the colors of Arizona and on impulse he wanted to see what it would look like around Xuan's lovely neck.

Thus laden, he flew back to Saigon and into the arms of Xuan. She was overwhelmed by his gifts and felt undeserving of them, but when she saw how much pleasure he derived from giving them, she accepted with gratitude and joy.

The piles of documents on his desk had grown taller during Cloud's absence in Tokyo. He plowed into them with renewed energy, but remembering his experience in the Japanese movie theater, a new attitude of skeptical humility showed in his evaluations of the contents of captured letters, operations orders, and cadre lists.

Three weeks after his return from R and R, Cloud and Xuan shared a customary simple dinner in her apartment. AFVN played quietly in the background, and when the Everly Brothers recording of "Let It Be Me" came on, Cloud turned up the volume and pulled Xuan into his arms for some American style slow dancing. At the conclusion of the song, Xuan did not follow what had become a pattern for them of moving to the tiny couch for a time of holding hands and kissing. This time she led him to her bedroom.

Without a word, she slipped out of her *ao dai* and slacks, and while Cloud began to disrobe, she dispensed with her undergarments. When Cloud, too, was naked, she rushed into his arms and pressed her body close to his. For a long time they stood together, reveling in the feel of skin on skin, and then their hands began to make exploratory sweeps over their respective backs and sides.

They moved to the bed where Xuan stretched out on her back, and Cloud lay on his side next to her. He began to caress her feet, calves, and thighs, tickling the lines of her hipbones with his fingers. For the moment, he refrained from exploring her pubic region, moving his hand toward her rib cage and then cupping her breasts one at a time, feeling her erect nipples press against his palm.

"I have never done this before," she said.

"Neither have I," he responded. "Please be gentle with me."

She laughed. "That is supposed to be...how do you say?...my line." Then honoring his request for gentleness, she ran her fingers delicately down the length of his erection, which caused him to croon with pleasure.

He explored her pubic hair in leisurely fashion before moving down to massage her clitoris. "*Co tran truong -dep lam!*" he whispered playfully. "You're very beautiful nude." Each felt exquisite arousal as the foreplay proceeded without hurry. And then with an unspoken sign exchanged through their eyes, Cloud shifted on top of Xuan and entered her.

Their lovemaking was not frantic, but a slow rhythm that increased in intensity until first he then a second later she burst into splendid orgasms that seemed in the condensed fruition of time to go on forever.

Of course, forever eventually came to an end, and in the stillness of satiation, they tarried in their connectedness. Cloud held Xuan in his arms as he rolled over on his back, so that the lovers were still linked but Xuan's weight was now on him. He loved the feel of her slender body resting on his.

She kissed him ardently. "I am so blessed," she said. "I love you more than I can stand." Xuan beamed, adding, "*Va anh dep lam tran truong*! -my beautiful naked man."

"I'm the one touched by fortune," he said. He began to laugh, a low, rumbling sound that originated in the depths of his psyche. "Oh God! How I love you, dear Xuan!"

Eventually they fell asleep in each other's arms. Cloud slipped away early in the morning, in time to get a shower at his BOQ and don a clean uniform. After this, Cloud often spent the night with Xuan, and kept shaving gear and a toothbrush at her place, along with extra uniforms and underwear.

Cloud took a deep drink of the ice water Xuan handed him. "Ah, sweet and refreshing," he said as he gave the glass back to her.

"Sweet water," she said in musing fashion. "I remember a story from the Christian Bible about sweet water."

"Have you read the Bible?" Cloud asked with genuine surprise.

"No, but a Thien monk told me a story from the Bible that his master assigned to him for meditation," she replied. "It is a story about Jesus making water become wine. Do you know it?"

"Oh yes," Cloud said. "I've heard multiple interpretations of that text over the years. Some of them strange. I'd like to hear what you make of it."

She thought for a moment and then said, "I think the Lord Jesus did not make wine from water but only tricked drunk people into thinking it was wine."

"Yeah, I've long thought of Jesus as a deft wielder of a good joke," Cloud said. "And I say that meaning great respect and admiration for Jesus."

"The story says the guests were drunk," Xuan continued, "and so they were...oh what is the word?...They could not fight against suggestions..."

"Susceptible," offered Cloud.

"I think maybe that is the right word," she said. "The people were susceptible to being fooled. They **desired** more wine and they were told it **was** wine, and so their drunken brains expected wine. So when they were given sweet water, their tongues tasted wine. They were fooled by the **illusion** that the water was wine."

"Your interpretation sounds like a good Buddhist critique of the wedding guests' lack of mindfulness. But initially, only one person was fooled -the steward," Cloud said.

"Yes," she said. "The steward was not attentive to the moment but was living in the future, in the world of expecting good things. It is not good to expect happiness. This Christian story is a good one, I think, for a Buddhist to meditate on. It is about the foolishness of illusions."

"But the steward and the rest of the people were happy with their illusions," Cloud noted. "Are illusions really so bad if they make people happy? And in this account, the result of their illusion turned out to be good for them. If they had imbibed more real wine, the guests would have gotten even more inebriated."

"Maybe illusions are OK in some cases for a little while," Xuan replied, "but eventually people are hurt more by hiding from the reality of suffering and comforting themselves only with illusions."

"Maybe this matter needs some sensible Buddhist balance," Cloud said.

"Yes," Xuan said and kissed him playfully.

— ☯ —

As December slipped away, Cloud realized he had only four months remaining on his tour, and he needed that time and more to make arrangements for their future together. Early in the new year he would talk with Colonel Melita about his options. Cloud was comfortable requesting an extension of his tour, and he knew that he was a valuable asset to the 1007th MI Battalion, and was thus confident that such a request would be approved.

On Christmas Day, Xuan took Cloud to visit a pagoda a few kilometers southwest of Saigon along Route 4. The building was decorated in red and yellow, the colors of the flag of the Republic of South Viet Nam, but this was not what Xuan wanted Cloud to see. She led him to a corner of the grounds and showed him an old Bo tree.

"This tree is a direct descendant of the tree in Nepal where Siddartha Gautama the Buddha reached enlightenment." She explained that it had been planted by monks who had taken a slip from another tree descended from the original Bo tree, from which slips had been taken and planted all over Asia by devoted followers of the Enlightened One.

"This sounds like an apostolic succession of trees," Cloud said.

"What's that?" Xuan asked.

"In the Catholic Church, bishops are said to be in apostolic succession. Jesus laid hands on Peter as his successor, who in turn laid hands on his successor, and each bishop since has had hands laid on by someone touched by someone who was, if you go far enough back, touched by Jesus," Cloud explained.

"I see," said Xuan.

"Actually, I like the idea of a succession of trees much better than a succession of hands on the back," Cloud mused. "There's a direct genetic relationship."

"I do not believe the tree the Buddha sat under talked to him and led him to reach satori," she said. "The meditation was all inside his mind. But it must have been a beautiful sacred fig tree to attract him to sit under it in long contemplation."

"By the way," Cloud said, "when are we going to Tay Ninh to see the Cao Dai Temple? I really want to see it."

"I think after the New Year we can go there," she said.

"Which New Year -American or Vietnamese?"

"The Lunar New Year -Tet," she clarified.

They admired the ancient and complex Bo for a time, and then Cloud spoke. "Standing before this venerable tree has brought me to a sense of enlightenment, not as profound as that of Gautama's satori, but as clear to me as anything in my life. Xuan, will you marry me?"

"I think it will not be easy to arrange, but yes, I will do whatever is necessary to marry you." She did not fall into his arms but stood facing him and added with calm realism, "Your government and my government will do many things to stop us from marrying. It will require much time to obtain the necessary documents and stamps."

He bent down and gently kissed her. "I know it will be difficult, but next week I'm going to request an extension of my tour. I really like my job, and I'm sure the United States Army will be happy to have me stay longer. Eventually, of course, I will be assigned somewhere else, but by then we'll be married, and you can travel with me. I promised to take you around the world with me, and we're going to do it."

Xuan then nestled into Cloud's arms and said, "Wherever you go, I will go."

CHAPTER TWENTY-FIVE

Stretched out on the floor in Xuan's apartment, Cloud said to his fiancée, "I'd like to learn more about Vietnamese history and culture. Teach me something important."

Xuan, sitting on the couch, said, "Clou', you already know a lot about our culture." She commonly dropped the final d sound from English words, including the name of her lover, when she was excited, tired, or speaking in a hurry.

"Yes, but there's a lot I don't know. Like Tet. Tet seems to be a much bigger deal here than New Year's Day is in America. Tell me about that," he said.

"You already know it is the New Year celebration, calculated on the lunar calendar, so it comes late in January or early in February by the Western calendar. It is the important celebration, when wandering family members return home."

"An annual family reunion?" he asked.

"Yes. Tet is like Christmas and New Year's Eve together, with maybe the American Fourth of July and Thanksgiving added in," she explained. "This Tet will begin the Year of the Monkey. Monkey people are unpredictable."

"Tell me about your most memorable Tet," he urged.

"Oh, the most memorable Tet was 1789," she answered.

"You weren't born then. I mean in your life."

"In my life, maybe the last Tet before my parents died. That was the last happy Tet. Since then the day has been very sad for me."

"Well, this Tet will be different. We'll really celebrate, you and I," Cloud said. "But you've intrigued me with the Tet of 1789. What happened then?"

"The events of that day are taught in every Vietnamese school," she said.

"Being a history major, I know that date well. That's the year the French Revolution began and George Washington became the first President of the United States," Cloud interrupted.

She continued, "In Viet Nam, Emperor Quang Trung led a surprise rebellion against Chinese occupation soldiers, while the Chinese were busy celebrating the New Year. This surprise attack is how Viet Nam gained its freedom from China. This is a very important event in our history, that every school child is taught."

"You see, professor, I learned something I didn't know. Thank you for the lesson. Is there anything else I should know, about this year's celebration for example?"

"Don't plan to sleep well when Tet begins. At midnight the firecrackers will start, and people will be out on the street going to temples. Children will stay up all night playing with firecrackers." A sly grin spread across her face. "This Tet I will see that you get no sleep, and then when you are worn out from making love to me, I will take you to My Tho to visit my sister and brother-in-law. She will be very surprised."

"I can't wait," he said. "That is I can't wait to meet your sister. We don't need to wait to get worn out from lovemaking."

"Not now. Wait until after dinner," she said, while at the same time making a suggestive gesture.

"Dear, I have something important to tell you," Cloud said.

Xuan noticed the change in his voice and suspected bad news. "Have you spoken with your *Dai ta*?" She avoided the word colonel because it was confusing.

"No, it's not about that. It's about me. Since you have already promised to marry me, I feel the need to confess something about me that I haven't told you."

Immediately her mind raced to the conclusion that he had been married before and had a child. She steeled herself for the news. "Yes?"

"It's a long story that began when I was six years old," he said. Cloud proceeded to tell Xuan about his out-of-body experiences. She sat in stunned silence as the words poured out of him in a torrent of release. "I have never before told a soul in this world about my floating. You are the only other person who knows."

"Do you believe this will harm my love for you?" she asked. "It will not. It only makes me love you more."

Cloud began to weep from the sheer relief of at last confiding in someone else, someone he loved and who loved him. Xuan slipped down onto the floor beside him and placed his head in her lap, stroking his hair. "It must be very hard to keep that secret so many years. Now I have something to tell you that I have kept secret for too long." She told him about her vision of a gecko that turned into a boy in khaki, who floated on her ceiling. "That boy was you, my dearest Clou'. I know it was you. And let me tell you something else. Your smile has not changed in all these years."

They forgot about dinner and went to their bedroom.

"What is it, Morgan?" Colonel Melita asked.

"Sir, I would like to talk with you about extending my tour," Cloud said.

"Come in and have a seat, lieutenant." The colonel sighed. He knew what direction this conversation would take and was not surprised that this time it was Morgan who would initiate it. Melita had gained experience with this kind of situation in Germany and Korea, but that didn't make it any easier to deal with. "Now, why do you want to extend?"

"Two reasons, sir. The first is that I really like my work, and I believe I'm good at it. It would be good for my career to have more overseas time. The second, to be honest, sir, is the more important. I want to request permission to marry a Vietnamese citizen, and I know that it takes time for all the necessary approvals."

"Well, Morgan, you're right that the red tape is pretty thick for a soldier who wants to marry a foreign national," Melita said. "But in your case it's even more complicated. You see, you have a Top Secret

Crypto clearance. And that adds a battery of investigations to the process. Her family and your family and just about anybody who has ever looked crosswise at either of you will have to be checked out. And not only does that take a long, long time, but if they find out that she has a third cousin she's never seen in Hanoi who once gave a hand job to an NVA flunky on the Ho Chi Minh Trail, the whole thing goes kaput, along with your career."

"I understand, sir. But in this case, Xuan works for MACV in a pretty sensitive area, so I'm sure she's been vetted already," Cloud offered with an air of hope.

"Yes, Morgan. I know the young lady. When I learned that you and she were an item, I had her checked out myself. She's a fine person. But the powers that be won't take my word for it. There will be no short cuts in a case like this."

"I may as well tell you now, sir, that her father played a part in the Diem coup," Cloud said.

"We know that, Morgan, and from my perspective, that's a plus. But I don't want to give you any false hopes. Let me pass on some advice I once heard a Master Sergeant tell a private during the German occupation. The young man wanted to marry a German girl. The sergeant said, 'If the Army wanted you to have a wife, soldier, it would have issued you one.' Now you and I both know that this is not factually true, but it is demonstrably true that the Army makes it excruciatingly hard for servicemen to enter into matrimony with women in war zones."

"What do you recommend I do, sir?"

"Well, Cloud," Melita said, addressing him by given name for the first time, "I recommend that you fill out your request for extension and put it on my desk. I will approve it, but I can't guarantee what they'll do upstairs."

"Thank you, sir."

"I gather you're intending to go for twenty years on active duty," Melita added.

"Yes, sir. My plan is to apply for a Regular Army commission when I get to my next assignment. If my record here is good, I think I have a chance. But if I don't get the RA, I still want to stay on as a Reserve Officer."

"That's a good plan for the Army," the colonel said, "but not a good one for you. My best advice, if you truly love **Co** Xuan, as I believe you do, is to extend your tour here to the end of your active duty commitment, then go home and leave the service. Once you're back in the States, with your experience and language skill you're practically guaranteed to be offered a contract to come back here as a civilian and stay as long as you want. Live with the girl as a soldier, and marry her as a civilian."

"Thank you very much, sir. I'll have the request on your desk tomorrow morning," Cloud said.

"That's fine, but it'll have to sit here unattended for a while, because I'm going to Honolulu for a little R and R with my wife. I'll sign it with my endorsement when I get back. Oh, by the way, Morgan, I'm putting you in for a Bronze Star. Your work has gotten better since you came back from Japan."

"What did **Dai ta** Melita say?" Xuan wanted to know.

Cloud told her.

"I think he is a wise man," she said.

"I still want both," he said. "I want to marry you and have a career in the Army."

"Sometimes you have to choose only one," she said.

"At least we know I won't be going back to the States in April. We have some time to work through the system," Cloud said with a sigh of relief. "And I want you to know that if I can have only one, I choose you."

Xuan kissed her soldier passionately, feeling for the first time that her bi-national, cross-cultural, inter-racial love affair might work out well after all.

They enjoyed a lovely evening together. After dinner they curled up on the couch and told each other funny stories from their childhoods, laughing until their sides hurt. They slow-danced to "Never My Love" when it was played on AFVN, and then went to bed, where they made love in leisurely fashion. Neither had any particular interest in reaching climax, nor in wearing themselves out with acrobatics, so they remained linked, side-by-side, moving their hips hardly at all. Instead, they used their free hands to caress each other's faces.

Cloud ran a hand through Xuan's straight black hair, continuing down to the small of her back. With his fingers wrapped in her hair, he lightly stroked her spine and neck. After an unhurried eternity of gentle delight in their physical bond, an interval of kisses led them to increasing movements at the other site of their union, which led them to simultaneous release. The lovers soon went to sleep filled with dreams of paradise.

Cloud had to work late on January thirtieth. A three-day holiday truce had been declared beginning the twenty-ninth, allowing Vietnamese combatants on the various sides in the war the privilege of going home for Tet celebrations. With the ARVN soldiers away on holiday, the Americans and other allied troops had to do double duty.

Cloud frequently pointed out to people who spoke of the war as two-sided that there were in fact layers of alliances and oppositions that made the war in Viet Nam truly multi-faceted. It was silly to talk about agreements between the two opposing camps, for there were a dozen or more camps. Nevertheless, a grand alliance of camps mutually opposed to American involvement in Viet Nam was at that moment working in concert to an unprecedented degree.

During the day, reports came in that North Vietnamese regulars had broken the truce in Central Viet Nam by attacking Da Nang, Qui Nhon, and other cities. Should American units from the South move up to help quash the attacks? If so, the South would be left wide open. Were further raids planned for Saigon and the Delta? Probably not.

It was half past eleven that night when Cloud, still in uniform, arrived at Xuan's apartment. In half an hour the noisy welcome to the Lunar New Year would begin. Xuan had bought a kumquat tree, and she invited Cloud to touch its leaves and admire its carefully trimmed shape. The two feet tall tree was rooted in an earthen pot.

"This tree is symbolic of the generations of my family," she explained. "It is traditional for Tet."

"You selected well," Cloud said. He tickled his palms by brushing them over the leaves. "Your beautiful family's past and future are nobly represented by this wonderful kumquat."

"*Co le,*" she said. "Maybe."

They went out on the balcony and surveyed the street, catching up on their respective days while awaiting the start of the celebration. Xuan told Cloud they would leave for My Tho around noon, so he would be able to get a few hours sleep before heading off to meet her sister and brother-in-law and their children.

After they listened to the initial round of midnight firecrackers, Xuan said, "You look very tired, Clou'. Why don't you lie down for a while and close your eyes. I'll wake you up if there is something special to see. I promise."

"If I go to bed, I may sleep way past noon," he protested.

"Get some rest. The Buddha said it is a duty to keep the body in good health in order to keep the mind strong and clear," she said.

Cloud compromised by slouching down on the couch to close his eyes for a few minutes. Xuan sat on the floor next to him, gently massaging his temples until he fell into a deep sleep.

Three hours later, he awoke with a start. A loud report sounded somewhere in the street below. That doesn't sound like firecrackers, he thought. It sounded like gunfire. Xuan was not in the room. He rushed to the balcony and saw her sitting on a rug, looking through the railing at the neighborhood she loved. She was wrapped in the full-length black silk robe he had bought her on a whim one day when they had gone to the Ben Thanh market together.

"Xuan, dear, I thought I heard gunfire." He reached down to her outstretched arm to lift her to her feet.

"How could it be?" she asked.

At precisely that moment, an American MP who was searching the street for remnants of a Viet Cong sapper unit that had just blown up an American facility a few blocks away, saw the rising movement of someone in black pajamas on a balcony. It looked like a VC struggling with an American soldier. He raised his M-16 and fired a burst at the target. "I'll get that son of a bitch!" he swore. At the opposite end of the block, the VC sapper being pursued by the MP saw an American officer on that same balcony fighting with a Vietnamese woman. "Death to Americans!" he yelled and pulled the trigger on his AK-47.

Cloud saw the effect of bullets from the M-16 splattering into Xuan's head the instant before a bullet from the AK-47 sliced his forehead, causing him to flinch backward, smashing the back of his skull into the wall. He slumped to the floor and everything went black.

—☯—

The eternal part of Xuan floated into the air above the street. She saw her beloved Cloud, lying against the wall, bleeding from the head, but still alive. She felt overwhelming love for him, which she expected to take with her into the next part of her journey. Surrendering to her karma, she rose into a tunnel of light and disappeared.

The fact that Xuan had been killed by an American soldier would never be whispered about, much less recorded anywhere. She was merely one of nearly six thousand civilians murdered during the Tet Offensive, in which 80,000 North Vietnamese Army and Viet Cong soldiers attacked sixty-five targets throughout South Viet Nam, including six major cities. In so doing, they violated the holiday truce, but that was hardly unprecedented, as soldiers of all sides had broken the holiday truce of the previous month in a hundred lesser ways.

The smell of disinfectant tickled Cloud's olfactory nerve. He opened his eyes and saw that he was in a hospital bed, with his forehead heavily bandaged.

The nurse standing over him said, "You were lucky. Only a flesh wound and a concussion."

"Xuan!" he cried out.

"Oh they found a woman with you. I'm sorry. She's dead," the nurse reported efficiently.

"I saw it happen," Cloud whispered. "Oh, God! Oh, God! Oh, God! Oh, God!" He started to raise his left hand to his forehead, but it caught on something sharp. He looked at the site of the snag and saw that a Purple Heart medal, the first one he would receive in Viet Nam, had been pinned to his hospital gown.

The nurse professionally patted his hand. "Colonel Melita is waiting to see you, if you are up to it. If you'd rather be alone, I'll tell him to come back later."

"I'd like to see him," Cloud said weakly.

Colonel Frank Melita got down on his knees beside Cloud's bed. "Son, I am truly sorry for your loss. I can't begin to express how terrible I feel for you. Your body will be fine very soon, but I suspect it will take a while for your soul to catch up." He rose to leave. "Get

as much rest as you need then report to my office. And by the way,
I've torn up your request for extension. If you decide you want to
stay, I'll sign a new one."

After his commanding officer left, Cloud lay in silent stupor for
a time. Then he became conscious of the pain. His forehead
throbbed with a dull intensity that seemed trivial to him. No doubt
medication, he thought. His mind, however, was a sea of agonized
turbulence swirling about in a frantic and vain search for some way
to deny what he knew to be true. This inner ache was almost beyond
endurance. When the nurse returned to check on him he looked
fiercely into her eyes and said, "Only one fig survived! I should have
known! Only one fig survived the truck!"

She wrote in his chart: "Not fully coherent."

CHAPTER TWENTY-SIX

Staring at a blank sheet of paper, Cloud sat glumly at his desk. Xuan had told him that the first writing one does in the New Year should be something beautiful and noble. But his mind denied him such thoughts. He grabbed his pen and in deliberate strokes wrote, "*TAI SAO*?" Why indeed, he thought. A cold premonition settled over him intimating that his first words would fatefully apply to the entire of Year of the Monkey.

Colonel Melita summoned him. "MACV has gone nuts over this Tet mess, Morgan. They're in shuffling and full ass-covering mode. I have orders to transfer some of my men to field units. You have less than three months till DEROS, but you need a change of scene. It won't do you any good to sit around here with your memories. So I'm sending you out to join elements of the 9th MI Detachment at Dong Tam, in the Delta."

Cloud spoke in a subdued, flat voice, "I know where it is, sir - near My Tho. I'll do my best. If others from my team are being deployed, may I take Shapiro with me?"

"I'm sorry, Morgan. Shapiro has orders to the 25th MID at Cu Chi."

"When do I report to Dong Tam, sir?"

"Day after tomorrow. They're sending a Huey for you." He

looked at a document on his desk. "A Lieutenant Zared will be waiting for you at the Dong Tam landing strip."

The key to Xuan's apartment was among the personal effects Cloud retrieved from the hospital when he was released. His khaki trousers were gone, but everything that had been in his pockets had been safely stored for him. He wouldn't need khakis for a while, anyway, because he would be switching to jungle fatigues in one more day.

He entered her apartment and found that nothing had been touched. Apparently the medics had removed them directly from the balcony to the street. Cloud sat on the tiny couch where he and Xuan had spent many hours of enchantment. He closed his eyes and breathed in the smell of the place. All he had to do now was open his eyes again and he would see her at work in the kitchen. The nightmare had not really happened.

When, at last, he did open his eyes, Xuan was not in the kitchen, nor was she in the bedroom. The flat was as silent as a mausoleum. A few weeks earlier, Cloud had sat on the floor in this room and wept with joy and relief, after telling Xuan about his out-of-body experiences. Once again tears flowed from his eyes, this time born of the deepest grief he had ever known.

He stepped into her bedroom -their bedroom- and opened the closet. Several of his uniforms were neatly hung next to her western style blouses and skirts and her Vietnamese slacks and *ao dai*. Cloud buried his face in her white *ao dai* and inhaled her scent, leaving the garment wet from his tears.

What among Xuan's possessions, would her sister Mua want to have, Cloud wondered. He had brought his duffel bag to pack with things to take to My Tho to give to the woman who would have been his sister-in-law. He filled the bag with an assortment of clothes, a photo album, and odds and ends that he knew had family sentimental value. He stuffed his uniforms on top. In a small cloth bag, he placed the few items of jewelry that Xuan had accumulated, except for the turquoise necklace he had bought her in Japan. The necklace and the small wooden Buddha statue he placed in another bag, for he intended to keep these himself. He would give Mua the key to the apartment, so that she and her husband could return for anything else they might want.

Searching at random through the kitchen, Cloud found the dried fig in a bread tin. Cradling the piece of fruit in his hand, Cloud stepped out onto the balcony. He had given no thought to what he might find there but rather homed in on the spot as if on automatic pilot. The medics had not cleaned up the blood. For an instant he felt sick at the sight of the now congealed and flyspecked bits of flesh and vital fluids on the deck. But then he noticed that a stream of what must have been his blood had mingled with that from Xuan's wounds, and the vision of these mixed pools of blood registered in his mind as an image to cherish. He would not remember this viewing as a sticky black repast for insects, but as pristine channels of their essences merging in the midst of tragedy.

Words he had heard years before in a very different setting came to his mind: "This is my body, broken for you. This is my blood, shed for you." No, he thought, these were not fitting words for an atheist and a Buddhist. Yet he could not separate them from his remembrance of this scene. These words enfolded his wounded psyche, granting him a momentary reprieve from grief. Reverently, he placed the fig on the spot where Xuan's blood and his blood had flowed together.

Colonel Melita escorted Cloud to the landing pad. The Huey from Dong Tam would be arriving in a few minutes. "Morgan," he said, "I have something for you. And I want you to know this is not in any way a sympathy gift. You have earned this." He opened a small jewelry case to reveal a set of silver Captain's bars. "Now, take that silver bar off your collar and let me pin these railroad tracks on you."

After the transfer of insignia had been completed, Melita said, "I want you to take care of yourself down in the Delta, Cloud."

"Good-bye, sir," Cloud said. "Thank you for...everything...for your wisdom...for caring." He saluted smartly.

Melita returned the salute and said, "Good luck, Captain Morgan. God speed."

Cloud stepped into the Huey for a flight from the Class A uniform world of Saigon to the jungle fatigue world of the Mekong Delta. He felt self-conscious about the new captain's bars on his collar, not least because when he scrunched his head down to look at them, it was clear that they had been hastily and incorrectly positioned.

One other passenger, who had previously boarded at Bearcat, the 9th Infantry Division headquarters base northeast of Saigon, sat quietly in the chopper's bay. This was an infantry second lieutenant in rumpled fatigues, flak jacket, and dusty boots, whom Cloud judged to be about nineteen. The platoon leader peered intently at Cloud and then abruptly turned his head away, satisfied that the new passenger was not worthy of deference or respect.

As soon as the Huey lifted into the air, the lieutenant removed his helmet and carefully hooked it beneath his seat.

Cloud could not refrain from staring.

The platoon leader stared back and said in a tone as if he were addressing a stupid child, "If we take enemy fire, it's going to come from the ground, from underneath us." He pointed downward in a mockingly exaggerated gesture. "I'm just protecting what's most likely to get hit. If I get it in the head, chances are I'll die instantaneously. If I get shot in the balls, I'll most likely live but wish I was dead."

Cloud, who at that moment had no helmet, nodded grimly and replied, "I'll try to keep that in mind."

Mercury Zared was waiting for Cloud when the Huey landed at the Delta base. "Well I'll be damned," he said. "Welcome to Dong Tam, **Captain** Morgan."

"Hello, Mercury," he said. "You probably will be damned, but I'm still Cloud to you, and if you call me sir, I'll probably have to kick you in the ass."

Zared explained that he was in charge of the IPW section - Interrogation of Prisoners of War. Cloud would serve as liaison between the Military Intelligence unit and the Brigade S-2 and S-3 shops, intelligence and operations, respectively. That is, Cloud would run interference between the conflicting demands of the work done by MI personnel and Infantry units. Differences of opinion often led to problems because the MI Detachment and the Infantry Brigade had separate chains of command.

"The S-2 is a lamebrain bullshitter," Mercury noted, "but the S-3 is strac. Sharp as they come. He knows his stuff. You can trust him to listen."

That night, Cloud poured out a carefully edited version of his relationship with Xuan as Mercury poured vodka into two somewhat clean tumblers. Mercury listened sympathetically as his friend unfolded his tale of love found and lost.

By the time Cloud climbed inside the mosquito net and settled into his cot, he was thoroughly intoxicated. In the middle of the night, he got up to pee. Staggering into the urinal, he vomited simultaneously with his urination. The emesis seemed to have a purgative effect on his troubled mind as well as his stomach, for when he returned to his cot, Cloud fell into a deep and restorative sleep.

Two days later Cloud located Mua's incense and charcoal scented home in My Tho. "***Chao Ba. Toi la Dai Uy*** Morgan," he said by way of introduction. Speaking in her language, but not knowing the softening euphemisms for death, Cloud explained in stark words that Xuan had been killed during the Tet Offensive. Mua wailed in grief.

After a time, Cloud said that he and Xuan had worked at near-by locations in Saigon. He planned to tell her in due course that he and her sister had been much more than friends, but Mua grasped the truth before he could diplomatically introduce the subject. She wanted to know the whole story, and Cloud told her a similarly edited version as he had with Mercury, omitting any word of their mutual extra-sensory experiences, and this time making no allusions to their physical intimacy.

Cloud gave Mua the key to Xuan's apartment and presented her with a cardboard box containing some of Xuan's things. Mua insisted on going through the carton right then. She glanced through the photo album and feeling obligated to provide him a gift, handed it to Cloud. "I would like you to have this," she said. Cloud took it gratefully.

As he watched Mua carefully handle each item from the box, Cloud took notice of the way she pursed her lips. With a pang of regret he thought that this is how Xuan might have looked in ten years. He liked Mua's strong and wise face.

"By the way," he said, "Do you have any idea where your brother is? Xuan told me she thought he had deserted from the ARVN."

"I wish I knew," she answered. "He is probably dead. I am certain he would never join in cause with the Communists. I pray and burn incense for him every day."

"It must be very hard not knowing one way or the other," Cloud said.

She took his hand when he left. "Thank you, captain. You are very kind, and I know my sister was blessed to be with you. You are welcome to return here any time."

A competent diagnostician would describe Cloud's behavior as clinical depression. He skipped meals because he had no appetite and went through the motions of work, but had trouble concentrating. He listened obsessively to a tape that Mercury lent him. The reel-to-reel recording, sent to Mercury by his rebellious younger brother in California, contained recent popular songs not approved for airplay by AFVN.

The psychedelic sounding "Incense and Peppermints" grabbed Cloud's mind and fed his depression while he internalized its nihilistic message. As with the song, Cloud didn't care what games he chose, felt his own innocence crippled, and brooded that the American Command was measuring the progress of the war with a yardstick for lunatics.

"Draft Dodger Rag" brought a brief smile to his lips as he wondered why the authorities would object to a song that, in his distracted view, mostly lampooned those who used every lame excuse available to evade military service. Anything to do with the draft must be taboo, he guessed. It's better not to encourage conscripted troops in a war zone to discuss the pros and cons of life in Canada.

Bob Dylan's "One Too Many Mornings" was also among the banned songs. There was nothing at all anti-war or subversive about it, other than Dylan wrote it. But Cloud didn't care about the official twists of logic needed to declare the song unsuitable for the troops, because the Beau Brummels arrangement offered him an aching reminder of too many empty mornings he had endured since Xuan's death.

A few nights after he returned from visiting Mua, a squad from the Viet Cong 514th Provincial Mobile Battalion launched a mortar attack against the Dong Tam base.

Everyone else in the 9th MI scooted into the sandbag covered bunker next to the interrogation tent, but Cloud sat still in his chair. He didn't care that a shell might fall on his head. It would be a mercy if one did hit him, he thought. Besides, chance was as likely for a mortar to strike the bunker as the tent.

When the all-clear was signaled, Mercury chewed him out.

"Leave me alone, *lieutenant*," Cloud retorted, pulling rank for the only time in his career. "It's no skin off your ass if I'm not afraid to die." There was no reasoning with him. He had turned his anger at Xuan's death onto himself.

"That's your asshole talking, *captain*, 'cause your mouth knows better," Mercury shot back.

For several days Lieutenant Busky Whiteroot had been observing Cloud from across the room at the Brigade Headquarters Officers Mess. Something about his melancholia powerfully attracted the Army nurse. She was sensually curious about him. This morning at breakfast she sat at his table and with some effort struck up a conversation with the taciturn captain.

She spoke and ate with gusto while he pecked at the toast and reconstituted eggs on his plate. When they had finished eating, she said, "I don't go on duty till this afternoon. Why don't we go for a walk?"

Busky was a tall, shapely blonde with a cheery and spontaneous personality. Cloud found her pleasant to sit with, particularly since he didn't have to do much to keep the conversation going. He loathed the competitive verbal machismo that military men brandished when talking about their work in the war. Having no specific obligations that morning, he found it easier to go along with her than to invent a reason why he couldn't. Over the course of their stroll around the base, Busky did nearly all the talking, and Cloud was content to listen to the upbeat flow of her words. He was most grateful that she didn't press him to talk about his feelings.

As they ambled past a bunker, Busky said, "Let's go in here for a little shade and privacy."

"It won't be private if there's a mortar attack," he said. This was the longest string of words he had put together so far that morning.

"We'll just have to take our chances," Busky replied and led him inside.

In the cool dampness of the bunker, she nuzzled herself into his arms and kissed him, making full use of her tongue. This startled Cloud, who had not picked up any of the erotic hints Busky had signaled during their walk. But lacking any reason to protest, he reciprocated her passionate gesture. After an interval of kissing and roaming hands, she broke the embrace long enough to unbutton and remove the tunic of her jungle fatigues and undo her olive drab bra. Cloud took off his tunic and olive drab tee shirt while Busky slid her slacks and olive drab panties down to the tops of her boots. Cloud dropped his pants, and Busky helped him do the same with his olive drab boxers.

The nurse settled back on a pile of their clothes, easing Cloud on top of her. Cloud's penis, however, remained limp, so Busky fingered his organ expertly. Still, there was no rising response. Following an uncomfortably long interval with no words or movement from either of them, she said, "Well, sometimes these things happen. Don't worry about it."

They fumbled for their clothing in silence, and then Cloud said, "You can go out first. I'll wait in here a while."

"Thanks, that's considerate of you," she said, patting him on the shoulder. "Don't do anything foolish while you're here."

As the day unfolded, Cloud did not worry about his encounter with impotence. He was too depressed to care about sex, much less think about this particular failure to function with someone he had just met.

It took a real tragedy to bring him out of this funk. An officer in the 25th MID at Cu Chi called Cloud at the request of Arquimedes Shapiro. The same night that Cloud had refused to take cover from a mortar attack against Dong Tam, Shapiro had taken a hit from a mortar fragment while running to a bunker at his base northwest of Saigon. His left arm had been badly mangled, and he had been evacuated to a hospital in Okinawa. Arquimedes would not be coming back to Viet Nam.

"The worst of it," the officer said, "was that his DEROS was the next day. He would be home already safe and sound and out of the

Army if he hadn't been hit. Now he'll be in a series of hospitals for months."

"Thanks for letting me know, lieutenant."

"You're welcome, sir. It was very important to him that I let you know. He hopes to see you again sometime."

Cloud decided that he also wanted to see Arquimedes, and for that to happen, he needed to live.

The next afternoon, a Chinook helicopter delivered a dozen suspected VC guerrillas to the base for interrogation. After the detainees were tagged and segregated in the barbed-wire prison compound known as the cage, a team of MPs brought them one at a time to the interrogation tent. Cloud sat in as an observer as Mercury and Sergeant Ho, an ARVN interpreter, questioned the first detainee.

No one was surprised that he claimed to be a simple peasant who knew nothing of Viet Cong activities in his village. They all said this, and a few of them were telling the truth when they did. In this particular case, however, Ho strongly suspected the man was VC, even though he had not been carrying a weapon when he was picked up in a general sweep. The questioning continued for some time without any progress.

Cloud stood up and walked over to the suspect. Speaking casually in Vietnamese, using the Delta dialect, Cloud said, "You seem like a good person. I would like to help you get back to your village. But you must be polite and address these two gentlemen by their proper positions." He pointed at Mercury and Ho.

The detainee was Pham van Hai. His given name, meaning "Number Two," signified in typically humble Vietnamese fashion that he was a first-born son. Hai was startled by Cloud's interruption, and immediately begged the pardon of the lieutenant and the sergeant. However, in his haste, he used nomenclature favored by the Communists, and this was the opening the interrogators needed to confirm Hai as a VC guerrilla.

When Hai at last realized that his fate was sealed and he would be spending the rest of the war in a POW camp, he spilled out a long tale of remorse for what he had done. He confessed to a series of atrocities and murders of village officials. Pham van Hai was tired of the war and wanted only to amend his karma.

As his monologue unfolded, he described the event that turned his life around. He had set a booby trap outside a hamlet and had gone to hide in a shack near Can Giouc. While there he experienced a vision of all the bad things he had done and ran away. As a result of this experience, he decided to repent and when he went back to disarm the booby trap, he found that it had been destroyed already. He thanked Buddha for this.

The prisoner smiled with relief as he was escorted back to the cage.

When not in the field, Captain Pride occasionally ate dinner at the Brigade Headquarters Officers Mess rather than with his own infantry company. One evening he sat at the table with Cloud and proceeded to enlighten the intelligence officer about the secret real reason the United States was engaged in combat in Viet Nam.

"Basically, this war is a Christian mission," Pride said. "We're in a crusade against godless Communists, pagan Buddhists, and the animistic Highland tribes."

"Oh?" said Cloud, unsure whether Pride was serious or facetious.

"Damn straight!" the infantry captain fired back. "Our government can't say so publicly, of course. Those ACLU assholes would be all over their butts like flies on shit if they told the truth in Washington. But our Armed Forces are here to spread the Christian gospel to these deluded people."

"Where would you get such a crazy idea?" Cloud asked. "The Constitution guarantees separation of church and state."

"It's not crazy," said Pride. "For one thing, these are slopes, not Americans, so the Constitution doesn't apply to them. Hey! Are you one of those Com symps or something?"

"I have no sympathy for the Communists," Cloud responded. "I voted for Goldwater for president, but that's beside the point. The Federal Government cannot favor one religion over another or proselytize while waging war."

"Oh yeah?" said Pride. "The United States Army can and does, all the time. The third verse of the *official* Army song 'The Army Goes Rolling Along' says, 'Faith in *God*, then we're *right* and we'll fight with all our might.' That proves that the Army wages war in the name of God. Jews and Moslems don't call God God; they call him Allah and Adonis or something like that. So by definition the song refers to the Christian God."

Cloud looked at his plate, shaking his head slowly. "Adonai," he said. "It's a Hebrew term of reverence for God, similar to Lord."

"Adonai, Adonis, what's the difference?" said Pride. "It's not God."

Cloud said nothing.

Pride continued, "My unit motto is 'Kill a Commie for Christ.' And we've given the Lord a shitload of dead Cong, which I'm sure he's pleased about. I pray with the men in my company before every operation. And I make it clear we go into battle under the sign and protection of Jesus Christ. You know what they say. There are no atheists in a firefight. But I'm not hard-shell about it. I let Jews and unbelievers in my unit stay for the prayers. Hell, I pray for them as much as for Christ's victory over the heathen Viets."

"Have any of your men been wounded or killed?" Cloud asked.

"Sure, lots of them," Pride replied. "That's life in a war zone."

"What happened to Jesus' protection of them?" Cloud pressed.

"God must've wanted them upstairs," said Pride. "Either that or they weren't very good Christians to begin with, so the Big Guy sent 'em packing to hell."

"I take issue with your claim about atheists in firefights," Cloud said. "It seems to me that the horrors of war often turn religious believers into religious doubters."

"Bullshit!" spat Captain Pride as he rose to leave. "And I see hell in your future."

Three days later, Busky Whiteroot joined Cloud for breakfast. They had not spoken since their unconsummated fumbling in the bunker. "I saw you talking to that Captain Pride the other day," she said. "They brought him into the hospital last night. He was badly injured in that explosion in one of the officers' latrines."

"I heard a rumor about fragging," said Cloud. "I didn't know he was the victim."

"The rumor is true," she said. "The word is that most of his men hated him. The problem is that there are so many soldiers with motives to attack him, and this makes for a very difficult CID investigation. There are hundreds of suspects."

"Which means, in effect, no suspects," Cloud said. "How badly was he hurt?"

"Very," Busky said. "He didn't survive."

"Oh," said Cloud. "I'm sorry." What he was genuinely sorry about was the pathology that created a world where soldiers murdered their own leaders. His feelings about the personal fate of Captain Pride were morbidly indifferent.

"Listen," Busky said, "I know the stress of war affects the whole body. If you'd like to try to get together again, in a more relaxed environment, I can arrange a place."

"That's very kind of you," said Cloud. "I like you. You're a very appealing woman. The thing is, I'm still mired in a Slough of Despond about the death of my fiancée during Tet. I don't think I'm up to any physical pleasure yet."

"I knew there was a secret grief gnawing at you. Thanks for confiding in me. Your secret's safe here," she said. "And by the way, you're a real poet with your words."

"Those are John Bunyan's words, not mine. Believe me, I'm no poet," Cloud said.

"OK, if you say so," Busky replied with a tone of skepticism in her voice.

"Really," he said. "Slough of Despond is an image from *The Pilgrim's Progress*. It's a Christian allegory, but just because I've read it, that doesn't make me religious."

"But spiritual for sure," she said. "And I think you're sweet. Just remember the offer stands if you begin to feel randy." She kissed him on the forehead, then took a piece of his toast and stuffed it in his mouth. "And eat something, for cryin' out loud!"

Among the detainees brought in one afternoon was a man who avoided being classified as Viet Cong by immediately confessing that he had run away from his ARVN unit. Jurisdiction in such circumstances belonged to the South Vietnamese government, so Sergeant Ho and an MP guard were dispatched to escort the deserter to an ARVN post in My Tho. Since his job was liaison, Cloud rode along to meet his counterparts in the local South Vietnamese intelligence section. Along the way, Cloud asked the deserter if he knew Xuan's brother, but he had never heard of him.

The broadly beaming intelligence officer announced to Cloud, "We have a female VC in custody, ready for ***cat van***. We invite you to observe our interrogation techniques. I think you will be impressed with the latitude and effectiveness of our procedures."

Mentally, Cloud noted that ***cat van,*** the Vietnamese verb to interrogate, literally meant to question the kidneys. This added painful nuances to the term absent in the English word.

The woman, unbound and without a blindfold, was escorted into the interrogation chamber by four ARVN soldiers armed with forty-five caliber pistols. The officer waved a stiletto tipped swagger stick in front of her face.

The prisoner, in her late twenties Cloud judged, wore cotton blouse and slacks, the outfit called black pajamas by American soldiers. Her face masked any emotion, but Cloud thought he detected mental strength -not defiance but more like determination- in her eyes. She remained standing, surrounded by the guards.

"Tell us the nomenclature of your unit and where your comrades are hiding," the officer instructed her.

"***Toi khong biet***," the woman answered.

The usual first response, Cloud thought. I don't know. He guessed this would be a long session.

"You must cooperate," the officer continued, "or I must find a way to make you cooperate. Perhaps you would like to share your cell with my horny guards?"

"***Khong. Toi khong biet***," she repeated.

The officer placed the tip of his swagger stick into her left nostril. "Let us not waste any more time. Remove your clothing!"

CHAPTER TWENTY-SEVEN

Unbuttoning her blouse with trembling hands, she stared at the floor. Shrugging off her shirt revealed that she wore no bra. With her whole body now shaking, the prisoner pushed her slacks to the floor. She paused then, leaving her underpants in place.

"Everything!" the officer insisted.

"*Khong!*" Cloud yelled. He picked up the woman's garments and handed them to her. "This is a violation of the Geneva Conventions," Cloud said to the officer with all the calmness he could muster. "You must not do this." Remembrance of a captured love letter flashed in his mind, and he wondered if this might be the Yellow River maiden he had met on paper in his previous life at the 1007th in Saigon.

"How squeamish and puritanical you Americans are," the officer replied evenly. "Very well, please captain, you interrogate this bitch. See how much information you can get out of her with your good cop game."

Though dressed once more, the prisoner's eyes now showed utter fear, for she knew what would happen to her when the Americans left.

"Alright," said Cloud. He turned to the MP. "Put her in handcuffs and a blindfold."

"Ah," said the ARVN officer, "I underestimated you. You intimidate by adding apparel rather than removing it."

"For the moment, yes," said Cloud. "We're going to take her to Dong Tam to interrogate her there. Would you care to follow along and observe?"

"You can't take my prisoner!" the officer shouted.

"I think I already have," Cloud said as Sergeant Ho and the MP escorted the woman through the door.

The woman wept quietly during the jeep ride to the American base.

At Dong Tam she was placed in a section of the compound separated from the male POWs, with private hygiene facilities. When she was brought to the interrogation tent, she looked at Cloud and said, "**Cam on, dai uy.**"

Cloud acknowledged her thanks, but beyond her name and home village, she refused to give her American interrogators any information. Cloud didn't care. Her comrades wouldn't be where they were when she was captured, anyway. And she wouldn't know any more of the infrastructure beyond the pseudonym of her cadre chief. But someday, when it really mattered, he thought, she would remember the compassion of her American enemy. Intellectually, he was clear that she was not the Yellow River maiden, but emotionally, he clung to a small fantasy that she might be.

Mercury was summoned to a rice paddy to interrogate a detainee whom a helicopter pilot had balked at transporting to Dong Tam. The Huey was standing by at the airstrip to take him to the site. Out of curiosity, Cloud invited himself along. On the way to the helicopter, Cloud stopped at a water truck to refill his canteen.

"We don't have time for a water buffalo stop," snapped Mercury. "The chopper's ready."

"Sorry," said Cloud. "I don't want to be stuck out there without water." He capped his half-filled canteen and followed Mercury at a trot.

"That stuff's no good anyway," shouted Mercury as they ducked under the whirling rotor. "You need lemonade powder or something to cover the disgusting chemicals the Army adds to make it allegedly potable."

"I know," Cloud shouted back. "But chlorinated water is better than what I might find in the village."

The pilot let them out in a rice paddy, where a squad of infantry was guarding a single detainee. The prisoner's arms were bound behind his back and a large red bandana covered most of his face as a makeshift blindfold. The unfortunate barefoot man wore a dirt encrusted white shirt and black shorts.

The squad leader approached Cloud and complained, "The chopper jockey won't take this gook to Dong Tam for interrogation. Claims he's a danger, just 'cause his ID card says he's got some kind of hooey. Says he's seen 'em before and won't have 'em in his aircraft. I apologize for calling you out here, sir, but we can't just let him go without your say so. He didn't have no weapon on him, though."

"Lieutenant Zared is the one you need to talk to," said Cloud. "But let's have a look at his ID."

Mercury was already talking to the detainee. "He's a *nguoi hui*," the interrogation officer announced. "A leper."

The squad leader stepped backward six paces. "Ugh! I put the blindfold on him. Who's got some disinfectant? I need to wash my hands pronto."

"Relax," said Cloud. "It takes prolonged exposure to Hansen's disease to become infected. Come over here. Look at the man's fingers."

"They look alright," the squad leader said,

Cloud squeezed the man's thumb, eliciting no reaction. "It's numb," he said. "Well, he's not much use to the VC. What do you recommend, Lieutenant Zared?"

"Let him go," Mercury ordered. "We'd have a devil of a time segregating him from the rest of the POWs in the cage."

"Stretch out your hands, corporal," said Cloud to the squad leader. When the soldier had complied, Cloud poured water from his canteen over his hands. "This is directly from a water buffalo, guaranteed to take the skin off an alligator."

"Thank you, sir," the corporal said.

Mercury untied the leper and removed the blindfold. "*Anh, di di mau!*" Mercury said to him. "Get out of here!"

"Tell him he can keep my bandana," said the squad leader. "To make up for the inconvenience and all."

Mercury stuffed the colorful cloth inside the leper's shorts.

The leper grinned, bowed his head in acknowledgment, and took off running across the rice paddy.

A chorus of laughter greeted this event. Cloud turned around and saw a score of children from the nearby village formed in a wide semicircle to watch the proceedings, apparently unafraid of the soldiers or their prisoner.

"There's no television out here," Mercury quipped. "This must be what they do for entertainment."

On a visit to the riverside park in My Tho, Cloud struck up a conversation with three Vietnamese soldiers. When he learned they were Cao Dai, his interest soared. They told him the Cao Dai had a private army, with their own chain of command, loosely affiliated with the ARVN. They were strongly anti-Communist, but favored reunification between North and South Viet Nam. They lived in a commune on an island in the My Tho River. Two twelve feet high temple towers on their island represented Christ and Buddha. These were overseen by a woman who served as their priest. The soldiers boasted of their independence and discipline and made dismissive remarks about their ARVN confederates, whom they characterized as weak and corrupt.

Cloud asked if he could visit their island and the soldiers said no. It was off limits.

During the jeep ride back to Dong Tam, Cloud mused about the ironies presented by these Cao Dai troops. They held to a universal vision, blending together many religious traditions, yet they were part of an exclusive army, segregated from their country's national armed forces. And they were anti-Communists who lived in a commune.

When he told Mercury about his encounter in the park, Mercury offered an account of his recent meeting with Hoa Hao soldiers. They too had a private army and shared the Cao Dais' negative attitudes about the ARVN. Hoa Hao were fiercely anti-Communist Buddhist warriors. The Hoa Hao sect opposed pomp and liturgy in worship, preferring simple, private devotions in their homes. They were the Puritans among Buddhist denominations in the country. With their disdain for ritual, they were the pietistic opposite of the Cao Dai, who loved elaborate, colorful ritual displays.

Cloud already knew a good deal about the Cao Dai religion and appreciated its egalitarian views about men and women, including ordained leadership for both sexes. Nothing he learned about the Hoa Hao inclined him to prefer the Buddhist sect. He still yearned to visit a Cao Dai temple, but this desire was now tempered with deep sadness that he would not be able to do so with Xuan.

This chance encounter with elements of a private army had another effect on Cloud. A vague idea swimming around in his mind was beginning to coalesce around a pessimistic assessment of the war. Two private Vietnamese armies operating at will exemplified the fragmented reality of Allied forces. On the enemy side, disciplined North Vietnamese regulars coordinated carefully with Viet Cong guerillas. Our side fielded international units with competing interests and differing military philosophies, including Australians, New Zealanders, Thais, Koreans, and Filipinos. The American commands, MACV and USARV, shared a single commander, but their staffs seemed to work at cross-purposes, with little mutual trust. Cloud wondered how any coherent strategy could survive this scenario.

Though his mind was reluctant to accept the idea, Cloud suspected they were set on a course in which soldiers in the field would soon begin acting like cornered rats, with no goal except personal survival. The vision for victory was narrowing rapidly into protecting individual interests. This was underscored for Cloud that night by a platoon leader in the officers mess.

The lieutenant bragged about his platoon's body count the previous day. There had been no combat that day, but a soldier found a dead Vietnamese man on the bank of the river. Though no wounds were visible and nothing about the man indicated any connection with the Viet Cong, following the rule that any dead Vietnamese was by definition Viet Cong, the lieutenant tallied one dead for his body count report.

The body was tossed into the river, where it washed up against the shore a few meters downstream. Another soldier spotted it and it was promptly recorded as another kill. Back in the river went the body, with the same result two hours later. So the platoon leader reported three VC kills that day.

The lieutenant boasted openly about his devious accounting, and everyone around him laughed heartily as if it were all a game. His body count numbers were accepted without question and passed up the chain of command, where they were added in with similar statistics from all over the country.

Cloud felt like vomiting.

The next day, the new Brigade Commanding Officer called a briefing for support and staff officers to inform them of a new policy concerning civilians. The colonel stood at the lectern, fumbling around in his pockets looking for something he obviously could not find. An attractive Vietnamese woman in a cocktail dress and high heels approached him deferentially and handed him his pipe, tobacco pouch, and Zippo lighter. He nodded silently and she quickly retreated from the room.

"Who's that?" Cloud whispered to Mercury.

"She's his live-in, full-service maid," Mercury replied softly. "He inherited her from his predecessor. It's in all our interests, don't you think, to have the Brigade CO satisfied and mellow."

The colonel tamped tobacco into the bowl of his pipe and lit it. After a few puffs, he exhaled the aromatic smoke of his favorite cherry and mint blend and began to speak. "It is of paramount importance to our success in this war that we interdict the flow of food to the Viet Cong units in our area of operations. There is no question in my mind that local villagers are providing food to the enemy, and this must stop. The simplest way for us to prevail in this conflict with the Communists is to starve 'em out.

"Therefore, effective immediately the following general order is in effect. Any Vietnamese civilian found in possession of more food than he or she can reasonably consume in one day will be detained for interrogation and the food will be confiscated. Possession of food for more than one person is prima facie evidence of supplying food to the Viet Cong. The Military Police will patrol all roads near this base and infantry units will enforce this order in the field. Any questions?"

Mercury raised his hand. "Sir, what about villagers taking produce or livestock they've raised into town to sell in the market?"

"They'll have to find alternative means of transporting their goods. Bus or truck or something," the colonel replied.

"What about carrying food to feed their families?" Mercury continued.

"They'll have to take their kids along," the CO explained. "One person, one day's rations. That's the rule."

"With all due respect, sir, this order is unrealistic and unfair."

The colonel turned to his aide and asked in a low voice, "Who is this uppity lieutenant?"

The aide answered, "Lieutenant Zared. He's an MI type, sir, in charge of the interrogation detachment."

"War is not fair, lieutenant," the colonel said addressing Mercury. "And I'll have your balls for dinner for your impudent and disrespectful behavior. Get the hell out of my briefing!"

Mercury left but Cloud stayed to the end. When they had been dismissed, the Military Police officers quietly grumbled about the idiocy of the order. They would deal with it, as they regularly did with other preposterous situations, by quietly ignoring it. If they found themselves in a situation where they were obliged to enforce the order, they would choose the most ludicrous case and give it maximum publicity. The MPs predicted the order would be quietly forgotten within two weeks.

After having his aide investigate Mercury, the new commanding officer learned that the MI Detachment was part of a separate chain of command and not under his direct authority. This news made him even madder, yet there was nothing he could do but complain to Mercury's commanding officer at 9th Division Headquarters at Bear Cat, which he did.

Two days later, Mercury received a letter from his CO stating that the Brigade CO would break his teeth trying to chew Mercury's brass balls for his supper.

In this instance, for the sake of his friend, Cloud was grateful for the Army's fragmented command structure.

The following week the MPs detained a seventy-two year-old woman caught with a large head of cabbage. They brought her to the interrogation tent with the explanation that she couldn't possibly consume the whole head in one day. The guards had a difficult time suppressing grins as they reported this information. Mercury ordered her transported to the Division POW compound at Bear Cat with instructions that per orders of the Brigade CO, this woman was a confirmed VC who was supplying cabbage to the enemy.

Three days later, after returning from a summons to see the Division Commanding General, without fanfare the new Brigade commander rescinded his order.

Cloud sat quietly in the S-3 tent, observing the planning for an air-mobile assault against elements of the 514th Provincial Mobile Battalion. A landing zone had been identified on a large aerial photo wall map of the Mekong Delta, but something about it didn't seem right to Cloud. Months of sitting in a windowless room reading captured enemy documents congealed in his mind, providing him with an intuitive sense of the situation.

"Pardon me, sir," Cloud said. "That location is exactly where the VC would expect us to touch down. They'll be waiting in ambush."

"Do you have any tactical experience, captain?" the S-3 asked.

"No, major, but I've read thousands of captured VC documents, and I have gained a sense of how they think. That spot is ideal for an air-mobile LZ, and the VC will expect Americans to take the easy path."

"Where would you recommend for our LZ, Captain Morgan?" the S-3 asked.

"Right here," Cloud said, pointing to a spot half a kilometer away from the proposed site. "There's just enough room for the Hueys to get in and out, with no room for error, but if you can pull it off, you'll catch them napping."

"OK, Captain Morgan. We'll use a smaller force and try it your way."

At dawn two days later, the operation was launched, and Cloud spent the morning in the operations tent listening to reports of its progress. It was proving to be a great success, with no American casualties.

The radio crackled and a voice from the field said, "Flamingo three this is Billygoat six, over."

The S-3 picked up the mike. "Billygoat six, this is Flamingo three. I read you lima charlie, over."

"Flamingo three, we've uncovered a large cache of VC papers, and our ARVN here tells us they might be very important. Can we get one of those MI dudes out here for a look-see? Over."

"I'll go, sir," Cloud volunteered.

Ten minutes later, Cloud climbed into a Sioux Scout helicopter to be whisked off to the operational landing zone. The Scout was known familiarly as a bubble, because its clear plastic dome resembled a soap bubble. There was room for one passenger beside the pilot, right in front of the engine.

The pilot, barely out of his teens, gave Cloud a ride worthy of the best amusement parks as he skimmed over the tops of trees and swooped up and down through the air for the sheer joy of it. A soldier on the ground threw a yellow smoke canister to identify the LZ, and the bubble touched down long enough for Cloud to alight and clear the rotors before the pilot started his ascent.

At that moment, crouching in a stand of reeds nearby, a VC with a hand-held grenade launcher fired at the helicopter. The projectile struck a corner of the engine, and the concussion caused the bubble to buckle into the ground, stunning the pilot. Acting solely on instinct and without any consideration of the nobility of his deed, Cloud turned and ran toward the bubble, and relying on a surge of adrenaline, unbuckled the trapped pilot. Throwing the young man over his shoulder fireman style, Cloud trotted away from the burning machine.

As he lumbered toward safety, a compatriot of the man who had fired the grenade launcher took several sniping shots at Cloud. One of the bullets struck Cloud in the left buttock, causing him to stumble, depositing his cargo and himself unceremoniously in a patch of sticky mud.

The arc of that bullet proved fortunate for Cloud and the pilot, for the moment they hit the ground, the helicopter exploded, sending fragments of metal in all directions, including over the low lying heads of the two recent occupants of the now destroyed flying machine.

Soon thereafter, Cloud lay prone on a poncho, naked from the waist down, as a medic dressed his wound. A box of captured documents was placed beside him, and Cloud read samples from it, stopping occasionally to wince.

"Well," he said, having read enough for a confident evaluation, "these would have been extremely important six weeks ago. This is all about preparations for the Tet operations."

The pilot and Cloud returned to Dong Tam on stretchers laid out in a Huey. It turned out that the pilot whose life Cloud saved was the son of a three-star general at the Pentagon. This is why the following week in a hastily convened small ceremony at HQ, the Brigade Commander pinned on Cloud's uniform a second Purple Heart medal and a second Bronze Star, this one adorned with a V for valor.

He was given a few days to rest his aching butt and thus had time for more brooding. "If I had finished flight training," he mumbled to himself, "I could have been that pilot. Would my passenger have rescued me or would I be dead now?" His world had certainly turned upside down, he thought. What was it that Miss Listerbaum had said to him before she died? When everything turns upside down, dance on the ceiling. He associated the ceiling with floating out of his body. "Is that what she wanted me to know?" he whispered. "In the face of ill fortune, leave my body for a while."

He lay in his cot curled up on his right side, so as to avoid pressure on his left cheek. From this fetal position he began deep, slow breathing and soon was hovering above his mosquito netting. Off Cloud went to explore the countryside, following an eastward course along the My Tho River. The brown, sinuous, dragon's claw of a stream flowed quietly toward the South China Sea.

Presently he encountered an American platoon engaged in sweeping a hamlet in search of any VC who may be hiding there. Cloud slipped into the first hut and observed a large corporal teasing an old woman, who was trying to prevent him from taking away her mentally retarded nine year-old grandson.

"Come on, mama-san, let's have the kid," the corporal demanded.

The boy was on his knees behind his grandmother. Roughly, the corporal grabbed him and pulled him outside. "You're not so smart, are you, kid? Ya wanna go for a ride in a Huey?"

The boy had no idea what this man wanted, and he shivered in terror.

"Hell, I don't want to waste a free ride on a freak like you. I'll just give you something to remember second platoon by." The soldier threw the boy to the ground and held him down with his boot. Casually he took a paper clip from his pocket and shaped it into a numeral 2, bending a piece at the bottom by which to grip it with pliers. Thus holding his numerical creation, the corporal took out a cigarette lighter and heated it. He rammed the makeshift brand into the boy's forehead. As the boy yelped in pain, the corporal said, "Now promise you won't forget me, huh kid?"

Cloud wanted to intervene but felt helpless without his body. All he could do was mentally scream at the sadistic soldier. The grandmother was now cradling her grandson, and Cloud could not bear the anguish in the woman's face, so he floated across a dirt lane into another thatched hut. Here a sergeant was interrogating an old man. "Tell me where Charlie's hiding!" he demanded. The old man cowered in a corner. "Where in this shit hole hamlet do you have them stashed?" In response to the man's silence, the American NCO kicked him in the groin, and as the grandfather rolled over in agony, the American kicked him repeatedly in the face.

"Hey sarge," a private said to him, "maybe he don't understand English."

"Oh, don't be stupid, dickbrain. All these gooks know English," the sergeant said.

Cloud floated out to the edge of the hamlet, where he found three soldiers gathered around a thirteen year-old girl. The girl was naked, her torn clothes thrown aside, except for a scrap of her blouse stuffed in her mouth as an improvised gag. By turns, the three held her down and raped her.

Cloud was sick and impotent with rage and did not want to see anymore. Before turning away, however, he glimpsed the nametag of one of the rapists: Wimple.

As he sailed back to the base to return to his body, he passed over a rice paddy, in the middle of which stood an American soldier handing out candy and plugs of chewing tobacco to a horde of eager children.

At the top end of an interesting inlet, Cloud discovered the decaying body of an American soldier, who had been the last man in a reconnaissance patrol. A VC squad had captured and tortured the man before killing him. The body was propped up against a tree, where it would be certain to be found by a future patrol. The soldier's genitals had been removed and stuffed in his mouth. This is certainly not what Miss Listerbaum had meant by dancing on the ceiling, Cloud thought.

The next day, Cloud tracked down Wimple's unit and made a visit to the company commander, Captain Krieg.

"Do you have a man named Wimple in your company?" Cloud asked.

"In second platoon," said Krieg. "He's a good fighter. We need more like him."

"I've received an anonymous report that three of your men engaged in a gang rape on your recent sweep," Cloud told Krieg. "One of them was named Wimple."

"Who's your anonymous source?" Krieg asked.

"I can't say," Cloud responded. "For security reasons." The circumstances of his observation made that impossible.

"Well, I'm not going to tear down unit morale on the basis of someone who's too chicken to step forward in person and state his case," Krieg said. "Unless someone has evidence, there's nothing I can do."

"I see," said Cloud. "I just thought you should know."

After Cloud left, Captain Krieg summoned Wimple.

"Your extracurricular exploits have been observed and talked about, Wimple," Krieg said.

"Sir?" Wimple responded.

"On the last mission. You know what I'm talking about," Krieg continued.

Wimple paled but said nothing.

"Now listen, you stupid shithead," the captain snarled, "Keep your stinking cock in your pants! I've got it covered this time, but I don't want CID swarming all over the company. And tell your pals too. Dismissed!"

On April Fools Day, Cloud visited Mua to say farewell. He was certain he would never see her again. At no time had he ever been in a position to protect them, but he was overcome with a sense of guilt that he was abandoning Xuan's family to a violent fate.

As she handed him a cup of tea, Cloud could not stop himself from looking directly into Mua's eyes, but then knowing how rude this was, he quickly turned away and peered through the chain link mesh covering the riverside window of the house.

Outside in the yard beside the river, he saw two girls. A toddler rode on the hip of an older girl, whom he guessed was about seven. The toddler was naked and the older girl wore only tan shorts. Both were laughing. How innocent they are, he thought, correctly surmising they were Mua's daughters. But for how long?

Tears formed in his eyes when he said goodbye to Mua.

At 0900 hours on the fourth day of April, Cloud boarded a Pan American jet at Ton Son Nhut Airport for his return flight to the United States. As the plane cleared the runway and rose into the sky, the cabin full of homebound soldiers burst into roaring cheers and whistles.

"We're going back to the World!" shouted a soldier at the back of the plane. A chorus of soldiers drunk on the promise of freedom chanted, "Back to the World, back to the World!"

When the captain announced they had cleared Vietnamese airspace and were now over international waters, more cheers erupted throughout the cabin. Through it all, Cloud sat silently lamenting all he had lost in that beautiful and tragic tan and green garden of a country.

Due to the International Dateline, it was still April fourth when the chartered plane, having refueled in Okinawa, landed at Travis Air Force Base in California.

Cloud had four months of active duty commitment remaining, and in his closing days in Viet Nam, he had decided not to stay in the service beyond that time. His dream of being a career Army officer was over. He was not, he came to believe, cut out for the work. On second thought, he concluded that he was quite good at intelligence work but did not fit in with the culture of the military. His discipline came from within himself and not from external authority.

After clearing customs, Cloud rode a bus to the Oakland Army Terminal, where he picked up his orders to Fort Bliss, Texas. His assignment was Adjutant at the Defense Language Institute branch at Biggs Air Force Base, next to Fort Bliss. This school offered an eight-week survival course in Vietnamese. It would be an easy post, allowing him time to contemplate future plans before returning to civilian life.

He considered taking a few days of leave in the Bay area to visit Gunnar and Irene. He no longer felt any romantic attachment to Irene and could not remember why he had once believed he loved her. The prospect of facing Gunnar was too painful, however. His friend's pacifism would cast an accusing shadow across Cloud's wartime experiences, and Cloud was not ready to deal with his growing feelings of guilt.

A cab delivered him to the San Francisco International Airport for a stand-by flight to El Paso. While Cloud stood waiting in the terminal, a troupe of anti-war protesters strolled by rapt in heated conversation. One of them, clad in jeans and a tie-dyed tee shirt, spotted Cloud in his now rumpled khaki uniform.

"Hey, soldier dude," the protester said. "Have you heard the news? Some racist warmonger just shot Martin Luther King in Memphis."

"Oh, no," said Cloud, shocked by the report.

"So, where have you been, lately?" the student asked snidely.

"I just returned from Viet Nam," Cloud said.

"Y'know what I think of you baby-killers in Viet Nam?" the protester continued. "I think this!" He spat, staining the fabric over Cloud's heart with a large gob of saliva.

Cloud's first reaction was to grab the young man by his throat, but he checked the impulse. Something snapped inside, and instead of defending himself against the insult he said to the protester, "You have every right to be upset with the war. I am ashamed of many things I saw there." Cloud extended his arms sideways in a gesture of openness. "I accept your contempt on behalf of every soldier in the war. Please, spit on me again. And the rest of you, you can spit on me too."

The protester said, "You're crazy, man."

"Come on," said Cloud, "who'll be next to spit on me? Will no one punish me?"

They turned and walked away in silence.

On the plane to El Paso, Cloud brooded about the stain on his uniform. It looked like a scarlet badge, a vivid gash, which everyone could see, even though people were too polite to say anything about it.

Deep in meditation on the subject of the spittle he bore, somewhere over Nevada, Cloud left his body and floated around the cabin. From his ceiling vantage point, Cloud noticed that all the passengers and crew had red stains on their shirts or blouses, right over their hearts. As he stared in wonder at the plethora of stains, they changed from scarlet to blue to white to purple to gold, including the one on his uniform. Then came a chorus of changes, like colored lights shining through a fountain of water. The stains flashed and shone in pulsing rhythms of brilliant hues.

Cloud returned to his body and noticed that the stain over his heart had disappeared. He looked around the cabin and saw that the glittering stains of all the others were gone too. Searching for a scientific explanation, Cloud decided that it had been an optical illusion due to atmospheric conditions. His stain had simply dried in the arid environment.

CHAPTER TWENTY-EIGHT

Adjutant -personnel officer for the DLI branch- was an undemanding job. Cloud had little to do, so he spent a lot of time at his desk daydreaming about what might have been. One morning he was grieving over the circumstance that he and Xuan had never visited the Cao Dai Temple at Tay Ninh. He was sure this omission would haunt him for decades.

Alone in a world of unfulfillment, he was therefore relieved when a visitor strolled into his office.

"Good morning, Captain Morgan. I'm Chaplain Crimond Greenpasture."

"Good to meet you, major. What brings you here?" Cloud said.

"I'm required to meet with each of the Army officers in the detachment for the quarterly character guidance lecture," the chaplain explained. "Besides, you're something of a celebrity around here, and I wanted to meet you."

"I can't think of anything that would qualify me as a celebrity," Cloud said, surprised such a term would be applied to him.

"Not so, my friend. Your reputation has preceded you here. Young captain, rising star, genuine war hero -and skilled linguist to boot," Crimond responded.

"Don't bullshit me, major. I'm getting out in three months," Cloud said.

"So I hear," Crimond said. "I also hear that certain influential people in your branch are trying to get you to stay in by offering you a faculty position at USAINTS."

"Are you sure you're a chaplain and not MI?" Cloud wanted to know. "Where do you hear all these things? Your information is accurate, by the way, but I turned it down."

"I suppose I would have made a good spy," Crimond confessed. "People just naturally confide in me. But alas, God called me to ministry."

"So, what is this character guidance business?" Cloud asked, changing the subject away from careers and the calling of God.

"Ah, well, here is a leaflet for you to read. I'll just mark down that I delivered it to you, and that will satisfy the requirement." The chaplain hesitated, weighing whether to proceed with opening a painful subject. He decided to do it. "Captain Morgan, I've also received a communication about you from a mutual friend. Colonel Melita wrote to me about the loss of your fiancée. I'm very sorry. He cares about you more than you know, and he asked me to look in on you to see how you're doing."

Cloud felt a flush of affection for his commanding officer at the 1007th and was grateful for Melita's request that a friend check on him. He doubted, however, that a chaplain was the right person to do that. "Thank you, Major Greenpasture. Under the circumstances, I'm doing pretty well. I'm not suicidal, at any rate." This last remark was not something Cloud had intended to say, but it popped out before his ego could censor it.

"Ah, yes, well, I'm glad you're OK," Crimond said. He started to get up from his chair, then hesitated and sat down again. "Th-th-there's something else I wanted to ask you about," he stammered.

"What is it?" Cloud said.

"I had a rough time in Nam, and you've just come back from a grievous situation there. I was wondering if we could sit down sometime and just talk about stuff," Crimond said. "No proselytizing, I promise."

"Like mutual therapy?" Cloud asked.

"Something like that, perhaps." The chaplain laughed. "I need to get some things off my chest, and I don't know anyone else I can trust."

"How do you know you can trust me?" Cloud said.

"I don't know. I just feel that I can," Crimond admitted.

"Let me show you something first," Cloud said. His dog tags were attached to his key-chain. He tossed the keys across the desk and said, "Look at what it says about my religion."

Crimond saw the words "No Preference" embossed into the metal.

"That's an Army euphemism," Cloud said. "I don't believe in God."

"I'm having trouble believing in God myself," the chaplain whispered. "That's why I need to talk with you."

They made arrangements to meet at the Officers' Club that night.

Major Greenpasture scooped a wad of guacamole dip onto a corn chip and held it in the air, halfway between the table and his mouth. "The thing is, I still believe in God, but not the same God I believed in before I went to Viet Nam," he explained to Cloud. "Before the war, I was certain God was on the side of America. I was a gung ho apologist for US military involvement in Southeast Asia. I still have trouble with the Communists, but I became greatly disillusioned by what I saw our side doing to that country. And it has affected my faith."

Cloud sipped a chilled glass of Lone Star beer. "In my case, I went there not believing in God, and came very close to becoming a believer in the midst of it all, and have returned a confirmed unbeliever once again."

Crimond finally chewed the chip, took a deep swig of beer, and said, "I'm convinced that whatever else may or may not be true about God, his favorite form of expression is irony." He then launched into a long tale about the horrors he had encountered in Viet Nam, as told to him by young soldiers who needed to confess the wrenching things they had seen and terrible deeds they had done.

"I found it very difficult to preach to them about personal morality, when they were forced into the most egregious ethical binds every day," the chaplain said. "How could I tell them it's a sin to go to the steam bath for a blow job but not a sin to burn down a village or spray napalm on kids?"

Cloud listened. "Hmmm," he said.

"I was getting pressure from my chain of command to support the war. Don't give the troops any support for pacifistic propaganda. Let them know that what they're doing to fight for freedom and democracy is moral and right. God approves of the terrible things they have to do for America to prevail. If they make a mistake and accidentally kill a baby or blow the brains out of an innocent civilian, God forgives them. God, however, is a very harsh judge of any soldier who disobeys a superior or expresses seditious thoughts."

"There's always a catch, isn't there?" Cloud mused. "So how did you handle the pressure?"

"I bit my tongue and gave them the party line. But I hated myself for it. I still do," Crimond confessed. "God forgive me for selling out to the system. But my concept of God changed in Viet Nam," he continued, "from the One who makes the rules and expects obedience to the One who weeps in the midst of the hells that humans create on earth."

"The God you describe must feel helpless in the face of evil," Cloud said. He was thinking of how he felt when he encountered gang rape and torture while he was out of his body. All he had to use was the suggestive power of his mind, but that wasn't very effective in those extreme situations involving people determined to hurt others. The sea lions in Monterey Bay had been receptive to his thoughts but the brutalized and brutalizing soldiers heard nothing.

"Not helpless so much as not omnipotent," Crimond responded. "The God I believe in now has influence in our lives but not absolute power. Does that make me a heretic?"

"Given your earlier comment about God's use of irony, it is ironic indeed that an ordained man of God should be asking an atheist if he's a heretic," Cloud said with a wry smile.

Narcissa sent Cloud a clipping from the Arizona Republic she was sure would please him. "**LOCAL CAPTAIN RETURNS HERO,**" the headline read.

Army Captain Evan Cloud Morgan, 24, of Phoenix, has been reassigned from the 9th Infantry Division in the Mekong Delta to Fort Bliss, Texas, where he serves as Adjutant to the Defense Language Institute. Morgan, a Phoenix native, received two Purple Heart medals and two Bronze Stars, one with a V for valor, while serving in the Republic of Viet Nam. He is a 1961 graduate of West High School in Phoenix and a 1965 graduate of Arizona State University. His parents, Narcissa and Lloyd Morgan, reside in the Palmcroft District of Phoenix.

As it happened, Narcissa misjudged her son's reaction to the piece. The epithet hero embarrassed him, particularly as he felt himself to be quite unheroic. And the more he thought about it, the madder he got at the gall of his mother to provide such self-serving information to the press. She had to have been the source, he thought. No one else would have done it. And as long as she was going to do it, why didn't she mention the 1007th? If he was proud of anything, it was his work with the MI Battalion.

To fill his time, Cloud began sitting in on language classes. He soon learned these classes were far different from those he had known at Monterey. The typical student here was not a linguist but rather a military advisor whose aim was to learn a few words and phrases to help him get around in-country.

Many of the students were literalists, who assumed Vietnamese was a variation on English. They could not comprehend that the letters in the Vietnamese alphabet did not have the sound values of the same letters in English. Thus they frequently mispronounced words, often in comic ways. Some of the humor only the teachers knew, however. Vietnamese is a tonal language, and a change in tone means a change in meaning. Since most students had little facility with tones, they were prone to pronouncing common words using the wrong tone, thus saying not what the instructor was trying to teach them but something entirely different. In a significant number of cases, what they actually said was obscene.

Cloud felt sympathy for the long-suffering teachers, as they tried hard to impart their beloved language to soldiers who had no affection for it. He loved the Vietnamese tongue as much as he hated the war. He hoped he would be able to retain fluency in the years ahead but had no idea where or how he would use it.

One thing he knew with certainty, however, was that his grieving for Xuan was not over. Most of his grief had been repressed while in the Delta because his life depended on it, but he fully expected that once he left the Army, the emotional pain would return stronger than ever.

On midsummer's eve 1968, Terp suffered a nightmare in which the soldier she had met the night of the blackout sat on an ash-heap with tears rolling down his face. She had seen him briefly in the elevator and had spoken with him only in the unlit hallway, but she had long since decided that the young man in the photograph her father had taken of her in the souvenir shop the day after the blackout was the lieutenant who conversed with her in the dark, and it was his image that filled her troubling dream.

Why she remembered him at all she did not know, but she suspected he represented in some cosmic way all the soldiers caught up in that terrible war. She desperately wanted all of them to come home and be at peace. But in her dream, this representative soldier was clearly not at peace, and this caused Terp to tremble.

Cloud returned to Phoenix on terminal leave near the end of July. Lloyd met him at the airport with significant yet not surprising news. He and Narcissa were separated. Lloyd had rented a townhouse in Scottsdale and lived there on what he expected to be a long-term basis. He had not filed for divorce and would not do so unless Narcissa wanted it, but he could no longer live in the same house with her. Cloud was welcome to camp out with him, if he wished, or stay with his mother, as he preferred.

Cloud said he would stay with his dad only until he found his own apartment. For several weeks, a broad plan for what he would do with his life had been developing in Cloud's mind, and an apartment in Tempe was part of it. He would take a couple of graduate courses in history at ASU while he fine-tuned the plan.

Most of Cloud's pay while overseas had been deposited in a

savings account at the Maricopa National Bank, and Lloyd had added the proceeds from the sale of Cloud's old Ford Fairlane. So he had enough money to live on for a good while, without having to look for gainful employment. The last thing he wanted right then was a professional job.

Lloyd drove Cloud to the house on Monte Vista so that he could greet his mother and collect his civilian clothes and assorted items. The first thing Cloud noticed when he walked into the foyer was the Arizona Republic article about him matted and mounted in a gold frame on the wall. Every sighted person who entered the house would see it.

After dutifully hugging Narcissa, Cloud said, "Mom, please take that thing down. It's inaccurate and embarrassing."

"Why nonsense, Cloud. It's a very flattering story. I want everyone to know that I'm very proud of you. You are my hero. And not only that," she added, tapping her knuckles on the glass, "this article makes you the most eligible bachelor in Phoenix."

If Cloud had needed a catalyst to unleash a wave of anger and grief, this was it. A fierce ache rose from his mind and rolled out of his mouth without prior conscious consideration. "Mother!" he roared, "I am NOT a bachelor. I am a WIDOWER!"

"Well, this is certainly news to me," Narcissa huffed indignantly.

Before that moment, Cloud had not thought of himself as a widower. He and Xuan had been engaged, but no wedding ceremony, official or unofficial had taken place. And yet his mother's presumption had brought to the surface a strong sense that in some undefined and universal way he and Xuan had indeed been husband and wife. And regardless of the technical category that would be attributed to their relationship, he certainly felt like a man who had lost his wife.

He considered explaining the situation to his mother but decided she would neither understand nor approve. Besides, he secretly enjoyed the shocked look on her face when he said the word widower. He would offer nothing about Xuan unless she asked, and he doubted that she would dare to seek such information.

"Look," said Cloud, "I don't want to get into an argument my first day back. Forgive my outburst. It'll take some time for me to adjust to being a civilian again."

Mollified, Narcissa said, "I hope you won't mind, but I sent the newspaper article to that Sergeant Frogger at West High. I thought he should know about his star cadet."

This made Cloud smile. "No, I don't mind that at all. Thanks, Mom." Now he hugged her with genuine affection. "But please don't send it to anyone else."

After a polite interval exchanging small talk, Cloud gathered a load of his civilian clothes and personal effects and headed off to Scottsdale with Lloyd.

Lloyd helped Cloud move into his new apartment east of the Arizona State campus on Apache Boulevard. Cloud had bought a double bed and a few items of furniture, but otherwise, the place was Spartan in its appointments. In a corner of the living room, the two men piled all the boxes of Cloud's pre-war possessions they had liberated from a closet and the garage at the Monte Vista house.

The day was hot, as befitted the Valley of the Sun, so after setting up Cloud's new bed and his old stereo system, they took a refreshment break. Lloyd had brought a cooler of homemade lemonade. Cloud pulled two glass tumblers from the freezer section in the apartment's ancient refrigerator, and Lloyd poured the drinks.

"I'd like to hear more details about your experiences in Viet Nam," Lloyd said. "But I know that I never leveled with you about what happened to me in World War II. I'd like to tell you now."

"I really want to hear your story," said Cloud. "All the time I was growing up I yearned to know what you did in the war, and you never talked about anything except a few funny anecdotes from your stateside training. What was it like flying over the Third Reich?"

Lloyd sighed. At long last, he was going to be brutally honest about himself, revealing to his son, who at this moment was the only person in the world Lloyd loved, the bitter secret that had cursed his life for nearly a quarter century. "You know that I was a B-24 pilot."

"Yes," said Cloud. "As a kid I thought that was the most romantic and heroic thing a man could do."

"Well, it wasn't," Lloyd said. He refilled his tumbler and began his tale. "I flew ten bombing missions over Germany with only minor flak damage to the plane and no casualties. The Luftwaffe fighters couldn't get near us. We reached our targets, dropped the bombs and flew back to England. But we knew our luck wasn't likely to last.

"The entire time in flight I lived in two worlds. I was fully conscious of the planes above and beside me and in front and behind. Every second I knew where they were in relation to my craft, and I was acutely aware of the laws of physics with regard to contact between heavy objects in midair. In training they harped on collisions taking more lives than enemy fire.

"At the same time I was in deep meditation, feeling disembodied, as if nothing existed except my mind. The sky and the cloud of bombers were illusions. I was merely floating peacefully in space and not on my way to rain destruction on buildings and people. I guess today you'd call it a state of Zen, and I became superstitious that as long as I could stay in this mental groove, all would be well.

"On the eleventh mission, after dropping our load on a marshaling yard, we turned for home and flew into a box of heavy and accurate flak. The plane above me to port was hit hard and two engines were on fire. It lost altitude and rolled in the direction of my craft. My mental groove instantly evaporated and I calculated the distance and trajectory and knew it would miss us. But then my rat brain took over and I pulled up and away from the damaged plane. What I didn't know was that after releasing the bombs, Tommy, the bombardier, had left the nose to use the relief tube and visually inspect the bomb bay doors. But I should've known. He was obsessive about those doors. When I banked, he banged his head and fell onto the doors and busted through. His parachute never opened."

"How awful," Cloud said.

"When we got back to base, I was a mess. I couldn't sleep that night. Tommy was dead, and it was all my fault. If the Germans had killed him, I could have accepted that, but *I* had decimated my crew. You know that decimate means to kill a tenth of a unit, and that's exactly what I'd done. Images of Tommy falling through the cold night air kept flashing through my mind.

"A few days later I flew my twelfth mission, and it went well enough, except that I was a mental wreck the whole time. I couldn't reach that meditative Zen state. I didn't give a damn about what might happen to me but kept worrying I'd kill another member of the crew. The eerie thing was we got a new bombardier, whose name was also Tommy. I'd just killed a guy named Tommy Olson, and his replacement was Tommy Person."

"Well, tragic accidents happen in war," Cloud said. He wanted to say more but could not find any suitable words and what he had just said felt trite to him. For a few moments silence prevailed.

And then Lloyd whispered, "That's not the end of the story."

CHAPTER TWENTY-NINE

Mechanically, as if he were an automaton, Lloyd refilled both glasses with lemonade and drained half his before speaking again.

"When the call came for the pre-flight briefing for the next mission, my thirteenth, I flopped. That is, I went into a blind funk and refused to get my ass out of bed. My co-pilot came and tried to jolly me into the briefing room, but I wouldn't budge. I had an overwhelming dread that I would kill Tommy Person just like I'd killed Tommy Olson. Eventually, the squadron CO came with two MPs, and they hauled me off to the psych ward at the base hospital.

"After eight weeks in the psych ward I was released to ground duty. I felt ashamed that my mistake had killed a man and worried that the real truth was that I was an emotional weakling. After a couple of weeks, I asked to go back to flight duty, but a sadistic colonel said no. He enjoyed calling me a coward and denying me a chance at redemption. I was assigned to S-4 and finished the war brooding about being a sad sack. I supervised the purging of personal effects of MIAs and KIAs before shipping them to next of kin. No photos or letters went back, because we didn't want a wife to accidentally get a picture of a girlfriend. And no rubbers or other embarrassing stuff, of course."

"Oh, Dad! I wish I'd known this a long time ago," Cloud

responded. "I wouldn't have understood back then how war can play cruel games with your mind. But I do now! You've got nothing to be ashamed of."

"I heard about the Pearl Harbor attack on the radio," Lloyd said. "While the local announcer was waiting for further information, he played patriotic songs. The first one was "Stout Hearted Men" by Nelson Eddy. It stirred my soul, and I said to myself 'I'm stout hearted, and I'm going to join the fight!' In the war I learned otherwise, and I've had to live with that ever since."

"Don't discount your courage, Dad," Cloud said. "But you're also tender hearted, and for my money, that trumps stout hearted any day."

There was another part of the story that filled Lloyd's mind, but he chose not to speak of it. It had to do with a vision he had seen in the 1930s, but this was too intimate a thing to reveal to his son. Even in the midst of this deep sharing of war experiences, Lloyd could not reveal what he perceived as the least manly aspect of his personality.

The Morgan genetic inheritance stretching back eons in the English county of Shropshire carried certain mystical traits. Lloyd became partially aware of this as a teenager but suppressed the knowledge because he wanted to be a regular guy in a strongly male cultural environment. The world where he grew up in Central Pennsylvania looked upon the mystical as purely feminine.

"There's a postscript that probably won't surprise you," Lloyd added. "What happened in England affected my marriage when I came home. Your mother wanted me to be a hero. Hell, she **needed** me to be a hero. You can imagine how disappointed she was when I came home in disgrace."

"That's hardly in disgrace," Cloud interjected. "You flew a dozen bombing missions over Germany and then served honorably on the ground. That's more than I ever did, and they gave me medals."

"Be that as it may, Son, your mother was deeply disappointed. I sometimes suspect she would have preferred my death in combat to my returning the way I did. At any rate, she tried to love me when I came home a lesser man than when I had left, but over time she became emotionally distant, and I came to believe it was only what I deserved." He took a sip of lemonade, waiting for a response from his son, but Cloud remained silent, so he added, "Of course, I don't feel that way now. Nobody deserves a loveless marriage, which is why I left your mother."

"I often wondered how you stood it so long," Cloud responded. "She can be rather manipulative."

"She's not a bad person," Lloyd explained. "She's just screwed up in her head. But then again, we all are, aren't we? So I guess it's no big deal."

"Yeah," said Cloud. "I'm beginning to think that all human beings are essentially flawed. The stuff I saw in Viet Nam shows me that basically decent people, put in the wrong circumstances, are capable of horrendous brutality. I wouldn't call it original sin, like the Christians do, but there's something not right in all of us."

Before leaving that evening, Lloyd said, "By the way, on a lighter note, a friend of mine who owns a car dealership just took a year-old VW Beetle as a trade-in. Believe me, I know cream puffs, and this is a doozy. As a favor to me, he would give you a great deal on it. Would you like to take a look at it tomorrow?"

Cloud did want to look at it, and the next day he bought the baby blue bug.

Cloud also realized that the growing bond of mutual understanding and affection that he and his father had enjoyed over the years in response to Narcissa's actions had been deepened by Lloyd's confession. So much of what he had misinterpreted as a child now made sense. Knowing that his father had spent two months in a psychiatric hospital during the war increased the esteem in which he held Lloyd.

The ringing phone shook Narcissa out of a daydream in which Barry Goldwater was pursuing her with passionate entreaties of undying love. "Hello?" she crooned.

"Narcissa, this is Dante Kherbet. I haven't seen you for a while, and I wanted to see how you're doing."

"Oh, hello Dr. Kherbet. I'm fine. I've been really busy. Not much time for hobbies these days."

"Well certainly, I understand that," Dante said. "Each life is full of its own particular busyness. Nevertheless, I would enjoy catching up with you sometime and learning what you've been up to. Not at the clinic. Maybe we could have dinner together some evening if you're free."

Narcissa was startled but quickly recovered and made a mental self-inquiry. Dinner? Does he know I'm separated? Is he interested in me? "Why yes, Dr. Kherbet. That would be lovely."

"How about tomorrow night," he asked. "And please call me Dante. We've known each other too long to stand on formalities."

"Let me check my schedule," she said, making no attempt to look at her leather bound calendar on the desk in her office (Lloyd's former bedroom). After a suitable pause, she said, "Yes, tomorrow will be fine. Shall I meet you somewhere?" She did not want him picking her up at home. Her nosy neighbors might take notice of a strange man calling upon her.

Dante was used to meeting ladies at neutral locations. "Eight o'clock at Durant's. Just give my name to the *maitre d'* and he'll take you to my regular table."

"I'll see you tomorrow night then, Dante."

At Kherbet's regular table the professional hypnotist was all charm and no past life regression. He uttered not a word about karmic wealth. Narcissa enjoyed a gourmet dinner, dry wine, and the attention of a suave man who appreciated the finer things in life. Dante, she decided, stood in stark contrast to her unsophisticated husband, who was content with a burger and fries.

Dante did not ask about the state of her marriage, and Narcissa did not volunteer any information. Instead, the two played a game of who's flirting with whom, which before the evening ended led them to a cheap motel on Grand Avenue. This was Narcissa's idea, believing that such a place would provide her protection from the eyes of anyone who knew her. As chance would have it, the motel clerk did know Dante, but Narcissa waited in her car and so was not aware that having eaten at Dante's regular table, she was about to have intercourse in his regular motel room.

Despite the illicit excitement of their coupling, it wasn't very good sex as far as Narcissa was concerned. Dante was interested in his own orgasm, which was by her standards significantly premature. Not that she was a sex maniac. She was not interested in sex often, but when she wanted it, she wanted it to satisfy her desires completely. In the context of being abandoned by her husband, she wanted to feel passionately alive, and Dante did not perform to her satisfaction. At least Lloyd knew how to make her climax.

One significant development came from Narcissa's tryst, however. On the drive home she developed a bout of paranoia. Starting with the hypothetical question, what if Lloyd had hired a private detective in search of grounds for divorce, she eventually convinced herself that Lloyd had done exactly that.

Believing that a good offense was the best defense, she called him the next day. "I've been thinking about why you left me, Lloyd. And I can't help but wonder if you have some babe shacked up with you in that fancy townhouse."

"Narcissa, that's ridiculous. There is no one else in my life," he said.

"So, you wouldn't mind if I hired a private dick to watch your movements?"

"Actually, I'd be flattered if you spent a whole pot of your Patriotic Ladies money on a private detective. But I'm afraid the report on me would be pretty boring."

Silently she mouthed agreement with his last statement. The next step in her plan would be a preemptive strike. "Well, I've given it a lot of thought, Lloyd. It doesn't make sense for us to stay legally married if you have no intention of coming back to me. I'll give you an uncontested divorce. All I want is for you to pay the mortgage on my house."

"Agreed," he said. And so it happened, except that Lloyd volunteered to pay not only Narcissa's mortgage but her property taxes as well. His business sense led him to give her more than she had asked for, so she wouldn't feel cheated later on.

ASU accepted Cloud as an unclassified graduate student. He registered for two courses, History of Modern Japan and History of Southeast Asia. Professor Aristotle Nestor taught both courses. When Dr. Nestor learned that Cloud was fluent in Vietnamese and had lived in Saigon, he took a special interest in the new student. Nestor encouraged Cloud to apply for a Master of Arts program, but Cloud said he was having trouble concentrating and didn't want to take on too much right away.

Nestor had observed this problem with concentration a decade earlier with students who were Korean War veterans, so he determined to be patient with Cloud. Also, he had seen the Arizona Republic article, for it had been reprinted in the alumni magazine, and thus guessed that Cloud had suffered significant trauma. Nevertheless, Aristotle Nestor did not want to let a promising graduate student slip away from his department.

Cloud enjoyed the history lectures, but apart from these classes, he spent most of his time alone in his apartment lamenting his loss by listening to what he called scab-picking music. The groove on his *South Pacific* album was nearly worn out from playing and replaying "This Nearly Was Mine." When the mood of his grief was less elegant, he played the Rolling Stones' recording "Paint It Black."

As Thanksgiving approached, Cloud visited the first of two fellow veterans he wanted very much to see. A visit to San Diego to see Arquimedes Shapiro would have to wait for another time. This day Cloud called on Quinn Queensbury.

The paraplegic veteran was living at his parents' home in the old neighborhood. "Hey, it's the conquering hero," said Quinn as Cloud stepped into his room. "Pardon me if I don't get up. There's no ejection seat on this wheelchair."

"Hi Quinn," Cloud said as he took his friend's outstretched hand. "But you have it all wrong. I am neither conquering nor a hero."

"That's not what the Arizona Republic says," Quinn retorted.

"My mother was responsible for that, and it's mostly inaccurate."

"Do you have two Purple Hearts?" Quinn asked.

"Yeah, but both were for surface wounds. Compared with what happened to you, I don't deserve them." He searched his brain for something to shift the conversation away from him. "I heard there was a master sergeant who received a Purple Heart for a hangnail he got sitting in a bunker during a mortar attack. And the medic got a Silver Star for cleaning all the shit out of his pants."

Quinn laughed. "Sit down Cloud, and we'll swap war stories."

Cloud listened intently as Quinn described in clinical detail what he endured in various Army and Veterans Administration hospitals but said nothing about combat.

"How did you get wounded?" Cloud asked. "I heard you have a

Silver Star."

"It's no big deal," Quinn said. "They passed those out like candy."

Cloud, knowing Silver Stars were rare, said, "Tell me anyway."

Quinn closed his eyes and spoke as if embarrassed. "I was point on a recon patrol and we walked into an ambush. Stupid of me, actually. Anyway, I did what I was taught and charged. I was pissed about getting caught in an ambush and hopped up on adrenaline and must have looked like a raging maniac to the Cong. Anyway, the rest of the unit followed through and we broke up the ambush. Killed most of the Cong. I was the only casualty on our side. The guys reported that I had inspired them and saved their butts, so they pinned a decoration on me."

"But how were you wounded?" Cloud asked again.

Quinn sighed and said, "As we consolidated after the fight, a ten year-old VC hiding in a tree used a slingshot to shoot shit-coated glass shards into my spine. Not exactly a heroic way to get crippled for life."

Though he had not planned to do so, in response to Quinn's honesty, Cloud felt the need to open up about his work in Saigon, Xuan and her death, and his disillusioning sojourn in the Delta.

"I've been doing a lot of thinking," Quinn said. "God knows I've had plenty of time to think. The Army ought to give Purple Hearts for the emotional wounds soldiers suffer in war. Those are the wounds that go deepest."

"You and I both deserve that kind of medal," Cloud said. "And thanks, Quinn. That gives me an insight." Cloud described his encounter with the amputee at the State Fair in 1957. "He said he hoped I'd go off to war and be injured like him. I think he got his wish...or his curse. Not in the flesh. I didn't lose a limb. But I'm sure as hell a casualty of this war inside my head, just like he was. I wonder if things would have come out differently if I had given him the dollar he asked for?"

"Hey, in a few months I'm breaking out of here," Quinn said, changing the subject.

"Where to?" Cloud asked.

"I'm getting my own apartment. There's no reason why I can't get around on my own now. I got wheels for legs, but my arms are still good, better than ever, actually. I've been working out. The government will pay for me to go back to school, and I'd like to become a vocational counselor."

"Good for you," Cloud said with sincerity.

"I wanna tell you something else, Cloud. I was angry at first. Really pissed off about getting wounded this way. Some gimps stay bitter all their lives. But not me. I have come to recognize the blessings that came along with my injury," Quinn said.

"What blessings?"

"The most prominent one is that my father leaves me alone now. He no longer expects me to be like him. He tells all his friends that I'm a war hero. It's a big pile of reeking bullshit, but that's what he wants to believe, and believing it allows him to let go of pushing me to fill his unrealized dreams."

"He was pretty mean to you, huh?"

"He used to beat me," Quinn said. "Remember that time I had a broken leg? I didn't fall down any steps. My father shoved me down those steps."

"I know," said Cloud. "I saw it in a dream." He realized as soon as he said it that he had revealed something private about himself to a person who had terrorized him during his childhood.

"I always figured there was more to you than you let on," Quinn said with perceptiveness. "What else did you dream?"

Oh well, thought Cloud. I may as well tell him. "I dreamed about Buddy Holly and those two other guys dying in a plane crash before it happened. And I dreamed about President Kennedy's assassination before it happened."

"Wow!" said Quinn. "A real psychic. Any unusual dreams lately?"

"You sound like a psychiatrist," Cloud retorted.

"No, I've had enough of those guys. They come with the physical therapy. I'll tell you what I am, though. And this is another blessing. For the first time in my life I am mellow. I can just sit back and be who I am without having to please anybody else or try to look tough for my old man. I'm really a softy inside."

"It takes an emotionally strong man to reveal his gentleness," Cloud said. "I admire you for that, Quinn. I only wish I'd known that about you a decade ago."

"If I'd shown any tenderness or sensitivity back then, my father would have called me a fairy and thrown me out of the house," Quinn said with a rueful laugh.

"It's not my place to criticize anyone else's parents, but I think that reveals a distorted view on his part of what constitutes true masculinity," said Cloud.

"Yeah," said Quinn, "I've met some gays who are so tough they make my dad look like a sissy and some straight guys with women hanging all over them who are the kindest, gentlest men you could ever meet. But they didn't live in this house."

"I need to get going," said Cloud. "It's been great to see you. Catch you later."

"Come visit me again when I get into my own apartment. We VVs have to stick together," Quinn said.

"Viet Nam veterans stuck together," Cloud mused. "That would make a good name for a lobbying group. I'll join if you organize it. In the meantime, happy Thanksgiving, Quinn."

"Happy Thanksgiving, Cloud."

Cloud was growing increasingly cynical about the world. In 1964 he had been eager to cast his first ballot for President of the United States. Now in 1968, with Vice President Hubert Humphrey running against former Vice President Richard Nixon, Cloud sat out the election. He could not bring himself to vote for either man.

In January 1969, he joined the Vietnam Veterans Against the War. Despair at the way the war was being waged drove him to align with some anti-war cause, and this one seemed the best of various organizations making waves on the national scene.

However, Cloud developed no supportive relationships among his fellow anti-war veterans, preferring to remain anonymous within the group. He developed proprietary feelings about his war memories and would not share them even with fellow veterans. When another young officer tried to draw him out and befriend him, Cloud stopped attending meetings.

The idea of revealing any of his experiences to fellow students or faculty members at ASU was beyond his comprehension. No war stories, even the humorous incidents, fell from his lips.

Most of the time Cloud simply wanted to be alone. Often he holed up in his apartment for three or four days at a stretch, venturing out only to go to class and pick up a little food on the walk home.

IV

TERP

Thou art so truth that thoughts of thee suffice
To make dreams truth and fables histories.
John Donne

Come to me in the silence of the night,
Come in the speaking silence of a dream.
Christina Rosetti

Let the torrent dance thee down
To find him in the valley.
Alfred, Lord Tennyson

CHAPTER THIRTY

Over the Christmas break in her junior year, Terp reflected on her development as a sexual being in a series of dreams. Studying the metaphysical poets in Advanced Placement English served as catalyst for these erogenic visions, for she had developed an attachment to mystical, erotic poetry. Ardently she sought these nocturnal explorations, identifying with the Song of Solomon maiden. "By night upon my bed I seek the man my soul loves," she recited longingly each time her head settled onto her pillow.

During this same period, she began brooding about her breasts, feeling they were too small. The dissatisfaction was in her mind only and bore no correspondence to general norms of beauty, for her curves were noticeably feminine. Nevertheless, she suffered heightened awareness that she would never be buxom, and this suggested to her that she was therefore not attractive to the opposite sex. The rightness of her conclusion was confirmed in her mind by the fact that halfway through her sixteenth year, she had yet to be asked out on a date or experience a first kiss.

Terp remembered vividly her first and only sexual experience. She had played doctor with Michelle's brother Will one summer afternoon when she was seven and he was ten. Tentative touching of exposed body parts had been involved but nothing else, not even kissing.

She was glad she never mentioned the episode to Michelle, because for years now her best friend had been telling tales about the raft of brokenhearted girls Will had left in the wake of his dating endeavors. On occasion Will had been dumped too, but in Terp's view being dumped at least meant there had been a romantic relationship. To her mind that was far better than being alone and undesired. Adding to her anguish, recently Michelle had begun confiding in Terp about her own petting experiences with various eager boys. Making matters worse, because she was now dating, Michelle was no longer available to go to the movies with her.

Following a characteristic pattern of introverts, Terp went by herself to see Franco Zeffirelli's **Romeo and Juliet** at the Forum Theater in Metuchen and ached all the more at the beautifully filmed tragedy because of her own deep longing for romantic love. In every other dimension of life, Terp was advanced for her age. In this arena she felt frustratingly retarded and ashamed at her lack of experience. It's not fair, she cried silently to herself. They have one exciting relationship after another and all I have are dreams.

The most memorable of her dreams involved a young, melancholy poet, whom she visualized as a twentieth century John Donne. By this she understood him to be both romantic and spiritual. He wrote her a poem, expressing deep longing for her, and she responded by dancing for the young man. "Lara's Theme" from **Dr. Zhivago** formed the soundtrack for the dream. As she moved in slow, elegant turns, her costume fell away, and she danced naked for the lovesick poet. She was fully aware of her nudity and was thrilled by the reflection of her body in his eyes. It was clear that he saw her breasts as perfect. Experiencing a sense of wild freedom, she continued to whirl and leap, her long hair brushing across her face as she spun. The sad poet smiled, and as the strumming of the balalaikas grew in intensity, he stepped forth undraped to join her in the dance.

At this critical moment she awoke and felt a surge of disappointment at not seeing the poet dance and make love to her, so she lay awake and lambently fantasized that prospect.

Two courses in Chinese history occupied Cloud's time in the new semester, although he continued to experience emotional restlessness and general malaise. As a result, he made no plans to formalize his program of study. He had no desire to work toward any particular goal, such as a Master's degree.

One sunny February day, feeling a bout of nostalgia, he decided to visit his old neighborhood. He drove up and down Villa Verde Street but recognized no one. Stopping in front of his former home, he perceived the place as smaller than he remembered it being. Two single men, both in their thirties, shared the rent on the house, which, Cloud knew, they paid regularly to his father. A young family had bought Miss Listerbaum's house. There was a different name on the mailbox at the Zadok place. He considered dropping in on the Verralls but remembered they both worked during the day.

He drove north on 19th Avenue past West High and up the street to Bill's Ranch House Burgers, where he stopped to ingest an onion-laden hamburger and an imitation chocolate milk shake. As he was preparing to leave, someone he recognized walked into the restaurant. The DAFT minister, T. C. Smith, entered the small dining room with the same expectation for attention that he received when entering the sanctuary of his temple on Sunday morning.

Cloud did not disappoint Smith's need for an audience. "Hey, Rev. Smith," Cloud said. "Do you remember me? I'm Cloud Morgan. My parents and I used to go to your church."

"Nope, I don't believe so," he replied. Smith stared at Cloud's face, searching for a visual clue to prompt his memory and soon an image of Narcissa's shapeliness came to him, but the preacher remained silent.

"We didn't go there very long. I had too many questions," Cloud said.

"What kind of questions?" Smith asked, intrigued by the conversation, and hungry for an opportunity to evangelize this good-looking young man. He was already mentally composing the preaching anecdote he would make of this chance encounter.

"In Vacation Bible School I asked your wife if Jesus and God are the same, how can Jesus be always loving and kind and God be always angry and ready to punish everybody? She told me to ask you, but I never got around to it till just now."

"Oh, that's an easy one," Smith said. "You see, God ain't really angry at all. God is pure love and only punishes people out of love.

It's for their own good. It's like what's going on over there in Viet Nam. They have to burn down villages in order to save them. God has to burn people in hell in order to save them. But he does it in love."

"That sounds like Calvin's rationale for burning Servetus at the stake," said Cloud.

"Who's that?" asked Smith.

"John Calvin was a sixteenth century Protestant reformer. A Spanish physician named Michael Servetus suggested a new understanding of the Trinity and expressed doubt about original sin, so Calvin had him burned alive as a heretic," Cloud recited in the fashion of a college history major. "Calvin thought it was the only way to save Servetus' soul."

"Say, I better look up this Calvin guy. I might pick up a few pointers. Thanks for the tip," Smith said coolly.

Years of childhood resentment dredged through the psychic trauma of war rose in Cloud's consciousness. "Naw," said Cloud. "He's too subtle for you. You'd better stick with Torquemada."

"Who?" said Smith.

"The head of the Spanish Inquisition," Cloud said. He walked to the door, turned and continued, "Torquemada believed there's a special place in hell for people like you." Cloud left, having enjoyed, however bitter, the last word.

The following weekend, Cloud drove his blue bug to San Diego to visit Arquimedes.

"I used to be left-handed," the former Army specialist told Cloud. "But now I've learned to be like the common majority and use my right for writing. I miss the distinctiveness of sinister dominance, but this is a lesson in humility for me." His left hand was frozen into a claw, with fingers separated, and his left arm hung straight and stiff at his side. "The doctors say I'll never regain use of my left arm, but I'm working with a spiritual nurse, doing my prayer exercises, and I expect to prove them wrong."

Everyone needs some basis for hope, Cloud thought. It would be cruel to challenge the validity of Arquimedes' quest for spiritual healing, though he suspected that his friend's doctors knew more than his spiritual nurse. "I wish I had your faith," Cloud said.

"I'm not sure my faith is good enough," confessed Arquimedes.

"So far I've made no progress with the arm. But I am consoled by the fact that the arm injury is an illusion. In the mind of God, where I truly exist, I am whole and unblemished." He lifted his left arm with his right hand and let it flap against his side. "I enjoy doing that," he laughed.

"I guess there aren't too many of us MI types in the Purple Heart club," Cloud offered. "Maybe we should start our own chapter."

"The club nobody wants to join," said Arquimedes. "By the way, I hope you don't mind me bringing up a painful subject, but I really miss *Co* Xuan. I think about you and her often. Her transition to a higher plane came way too early."

"I miss her more than I can possibly express in words, Arquimedes," Cloud said. His eyes filled with tears.

"I understand, sir," Arquimedes said, reverting to military address. "You two were perfect for one another."

"We're civilians now. Call me Cloud," the former officer said. "And thank you for remembering us. No one at home ever met her."

"She was a lady in every good sense of that word," Arquimedes said.

On the return trip, Cloud reflected that the Buddha was right about one thing. People organized their lives around illusions. But some may be beneficial, while other illusions are clearly pernicious, he thought, with Arquimedes and T. C. Smith in mind.

When Cloud got back to his apartment, he pulled out the photo album that Xuan's sister had given to him. He had looked through it many times, visually absorbing the images of Xuan at various stages of her childhood and teen years, studying what she looked like in the time before he knew her. Cloud linked certain photographs with the visions she had experienced at particular ages.

But the picture he treasured most was the last one. A secretary at Xuan's office snapped it six weeks before Tet. Cloud stared at the picture of Xuan and himself standing beside her desk and felt a sudden inspiration to matte and frame it. The walls in his place could certainly use a little decoration, he thought.

When he pulled the photo from its sleeve, a half-sheet of dry onionskin came out with it. Cloud gingerly unfolded the paper and found that it was a letter, dated 26 December 1967. Xuan's voice rang in his mind as he read:

> My dearest Cloud,
>
> I do not know where you or I will be when you read this letter. You may be back in America while I am here in my homeland. I may be dead, or I may be nursing our son or daughter. I speak of the child I dream to carry someday and not one growing in me now. In front of the Bo tree yesterday, you asked me to marry you, and I said yes. I pray that we become one. Yet I have lived with war far longer than you, my beloved, and I know that we cannot rely too much on the happy endings of American cinema.
>
> If we are apart when you read this letter, I want you to know that I cherish (you taught me this word) every minute of my life with you. Knowing your love today is all that matters to me. I do not want to lose you, but if fate ever separates us, I would fall in love with you again and again in every new lifetime, even if I knew it would lead to tragedy.
>
> I love you forever, my beautiful Cloud.
>
> Xuan.

Tears streamed from his eyes, generated from raw grief and from gratitude that her last words to him were not a question about gunfire but an expression of undying love. He did not believe in reincarnation, particularly the egocentric form his mother had brought to the dinner table. Yet he felt comfort in the idea that some kernel of their love was somehow universally eternal. The fact of their love could not be repudiated by death.

This day marked the beginning of Cloud's ascension from grief. The rise would be choppy, with ups and downs, but now he played wistful love songs on his stereo, savoring the joy they had known. "Younger Than Springtime" and "I'll Be Seeing You" replaced the keening dirges he had lived with for months.

In April, Cloud was formally accepted into a Master of Arts in history program. With this official recognition, he applied for GI Bill education benefits and in due course began receiving a government check each month. As frugally as he lived, he was not worried about money, but the GI Bill stipend was a nice bonus that paid his rent and groceries and kept his savings account from further depletion. Apart from classes and occasional visits to see his dad, Cloud passed his days like a hermit. He was feeling better but avoided emotional entanglements.

Narcissa sent Cloud a note with a newspaper clipping in late May. The note chided him for not having a telephone, thus requiring her to communicate with him through the services of the Post Office Department. He did not want a phone because if he had one, she along with strangers trying to sell him things, would disturb his peace. He did not have a television, either, although he did stay connected to the wider world through radio and a subscription to Newsweek.

After her opening criticism of her son's introverted ways, she wrote that Onan Verrall had died of a massive heart attack. With no concern about contradictory messages, she described the death as an unexpected bombshell and also something she had seen coming for years. There had been a funeral service at the Natural Christian Church, but Narcissa had not attended. Onan had been buried in the buff in the church cemetery. The clipping was his obituary from the Arizona Republic. The article indicated that memorial gifts should be made to the NCC in New River.

The news saddened Cloud, and he sent Nissa a letter expressing his condolences and then mailed a check for fifty dollars to the NCC in memory of his former neighbor. Never before had Cloud personally contributed any amount of money to a religious organization, and he was not clear why he did so this time. All he knew was that he felt a strong urge to make the gift, and he suspected that his mother would not approve of the gesture. This latter thought was motivation enough, and brought a smile to his face.

CHAPTER THIRTY-ONE

Darla Zadok stared at Cloud. They were in the University Bookstore, and he had not yet seen her. "Cloud!" she shouted across two racks of textbooks.

He looked up. "Darla! How are you?" He bumped his way through the crowded aisles and took her hand. "What a pleasant surprise! What are you up to these days?"

"Nothing conventional," she said. "What about you?"

They quickly agreed to walk to an ice cream parlor on Mill Avenue so they could talk at leisure in a quiet booth.

"You look great," Cloud said after they had ordered sundaes.

"Thanks," she said. "I feel pretty good about myself right now."

"So," Cloud said, "You went off to Kenyon College, then what?"

"I majored in English and dabbled a bit in the theater program. Mostly I worked behind the scenes. I wrote a couple of plays that were staged on campus. Two years ago I graduated, moved to LA, and got a job as a gopher in the scriptwriting department at Cosmic Hound Studios. I figured it would lead to writing jobs, but unfortunately all it led to was coffee stained blouses and propositions from horny male writers. This month I gave up that particular dream and moved back to Phoenix."

"What writing have you done?" Cloud asked.

"Short stories, screenplays, things like that. I have a great idea for a novel that I'd like to write one day, but first I have to pursue something else," she said.

"I'd like to read your work sometime," Cloud said with genuine interest.

"That's a sore point with me," she said. "One of the writers at Cosmic expressed interest in my writing, and I ended up having an affair with him. It turned out he feigned interest as a ploy to get into my pants, and after he'd had his way, he stole a treatment I had written for a sitcom. You may have seen my work on TV, but I got no credit or pay for it. I literally got screwed out of my work."

"I don't have a TV," Cloud said. "After what you've told me, I'm glad I don't."

"What about you?" Darla asked.

"I'm working on an MA in Asian history here at ASU," Cloud explained. He told her about his experiences as a Military Intelligence officer in Viet Nam, including his relationship with Xuan and the circumstances of her death. He said nothing about his wounds or medals.

"A truly sad story," Darla said. "I'm sorry for your loss, Cloud. You deserve some happiness. You're a real *mensch*."

"You said you had to pursue something else before writing your novel. What's that?" Cloud asked.

"It's a good thing you're sitting down, Cloud. I'm thinking of becoming a rabbi. Actually, I'm more than thinking about it. I am determined to become a rabbi."

"Do they have women rabbis?" Cloud asked.

"There's a lot of serious talk in Reform Judaism about allowing women rabbis. I've been accepted at the Reform Seminary, Hebrew Union College in Cincinnati, starting this fall to begin studying for the rabbinate. I'm optimistic that by the time I graduate the way will be clear for me to become Rabbi Darla Zadok."

"I hope so too, Darla. You'd be famous. Then I could tell everyone that I knew you when. I would come to your synagogue and tell all your parishioners that you went to the prom with a *goy*," Cloud said.

"You wouldn't dare," she laughed.

"I would, but I'd do it reverently, and then I'd tell them what a great kisser you were in the old days."

The two old friends, each in need of relief from painful memories, laughed at considerable length. When at last she regained equilibrium, Darla said, "Running into you was just what I needed."

"Well, I'm still interested in reading what you've written," Cloud said. "And I promise I'd stay outside your pants while doing it."

Darla burst into laughter once again, this time with a scoop of ice cream in her mouth, some of which ended up on Cloud's shirt. "I'm sorry," she said between gasps.

"No problem," Cloud answered. "It's a stain to remember you by."

"Stop," Darla pleaded. "I can't breathe."

Both were once again lost in laughter.

The table was awash in spilled and spewed ice cream when they finally departed, so Cloud left a generous tip as a peace offering. Cloud walked Darla to the parking lot, where they hugged good-bye. As he hiked to his apartment, he wondered if he would ever see Darla again. He hoped he would, for he thought of her as a dear friend, but he knew the path she was preparing to take was one where he could be no more than an interested by-stander.

She was a beautiful woman. Her face was lined with intelligence, determination, and a sense of grace. Cloud speculated about all that comes with a pretty face or a beautiful body. What structure of mind, what expectations, what defense mechanisms, what control needs, what intellect, what curiosity, what guilt, what passions abide behind the eyes and skin of a beautiful woman -or a beautiful man?

So much of human behavior is influenced by visible physical attributes, yet what lies beneath shapes external beauty in powerful ways. A dull curiosity and fearful mind inside a gorgeous body seriously diminish a person's outward appearance. As far as Cloud was concerned, Darla was more beautiful on the inside than the outside, and this was the highest praise he could give to a woman.

Shortly before 8:00 p.m. Mountain Standard Time on July twentieth, Cloud broke his habit of not watching television. He joined a student gathering at the Memorial Union to watch first Neil

Armstrong and then Buzz Aldrin descend from the Eagle lunar-lander and walk on the Sea of Tranquility.

That morning, the members of Webster Presbyterian Church in Houston had celebrated the Lord's Supper, but when Rev. Dean Woodruff had lifted the loaf of communion bread, they saw that a piece was missing. The congregation soon learned that one of their absent members had taken a chunk from the loaf to carry with him on a long journey. It was not until Buzz Aldrin stepped onto the surface of the moon that he belatedly ate the sacramental bread, after which the pastor on earth pronounced the benediction ending the day's service of worship.

Cloud knew nothing of this long-distance Christian rite, but the scene unfolding on television was nonetheless a spiritual experience for him. The giant leap for humankind these two astronauts made that day seemed to Cloud the ineffable marriage of practical engineering and the whimsical mystery of science fiction. Watching the moon walkers provided him a rare burst of joy.

Late that night, as he lay in bed, he decided to leave his body. When he had done so and was floating above the roof of his apartment building, he mentally rolled over and instead of examining what was below him, as he had always done in the past, Cloud took in the heavens, paying particular attention to the now inhabited moon.

If Neil Armstrong and Buzz Aldrin could hike across the surface of the moon, he thought, then Cloud Morgan could float upside-down into the upper atmosphere of earth. He wondered how high he could go without his body. One factor, he surmised, was keeping track of the location where his empty body rested. He must not venture so far that he lost his bearings. Another limiting factor was speed. To that date, Cloud had soared only about twice as fast while outside his body as he had been able to propel himself by sprinting while in it.

Leaving thoughts of time behind, he floated higher and faster than ever in the direction of the moon, sensing as he rose into the ether that eventually he could reach it and watch the astronauts close up. Perhaps he could ride back with them. That would be great fun. He wondered if they would sense his presence in the capsule. Then it occurred to him that in the meantime his body on earth would dehydrate and die.

Cloud turned his orientation back to earth but did not recognize where he was. Only a few dim patches of light pierced the darkness. Exuberance had gotten him lost. Careful, Cloud, he thought. Move closer to the earth and something recognizable will appear. He dove down and down until he began to perceive a dark ragged protuberance of mountains. As he came closer, he saw the familiar surfacing submarine profile of the Superstition Mountains, and to the west, the faint lights of Apache Junction.

Soon he floated above the Apache Trail and followed it to the center of town, then westward to Mesa, Tempe, and the safety of his apartment. It was good to be back in his body, yet it had been exhilarating to set out for the moon. He would try again soon to push his out-of-body limits, being more mindful next time of where he was going.

Terp stayed up late to watch Armstrong and Aldrin make their first leaping moonwalks. Outwardly, she crowed with delight that this was the fulfillment of a challenge her favorite president, John Kennedy, had made to the nation before he was assassinated. Yet the event also teased that section of her brain that spins out wonder and generates restless awe. The choreography of it all astounded her soul.

Three hours elapsed before she reluctantly abandoned her chair in front of the television, bounded upstairs to her room, and slipped out of her clothes for bed. But she was not able to sleep for sheer mirth. Her head shimmied around her pillow, while her arms and legs twitched rhythmically beneath the cotton sheet.

Terp got up and turned on a lamp long enough to place a record on her turntable. She set the volume low enough not to attract attention from her mother at the opposite end of the house. In her night-clad room, Terp danced naked to Oliver's campy hit recording "Good Morning Starshine" -from the Broadway musical *Hair*- in honor of human feet dancing on the moon. After that, she was able to drift contentedly to sleep.

Unlike her son, Narcissa's reaction to the lunar landing took her deeper into the earth in search of the mysteries of the heavens. A former associate of Dante Kherbet invited her to a private orientation session of the Northern Arizona Trans-Solar Alien

Service Society. The leader of the society, Malachi Hinny, drove down to Phoenix from his headquarters in Winslow to meet with a carefully screened group of potential seekers.

The common characteristic among the three women and one man who constituted this carefully screened group was physical attractiveness. At forty-seven, the trim and carefully coiffed Narcissa was the oldest and most comfortable in the role of leader. The other women hovered just under and over forty, while the soft-spoken man was in his mid-twenties. They met in a suite at the Mountain Shadows Resort.

Malachi Hinny radiated intensity. He had been in this world forty-five years, stood five feet eight inches tall, and was completely bald. His entire head and face had been closely shaved, so that not a trace of hair intruded through his taut pale white skin.

"We have been watching the four of you for many years," Hinny began. "Not in the unconstitutional way that government agents spy on free citizens, but through family communications." Narcissa leaned forward in her chair, followed in quick succession by the other three, and Malachi knew that they were his. "I am the direct descendant of Stejrne, who came to earth from another planet a thousand years ago."

No one spoke, so he continued, "You four are descendants of other colonists who came with Stejrne on that fateful visit to Earth. That's why we have been tracing your journeys through terrestrial time. The signal to bring you back into the family was recently given. One of our relatives, Neil Armstrong, waved from the surface of the moon. This was the signal."

"How do we know we're related to aliens?" the young man asked.

"Hush," Narcissa said. "Let him tell his story."

"Oh this is a necessary and astute question," Malachi said. "If you hadn't asked it, David, I would have invited you to ask it. There is a long answer which I am not at liberty to share with you at this moment. But I can offer you a way to test my veracity. Before the summer is out, you will look upon unprecedented photographs of the planet Mars. If you doubt what I'm about to tell you about your ancestry, and my words concerning Mars do not come to pass, then by all means, consider me a phony and a kook. But if any part of what I say resonates within you, connects with secrets buried deep in your minds, and my prophecy proves true, then you can be certain that what I will tell you is fact."

"I'm listening," the young man said. "Go on, go on!" the women said in unison.

"In what the people of Earth call the Alpha Centauri system, a beautiful aquamarine planet circles a sun very much like Sol. The name of this planet is Synnssjukasyl. Ten earth centuries ago a small party of brave pioneers from this planet boarded a floating space city to explore other star systems, looking for congenial planets to colonize. Synnssjukasyl had become overcrowded.

"They discovered planet Earth to be nearly as beautiful as their home. On a high mesa in what is now known as Northern Arizona, they used lasers to prepare a nest for their floating city. My home today is near that original landing spot."

"Where is it?" Narcissa asked.

"It is the place known popularly as Meteor Crater. Actually, we prefer that it be known that way, because it allows its true purpose to be disguised from ordinary people. The scientists say that a giant meteorite struck the sandstone desert about 50,000 years ago, creating the mile wide and nearly 600 feet deep crater. They point to the out-of-place nickel-iron elements there as proof of an extraterrestrial impact. They are right that the hole was created from space, but what they don't know is that our people deliberately camouflaged the site."

Malachi produced an aerial photograph of Meteor Crater. "Here is what the scientists overlooked," he said. "You would expect a crater made by a meteorite to be round, but you will note that this site is square with rounded corners. It was made thus to house, temporarily, the floating space city, Yomi. They remained at this place for less than a century, then dispersed throughout the world, taking pieces of their nickel-plated city with them."

"So, how are we related to all of this?" the youngest woman asked.

"You four were either born in Arizona or migrated here out of subconscious need to return to the site of the original colony. You are not full-blooded Synnssjukasylians, but each of you is at least half. I myself am three-quarters. There is an annual pilgrimage to the home site near Winslow, and if any of you would join me in that sacred visit, you will learn more from other members of your family. You will also be invited to participate in some of our ancient customs. But I cannot speak of those at present."

Narcissa was hooked. And the fact that a few days later NASA's unmanned Mariner spacecraft radioed spectacular pictures of Mars confirmed in her mind that she was indeed descended from a majestic alien race.

Cloud searched through the long magazine display, looking for an obscure Zen Buddhist publication, when his eyes fixed on the cover of Songsmith Digest. A smiling face looked back at him, and for a second he thought he had met the person on the cover sometime in the past. But he could not remember when or how.

The face belonged to Colin Glee, whom Cloud had never formally met. However, the two had passed by one another in Greenwich Village the day after the power blackout in 1965. The force of recognition derived from their mutual experiences with the Old One. But none of this registered in Cloud's mind.

Out of curiosity, he opened the magazine and read that the artist featured on the cover had written the enormously popular "Dancing with Lady Luna," which celebrated the moon landing earlier in the summer. Cloud had heard the song on the radio and liked it a lot. Its lyrical image of dancing on the moon tickled his consciousness, reminding him of the dancing girl he had dreamed about. This in turn led him to wonder who the first woman to walk -or waltz- on the moon would be.

"I owe it all to my business partner, Asher Shepherd," the article quoted Glee as saying. "I was starving in Greenwich Village at the time of the blackout in New York, and he rescued me." The article went on to note that Shepherd was carving out a successful career as an entertainment attorney and agent.

Cloud put the magazine back in its place. Somehow the story of Colin Glee reminded him of the phonograph records he had inherited from Miss Listerbaum, and he decided to sort though the discs in the week remaining before classes resumed.

— ☉ —

"Wow!" Cloud exclaimed to himself while sitting on the floor of his living room amidst stacks of 78-rpms. "You can learn a lot from a person's record collection." He looked up and spoke to the heavens. "Miss Listerbaum, I hardly knew you!"

In addition to many popular ballads of love, loneliness and longing, there were jazz and blues recordings, and numerous risqué novelty songs. Miss Jael Listerbaum's legacy included a Sophie Tucker ode to ancient Egyptian nudism, "In Old King Tutankhamen's Day." Also "Nellie, the Nudist Queen" performed by Ross and Sargent, as well as Irving Kaufman's "Masculine Women! Feminine Men!" and Gracie Field's "What Can You Give to a Nudist on His Birthday?"

So many titles intrigued him that he spent hours listening to records that judging from the wear on the grooves had been played many times by their original owner.

Cloud thought he knew Cole Porter's "Anything Goes" but discovered from a 1934 recording by an artist named Ramona that the original lyrics included references to nudist parties and meeting no opposition to a desire to see the singer undressed.

When he played "Tain't No Sin" Cloud's mind filled with a vivid image of his ersatz mother dancing to the song while joyfully flinging her clothes across her living room. "I hope you enjoyed dancing around in your bones, Miss Listerbaum," he said aloud with a chuckle in his voice. "I would love to have danced along with you if you'd been bold enough to ask." An intuitive flash of understanding told him her interior mind was far bolder than the inhibited social world of her physical body.

Looking upward again, he addressed her in spirit. "I'm sorry I never told you about my habit of slipping out of my skin and dancing in air. And if I'd known about your interest in the clothes-free life, I would have invited you to join me dancing naked in my back yard. Wouldn't that have been a hoot?" A sudden wave of filial affection washed over him. "I miss you very much," he said.

CHAPTER THIRTY-TWO

Encountering Cloud in the first month of the new decade of the 1970s, people on the street might have been tempted to think he was a well-scrubbed hippie or perhaps a displaced beach bum. Though his dress was conventional -jeans and sedate sports shirts- his hair now reached his shoulders. The previous summer, he had decided to economize by eliminating the costs of regular visits to a barber. As the months passed, he grew to like his lengthening locks. Since he had been spending a good deal of time hiking outdoors, the bleaching sun had lightened his mane, adding blond tones to it. Every night he carefully brushed his straight fine hair to keep it clean and unmatted. This was his only evident vanity.

Looks, however, can be deceiving, for Cloud had become neither hippie nor beach habitué but an ascetic scholar who took into his body no recreational drugs, very little meat, and drank only water and fruit juices. His sole method of getting high was out-of-body experiences, which of late he used as a means of studying people's faces.

On weekends, Cloud slipped out of his body and into synagogue services, Catholic folk masses, Quaker meetings, and assorted Protestant services. He told himself he did this because a historian needs to know about the ritual practices of various religions. He eschewed appearing at church in the flesh because worshipers might welcome him and invite him back, and he wanted the freedom of anonymity to come and go according to his own schedule without dealing with the desires of believers to be hospitable. Rarely, however, did he leave a service before it had concluded. Apart from his doctrinal disbelief, he treated the sacred traditions of others with courteous respect.

At an independent fundamentalist church he nearly left in the middle of the sermon in which the preacher ranted about how people deserved God's wrath because they weren't strong enough or smart enough to stand up to the silver-tongued cleverness of Satan. But something -inertia or intuition- made him stay, and after the lurid sermon, the choir sang "Beautiful Isle of Somewhere" with innocent wistfulness. The late nineteenth century hymn expressed yearning for a bright land where "God lives and all is well."

Cloud was captivated by the anxious hope in their voices. Everybody longs for a beautiful place of peace and joy, he thought. Why does the church always project this to heaven? Why not strive to create an Eden on earth? The more he reflected on this, the surer he became that the only way he would ever see such a beautiful isle was through dreams and imagination. However, he would not dream of the theologian's moralistic heaven but of an earthly paradise to satisfy his own heart.

His study of human faces seemed somewhat voyeuristic to him, but he rationalized that he did not invade anyone's private sanctuaries. He was not interested in seeing naked bodies in bedrooms or bathrooms. He already knew what unclothed bodies looked like. Cloud was instead drawn to reading faces. Years earlier he had painfully discovered that he made people uncomfortable and sometimes hostile if he gazed at them. Over the years close friends reported that when he looked at them it felt like his piercing eyes bored right through them. It seemed to Cloud that his eyes were addicted to human faces and his mind to what ticked behind them.

At any rate, he now retreated from his body when he wanted to examine and absorb the lives that human beings revealed through physiognomy. He found this exercise endlessly fascinating, informative, and mystically nourishing.

Narcissa had not yet penetrated to the innermost circle of NAT-

SASS, where the most ancient, holy, and secret customs were practiced, but she had progressed through five of the seven degrees of purification. With the help of Malachi Hinny she completed her genealogical chart, tracing her Synnssjukasylian heritage through her mother's lineage back to the Yomi pioneer woman Jagrat.

Along the way, she and Malachi had shared a few stolen kisses, and she expected these would lead to further caresses. Being desirable was a feeling she enjoyed, and his kisses proved that Malachi found her attractive. She had also learned that the sixth degree involved casual nudity, but this was nothing new to her. Narcissa didn't object to nakedness among friends, and she thought she knew how to handle men if they got frisky in such environments.

What she did not know was that Malachi had also enjoyed more than stolen kisses with David, the young man in her initiation class. The two other women in that class had dropped out during second-degree training. But Narcissa was a survivor, not a quitter, and planned to get into the innermost circle if it cost her every dime she had.

On Saturday, May 2, 1970, Terp participated in a peace rally at her church to protest President Richard Nixon's escalation of the war into Cambodia. She was approaching the end of her senior year at Edison High School and looking forward to going away to college in a few months. Nevertheless, the war weighed heavily on her conscience, as if she personally bore responsibility for convincing the president to change course and stop the fighting.

She was therefore devastated by the news the following Monday afternoon that Ohio National Guard troops had fired into a crowd of student demonstrators at Kent State University, wounding nine and killing four. The bullets and blood of the war had now expanded into the green hills of the American Midwest. That night Terp joined with a multitude of students and faculty for a candlelight vigil on the campus of Rutgers University. As protesters chanted defiance of the president and pronounced anathemas on the National Guard, Terp mentally absorbed the expressed rage of the crowd and simmered in deep sorrow for all the lives lost and damaged by the violence of war.

— ☉ —

On the other side of the country, Cloud stood in respectful silence at a campus rally at ASU in protest of the killings at Kent State. He had considered attending out-of-body but decided that this event required his complete presence. He wanted to be seen and counted among those who opposed this brutal suppression of free speech.

Second only to an end to the war, the thing Terp most wanted as May ebbed away was for a kind-hearted boy to take her to the prom. There were, however, several elements operating against this eventuality.

The fact that she wore glasses was not a hindrance at all. The fact that she had reached five feet nine inches in height limited her chances only slightly. Her slender body, firmly muscled from years of dance lessons, was an attractive asset, as was her long brunette hair, which on her left side fell down her front past her breast and on her right down her back, descending past her shoulder blade. This was an affectation in imitation of Judith Durham, the lead singer of the Seekers, an Australian folk group she admired. These things were all to the good.

Problematic, however, was Terp's academic standing, having been named class valedictorian. She was articulate and quick-witted, and if these were not enough to intimidate the most confident prospect, her even-featured countenance radiated a spiritual depth that created an image of untouchability in the minds of seventeen and eighteen year-old boys. All things considered, there were young men at Edison High who were in awe of her, even some who worshiped her from afar, but none daring enough to ask her to the prom. Therefore, on the night of the senior dance, Terp sat alone in her room, listening to wistful songs on her stereo between episodes of tears.

Terp placed her original cast album from *Flower Drum Song* on the turntable and set the arm to hear Arabella Hong sing "Love Look Away." She repeated this a half dozen times, wallowing in the painful acknowledgment of unrequited love. When she was sated with Arabella's voice, Terp put on the cast album from *The King and I* and listened to Doretta Morrow fantasize melodically about tragically denied love in "I Have Dreamed." But mostly that evening, Terp played her favorite pop recording by Merrilee Rush, "Angel of the Morning." With all her might she yearned to be that grounded angel, but no one would touch her.

— ⊙ —

A Master of Arts degree was conferred upon Cloud at the end of May.

His advisor, Aristotle Nestor, encouraged him to apply for the PhD program at Stanford. "With your mind, Cloud, you can rise to the top of the profession in Asian history. You would benefit greatly from the prestige Stanford has to offer."

Cloud was not inclined to apply to Stanford. "Thanks for the vote of confidence, Dr. Nestor," he said. "But right now prestige does not appeal to me, and I have no interest in going to the top of the profession. The emotional energy needed for such a track seems overwhelming. I love intellectual pursuits and glory in research, but at the moment I'm content without credentials or position."

"What do you plan to do, then?" Nestor asked.

"I don't know," Cloud confessed. "I wish I did. Essentially I'm an autodidact who wants to follow whatever mystery my mind perceives. I suppose I'll continue to study in desultory fashion. I have unfinished emotional business with Viet Nam. I might go chasing an unfulfilled intellectual dream about utopian syncretistic temples."

Nestor was not surprised at Cloud's lack of direction and believed that in time the traumatized veteran would become more focused. "Though vague, that idea is not without merit," he said. "It wants honing, of course. Let me propose a back-up plan. I can get you into a PhD program here at ASU with a good balance between structured study and autodidactic freedom."

"OK," said Cloud. "That sounds like a good plan. It would be gratifying to do a dissertation on the Cao Dai religion."

"Don't get ahead of yourself, Cloud. You'll have a lot of course work and comprehensive exams before getting to your dissertation," his wise advisor said.

Edison High School Valedictorian Terry Person had been accepted by Princeton and the University of Pennsylvania, but she had another school in mind, and her mother was not happy about it.

"Why can't you go to an Ivy League university in your own backyard?" Penny whined. "Why are you so intent on going to a party school out among the cacti?"

"They have a fine honors program at ASU, Mom, and I really want to learn to live on my own for a while. Princeton and Penn are too close," Terp explained. She would never tell her mother her deepest motivation for wanting to attend college in Arizona. Over the past year she had been meditating again about her experience of meeting the Old One in the desert. She did not know the exact location of that oracular encounter but had mapped out the general area. Intuition or perhaps wishful thinking told her she would meet someone out there who could help her find Big Head.

Penny knew she could not win a debate with her older daughter and caved in quickly. "At least promise you'll apply to an East Coast university for graduate school."

"Yes, Mom, I promise," Terp responded.

Penny then revealed Terp's graduation present. "I'm taking you and Mary to England," she announced. What she did not say was that the trip was a gift to herself as well. Tom had talked so much about being stationed in England during the war that every mention of the country reminded her of him. Visiting the place would diminish the sting of his death, she reasoned. In the future she would have her own memories of England that did not depend on Tom.

None of this would have mattered to Terp. She and Mary were ecstatic about the trip. Penny set the passport applications before her daughters that day, and four weeks later the three attractive women flew to London.

Terp, whose graduation gift the trip ostensibly was, wanted to visit the British Museum, Saint Paul's, where her favorite poet, John Donne, had preached in the seventeenth century, the bookshops along Charing Cross Road, and at the recommendation of Argyle Watts, Salisbury Cathedral. Mary wanted to go to the clothing shops in Soho, Hyde Park, the Tate Gallery, and Stonehenge. Penny wanted to see Piccadilly Circus, Ten Downing Street, the Tower of London, and Windsor Castle. In turn, each would have her way.

Their second day in London, Penny and Mary voted for shopping, while Terp argued for a pilgrimage to Saint Paul's Cathedral. Rather than create a fuss, Terp arranged for a taxi to St. Paul's while her mother and sister searched for souvenirs. It proved to be a good arrangement, for it allowed Terp unpressured time alone.

She stood for a long time in the cathedral's south aisle in front of John Donne's memorial statue, imagining him as variously a poet and a preacher. She marveled at his ability to be authentically both. "Where are the John Donnes of the world now when I need someone like him?" she whispered to herself. A tide of aching loneliness washed over her. From memory she quoted aloud the end of one of his holy sonnets: "For I, except you enthrall me, never shall be free, nor ever chaste, except you ravish me." Reverting again to a whisper, she said, "Oh, John Donne, I don't want God to make me chaste. I want a man like you to ravish me."

The three American ladies were captivated by an amateur troupe's free-flowing outdoor performance of *A Midsummer-Night's Dream*. It was a public show, mounted across acres of grass in Hyde Park. The frenetic staging of the play required considerable movement on the part of the audience. Terp loved the flippant delivery of lines, Mary enjoyed the colorful costumes, and Penny savored the idea of telling her friends in New Jersey that she had seen a Shakespearean drama in London.

Because of the anachronistic festivity that day, the crowd paid no attention to an unusual character with a large head meditating serenely in a grove nearby. The Old One, garbed in a loose-fitting white alb, ignored the actors, concentrating instead on a former RAF officer, who at that moment was brooding in his office in Harley Street. When the play ended, Terp noticed but did not recognize the Old One. She associated Big Head solely with the Arizona desert so this London context made identification unlikely. Nevertheless, feeling curiously drawn in that direction, she started to move toward the individual with the large cranium. Penny, however, took her arm. "Come on, Terp. I promised Mary we'd go over to Soho to look for fashion treasures."

As she dutifully followed her mother, Terp said, "Shakespeare knew how to shop. He had Titania say, 'I have a venturous fairy that shall seek the squirrel's hoard and fetch thee new nuts.' Are you looking for new nuts, Mary?"

Mary chortled and quoted Bottom in reply: "'Methinks I am marvelous hairy about the face, and I am such a tender ass.' I must to the beauty parlor!"

"What in heaven are you two raving about?" Penny asked.

The girls giggled all the way to Soho.

Without breaking concentration, the Old One by means of a tiny smile took note of Terp's mirthful presence. Primary attention, however, was aimed at Dr. Clark Hyfrydol, a distinguished psychiatrist who was seriously depressed. He'd wasted his life, he thought, babysitting wealthy neurotic women. They didn't want to get better. They liked paying him large sums of money to indulge their feelings of dependence. He was merely a status symbol to them -their Harley Street analyst.

Believing he had thrown away his life, he considered two options: retire and play golf or commit suicide. The latter seemed more attractive to him. His major task was deciding among the various available means. At that moment, the Old One added a clarifying notion into the psychiatrist's brain. Being an efficient person, Clark should put his files in order before acting on either course.

Clark walked across his spacious office to a bank of expensive mahogany filing cabinets. Thinking in his usual methodical way, he opened the drawer where he kept his oldest files, those he had taken with him a quarter century earlier when he left the RAF at the end of the war. Inside the elegant drawer, the manila folders were in a jumble. Egad, he thought. He'd have to get after his secretary about this disorder. But he couldn't resist the urge to tidy them up himself. He pulled out a load of folders but in his haste they slipped from his hands and scattered across the floor.

Uncharacteristically, Clark sat on the carpet and reached at random for a file. It belonged to First Lieutenant Lloyd Morgan. Ah yes, the Yank, Clark thought. A decent chap. He wondered whatever became of Morgan.

After reading at random through a dozen files from his wartime service, Clark developed the idea of refocusing his work. He would begin research on the subsequent lives of servicemen who suffered psychiatric symptoms as a result of combat, looking for patterns of recovery or recurrence of illness. It made sense to start with his own patients. He would trace as many as possible and invite them to participate in his research. His mind was buzzing now. He could put ads in newspapers seeking information from veterans about their post-war emotional experiences.

Dr. Hyfrydol forgot about retiring or suicide. He would start with the Yank. In Lloyd's file, he found a notation that the pilot had a wife and infant son in Phoenix, Arizona. That was a starting place for his search. The next afternoon, his secretary, with surprisingly little effort, produced Lloyd's address in Scottsdale, and Clark wrote to his former patient.

At the time Dr. Hyfrydol's letter was en route across the Atlantic, Lloyd was preoccupied with a major change in his life. He sat in Cloud's apartment, sipping the limeade his son had offered him. Wasting no time on preliminaries, he said, "I'm getting married again, Cloud."

"Congratulations, Dad. Who's the lucky lady?" Cloud had not known his father had been dating but was pleased with the news.

"Nissa Verrall," said Lloyd.

"Wow, Dad! She's a neat lady. Good for you. I'm happy for both of you," Cloud said with more enthusiasm than he had known for some months.

"Adam and Evelyn Rarom will perform the ceremony at the NCC chapel," Lloyd added, "and I want you to be my best man."

"I'd be honored," Cloud said.

"By the way, you may be interested to learn that your old man is the cause of a doctrinal change at the NCC," Lloyd said.

"How's that?"

"I plan to join the church after the wedding, but I'm still opposed to re-baptism. Adam and Evelyn took the matter to the church's National Assembly. It turns out that other congregations have been faced with the same situation. So the National Assembly created a special rite for people like me. I can join the church through something called renewal of baptism."

"What's that?" Cloud asked.

"A pastor announces to the congregation that a new member - me in this case- had been baptized previously. The pastor then pronounces the baptismal formula that had been used and the new member is asked to affirm this. The pastor and the new member then re-enact the baptism with the NCC authorized questions and nude immersion, except that the actual baptismal words are not spoken during the rite."

"That sounds like a sensible solution to the impasse," Cloud said.

In fact, it would prove to be the first of many ecclesiastical and doctrinal reforms ultimately made by the young denomination.

Looking up from the nave of Salisbury Cathedral, Terp noticed a wooden angel attached to an arch support. It was clearly out of place, which fascinated her. It did not belong on that otherwise unadorned arch. As she focused on the artifact, she imagined the tiny angel coming loose from its mooring and floating around the sanctuary. The carving immediately responded to her thoughts, smiling impishly and then sailing aimlessly around the room.

Amused by this turn of events, Terp imagined the angel turning a somersault in the air, and it promptly did so. As if this were something she did every day, Terp mentally sent the angel on a series of twists and spins throughout the huge hall.

To her right stood a particularly obnoxious tourist, who had ridden with the Persons on the same tour bus from London. The woman was loudly pronouncing her distaste for English architecture, which caused Terp to think about the angel nipping at the woman's backside. No sooner had the image entered her mind than the angel swept down and pinched the complaining tourist's ample fanny.

"Eek!" she screamed and swatted at the offending object. But nothing was there. The others in the touring party stared at their bus-mate, who was thrashing around in a vain attempt to rid herself of an invisible nemesis.

Terp tried hard not to laugh but failed at the attempt. She had sufficient presence of mind, however, to move the angel back to its original perch. Before leaving the sanctuary, she tested her vision.

"Mary," she said, "look up there. What do you see?"

Mary stared at the arch and said, "Just a beam, as plain as the rest."

"Do you see anything else?" Terp asked.

"No. Do You? Are you seeing things, Terp?"

"I thought I saw an odd shape. It must have been a shadow," Terp said. Obeying Terp's fancy, the wooden angel bowed and melted into the high beam.

— ☉ —

It had been Mary who most wanted to see Stonehenge, although Terp was happy to do so, anticipating that the experience might be a useful touchstone for her planned study of religion in college. She was not prepared, however, for what happened when she actually saw it.

Terp stopped walking and cast an unfocused gaze at the megalithic circle, while Penny and Mary continued around the grounds listening to the tour guide tell a tale of the mysterious Druids who had worshiped at Stonehenge in the mists of antiquity. Terp's attention was drawn to a particular capstone resting atop two large pillars of rock. For a moment she thought she saw a Druid priestess wearing a long diaphanous gown standing erect on the capstone. The nubile woman's arms extended forward at a forty-five degree angle from her shoulders, so that her palms were visible to anyone below.

Terp closed her eyes in an attempt to clear her mind and refocus, and as a result, with her eyes shut she saw even more clearly the vision of the priestess whose skin was pale white, whose hair gleamed black, red, brown, gold and silver, and whose gown, Terp noted, hid nothing at all of the woman's physical attributes.

Now Terp's peripheral vision detected a tall and tanned youthful looking man wearing nothing but a crown of orange blossoms on his head and a sash of ferns around his waist. In stately manner, he processed across the grass approaching the priestess. When he reached a spot three yards away, the young man stretched his arms into the air as if he were Moses commanding the sea to part, and silence fell over the scene. This struck Terp as odd, because there was no sound to the vision anyway.

Then on both knees he knelt in the wet grass and bowed his head in respect. At her wordless bidding, he rose and removed his sash and crown. Thereupon the man levitated to the base of the capstone and placed the sash and crown at the feet of the priestess.

She, in turn, gracefully bowed and placed her delicate fingers in his light brown locks and began to massage his scalp with tender strokes. Holding the sides of his skull, she then lifted him higher so that they were face-to-face, he in the air and she on stone.

When their lips touched, her gown dissolved. Whereupon he invited her to step into the air, and they flew hand-in-hand above the field, first in lazy wide orbits around the megalith, and then shooting like arrows across the plain. For a time they hovered conspiratorially inside a billowing white cloud cocooned within the cottony mist, until they burst out and swooped down into the river to bathe.

After what felt to Terp like many minutes, she opened her eyes, guilty and apprehensive about the sight of frustrated family members that were likely to greet her. But her mother and sister were nowhere to be seen. This discovery initially relieved her mind that she had not been caught dawdling in a fantasy world.

Within seconds, however, across the mystic plain Penny's motherly voice permeated the atmosphere with a loud, "Terrrrp! We're getting on the bus now!"

CHAPTER THIRTY-THREE

Flying from London to Newark, a chain-smoker sat across the aisle from Terp. After several hours enduring the acrid fumes, Terp got up from her seat to visit the restroom. Her leg muscles were wobbly from the physical effects of the cramped space, thus she bumped into the smoker, brushing the back of his head with her right hand as he was reaching for another coffin nail. In that moment, her mind was filled with distaste and sorrow concerning the habit that had killed her father.

"Pardon me," Terp said.

"No problem," the smoker responded. He tamped the cigarette back into its pack and stowed it in his suit pocket. For some reason he did not understand, he no longer felt like smoking, and this feeling remained with him for the rest of the flight.

"The thing is," the blonde woman said, waving her large breasts close to Narcissa's face, "those alien kooks in Roswell are doing us a favor."

Narcissa impatiently brushed some invisible crumbs from her own bare breasts and said, "I have no idea what you mean."

"They claim over in New Mexico that an alien space ship landed there in 1946 and the government is covering it up," Undine Greko explained. "Well, I have it on good authority that Malachi arranged the whole thing as a diversion, to keep nosy people away from NAT-SASS." The good authority had been Malachi Hinny himself, who had told the well-endowed blonde this bit of news in the afterglow of an extremely passionate coupling.

Narcissa was stretched out in a lounge chair awaiting the slide show that would serve as introduction to the seventh circle.

Malachi Hinny called for quiet, and the three sixth-degree students who were being recommended for initiation into the seventh most secret circle -Narcissa, David, and Undine- immediately stopped talking.

"The most sacred Synnssjukasylian customs are the exclusive possession of the seventh circle elite," Hinny intoned. "Candidates who have reached the sixth circle may, upon nomination by the Inner Glebe, preview carefully selected images of a few of these rites, but under no circumstances may they divulge what they have seen to anyone else. The penalty for unauthorized disclosure is expulsion from NAT-SASS and permanent removal from the genealogical records of Synnssjukasylian descendents."

For the first time since she had met Hinny, Narcissa felt uneasy. The slide presentation proceeded through a series of slides of naked people cavorting in innocuous dances. Big deal, thought Narcissa. The next slide showed two seventh circle members, one male, one female, lying spread eagle on a bed while Malachi tickled their respective genital areas with large feathers.

"Note the use of the sacred ostrich feather," he explained. "The ostrich is very like a bird found on Synnssjukasyl, and is therefore vitally important to members of the society."

Without a word of preparation, Malachi dropped in the next slide, which showed him engaged in sexual acts with a man and a woman simultaneously. David and Undine Greko purred approval. They had been anticipating this ritual. Narcissa was stunned. Is *that* what he's been hinting at? How could she have missed the signs? This was the most disgusting image she had ever seen, she thought. In that judgment, however, she was premature, for each of the next five slides revealed acts she found increasingly more unpleasant to contemplate much less view.

When the preview ended and the lights turned on, it was evident that Malachi, David, and Undine were physically ready and eager to practice some of the seventh circle rituals they had seen. Narcissa was sick at her stomach.

"I don't know what's come over me," she said. "It must have been something I ate. I think I'll go to my room and rest a while."

Malachi knew that he would never see Narcissa again. He didn't care. He had two new recruits who promised to be spectacular inner circle athletes. And he believed that Narcissa would never breathe a word to anyone about NAT-SASS.

The day was perfect for a late morning wedding. Nissa was resplendent wearing a garland of chrysanthemums in her hair and nothing else. Lloyd wore only a bow tie made of palm fronds and willow. Cloud was dressed the same as his father, and Nissa's matron of honor, her friend Sandy, was clad in similar fashion to the bride.

Lloyd stood at the base of the chancel watching Nissa process barefoot and unescorted down the aisle toward him. His heart was bursting with joy because she was intent on vowing before all these people that she loved him and wanted to become one with him in matrimony. Corresponding feelings circulated through Nissa's mind as she reached Lloyd's outstretched arm and stepped forward to face the pastors.

Adam and Evelyn proceeded through the worship litany by turns. "Dear friends, we are gathered for a wedding wearing none but God's garments," Adam intoned. "No human made fabric could ever shroud the glory of God, so we pursue this sacred purpose humbly clad only with the image of God created in us."

Soon the vows were made, and Cloud and Sandy produced the rings to be exchanged. Sandy's twelve year-old twins, a boy and a girl, sang Malotte's "The Lord's Prayer" in a duet that filled the chapel with their high, soaring, and innocent voices.

Lloyd kissed Nissa Morgan and took her hand for the recessional, up the aisle and out into the warmth of a bright day.

At the reception, Cloud said, "I didn't know what to get you for a wedding gift, so I decided to give you something of myself." He handed small parcels to each of them.

Nissa unwrapped her present and opened the box lid to discover a turquoise necklace. "It's beautiful," she cooed.

"I bought it in Japan. It was a gift for Xuan," Cloud said.

"Oh, Cloud, I know how much this means to you. I'll treasure it always," Nissa said, deeply moved at her stepson's gesture. She hugged him, kissing his cheek.

Lloyd peeled away the wrapping on his box and found inside a Purple Heart medal.

"You deserve it, Dad," Cloud said. "You were wounded too."

Lloyd was speechless, but water seeping from his eyes communicated a great deal. He wrapped his arms around his son and mumbled, "I love you." When he had recovered his composure, Lloyd said, "I know it's not the usual thing to do, Cloud, but we have a wedding gift for you. Nissa and I have talked it over, and we both want to share some of our happiness with you."

"You don't have to give me anything," Cloud said. "I have plenty."

"Let's go sit by the pool for a minute," Lloyd said. "I want to tell you a story." Cloud, Lloyd, and Nissa sidled through a crowd of wedding guests and found chairs on the pool deck. "Do you remember your mother and I arguing about money when you were small?" Lloyd asked his son.

"You argued about a lot of things," Cloud answered.

"Well, one of the things we argued about was land. I wanted to buy it and she thought it was a stupid thing to do. She wouldn't listen to reason, so I gave up talking to her about it. But I didn't give up the idea. A friend at the bank and I set up a private corporation to buy cheap land. We started in 1946, and over time, we bought quite a bit. It was easy to get small loans and pay them off in installments. Your mother never found out about my side investments.

"Recently, we sold some of our holdings. And by the way, Nissa didn't know about this either when she agreed to marry me. She was shocked when I told her."

"That's for sure," Nissa said.

"The bottom line, Cloud," Lloyd continued, "is that your father is now a wealthy man. I have paid off your mother's house and set up an account to pay the property taxes on it as long as she lives there. And Nissa and I want to give you something to help you with your further education. We have added some funds to your savings account at the bank. Whatever you don't need for current expenses, I suggest you invest in something more profitable than a passbook savings account. I can give you the names of some very good investment advisers."

"Thanks, Dad and Nissa," Cloud said. "A little extra money will come in handy around tuition time. I'd be happy to have you manage my account, for a fee of course, if you'd be willing to do that. But let's not talk about business. This is your wedding day! You two had better get back to your reception."

"OK, no more business, Son. I'd be honored to manage your money," said Lloyd.

Two weeks later, when Cloud received his bank statement in the mail, he discovered that a deposit had been made into his savings account for two hundred fifty thousand dollars. He sat on the floor stunned by the gift. It's a damned good thing Dad is going to manage this, he thought, because I wouldn't know where to begin.

Lloyd waited to respond to Dr. Hyfrydol's letter until he and Nissa had returned from their honeymoon on Maui. He was thus in an excellent frame of mind when he wrote back to the physician who had helped him work through his guilt at causing another man's death. He would be pleased and honored to participate in the doctor's research project, he said.

A series of questionnaires, multiple choice as well as narrative, followed Lloyd's return letter, which the former pilot dutifully completed. In the process he came to recognize how long his post-traumatic suffering had lasted. In some ways he was still not fully recovered and never would be. The Hyfrydol research project proved to be as therapeutic for Lloyd in addressing his wounding war guilt as marriage to Nissa was at restoring confidence in his ability to give and receive affection.

The marriage was a blossoming for both of them. Nissa taught Lloyd how to be emotionally expressive and how to trust a lover. Lloyd encouraged Nissa to explore intellectual interests, to expand her mental horizon. This was something Onan had discouraged, even disparaged. At first, Nissa needed Lloyd's permission to follow her yen for learning, but when she realized that he enjoyed her pursuit of knowledge, that in fact it gave him much pleasure, she invested torrents of energy and attention into catching up on decades of books she had wanted to read. There were weeks at a stretch when she had difficulty pulling her eyes away from one compelling book after another, especially in the areas of history, psychology, theology, and sexuality. She did not stop to eat. The only thing that enticed her from the mind-expanding pages was curling up in Lloyd's arms when he came home from work, and when she did that, books be damned!

The woman sitting next to Terp on the flight from Newark to Phoenix suffered an obsessive-compulsive disorder. Before the jet took off, the woman needed to complete a ritual of buckling and unbuckling her seatbelt exactly thirty-eight times before the final buckling. Once completed, she would not undo the belt until the plane landed. She had not had anything to drink for twelve hours, and would not drink any beverages during the flight, for she could not allow herself to unclasp the buckle even to go to the lavatory. She counted to herself in an agitated whisper as the ritual proceeded.

Terp had no idea why the woman was playing with her seatbelt in this way, but when she reached the thirty-first set of couplings, Terp's patience gave way. Gently Terp touched the woman's shoulder and said, "Here, let me help." Terp clicked the male and female ends together and said, "There, it's secure now."

"Thank you," the compulsive woman said. Immediately she became calm and felt no need to continue the ritual. During the flight she drank two cups of coffee and a soft drink and got up twice to visit the restroom.

Terp did not realize that something extraordinary had happened. All her attention was focused on starting classes at Arizona State. What would her roommate be like? Would she feel at home? Would she make friends? Within two weeks, her questions would be answered. Yes, she felt at home. Yes, she made new friends -two of them, who would play dissimilar roles in Terp's life at college.

The first friend she made was her dormitory roommate in Palo Verde West, Dagmar Solbrent. To their mutual satisfaction, they quickly learned that neither was interested in pledging a sorority. Dagmar was a fine arts major, focusing on drama. She was stunningly beautiful, with long blonde hair, full breasts and a carefully acquired tan. Their first night together, Terp discovered through observation and subsequent conversation that Dagmar eschewed wearing undergarments of any kind and her tan was comprehensive.

"I'm envious of your tan," Terp said with unusual spontaneity. "I wish there were some private place around here where I could experiment with sunbathing nude."

"If there is, I'll find it," Dagmar replied. "Mine could use some maintenance. Let's check out the dorm roof."

Terp started to ask where her roommate had been able to sunbathe nude previously but intuitively held back, thinking this might be probing into a sensitive area. She did not want to start off the relationship with her roommate by being too nosy.

As it happened, Dagmar had acquired the all-over tan in her backyard, during hours when her overtly pious parents were away from the house. But Terp's intuition was well tuned, because Dagmar was anxious to avoid discussing her family life and did not want Terp or anyone else she met at college to know anything about much less see her modest home in the Maryvale section of Phoenix.

She wasn't embarrassed by her family's limited financial means, and she was proud to be attending college on a National Merit scholarship. But she was ashamed of the general shabbiness of the house she grew up in. And under no circumstances would Dagmar allow even the slightest possibility that her roommate and her parents would meet face to face. Though she had a car, a hand-me-down 1962 Rambler Classic, Dagmar would not be inviting Terp home for any weekend visits, nor would she be making many by herself.

In the event, after scouting expeditions to the dormitory roof and other locations, they found no safe and private venue on campus for nude sunbathing. Thus Dagmar was obliged to defer maintenance on her tan, and Terp would have to wait for a more opportune time to pursue her goal of experiencing the glow of sunshine on her entire body.

Their relationship quickly evolved into one in which Dagmar was the primary talker and Terp the primary listener. Within a week Terp learned that Dagmar was sexually active, and within two weeks she knew that Dagmar used her sexuality to attract and control people, both men and women.

Dagmar had never had sex with a woman, but she talked to Terp about wanting to try it someday, just to know the sensation of it. Drama majors, she declared, need to experience life in all its dimensions, beyond conventional boundaries, and bring what they discover to their art. Terp felt both intimidated and captivated by Dagmar's erotic earthiness.

The other new friend came into Terp's life as a result of her academic track. As part of the honors program, she chose two fields for major study: English and religion. The choice of religion brought her to the attention of the Reverend Doctor Kirkegaard Trilby, adjunct professor and Director of the ASU Christian Student Ministry.

The Reverend Doctor Trilby, ordained by the Northern Reformed Congregational Church, stood five feet six inches tall. He was thirty-seven years old and favored pale blue button down Oxford cloth shirts and a tweed sports coat with leather patches on the sleeves. A briar pipe appeared to be either in his left hand or his mouth at all times. The charming pastor attracted a large following of students, disproportionately female, into the Christian campus fellowship he had founded five years earlier.

Trilby sought out Terp and invited her to attend the first program of the new school year. As a religion major, he assured her, she would be an important asset to the organization. She soon became a regular participant, facilitating a small group theology discussion and leading opening devotions at ministry meetings.

At Terp's urging, Dagmar reluctantly attended one meeting at the campus ministry building but declined to return. "Religion is not my thing," she said.

"But what about gaining new and different experiences for the sake of your art?" Terp replied.

"Oh, I've had plenty of exposure to church," Dagmar said. "And none of it any good. There's already plenty in that vein to feed my art."

"Like what?" Terp asked.

"I really don't want to talk about it," Dagmar said with suppressed anger in her voice. She paused and sighed. "OK, I'll say this much. I believe in an abstract God, not a personal one, not some deity who gives a crap about what individual humans do with their lives. And all this holiness language gives me the creeps. Let's just leave it at that."

Terp was greatly curious about Dagmar's religious background but did not press her roommate on this obviously painful subject. Hoping to gather more intelligence for her floating boy search, however, she turned instead to what she thought would be a more productive area of conversation. "Did you ever see the mothballed World War II airplanes in the desert west of Phoenix?"

"Oh, sure," Dagmar said. "A long time ago. But I don't think they're there anymore. You're probably out of luck if you want to see them."

"I saw them when I was a kid," Terp said. "And then we went out in the desert northwest of there for a picnic. Did your family ever go on picnics in that area?"

Dagmar let out a bitter laugh. "My parents believe picnics are sinful."

"Oh," Terp responded with a start. "I'm sorry. I really wasn't trying to bring up religion again." A spasm of disappointment ran through her chest.

CHAPTER THIRTY-FOUR

Stop-the-war rallies popped up all over campus in October. Despite disdain for what to him were self-righteous, smart-ass protesters who knew nothing of the real cost of war, a sense of moral responsibility led Cloud to attend one in the flesh. On the far side of the crowd he caught sight of a tall, slender young woman. He did not recognize her, but a gold aura circled her head. Fascinated, he edged through the field of peace-minded students, intent on finding a way to meet her, but someone with a large sign stepped in front of the woman, and when the sign-bearer moved on a moment later, she was gone.

Terp's eyes fell on a longhaired man across the way and a sense of *déjà vu* filled her mind. There was something familiar and appealing about the man, but she could not put a name to his face. Before she could make a mental inventory, Dagmar called and waved for Terp to come meet the enraptured young man clinging to her arm. Terp sidled over to be introduced to Dagmar's latest conquest.

Seeing the student with the golden aura caused Cloud to consider that he might at last be rising out of his grief for Xuan. It was now three months shy of three years since her death, and this was the first time since that tragic night that he had looked at another woman with any interest in a possible romantic relationship.

Of course, he did not know if she were indeed a student at ASU.

These protest rallies attracted a lot of non-students. She might be passing through town and he'd never see her again. He had only glimpsed her for a moment, but that was sufficient to form a lasting image in his mind, and hope rose in his chest that he **would** see her again. That night he sat in his lonely apartment and composed a poem to this unknown woman.

TERPSICHORE

She danced across my field of sight,

    her aura golden over darkened mane.

And then Terpsichore took flight,

    yet left her visage swirling in my brain.

An age ago before the war,

    I conjured once a dancer in a dream.

Entranced by her kinetic lore,

    I'm waiting still to see her body stream

Across my field of sight and stay.

    Could this be she who flitted past my eyes?

If so, why did she dance away?

    I long to float with her across the skies.

Not bad, he thought, for a first poem. He had no idea why the image of the dancing girl came to him as he tried to capture the essence of his glimpse of the woman with the gold aura. Yet it seemed to fit the moment. In time he would try his hand at other poems, but for the present, this one would reside in a manila folder along with assorted notes from history lectures.

For several months, Cloud visually searched for his imagined Terpsichore whenever he was on campus, but their paths did not cross again that year or in the next. Eventually, he stopped looking and let go of the hope of meeting her or any other woman he could fall in love with and instead invested his emotional as well as intellectual energy in pursuit of a PhD in Asian history and religion. His life unfolded prosaically in the familiar space between his library study carrel and his apartment.

The city park in Tempe was unremarkable for the area, but it seemed mystical to Terp, out for a Saturday afternoon stroll in January 1971. A strong desire to be alone and away from everyone on campus competed in her psyche with an abysmal loneliness. Somehow, the park's atmosphere managed to appeal to both sides of her mental struggle.

A deep expanse of yellow-white grass and scattered pale eucalyptus trees spread before her, and she felt an urge to disappear into the field and be veiled by its bleached hues. In her reverie she saw a vision of Big Head waiting for her in a circle of gum trees, chatting amiably with the floating boy. As she approached, Big Head smiled and casually introduced him to her. More than anything, she ached to put flesh on that elusive lover-partner-savior abiding in the depths of her mind. The floating boy was all she needed to burn away the mist of unrequited longing and dismiss the melancholy that clung to her. This dream, however, would not be realized in the still young year ahead.

Late April turned warm that year, so as Dagmar strode into their dorm room one afternoon, she was not entirely surprised to see a nude Terp sitting at her desk intently concentrating on a typing project. "Too hot and stuffy for clothes?" she asked dryly.

Terp dropped her hands from the typewriter keys to her lap and peered blankly at her roommate and then glanced down at her own body. "Oh no it's not the weather; it's the subject matter. I'm writing a paper on Melville's *Typee* for my nineteenth century American lit class."

"Well, that certainly explains it," said Dagmar. "Whales swim naked so Terp gets naked to write about them."

"Right author, wrong novel," Terp said. "Actually, I'm focusing on Fayaway, the blue-eyed native girl who is the love interest in this novel of South Sea manners. When *Typee* was first published in the 1840s, she captured the hearts and imaginations of the American reading public. *Typee* was Melville's first and most popular book, and the character Fayaway was a major reason for that. Here, let me find a quote..."

Terp ruffled through pages of notes until she found what she sought. "Listen to this. The narrator writes, 'Fayaway -I must avow the fact- for the most part clung to the primitive and summer garb of Eden.' So the biblical metaphor was transferred to a tropic isle but without the symbol of sin."

"Wow! A naked native girl capturing the imaginations of armchair American men. Who would ever believe such a thing?" Dagmar said sarcastically.

"Yeah, yeah," said Terp. "The book is fiction but based on Melville's actual experience in the South Pacific, and for decades a lot of readers thought it was a true story. Anyway, that's why I'm naked. I want to get into the spirit of Fayaway as I write about her.

"The book was ahead of its time in looking favorably on non-Western cultures. That's the most significant part. For Melville, primitive was not a derogatory word. It's also a return to nature kind of work. Those are always popular. And he was very critical of the efforts of pious missionaries to civilize so called savages.

"At any rate, Fayaway greatly intrigues me. I admire the way she is innocent and sexy at the same time, very natural and unashamed, a Pacific island Eve. But I'm disappointed too, because Melville didn't give her much to say. Unlike the Hebrew Eve, she's not curious. She doesn't think complex thoughts."

Dagmar responded, "A nineteenth century male writer describing an ideal female wouldn't make her too bright. Especially if he could have her running around without clothes. Men are easily distracted and satisfied with physical charms alone. They don't want women who ask deep questions."

"I don't believe that. Not all men," Terp said almost defiantly. Silently she continued the thought: "Not the sad poet in my dreams." She exhaled a long sigh. "It's just that I want Fayaway to be naked in nature and articulate about what that means, to defend her society's ways intellectually as well as in practice. And I know I'm asking too much of the book, so I must be asking it of myself. Anyway, the paper is due to tomorrow, so I'd better get back to work."

"Let me know when you find an intellectual Fayaway," said Dagmar. "I won't hold my breath on you finding a guy who gets off on smart women."

A rare confluence of schedules found Terp and Dagmar studying together in their dorm room after lunch a few weeks later, on a sunny Tuesday in May. After an hour of diligent bookwork, Dagmar looked up and said, "I can't concentrate on such a nice day. Let's go outside and get some sun."

Terp had finished the book she was reading and wondering what project to start next and was thus open to putting aside academic assignments. "Well, OK. What do you have in mind?"

"A bit of exploration off campus," said Dagmar. "Get your sneakers on, grab a beach towel, sunglasses, and a hat, and I'll show you a secret place."

"You have me intrigued," said Terp. "How far are we going? Are we taking your car?"

"Nope, we're going on foot," Dagmar replied. She pulled a backpack out of the closet and loaded it with her towel and Terp's, along with sunscreen and two bottles of artesian well water.

They made their way north past Sun Devil Stadium and climbed down the bank of the Salt River into its broad, dry bed and turned to the east. Dagmar led the way through the sand, weaving around bushes and stepping over rocks.

"How far are we going?" Terp asked.

"I don't know exactly. Less than a mile, though," said Dagmar.

After fifteen minutes of hiking, they reached a thirty feet long row of mature cottonwood trees that lined the north bank of the waterless river course. A thick stand of Palo Verde trees formed a rough semicircle connecting at each end of the cottonwoods, creating a sylvan fence in the shape of a capital D. A raised patch of sand formed the interior of the D, with a campfire pit circled by a ring of stones in the center of this enclosed beach.

"Wow!" said Terp. "How did you find this place?"

"A date brought me here two days ago," Dagmar said. "I think it's used a lot on weekends and some nights, but it's quite deserted on weekdays." She took the towels from her pack and tossed one to Terp. "Here, find a nice spot and we'll get in some first class sunbathing."

"We didn't bring bathing suits," said Terp.

"We don't *need* bathing suits here," Dagmar responded.

"Oh," said Terp, the purpose of the expedition now dawning on her. "Right. But what if someone sees us?"

"Did you see any other people in the riverbed? There's no one else around at the moment, Terp. And no one can see us unless they come waltzing inside these trees. And if they do...well, they'll get a very nice view," Dagmar said with a grin. She was already out of her blouse and working on the zipper of her jeans.

Terp hesitated for a few seconds and then began undressing. "If anyone was coming this way, I suppose we'd hear them crunching through the sand long before they arrived," Terp said with a philosophical sigh.

Dagmar stood on her towel and applied sunscreen liberally to her body and then tossed the plastic container to Terp. As she too added the protective lotion to her skin, a passenger jet flew directly overhead, making its landing approach to Sky Harbor Airport.

"I wonder if *they* can see us," Terp said with a nervous laugh.

"Only if they have windows in the floor of the cabin," Dagmar retorted. "But even if the viewing angle permitted it, they're too far up and moving too fast to see what we're not wearing."

"You seem to be quite knowledgeable of lines of sight," Terp said, as she settled into a comfortable position on her towel.

For a moment Dagmar said nothing and then responded in teasing fashion. "I'm a drama major. I need to know how much people can see from various vantage points...and what I can get away with in moments of opportunity."

Another plane made a landing approach above them, and Terp, reassured by Dagmar's assessment, waved playfully and said, "Hope you had a nice flight."

Nevertheless, for the first few minutes of her tanning adventure, Terp continued to feel anxious about possible intruders on foot.

Soon, however, she forgot to worry as she relished the feel of sunlight on her bare breasts.

"Fifteen minutes on a side and then flip," Dagmar instructed a short time later. "Time to turn the meat and let the other side take the heat."

"Nice rhyme," Terp said with a relaxed laugh.

Altogether they enjoyed two fifteen-minute sessions supine and two prone before dressing.

On the hike back, they saw no one else in the riverbed.

After a shower that evening, Terp noticed with pleasure a pink glow on parts of her skin that had not previously known sunrays, although nothing approaching a well-established tan. She made mental plans to go back to the tree-ringed beach for more sunning the following Tuesday, with or without Dagmar.

Curious about how far from campus the hidden arbor was, that night Terp peered out her dorm window, which provided a view of the Salt River, and tried to gauge where her basking place was located. It did not take long to find it, for a slender column of smoke from a campfire rising in the east marked the spot.

The following week, Terp, by herself, made a late-morning visit to the arbor and sunbathed nude for an hour. Then the term came to an end and she flew home to New Jersey.

Terp's summer visits to the Jersey shore, wearing a bikini, resulted in a deep tan that made the now covered parts of her body that had been lightly tanned in Arizona look pale by comparison.

When she returned to school in September, Terp and Dagmar hiked out to the arbor a few times for tan maintenance, but the press of studies and extracurricular activities soon made it difficult to find time to continue nude sunbathing.

A few days before Terp's twentieth birthday, in May 1972, the campus ministry sponsored a day of tubing on the Salt River. The Rev. Dr. Kirkegaard Trilby had gathered dozens of old car and truck inner tubes, which the students inflated and threw in the back of a borrowed van. One tube was fitted with a canvas bottom to be filled with ice and soft drinks. The others were parceled out as vehicles to transport soon to be sunburned students downstream over small rapids and around gentle eddies. The caravan drove northeast to a stretch of river above the dams where the water flowed briskly.

Terp launched her tube next to Trilby's, and they followed the current in tandem, about twenty feet apart. She wore a bikini under a baggy tee shirt, intending to remove the shirt at intervals to get some sun without burning. Reflecting on the secluded place Dagmar had found in a dry section of this very river where they had enjoyed sunbathing nude, Terp momentarily entertained the idea of how much fun it would be to tube naked, and a wide grin spread across her face. Then she nearly capsized in an eddy and lost the thought.

Halfway downstream from where they had dropped off a car for getting back to the van, the campus minister began lustily singing "Cruising Down the River." However, he failed to remember the correct lyrics, so instead of cruising, he bellowed in his usual off-key chapel service voice, "Floating down the river, on a Friday afternoon..."

Terp flinched at his use of the word floating, for she still brooded periodically about her as yet unrepeated encounter with Big Head. Could Kirkegaard Trilby be the floating boy? He certainly had a boyish charm. Despite his tendency toward pompous intellectualizing, she liked him. A rumor circulated that he was married, but he wore no ring and never spoke of having a wife, and no wife had ever appeared at the campus ministry programs. She asked him if he had ever gone on outings near the White Tanks, but he said he had never been to that area. She would have to contrive a way, she thought, of subtly asking him if the words floating boy meant anything to him.

A week later her sophomore year came to an end and she flew home to New Jersey. During the summer respite she volunteered two days a week as a receptionist at a birth control clinic, and temporarily put the Rev. Dr. Kirkegaard Trilby out of her mind.

In June, Firstlaugh Begay tracked Cloud to his apartment in Tempe. The two old friends drank a fruit juice and grated ice concoction as they talked about the unfolding of their respective lives since graduating from college.

"I graduated from Flag in sixty-five and got a Navajo Nation job in Window Rock," Firstlaugh explained. "It was OK. Pretty good money for an Indian. But Indian bureaucracy, if you can imagine.

Three years later the Federal Government declassified the work my dad had done in World War II. For the first time, he was free to talk about it."

"What did he do?" Cloud asked.

"Have you ever heard of the Navajo Code Talkers?" Firstlaugh responded.

"He was a Code Talker? They're the most famous war heroes in Arizona!"

"Ira Hayes was more famous for raising the flag on Iwo Jima," Firstlaugh said. "He was a Pima, but the Code Talkers are the best known Navajo war veterans."

"So, what effect did this news about your dad's heroism have on you?" Cloud asked, intuitively certain what the answer would be.

"Well, it boggled my mind. I was so proud of him, especially when I thought about him keeping it secret all those years. So I went right out and enlisted in the Marines." Firstlaugh had confirmed Cloud's guess. "My father tried to talk me out of it. He told me how hard it was to maintain *Dine* traditions in a foreign war. In fact, he said it was impossible. But I was in awe of his legacy -and stubborn too. After I signed up, I was accepted into OCS and was promoted to second lieutenant in 1969."

"Well, there was only one place that Marine second lieutenants were being sent in 1969," Cloud said.

"Yeah. I was a platoon leader in Nam," Firstlaugh said. "It was the most gruesome experience I could ever imagine. Really brutal! I saw so many dead people. Some of them I killed myself. It was a good thing that I'm not a Traditional Navajo, because the many *chiindi* over there made it impossible to walk in beauty. A *chiindi* is a malevolent ghost, by the way. I would have gone nuts trying to be faithful to our ways. I think the thing that saved me was all the years I spent with you white guys in Phoenix. That prepared me for the barbarity I experienced in Viet Nam."

"Were you wounded?" Cloud asked.

"Yeah, a couple of times. Nothing major," Firstlaugh said. "The big wound was to my spirit. When I got back to the Navajo Nation I went through an Enemy Way ceremony, three days and nights, and that cleared my head of the contamination of battle and contact with dead bodies. I'm OK now. I don't think about it much."

Cloud told Firstlaugh about his experiences in Viet Nam. "I wish I could get it out of my system as neatly as you have," he said. "Do they have an Enemy Way ceremony for *bilagaana* vets?"

Firstlaugh laughed. "For you, Cloud, they might make a special ritual. Actually, you don't have to be present for the ceremony. It can be done on your behalf. When my father was in the Pacific Theater, the Tribe conducted a group Enemy Way for him and over a hundred other Navajos stationed overseas. The singer used their photographs to sing the ceremony."

"I'm still brooding about Viet Nam four and a half years later. Most of the time it's bearable, but every once in a while I get really down," Cloud confessed.

"What you need is a good woman," Firstlaugh said. "I got married in February, and she helps keep my head straight."

"Tell me about your wife," Cloud said.

"I married outside the Tribe, so I don't have to worry about clan incest. Her name is Cedar Cradle. She's Lakota. We met in Window Rock, where I'm working again. She came down there to organize some people for the Indian rights movement, and she organized me right into matrimony."

"Congratulations," said Cloud. "I'm really happy for you."

"Well, I gotta get over to my parents house," Firstlaugh said. "I need to break the news to them that they're going to be grandparents around Christmastime."

"If clan membership is matrilineal," Cloud asked, "what clan would the baby be?"

"That's a gray area. He -or she- will be enrolled as a member of the Navajo Tribe. It only takes a quarter Navajo blood to qualify for that, as long as one parent is at least half -and I'm full. But the Lakota don't reckon clans the way we do. Down the years, we'll probably have to go through elaborate family tree explanations when the time comes for our kid to date other Navajos. Or *if* I should say, considering my track record."

"I envy you the complications," said Cloud.

The two veterans embraced and promised to keep in touch. Cloud walked out to the parking lot with Firstlaugh. "What do you think of my blue Beetle?" he asked.

"Nice color," said Firstlaugh and then he chuckled. "Navajos have a word for that car. We call it *chidi ne'eshtili* –a booger car."

Cloud laughed in turn. "So, I'm driving a blue booger, huh?"

"Only if you take it up to *Dinetah*," said Firstlaugh.

"I'd like to do that sometime," Cloud said, "even at the risk of my beautiful car turning into a ball of snot along the way."

The August weather in Central New Jersey was hot and humid, and the air conditioning in her house was pleasant, but Terp was bored and restless and needed to get out of the house for a while. The beach was always an appealing possibility, but she was weary of the crowds at Asbury Park. Even the private beach at Loch Arbour that she sometimes went to seemed to admit more people than she felt comfortable with.

Pursuing an activity that promised solitude as an ultimate reward, she drove to a used book store in Edison to pass time browsing for anything that might strike her fancy. Poking around the shelves in anticipation of finding some wonderful and heretofore unknown novel, biography, or volume of poetry sent pleasant tingles down her spine. She loved the ambience of old books and magazines arranged in prodigal piles and stacks. The smell of musty paper was incense to her nostrils, and she breathed it in deeply.

On this visit she found a novel written during the roaring twenties by Thorne Smith. Terp recognized the title but had not known that *Topper* was anything other than a television program. "I used to watch this on TV when I was a kid," she said half-aloud to herself. A wave of nostalgia flooded through her as she remembered a time in her life when everything felt secure and tinged with laughter. She pulled the book from the shelf with the excitement of a successful treasure hunter and danced to the counter.

Once home, she curled up in her room and delved into a story that was far more free-spirited than the sanitized television series. Topper was a man in mid-life crisis, who encountered husband and wife ghosts who led him on a prohibition-era spree of libidinal self-discovery. Terp was charmed by the Sybaritic inclinations of the ghosts, George and Marion Kerby, who led Topper delightfully astray.

She enjoyed the novel so thoroughly that she went back to the bookshop the next day in search of anything else by Thorne Smith, returning home with **The Bishop's Jaegers.** Smith penned this novel later, in the depths of the Great Depression, after the larkishness of the flapper era had taken a more serious turn. The author had changed with the times, but not in the direction of more serious themes. Instead, he provided readers even more fantastic escapes from the bleakness and drudgery of their daily lives.

From the title, a reference to the cleric's long underwear, Terp surmised the bishop would undergo a loosening transformation similar to that of Cosmo Topper. But the prudish bishop, who as a missionary had clothed South Sea natives, provided contrast to the more eccentric and libidinal characters. Terp remembered Herman Melville's dislike of Pacific island missionaries, which led her to find the bishop even less sympathetic.

The plot grew from the Staten Island Ferry becoming stranded in heavy fog. Six passengers, including Bishop Waller, left the ship in search of assistance and found themselves trapped in a private nudist colony. While others ran about naked, the bishop stayed in his jaegers throughout the farcical romp.

Terp chuckled aloud at the philosophy of the nudists, that clothing -not skin- was titillating, that people dressed to enhance their sexual appeal, and thus the way to handle lust was to undress. They put their clothes on when they wanted to act out sexually. On the other hand, she felt perturbed by the presentation of the naturist children as embarrassed prudes who wanted their parents dressed in the presence of visitors. When I was a kid, she thought, I would have loved the chance to go running naked through meadow and forest.

She was encouraged, three quarters of the way through the book, when the bishop said he almost felt like taking off his drawers and leading the group in prayers. "Oh why not, bishop?" she sighed. "Redeem yourself. For once in your life, go for it!" She reflected that she was usually nude when praying before going to sleep at night. Nudity is actually quite spiritual, she thought, a boon to praying. In the end, much to Terp's disappointment, the bishop did not follow through on his urge to disrobe and lead devotions.

For a moment, she wondered what the clerics she knew, Argyle Watts and Kirkegaard Trilby, would think about conducting worship without clothing. She had a difficult time imagining her pastor at home approving of such activity but thought the intellectually adventuresome campus pastor might deem it acceptable.

"As for you, Bishop Waller," she announced aloud as if he were present in her room, "I'll just have to do it for you." Terp proceeded to slip out of her jeans, tee shirt, bra, and panties. Assuming the lotus position on her bed, she entered into silent meditation, listening for God. After a quiet interval, she distinctly felt something in her brain smile warmly.

Mary and Penny had gone back-to-school shopping for Mary's senior year at Edison High. Now Mary burst joyfully into Terp's room carrying bags loaded with new apparel.

"Doing yoga again?" Mary asked.

"No, I was doing spiritual meditation," said Terp dryly.

"Sorry to interrupt. Are you finished?" asked Mary.

"Apparently," said Terp, resigned to the interruption but feeling a residual glow from the mental smile evoked by her time of listening for God.

"Let's have a fashion show to model my new outfits for school. I got new under-things too. Lace panties and matching bra," said Mary.

Mary disrobed and was in the process of removing sales tags from various items when Penny entered the room.

"Fashion show, Mom. Want to see my new clothes in the flesh?" Mary said.

Penny laughed. "Well, I see plenty of flesh on both of you but no clothes covering any of it." She then turned to address Terp. "Mary's going to need a new closet for all this stuff. But I still don't understand why you didn't come along with us. Don't they wear the latest styles on your college campus anymore?"

"Sure they do, some of them, but I'm not into fashion these days, Mom," Terp replied. "My current wardrobe is sufficient for school. I prefer to dress simply."

"That's for sure," said Mary. "Terp doesn't have a single nightgown or teddy or any frilly underthings at all."

"Yes, and I threw out all my teenybopper pajamas years ago," Terp shot back. "So what? I happen to be a no frills basic woman. Bare skin is far more elegant than a nylon nightie any day."

Penny ignored her daughters' interchange about bedclothes and returned to the subject of fashionable outerwear. "Well, it's a good thing you and Mary are the same size, so you can borrow from her if the occasion calls for dressing up a bit."

Terp gave her mother a dismissive look and Penny withdrew from the room.

Mary stepped into her new lace panties and twirled her hips to admire how they looked. "Pretty sexy, huh?" She looked at her naked sister and a different thought came to her. Mary said, "Would you sit in that yoga position again?"

Terp did so.

"Ethereal," said Mary. "Some day I'd like to paint you like that. Would you consider posing for me?" Mary's artistic ability was as advanced as Terp's intellectual prowess and she planned to major in art when she got to college.

The prospect pleased and intrigued Terp but she did not admit this to her sister. "Someday, perhaps," she replied while nodding her head in affirmation.

"To be clear, I mean with you nude," Mary added.

"I know what you mean," said Terp, now smiling. "With or without glasses?"

"Hmmm, let me think," said Mary. "Take them off for a minute."

Terp removed her glasses and Mary peered into Terp's face.

"With your specs, definitely," Mary pronounced. "They add spiritual gravitas to your appearance. But I would probably depict them as antique eyeglasses."

"Yes, well as I said, someday maybe," Terp responded.

That night, Terp dreamed of posing nude not for Mary but to provide inspiration as a mysterious and equally unclothed reincarnation of John Donne wrote a sonnet about her unadorned beauty.

CHAPTER THIRTY-FIVE

September fifth proved to be a troubling day for Cloud, as he suffered a severe bout of post-traumatic depression. While he was cleaning up in his kitchen, the radio kept him company. A news bulletin interrupted his sink scrubbing with a report that Arab terrorists had murdered eleven Israeli athletes at the Munich Olympic Games. The story immediately connected Cloud with memories of wanton violence in Viet Nam. He had tried to bury these images, but when the synapses that led to those sore places in his brain conveyed them from darkened cells to the light of consciousness, he found they were still raw, pulsing with psychic infection. The mental mausoleum where he had confined these thoughts came unsealed, and he descended into weeks of unwelcome and bitter grief.

The Olympic massacre caused him to believe all the more strongly in the essential depravity of humankind. This was a symbol and symptom to him of something dreadfully wrong with the world. And religion was at the heart of it. He made a historian's mental inventory of the unspeakable violence perpetrated upon millions of people over the ages in the name of God. The list was long, and no major world religion was exempt from it.

He stayed up late into the night composing rambling, nearly

incoherent poems about the Great Cosmic Indifference that suffering people naively dared to call God. "A wild and evil reality is loose upon the world," he scribbled, "and God is AWOL. Absent the holy, the people make their own wrath." Cloud found himself crying out for God to report for duty, and then lapsed into despair when there was no response. He wrote, "Is God a sadistic projection or simply a sad desire?" The silence, not in the room but in his mind, mocked him.

The idea of suicide circulated seductively through his brain. He brooded about it for weeks, and eventually decided against killing himself out of mere curiosity. He wanted to find out how the painful drama of his life would ultimately play out. A huge mystery lay before him and he wanted to discover as much of the answer to it as possible in the years remaining. He would tough out the mental agony for the sake of finding what was on the other side of it.

His father once said the cure for a hangover was a hair of the dog that bit you. Take another drink of what caused the drunkenness. Cloud thought that military service was responsible for his psychic hangover, and taking the hair metaphor to heart, he cut off his long locks, giving himself an Army style buzz cut. He regretted this rash act the next day, but there was nothing for him to do but let it grow back. As it did, he reverted to the habit of keeping his hair moderately short and neatly trimmed.

When Terp returned to campus in September, a letter was waiting for her from Kirkegaard Trilby. It was an invitation to dinner. Good, she thought. This will give me a chance to slide in a reference to the floating boy and see if he reacts to it.

They met at Monti's La Casa Vieja, and once seated, he presented her with a single white rose. "I have a big favor to ask you," he explained. "This rose is a symbol of the purity of my intentions."

"What is it you want?" Terp asked.

"Some of the ministry work I do involves counseling troubled students. But I'm not always up to date on the mindset of collegians these days. I'd like you to be my assistant. We could meet to discuss cases and you could give me your insights. I trust your judgment. It would be a big help to me."

"Wouldn't that be a breach of confidentiality for you to talk about your counseling with other students?" Terp wanted to know.

"Oh, I would never reveal their names, just the circumstances and the puzzling aspects of the case," the minister explained.

"Well, OK I guess," she said.

"Good," he said. "And now that we're colleagues in ministry, I want you to stop calling me Dr. Trilby. Call me Kirk."

"That'll be hard for me to do Dr. Tr...er...Kirk." She smiled at him.

"I think we'll have a lot of fun working together," Kirk said. He lifted her left hand and kissed it.

"Oh **boy**," she said. "It'll be great. Just like *floating* down the river." She listened for his response to her carefully prepared remark. "Floating...boy," she repeated.

"Oh yes," he said. "We shall float through the rapids of campus ministry together."

Kirk's response did not give her any clue about his relationship to the floating boy. Nevertheless, Terp assented to spending time with Kirk discussing case histories of the confused lives of college students.

For their first session, Terp sat at one end of the couch in Trilby's office and he at the opposite end. Each was half turned toward the other in order to make eye contact. Though she felt honored to be included in such a professional encounter, she could not entirely dispel a modicum of anxiety.

"Here's a case that's bewildering me, Terp," Kirk said. "I'd like your take on it."

"Well, that's what you invited me here for, so let's have a go at it," she said.

"There are, of course, theological implications to the case. Biblically proscribed carnal acts stand over against the spiritual and incarnational needs of the student involved," he drawled. "I see issues of individuation as well as contrasting moral imperatives. The exegetical question we need to frame the issue with is 'where is God in this situation?'"

"Yes?" said Terp, not sure she grasped what he had said.

"There is a student, let's call her L. She's nineteen and a

sophomore here at ASU. I've been counseling with her for a month. Her mother is dead and she has no siblings, so she lives at home with her father, who is a— a— let's say ecclesiastical professional."

"Do you mean a church worker or an ordained minister?" Terp asked for clarification but then intervened before he could respond. "Wait. Stop a minute. Is all this detail necessary? It wouldn't be too difficult for me to figure out who L is if you say much more."

"I fully trust your discretion, Terp. Not to worry," he responded in a reassuring manner. "He happens to be a minister, non-denominational. At any rate, last week L confided in me that she has been involved in an incestuous relationship with her father for some months. She told me that she had been flirting with him off and on for years and one evening she escalated the level of teasing by climbing into bed with him, wearing only a nightgown. She asserted that initially she had no intention of having sex with him, but only to take the flirtatious behavior to a new and in her words dangerous level. One thing led to another and she became fully aroused and enticed...I mean to say invited him into intercourse. Since then they have repeated this behavior on a regular basis."

Terp had blanched at the mention of incest. As she listened, her intuition led her to doubt that L had initiated the behavior, but she felt insecure about challenging Kirk's description.

"In the spirit of honest self-disclosure," said Kirk, "I'm an only child of a divorced mother. I never knew my father as I was growing up and therefore lack insight into father-daughter affections. Can you shed any light on the ways in which a daughter may develop erotic feelings for a father?"

Terp was abashed by the question. "Not erotic, no," she stammered. "Affection, deep bonding yes, but certainly not sexual feelings."

"What if such feelings were mutual?" Kirk continued. "Any insights into how a father could feel a sexual attachment to a daughter?"

The idea nauseated Terp but she felt defensive in the face of the reverend doctor's apparent clinical dispassion. "Well, I'm clearly no prude, and my views about what consenting adults do are pretty liberal, but incest is...just ...wrong."

"For the moment, try to set aside the superego task of passing judgment," Kirk said. "What if I told you that L was adopted? So there would be no biological issues in the relationship. And to use your terminology, they are both consenting adults."

"Is that true?" she asked. "Is L adopted?"

"Let's say that it is. Would that change your view of the situation?" he pressed.

Terp paused and made an attempt to consider the matter with an open mind, but this was too high a hurdle. After a period of uncomfortable silence, she said, "No. It wouldn't make any difference at all. And I can't exactly put my finger on it, but something doesn't add up in L's behavior."

She thought she detected a shadow of disappointment in Kirk's face.

"I see," he said quietly. "Well, that's very helpful. Very helpful indeed. I would have expected a different response, some intuitive sense, so you can see that I am completely inadequate when it comes to coed behavior. I really need your insights."

Terp did not speak. In her mind, the subject was not coed behavior.

"Well OK I guess that's all for tonight," he added.

"But what about where is God in this situation?" she asked.

"Yes, well that's your homework, Terp," he said. "Reflect on that overnight and tomorrow evening we can try to identify God in the midst of sexual conundrums."

Misgivings flooded Terp's mind about the wisdom of another session with Kirk, but she decided to give him the benefit of the doubt, and in their next meeting all their time was taken up with compelling conversation about the radical grace of God. This kind of theological discussion excited her imagination, and she found herself returning to his office two or three evenings a week.

Apart from revealing more intimate details about the lives of counselees, Kirk acted the perfect gentleman. One Friday evening, however, he reached across the couch and placed a hand over hers and whispered, "Terp, I need to confess something. I think I'm falling in love with you."

She was stunned. "Kirk, I don't know what to say. I'm– flattered, but– well– you– uh– "

He slid over the cushions, took her in his arms and kissed her passionately, parting her lips with his tongue.

Terp was confused. Rather than make a scene, she allowed the kiss to continue, although she was not skilled in the art, and thus she was more a passive vessel than an active participant.

Kirk had another confession for her. He was married but had been separated for years. "It's not a real marriage in any spiritual or religious sense," he explained. "My wife hates the ministry and the church and won't live with me, but I haven't divorced her because the denomination doesn't like its ministers being divorced. But now that I've been blessed with these feelings for you, Terp, I'm prepared to risk my career. You, my dear, have given me the courage to face up to the displeasure of my superiors and do what I should have done a long time ago."

Her mind was a jumble as she walked alone to her dorm. Kirk explained that he had time-sensitive work to finish that night and was thus unable to accompany her across campus. Mentally, she questioned herself. Is Kirk the one I'm supposed to find? He's a little shorter than I and almost twice my age. He's not my type at all, certainly no John Donne. But he said he's in love with me. Nobody has ever told me that.

Terp told Dagmar about Kirk's words and kiss, and Dagmar said, "Watch out, Terp. He's no good. I don't trust him. He's just after your body."

"How can you say that, Dagmar? Of all people! Don't you play the prude with me!" Terp spat out angrily. She had expected her roommate to be happy for her. "How many boyfriends have you gone through in the last two years? Why do you begrudge me one little romance?"

"I'm sorry, Terp," Dagmar apologized. "It's just that I know the male species better than you do, and I feel kind of protective of you."

"I can take care of myself, thank you very much," Terp responded. Until that moment, she had been ambivalent about beginning a relationship with Kirk Trilby, but Dagmar's motherly behavior pushed her toward defiance. The next night, she met Kirk in his office and practiced passionate kissing techniques with the older man. She rather liked the kissing and liked Kirk too, although she did not feel any sense of loving him. One thing was certain, however. She loved being loved. She basked in the glow of believing that an accomplished, erudite, and somewhat attractive man loved her.

A week later she and Kirk ate dinner at his apartment. Two candles flickered teasingly on the table as the host poured wine generously. The time soon arrived when Kirk uncorked a second bottle and held it up for Terp's inspection.

"Here, beloved, let me refill your chalice," he said warmly. "Jesus demonstrated at Cana that he approved of more wine for special occasions. This is a wonderful vintage, the finest wine that I have saved for a sublime moment such as this."

Terp said nothing but allowed her glass to be refilled and then sampled the red liquid. No words came from her mouth, but she nodded and smiled.

"You are so beautiful, Terp," Kirk purred. "You're an enchanting Nimue who has captured the heart of this fumbling old Merlin."

"You can keep talking," Terp mumbled, the power of the wine now affecting her tongue. "I like romantic literary talk." A seductive memory of the musical **Camelot** radiated from her brain to her skin.

But he did not keep talking. Instead, he escorted Terp to his bedroom and helped her disrobe. In the end, Kirk proved to be a gentle lover and expert in using a condom. Clearly he was no old fumbler in the arts of sex. He thought of himself not as a rough thief of virginity but rather a deft artist at the holy task of deflowering maidens.

Terp decided she liked sex and wanted to do it again, without the assistance of alcohol. The affair continued for some weeks. One night, remembering **The Bishop's Jaegers**, Terp asked Kirk what he thought about worshiping nude.

He replied, "I worship your nude body." This ended that discussion.

In late October, lying abed in the afterglow of sex and wishing their relationship could be public, she asked him how long it might be before he would be legally free of his wife.

"Not too long," Kirk said. "I talked with her about divorce, and she seems open to letting it happen without a fuss." Knowingly, he accepted Terp's inquiry as a signal that the time was nigh for another transitional event.

The next afternoon, Kirk telephoned Terp in a well-rehearsed panicky voice. "Come over to my office right away. I'm really shaken up, babe. I need to talk with you. It's really important."

When she arrived, he looked grim. "What's wrong, honey?" Terp asked.

"My wife is what's wrong," he said. "She informed me this afternoon that she wants to reconcile. She refuses to give me a divorce, and if I proceed with filing, she will hire a private detective to watch my movements. She suspects there is someone else."

"Well, there is someone else," Terp said defiantly.

"But don't you see? If she finds out about you it'll be in all the papers. I don't want to see you get hurt by all this. She's a malicious woman," Kirk explained.

"What are you saying?" Terp wanted to know. "Are you going to let your estranged wife destroy our happiness? Why can't you stand up to her?"

"It's not as simple as that," Kirk said. "What we need to do right now is play it cool. We need to stay apart until she calms down. I'm sure in time I can reason with her. But not if she suspects or, God forbid, has proof there's another woman in my life. For your sake we have to stop seeing each other for a while."

"For how long?"

"I don't know. It could be months. But trust me, it has to be this way."

Terp wanted to cry but a numb anger shut off the tears before they could start.

"Terp, I'm sorry," Kirk said in a throaty whisper. "I can't see you for a while. We have to pretend we've never known one another -in a biblical sense. Maybe you should take a holiday from the campus ministry program for the time being. If there's any change, I'll send you a discreet note, but say nothing to anyone until you hear from me."

Kirk had planned to ask Terp to return the office key he had given her, but seeing the pain in her face, decided it would be more prudent to pass on that and simply have the lock changed in a few days. That approach to security had worked before.

She left his office seething with rage at Kirk's manipulating wife. As she walked across campus to her dorm, she realized she didn't even know the woman's name. Dagmar was not in the room, being off on an overnight stay with her latest boyfriend. So Terp sat alone in stunned grief, mentally berating herself for whatever it was she had done wrong. Maybe she would write a letter to his wife and explain the situation. Perhaps the woman had a compassionate heart and would understand the need to let Kirk go.

Terp was not hungry but forced herself to eat cheese and crackers, hoping that a bit of food would lighten her mood or at least ease the ache. It didn't help. Around nine in the evening she remembered that she had left at the campus ministry office a novel she was reading for an American lit class. Surely it would be alright to slip over there and retrieve the book. Kirk wasn't likely to be there this late. She still had the key he had given her as a secret sign of what he had called her mantle of leadership.

Entering the building quietly, she found the book on the table where she had put it and picked it up with her left hand. Noticing a light emanating from the crack under the door of Kirk's private office, she made her way toward it but stopped when she heard a vaguely familiar female voice.

"This white rose is so beautiful, so romantic, Dr. Trilby," the woman said.

Whose voice was that? It sounded like Linda, a sophomore student in the campus ministry program. In the last few days, Linda had been hanging around the office a lot more than usual, Terp noted mentally.

"The thing is, Linda," Kirk said, "I think I'm falling in love with you."

CHAPTER THIRTY-SIX

Stunned by a blow of awful recognition, Terp knew that Linda was the L whose incestuous relationship Kirk had described in their first counseling assistance session.

Numbness progressed to paralysis. Terp's muscles would not move and she could not breathe, but her mind raced. How many other women had he seduced? How could she have been such a fool? Nimue indeed! Merlin? Hardly! She fiercely craved a return of physical control so she could kick in his door and (following the idiom that scrolled across her brain) scare the living shit out of the Reverend Doctor Don Juan.

The mental image of the campus pastor soiling himself was quickly displaced by one of Kirk and Linda engaged at that very moment in passionate kissing. This thought sent a hot surge of oxygen storming through Terp's system, restoring her muscular movement. Taking two swift and angry steps toward his office door, with her right hand clenched in a hard fist, she abruptly spun around and reeled out of the building.

What sent her out into the night was not fear of a scene or reluctance to face a false lover but a rising tide from her stomach. As soon as she stepped onto the grass, Terp dropped the book locked in her fingers, fell to her knees and vomited. Regurgitated cheese and crackers and bile erupted from her mouth. After a terrible interval of retching, she forced herself up and staggered back to her dormitory, taking small comfort that no one in the lobby or hall saw her enter and that her roommate was not there.

Dagmar found her the next morning, still dressed. Bits of vomit speckled her blouse, and grass stains streaked her skirt like skid marks where her knees had pressed the fabric into the earth. Terp lay sprawled on her back across her bed, a sour stench emanating from her gaping mouth.

Dagmar cleaned Terp's face with a warm wet washcloth and then said, "OK, kiddo, time to wake up."

Terp stirred and with Dagmar's help rolled into a sitting position. "I feel so awful," she said.

"Here, I've made you some broth. You need to get some sustenance in you," Dagmar said. Little by little she spooned the warm soup into Terp's mouth. "Now, tell me what happened, although I can guess that it involves the sainted reverend."

Terp told Dagmar the events of the previous afternoon and evening. "Why does it hurt so much? You don't seem to have any trouble dumping or being dumped by anyone, Dagmar. What's wrong with me?"

"There's nothing wrong with you, Terp. It's me and Trilby who are screwed up. Let me tell you something about me. You want to know why I sleep with so many men?" Dagmar decided that revealing her own experience might help Terp deal with her trauma. "From the time I was five until I turned fifteen, my father used to beat me with his leather belt. It didn't matter what I did or didn't do. He would find a reason to punish me, at least once a week. But he didn't just give me a whipping. He made me take down my underpants so he could beat me on my bare flesh. That's why I don't wear panties, so I don't have to experience the humiliation of pulling them down.

"When I was fifteen I was as tall as he was and I stood up to him and said, 'No more!' That same year his brother, who was thirty-two at the time, came to stay with us for a while. He'd been booted from the service and was looking for a job. Anyway, he seduced me, and what he did to me felt so much better than what my father had done to me, that I started using sex as a way to cover up for pain. Even now, whenever I feel a little depressed, I go out and find someone to give me a good orgasm."

"I'm sorry, Dagmar," said Terp. "I had no idea."

"Well, nobody does," Dagmar asserted. "My mother knew all about the beatings but closed her eyes to it. And she once caught me and her brother-in-law in bed, when I was sixteen. She walked right into my room and saw him humping me but backed out without a word and never mentioned it. So you're the only person I've ever told, and I'm not sure why I'm even telling you. I guess I want you to know that you're not alone in this rotten world."

"I guess if misery loves company, we're well suited," Terp said, smiling weakly. She stood up but her legs were unsteady, and she plopped back onto her bed.

"Time to get you cleaned up, kiddo," Dagmar said. She boosted Terp onto her feet and led her down the hall to the showers. Terp's hands shook as she tried to unbutton her blouse, so Dagmar helped her undress. While Terp was removing her panties, Dagmar started the water in the shower stall. "In you go, Terp," she said, piloting her friend into the stream of hot water. "Wash up!" In the process, Dagmar's left sleeve was soaked. "Oh what the hell," she said, pulling her dress over her head. "Make room for Dagmar. Here, let me have the soap." Dagmar broke the cake in two and handed half to Terp.

The roommates individually scrubbed themselves, each one intent on washing away various residues of bodily fluids and manly scents that were in some ways more than skin deep. Dagmar stepped out of the stall and returned a moment later with a bottle of shampoo. "Here, Terp, you need to get the puke out of your hair," she said. While Terp lathered her tresses, Dagmar dried off and waited for Terp to finish.

Once back in their room, Dagmar dried Terp's hair and brushed it. As she stroked the long brunette locks, Dagmar said, "I'm jealous of your hair, Terp. It's so beautiful."

"I can't imagine why someone as gorgeous as you is jealous of me," Terp said.

"Don't be so hard on yourself. You're an attractive woman, Terp," Dagmar said. "Hey, if you'd ditch those glasses and get contacts, you'd be stunning."

"Well, I can't stand the idea of putting anything on my eyeballs, and I'm kind of attached to my glasses. They're like little shields over my eyes," Terp responded.

"Forget what I said about contacts. There are plenty of guys out there who are turned on by girls in glasses," Dagmar said.

Terp enjoyed having her hair brushed, but began to fret about where this might be leading. Here I am sitting naked on my bed being groomed by another naked woman who once told me she'd like to experiment with lesbian sex. Is Dagmar also, like Kirk, out to seduce me, she wondered? Don't be silly, she answered herself. Dagmar and I have been naked together in this room plenty of times and nothing sexual has ever happened. Just relax and enjoy the nurturing attention. But her anxiety level was too high and she was unable to relax. Oh, God, she prayed silently, I can't handle this now. Please give me a sign about Dagmar's intentions.

Immediately, Dagmar said, "There you go! Your hair looks great. Enough playing around. Get dressed, lady. You've got classes to get to and so do I."

A few minutes later they were en route to their respective classes. Terp had the presence of mind to detour by the campus ministry building to retrieve her copy of Kate Chopin's **The Awakening** from the grass a few feet from the place where she had thrown up the night before.

She muddled through two classes, and managed to eat a salad for lunch, but late in the afternoon, a wave of depression washed over her. Sitting alone in her room, she felt physically stained, aching to scrub her insides clean. It was not the loss of virginity she rued. Sex was good, she told herself, but not if it was based on lies. Thinking about Dagmar's sexual history caused her deep sorrow mingled with sisterly affection. But apparently misery didn't love company as much as she had first thought, because learning of Dagmar's traumatic childhood did not alleviate the pain of her own shame-laden experience of abuse. Terp was angry at Kirk, but angrier at herself for being so gullible as to be taken in by him. She searched her mind for some way of punishing both of them.

The solution she came to was a suicide gesture. She remembered a bit of lore that over-the-counter pain pills, if taken in sufficient quantity, could kill a person. She had no genuine desire to die, but the image of a frightened and remorseful Kirk pacing fretfully outside the Emergency Room while Terp was having her stomach pumped satisfied an inner need for revenge. That it would be painfully purgative for her only added to the appeal of the idea. Terp set out on foot for a drug store on Mill Avenue.

Cloud was feeling blue. His anguished depression from wartime flashbacks had lifted, but he very much needed another, brighter world to escape into for a while. Indulging a life-long habit, he hiked over to Mill Avenue in search of a paperback novel that would offer emotional relief. He stood in front of a rotating rack of science fiction novels, peering intently at titles, looking for a promising one that might satisfy an urge to fill his mind with fantasies of Utopia on some other planet.

Terp stepped into the store and surveyed the room. The pain-reliever aisle was across the way, just past the bookstand. A tall, slender man was browsing at the rack, partly blocking her path. Without speaking, she tried to squeeze around him, in the process bumping buttocks with him. She then pivoted in an attempt to recover from the unintended body contact but lost her balance and hit his right shoulder with her left arm. Her right hand reached out for the bookrack to steady herself, but this only set it spinning, causing the man to drop the book he was holding. Years of dance lessons provided Terp the grace she needed to recover and stay on her feet.

Cloud squatted down to retrieve the new Isaac Asimov novel that had caught his fancy, from which vantage point he looked up into the face of the apparently klutzy coed who had knocked it loose. Immediately he knew she was the woman he had seen at the peace rally two years earlier. Out of respectful habit, he carefully placed the book back in the rack, thinking Asimov could wait. "This sounds like a line from a movie," he said while rising, "but haven't we met before? Have you been at any war protests on campus?"

Before he had finished speaking, a long shuttered memory opened in her mind, and Terp realized she had seen this man long ago in another setting far away. "The Edison Hotel during the blackout," she blurted out.

"Was that you?" he asked in a flash of remembrance. "With the transistor radio?"

"Yes, and you were a soldier, a lieutenant," she said.

"Listen," he said, "I don't know your name or anything about you, but we need to talk. By the way, I'm Cloud Morgan." He extended his hand.

"Terp Person," she said, taking his hand and not releasing it.

"Terp?" he asked. "How do you spell that?"

"T-E-R-P," she said. "As in Terpsichore, the Muse of dance."

If she hadn't been holding his hand, he might have tumbled backward into the bookrack. "We need to find some place to sit down. My mind is spinning," he said. "This is...an amazing encounter...and surely no coincidence."

"There's an English tea shop a couple of blocks from here," Terp said.

As they walked together, Cloud told Terp about seeing her at the anti-war rally and how he felt an immediate attraction to her. He did not mention seeing her aura. She told him she had had a dream about him two and a half years after the blackout, seeing him in pain sitting on a pile of ashes. He told her that would have been about the time he returned from Viet Nam, and he was indeed in pain at that time.

Cloud ordered two cups of green tea, but they let their steaming beverages go cold. They spoke rapidly in broad details about their lives before and since the blackout. When Cloud told Terp about Xuan, she wept and had a hard time getting the tears to stop. Something about his devotion to the Vietnamese woman touched her even more deeply than the aching tragedy of her death. The owl-eyed man sitting across the table from her enchanted Terp's mind. She felt herself becoming absorbed into the depths of his being and not at all frightened by the prospect.

Cloud felt that he could trust Terp with anything and knew that in time, he would tell her everything. But there was so much to say that he didn't know where to begin. He also sensed that he ought not overwhelm her with too much right away. He perceived a lingering aura of grief around her, which led him to ask, "How did it happen that you came to the drugstore tonight?"

Had he not already told her about Xuan, Terp might have evaded the question. Then again, there was something about Cloud that she trusted far beyond reason. She had known him by name only an hour, yet she was convinced she could hold nothing back from this man.

"I was looking for something -some pain medication- that I could use to overdose on," she said almost matter-of-factly.

"I see," he said, showing no surprise. "During my bouts of brooding about suicide, I've tended to conjure more drastic methods. But rabid curiosity about how all this tangled human farce will turn out has kept me from following through with any of them." He reached across the table, took her hands in his, and looked into her eyes with luminant compassion.

Terp quivered in delight from his touch. She proceeded to tell him about Kirk Trilby seducing and then dumping her, feeling far more relief in relating the story to Cloud than she had with Dagmar. "When I was a kid," she continued, "whenever I felt sad, I'd put on a record and dance around my bedroom. It always made me feel better. Now everything in my life seems turned upside down, so I guess it's time to dance on the ceiling."

Miss Listerbaum's deathbed message came back to him. "You're not going to believe this," Cloud said. "No, I'm wrong. *You* will believe this. In 1964 I had a dream about a dancing girl from the East. She had long, dark hair, and I couldn't see her face, but there were palm trees in the background. In the dream I was told she would appear in dark times. And the next year, just before my next-door-neighbor died, she said she had a message for me. That message was 'When everything turns upside down, dance on the ceiling.'"

"I believe it to the bottom of my toes," Terp said, brightness returning to her voice.

They continued to talk until the shopkeeper shooed them out and turned out the lights. Cloud walked Terp to her dorm lobby.

"Wait here. I want to show you something," she said. He sat on a couch while she scurried to her room, rummaged through a trunk in search of her photo album, and returned to the lobby.

"Here it is," she said. "Look at this." She pointed to a snapshot of herself in a New York theater merchandise shop. "Dad took this the day after the blackout," she explained. "Can you identify that man in the background?"

"Oh wow!" he exclaimed. "That's me."

"This is the man I saw in a dream, mourning on an ash heap," Terp said.

He glanced back and forth between the image of thirteen year-old Terp and the actual twenty year-old woman standing before him, trying to absorb the essence of all the changes in her over the elapsed seven years. "Your inner beauty has not faded," he said, "and your exterior physiognomy remains irresistible too."

She blushed and grinned from his erudite compliment.

He stood and faced her. "We have a whole lot to talk about, Terp, more than we could ever get to tonight. You've had a traumatic day and look worn out. Get some sleep, and I'll come by tomorrow and take you to dinner."

"Not Monti's," she said.

"I wouldn't dream of it," he responded.

"As far as I can tell, you never know what you may dream," she quipped.

Cloud enfolded Terp in his arms and gently kissed her forehead. "Tomorrow evening, then, at six o'clock. OK? I'll pick you up here in your dorm lobby."

"I'll be ready," she said.

Before falling into a deep, restorative sleep, Terp noted that she had said nothing to Cloud about Big Head or the floating boy. She would have to remedy these omissions tomorrow. She had no doubt now that he was the one the Old One had told her to look for, but she had no idea what floating meant. Soon she'd know, she realized as her mind gave way to profound slumber.

Cloud practically danced back to his apartment, feeling more alive than he had in years. Along the way he determined that he would throw caution to the wind and tell Terp about floating out of his body. He, too, slept soundly and woke refreshed to the sound of the Stampeders singing "Sweet City Woman" through his clock radio. He grinned broadly. A good omen, he thought. Sweet indeed.

CHAPTER THIRTY-SEVEN

Cloud had no classes scheduled that day, so in his usual morning nakedness he did a series of calisthenics before turning his bodily attention to seven yoga asanas. These particular postures were his favorites, and he did not rush through them. First he lay on his back in the dead body asana and became mindful of his breathing. Not wanting to float from his body on this occasion, when he was sufficiently relaxed, he shifted into the shoulder stand, followed in due course by the plow, and then he turned over to get into the cobra position. After holding that a minute, he did a scorpion, a headstand, and finished the series by assuming the lotus posture.

According to his habit, while in the lotus asana, Cloud meditated, first clearing his mind and then allowing it to free associate. On this morning, an image of the dancer from the East filled his consciousness with sunlit clarity, and for the first time since he had met her in a dream eight years earlier, he could see her face.

He ate a leisurely breakfast of raw walnuts and fresh blueberries stirred into oatmeal and invested thirty minutes cleaning his apartment. Along the way, he searched for the poem he had written two years earlier about Terpsichore. He wanted to take it with him and show it to Terp at dinner.

Terp slept late and upon arising felt a pleasant aura, tactile rather than visible, pulsing around her body. Remembering Cloud's kiss, she decided it was responsible for the feeling. Silent meditation seemed to her the appropriate way to begin this day of sublime expectations. She often did this on mornings when she was alone in the dorm room.

Assuming the lotus posture, she let her mind go blank and then invited her subconscious to choose any desired thought to bring to the surface for contemplation. This time, a remembrance of her admiring the statue of John Donne at St. Paul's arose from her mental storage cells. But the image was mixed with another one, for the metaphysical poet's face looked like a different poet.

By the time she had showered and eaten yogurt mixed with bran flakes, she had missed half of her first class. Dagmar was sleeping elsewhere, so she had no one to tell about meeting Cloud. Knowing she wouldn't be able to concentrate on literary tropes and Reformation doctrines, Terp decided to skip school. There was something else she preferred to do. She stepped into plain white panties, shimmied into a pair of denim bellbottoms, and half emulating her roommate, opted to go braless under a Sun Devil sweatshirt. After pulling white sneakers over white socks, she set out on a hike, whistling the recent hit song "Too Late to Turn Back Now" in a self-satisfied manner.

In the shower, Cloud reflected on how difficult it would be to wait until six o'clock to see Terp again. He wanted to see her right away and wished she would magically appear at his door. But she had morning and afternoon classes, and that aside she didn't know his address. Just as he stepped out of the shower, he heard a knock at the door. "Hold on," he yelled. "I'll be there in a minute." Quickly he toweled off, ran a comb through his hair, and donned khaki shorts and a white tee shirt.

"Hi," Terp said when he opened the door. "I couldn't wait till dinner."

Cloud produced a wide smile. "How did you find me? I'm not in the phone book."

"You gave me enough clues last night. Your name is on the mailbox," she said.

"You'd make a good MI officer," Cloud said while escorting her in. "It's not much, but it suits me for the present." He invited Terp to look around while he brewed two mugs of hot chocolate.

She quickly gravitated to the bedroom and two minutes later came out holding the framed photograph of Cloud and Xuan. "She was beautiful," Terp said. "I can see you two were very much in love."

"It's true," he confessed. "And she'll always be a part of me. But the love that Xuan and I knew now abides in eternity, where it rejoices for all new affections that grow in this world. All true love adds something good to life and takes away nothing."

"Wow," Terp said. "A real poet."

"That reminds me," Cloud said. "I have something to show you." He pulled open a manila folder and handed her a handwritten page.

When she finished reading the poem, Terp said, "Whew! I have to sit down. This is the most incredible thing I've ever read. It makes me blush."

"That's high praise coming from an English major. I thought it was OK for a first poem," he said.

"It blows me away," said Terp. The word float in the last line made her heart race.

Now Cloud blushed and with evident eagerness in his voice asked, "Any thoughts on the questions in the poem?"

"*Could this be she who flitted past my eyes? If so, why did she dance away?*" Terp read aloud. "Hmmm. To the first question, I'm certainly drawn toward the affirmative. As to why she..." She paused and with intuitive assurance rephrased her response. "As to why *I* danced away, I suspect the time wasn't right, wasn't..dark enough. Perchance there were things I needed to learn, events I needed to experience first. As eager as I was to meet the flo...uh...the man of my dreams, I don't think that two years ago *I* was ready for *you*."

A grin spread across Cloud's face. "The man of your dreams?"

"You're not the only dreamer in this room," she declared. "I once had a dream involving a sad poet. It was a glorious dream that I never wanted to tell anyone about, because it was so beautiful. This was my private reverie. It's funny, though, because right now I feel completely comfortable telling you that I danced naked for this poet. I won't reveal the rest of the dream, not yet anyway."

"You don't need to," Cloud said. "I think I know already."

Terp sat in the rocking chair and sipped the steamy cocoa beverage. Cloud sat facing her in a stuffed chair. For a time, neither spoke, both savoring the comfortable domesticity of the scene.

"Oh, I meant to tell you something else last night, and just remembered it again," Terp said, breaking the silence as if they had been married for decades. "Actually, I would've told you last night except you made me go to bed and get some sleep."

"Well, you were exhausted and needed rest," he replied. "What is it that you remembered to tell me?"

"Only my deepest secret, much deeper than my sad poet dream. It's something I've never breathed a word about to another human being. It seems really strange -almost reckless- to be telling it to someone I've just met, but I feel **compelled** to tell you. I have this sense there's only one person on the planet who will understand my story and that is you."

The back of Cloud's head tingled in anticipation of her words, and he said, "When you're done, there is something I feel compelled to tell you also, and intuition tells me our secrets may be related."

Terp described the trip to Arizona when she was almost five and her encounter with the Old One. "Look for the floating boy, Big Head told me. Do you think I'm crazy? Could I have been hallucinating?"

The tingling sensation radiated in a circle around his head, and the top of his skull felt open and pleasantly connected to the atmosphere. "You're far from crazy, Terp, and now I'm going to explain what it means to float."

He told her about his first out-of-body experience when he was near death from the measles, and about his imaginary friend who somehow knew how to send him back into his body.

"Since I was a teenager," Cloud continued in a meditative voice, "I've thought of my mental friend as a manifestation of my own brain and not a separate entity. But your tale registers so authentically true in my mind that you have convinced me otherwise, and in the process, you have overwhelmed me with awe."

Terp beamed at his words and replied, "That awe is incredibly mutual."

Then he took her on an armchair tour through his floating expeditions over the years. When he finished the story, Terp found she had fallen into a trance in rapt attention to his words. Heightened consciousness seemed to permeate every cell in her body. The two remained silent for some minutes, neither feeling any need to speak. Each seemed weightless, as if suspended in the atmosphere of a delightful alternative universe.

And then she said, "Do you think we can find the place where I met Big Head?"

"I think we might be able to do that," Cloud said carefully. "I know where the mothballed airplanes used to be parked, and I once had a floating experience north of there in the White Tank Mountains. All these things may well be connected in some way. Let's go take a look."

"For years I've yearned for someone to help me search for that place," Terp said.

"Let me change clothes and we'll be off," Cloud said.

He went into the bedroom and without closing the door, slipped out of his khaki shorts. From her vantage point in the rocking chair, Terp saw Cloud's bare buttocks, noting the wound on the left side, and instantly imagined her right index finger reverently tracing the faded red length of the scar. Someday she would have to ask him about that, she mused. With the right circumstances, someday soon.

Cloud pulled slim white boxer shorts from his dresser and put them on, stepped into a well-worn pair of Levis, efficiently buttoned the fly from bottom to top, donned a flannel shirt, and put on white socks and hiking boots before returning to the living room. "I always keep a couple of full canteens in the car," he reported. "Ready for a quest?"

"It feels more like a pilgrimage," she said. "And yes, I'm ready. I've been ready for fifteen years."

They piled into his blue Volkswagen and headed west toward Goodyear. Along the way, Cloud said, "Pilgrimage and quest are not mutually exclusive. So, in the context of your Christian faith, who do you believe this Big Head is? God maybe?"

Terp said, "Certainly not God. I really don't know. For a time I thought maybe the Holy Spirit. Reverend Watts told me that the Holy Spirit described in the Old Testament is a she and in the New Testament an it, but the learned scholars who translated the Bible into English insisted on translating all pronouns referring to the Spirit as he. Since I couldn't tell whether Big Head was male or female, for a long time I thought maybe he, she, or it was the Holy Spirit. I don't think that now. Perhaps some sort of angel."

She paused to consider how to ask Cloud a question in the most tactful way. Following his lead, she said, "Given your lack of belief in the existence of God, who or what do you think is responsible for your extra-sensory experiences?"

"Fair question," Cloud responded. "I've asked myself that many times. I simply don't know. I used to think it could all be explained scientifically. After listening to you, I'm not so sure anymore. It could be Big Head, I suppose, but I'll withhold judgment for the time being. Maybe I'm looking for a sign."

Past Goodyear heading toward Buckeye, Cloud and Terp agreed to navigate via their combined intuitions. Thus they followed an old farm lateral to a dirt road that led them into the desert southeast of the White Tank Mountains. As the Volkswagen crossed a dry wash, Terp shouted, "Stop the car! This feels like the right place."

In the dry bed of the Todd River west of Alice Springs in the Northern Territory of Australia, the Old One sat, concentrating intently on six year-old Amoonguna, an Aboriginal girl whose drunken father, without intending to do so, was on the verge of beating her to death. An irresistible odd thought entered her father's mind from out of nowhere, and he put down his stick to muse on it. The girl scampered away.

The odd thought involved white people going on walkabout without their clothing. This seemed bizarre to him. The whites, he judged, were obsessive about covering their soft bodies and lacked both inner and outer strength for traveling by foot over the harsh environment. But the image that had invaded the intoxicated man's brain was so insistent that he couldn't help believing that such an event was bound to happen, and probably soon. This was not a prospect he was eager to encourage, however, for the stupid Europeans were likely to become wounded, burned, or maimed while wandering nude around the land, and then he and the other men of his tribe would be obliged to come to their aid.

This mental scenario added a new and difficult to integrate element to his conceptual world. On the other hand, he acknowledged to himself, he did know one white person who sometimes disrobed without difficulty when visiting the Arrernte, and this seemed good to him. But she was a rare exception among the vast, indecently modest tribe of the whites.

Amoonguna retreated to a stand of River Red Gum trees, where she comforted herself by meditating on a recent nocturnal vision. Her dream was more specific than her father's odd thought, for it included a pair of unclad whites hiking across the sand in the riverbed, and she distinctly saw their strange but friendly faces.

A family from Amoonguna's Arrernte Tribe passed within a few yards of the Old One, but they were so busy chattering about their trek into Alice Springs that none of them looked in that direction and no one saw the Old One sitting cross-legged and naked in the warm sand.

Terp led Cloud along the wash on foot. After a short distance she saw a depression of land to the left, and she took Cloud by the hand and they climbed over the bank and down the slope. No shack was in view, but they continued to hike on a northwesterly course and soon spied a pile of bleached white boards.

The hair on Terp's arms and head stood up and she cried excitedly, "This is the place! I know it is!" Bending at the waist, she pulled a shard of sun-blued glass out of a patch of flaky dried mud. Immediately, her memory glowed with images of blue sky and blue glass blazes. "A trail of these shards led to the cabin!"

Cloud found a rib from a dead Saguaro cactus, which he used to probe among the boards. He wanted to give any poisonous desert denizens that might be resting in the dark shade under the lumber the opportunity to leave via some route other than his hand. When he was confident that no such creatures lurked there, he reached down and pulled up several scraps of wood.

"What's that?" Terp asked.

In the open space he had created by removing the boards, a piece of dark fabric lay exposed to the sun. Cloud used the cactus stave to lift out a long scrap of finely woven purple cloth.

"That's what Big Head was wearing," Terp said, a note of restrained awe in her voice.

Cloud then fished out a piece of dirt-encrusted canvas that appeared to be a shirtsleeve. "Does this look familiar?" he asked.

"No," said Terp. "All I remember is the purple robe. I suppose Big Head was wearing something besides the robe, but this doesn't look like a very comfortable undergarment."

As they continued to poke through the remnants of the shack, Cloud and Terp began to feel euphoric. Terp uncovered a length of purple satin that looked like the hem of a robe. After gathering a small pile of wood scraps, pieces of cloth, and a handful of triangular blue shards, they carried the treasure to the car. Cloud opened the trunk in the front of the Volkswagen and arranged the relics inside.

He walked around to the driver's side, but instead of opening the door, he turned and leaned back against the vehicle and began to laugh, quietly at first but increasing in intensity. The laughter seeped from a secret place in the depths of his mind and grew in power as it reached the surface of consciousness. It flowed with joy and streamed with irony. Cloud couldn't stop laughing.

Terp marched up to him and stood with her feet apart and hands on her hips, a wide grin revealing delight at the sight of him. She stared not at his bellowing mouth but into his radiant blue eyes. At last the floating boy, she thought. But this is no boy. His eyes are ancient, and so is the sound passing his lips.

"Peaceful, Easy Feeling," a song from Dagmar's Eagles album, arose in Terp's consciousness. Dagmar had been playing the record repeatedly in their dorm room since returning to school the previous month. This number was Dagmar's particular favorite, and Terp also delighted in its energetic melody and earthy imagery. And now, as she heard the sensual lyrics reverberate inside her head, Terp attached them to a real person, experiencing a sudden powerful urge to stay where they were all night and sleep in the desert under a quilt of starlight, enfolded in Cloud's arms.

But the desire, as compelling as it was, soon dissipated as she began laughing too, in resonant harmony with Cloud. She plopped beside him on the left and continued to laugh in a prolonged and cleansing release. They laughed so hard their sides ached, but still the mirthful roaring poured forth into the desert air. An eon later they stopped, sighed, and rested in smug silence. Then Terp started laughing again and Cloud followed suit.

Eventually their unrestrained outbursts abated, and for a long time they did not speak. Cloud extended his left arm around Terp's shoulders, and she snuggled in to his side, pleased and at peace.

The dancer from the East, Cloud thought, mentally composing a poem, offers beauty with her art but also knowledge more profound. Another thought sifted through his mind, and he spoke it out loud. "All shall be well."

HERETICS IN OCCUPIED EDEN

CONTINUES IN BOOK TWO,

THE STRANGE ANGELS

About the Author

Photo courtesy of Shelly Moe

Kenneth Alan Moe was born in Phoenix, where from an early age he experienced mystical events. At age ten he began writing poetry. His working life has included service in the US Army as a prisoner of war interrogator, in the corporate world as an insurance investigator, and as a mainline Protestant minister.

Consistently underscoring it all, for more than half a century he has practiced the vocation of writer, evolving through pencil, pen, manual and electric typewriter, and computer to produce reams of fiction, non-fiction, and poetry.

About Strange Angel Press

Strange Angel Press is a consortium of writers who act as editors, advisors, and cheerleaders for one another. We pool our collective experiences and talents to help participating writers with the art, craft, and discipline of fully telling the stories that have inspired us to put words to paper.

Visit our websites:
strangeangelpress.com
facebook.com/StrangeAngelPress
facebook.com/HereticsInOccupiedEden

TAKE A WALK ON THE SPIRITUAL SIDE

with

KENNETH ALAN MOE

And the

HERETICS IN OCCUPIED EDEN

THE STRANGE ANGELS – Cloud pursues a career as a history professor, while Terp serves as a mainline parish pastor, until peculiar circumstances draw them toward a previously unimagined vocational partnership.

THE DANCING CHURCH – Rebuffed when seeking to join an ecumenical pastors organization in Sedona, Cloud and Terp launch their own unorthodox group of spiritual leaders, from New Age to Native American. These efforts soon attract the malicious attention of local fundamentalists.

Praise for the Series

"A special genre of fiction that gives respect to our psychic and paranormal world and our need to demystify the body…"- Lawn Griffiths, Journalist

"I have not felt a connection to fiction like this in some time. Perhaps you could say it is a Harry Potter for adults."- Amazon Reviewer

Available in Paper and Kindle editions on Amazon.com

STRANGE ANGEL PRESS

NO SUCH THING AS COINCIDENCE...

The Rider had chosen him. The knot of darkness would billow out of his chest like a mist of writhing tentacles, to feed, flay and kill. Its goal, its need... its passion bled through his dreams as he slept. Salvation would only come once he brought the Rider to its desire.

Now bound to the deadly spirit, Evan Michael's only chance for survival lay with two witches from the Order of Magdalene: women who could bind the Rider to prevent it from feeding and help him avoid the authorities.

If they failed, he would be executed in front of a live television audience.

But, the Rider's passion was to kill the Abbess, the leader of the Order of Magdalene.

If they succeeded...

Available in Paper and Kindle editions on Amazon.com

STRANGE ANGEL PRESS